ONCE A CRIME LORD

Crime Lord Series, Book 3

Mia Knight

Mia Knight

Cover Art by Kellie Dennis at Book Cover by Design
www.bookcoverbydesign.co.uk

DEDICATION

To my fans who have made all of this possible.
I appreciate you so much!

CHAPTER ONE

Lyla

Lyla Pyre rocked her four month old daughter as she nursed and ran her hands through Nora's full head of jet-black hair she inherited from her father. Nora's eyelashes fluttered, revealing silver blue eyes identical to her own. Nora was perfect from the top of her head to her tiny, pudgy toes. Lyla couldn't imagine life without her, yet she had come so close to never experiencing this. She held a miracle in the crook of her arm.

What sounded like a pig snort interrupted Lyla's thoughts. She glanced down at Beau, a gray Pit bull, who was fast asleep at her feet. She saved Beau from a dog shelter after volunteering there for several months and he had become a loyal companion. She ran her foot down his back and felt the ridges from bullet wounds. Beau got shot trying to protect her the day a handful of bodyguards turned on her. It had been a long recovery for Beau, but he was alive and that's all she cared about. He spent most of his time in Nora's nursery, keeping guard.

Lyla switched Nora to the other breast so she wouldn't have to pump. There weren't many things she was proud of, but creating a human being was a pretty big deal. Having a baby with Gavin Pyre, the man she loved, was a blessing. She wanted to offer Nora the world, but first her daddy had a few things to take care of. Gavin's first priority was killing the man who bribed her guards to gun her down while she was seven months pregnant and who brutally murdered his father, Manny Pyre two years ago.

Nora fell asleep with her mouth open. Lyla dabbed Nora's mouth with a bib, smoothed her top down and rested Nora on her shoulder, rubbing her back lightly. She closed her eyes as she rocked, taking comfort in the quiet. The nursery had become her sanctuary in the past four months, a peaceful room untouched by the horrors of the outside world. Here, they were safe.

Beau's head rose suddenly, which caused his dog tags to clink together. A man stood in the doorway. Even as her heart jumped into her throat, she recognized her husband. She'd seen him only a handful of times over the past four months. His scruff made him look even more dark and dangerous than he already did on a regular basis. The air around him simmered with a coiled tension that made people get out of his way.

Beau trotted over and sat in front of him. Gavin looked down at the dog for a moment before he pat him on the head and then scratched him under the chin. Sometime during Beau's recovery, Gavin had

2

finally accepted him as part of the family.

Gavin strode forward, hazel eyes glinting in the dim light. He set his hands on the arms of the rocking chair and stared at her. Her heart stuttered.

"Gavin?" she whispered.

His eyes moved to Nora. He reached for her, gently lifting the baby from her shoulder. He cradled Nora's head in one hand and her body with the other. He scanned his daughter, taking in every detail he missed in the three weeks he hadn't seen her. Nora frowned, hands reaching out for an anchor. Gavin kissed her forehead and then placed her on his chest, her little face tucked against his neck. Nora relaxed instantly and let out a shuddering breath as she drifted back to sleep.

"Everything okay?" Lyla asked.

It was hard to determine his mood. When Gavin came home, he was capable of anything. The aggression and brutality he exerted in the underworld clung to him. The most communication she had with Gavin was over the phone and that was infrequent. Gavin spent ninety percent of his time in the underworld and the rest in the business world where he was CEO of Pyre Casinos, a chain of casinos on the notorious Las Vegas Strip. When he could carve out time, he spent only a handful of hours at home before he was gone again. It had been hard on both of them. Lyla reassured herself that this was temporary.

Gavin stared intently at her. "Did you have a good day?"

Lyla rose from the chair. "What are you talking about? What's going on?"

3

Gavin walked towards her, cupped the back of her neck and hauled her against his side.

"Gavin—"

He kissed her, a deep and carnal kiss that made her body go up in flames. She clutched his arm and dug her nails into his chest, very aware of Nora's weight against her arm. Apparently, he was capable of kissing her mindless and holding Nora without a problem because he did so until Lyla forgot her own name. When he pulled back, she stared at him with her body throbbing.

"I watched you in our bedroom this afternoon," he said.

"What are you—?" Her voice died out and her face went up in flames. "Oh my God."

She tried to push away, but his arm kept her banded against him. He kissed her forehead, cheek and then jaw.

"You had your checkup with the doctor, but you didn't say we could have sex," he said against her temple.

"I—" she fumbled and then swallowed. "You've been busy." She couldn't ask her husband to come home to have sex when he was trying to find a serial killer.

"I'm never too busy to make you come."

"Gavin!"

"What?" He captured her lips again and squeezed her ass. "You're ready, right?"

She still had her pregnancy weight and her body definitely wasn't something most men would call beautiful since her chest and abdomen were marred by gruesome scars. It should have been impossible for her to feel sexy in sweat pants and a loose top, but the way Gavin was looking at her made her feel like the most desirable woman in the world. Lyla winced as her breasts began to leak. That was definitely *not* sexy.

"I'm, um—" she stammered.

"I'll make you ready," he said and moved towards the crib.

Deprived of his heat, Lyla swayed before she found her balance. Gavin nuzzled Nora and kissed her on the mouth.

"Sleep, baby girl," he murmured before he set her in the crib. He turned and then strode back to Lyla. "Bedroom."

"Gavin, you haven't—" She bit back a shriek when he picked her up and strode to the master suite.

"You don't want to fuck, then I'll go down on you and you go down on me."

He kicked the bedroom door shut, dumped her on the bed and braced himself over her, hands on either side of her head. His face was hard and drawn with lust. He definitely didn't look like a sweet lover.

There had always been something dark about Gavin, but now that he was back in the underworld, the feral part of him was close to the surface. There was a storm inside of him, fighting for release. Desire warred with insecurity. Her body tingled with the knowledge that if she let him, she could be thoroughly fucked tonight.

"What's it gonna be?" he asked.

"Gavin—"

He straightened and yanked her sweat pants off. In the next second, her legs were being spread as Gavin knelt beside the bed and bent his head. Her body convulsed at the first lash of his tongue. Gavin went *deep*, gorging on her while she sank her hands into his hair and closed her eyes against the lash of pleasure. His fingers intruded as he lapped at her clit, driving her crazy.

"Gavin."

His fingers curled and she erupted beneath him. He growled and did it again.

"Gavin," she panted.

He didn't speak, didn't stop.

Her hands slid from his hair to the back of his neck, dragging him into her heat, raising her legs high. His eyes flashed up to hers. Those mesmerizing lion eyes commanded she give herself to him. He sucked on her clit and curled his fingers again. Her heels slammed down on his shoulders and she arched. Gavin's hands cupped her ass, grinding her against his mouth. She collapsed on the bed as the orgasm passed. Gavin didn't move his mouth from between her legs. He continued feeding from her. She tried to squirm away, but his hands flexed on her hips, keeping her in place.

"Gavin," she moaned.

She jerked, shuddered and ran her hands through his silky hair. When he stopped, she opened heavy eyes and saw that his were dark and hungry.

"What do you want?" she whispered.

He yanked and she slid off the bed onto his lap. His hand sank into her hair, gripped and held her still for his kiss. He drank from her as if she was life itself. She ran her down his chest and felt him shudder. He clutched her tight as if he wanted to absorb her.

When he pulled back, her lips were swollen and pulsing. Gavin rose and left her on her knees in front of him.

"Suck me," he ordered.

Her mouth quirked. She ran her hand over his crotch and felt the hard bulge beneath. She traced the length of him through his slacks and tempted the beast by nuzzling him. Gavin stood with his legs braced apart, arms clasped behind him like a soldier. He said nothing, but a muscle in his jaw locked.

Lyla took her time exploring him through his clothes, even reaching down to cup his balls and give them a gentle squeeze before Gavin's control snapped. He gripped her hair and gave her a punishing kiss.

"I'm not in the mood to be teased," he said against her mouth.

"I am," she said as she traced his jawline.

Gavin resumed his pose. "You know the consequences."

She sure did. She was getting wet just thinking about it. She undid the buckle, slowly dragged the belt free and unhooked his slacks. She dragged the zipper down, the sound magnified in the hushed quiet. His cock, unencumbered by boxers, fell into her hand before the zipper was all the way down. Lyla ignored his erect dick and reached up to unbutton his shirt. A low growl of impatience filled the room and she ducked her head to hide her smile.

Lyla wrapped her hand around the base of his cock and slowly stroked him. A drop of precum formed at the tip of his penis. She captured it and Gavin bit back a groan. Her body began to heat again and milk leaked from her breasts. She ignored the sensation and tugged his pants down so she could cup his balls. Gavin obligingly spread his legs and rocked forward, imbedding half his length in her mouth. Lyla groaned and heard him swear as the sound vibrated along his sensitive cock. Lyla leaned back and swirled her tongue around the tip and then traveled along the length of his shaft to his balls. She licked delicately.

"That's it," Gavin hissed.

Gavin yanked her up. Even as she braced her hands against the wall, Gavin lifted and then sank his cock into her. He gripped her hips and didn't stop until he was fully imbedded inside of her. Her body stretched and yielded. She panted as Gavin dropped his face in her hair.

"I need this," he growled before he pulled out and slammed home with such force that she cried out.

Gavin moved, deep thrusts that made her teeth clench. He was a man possessed. Lyla took everything he gave and asked for more by arching into his thrusts. Gavin brushed her hair to the side and bit her neck, hard enough to shock her.

"You'll never be free of me." He collared her throat as he continued to plunge home. "I'll never get enough of you."

"Gavin!"

His hand moved to her chest. Lyla panicked and

shoved his hand away before he could feel her damp bra. Gavin's rhythm faltered. Without warning, he pulled out, whirled her around and pinned her back against the wall. Gavin was a carnal beast and not about to be denied anything. He looked half savage, half warrior in his unbuttoned starch white shirt, suit jacket and nothing else.

"You don't push me away," he ordered and went for her breasts again.

Lyla knocked his hand away and he bared his teeth.

"What the fuck did I just say?"

"I-I'm leaking," she muttered, mortified and turned on at the same time.

She wasn't prepared when he ripped her loose top in half. She wore a nursing bra, which wasn't even close to cute. Why the hell did he have to see everything? She raised her hands to cover herself, but he wasn't deterred. He deftly undid the hooks on her bra and it fell away. Lyla tried to escape, hands clamped over her damp breasts, but he boxed her in.

"When I get aroused, I start leaking. It's embarrassing—" she began.

Gavin gripped her wrists, spread her arms and examined her breasts, which definitely weren't as perky as they'd been before she gave birth. Sex was about fantasy and her post pregnancy bod, scars and leaking breasts dimmed her libido significantly.

When his head ducked down, she collided with the wall. She sucked in her breath, which did nothing to prevent Gavin from capturing her nipple in his mouth. He suckled. Lyla screeched and tried to stomp his foot. Gavin dragged her up so her breasts were at the perfect height for him to feast. Lyla shoved at his head, but he didn't budge.

"Gavin, stop!" she shrieked.

He ignored her. As he sucked, more milk gathered heavy in her tits. Gavin switched to the other breast and she fought the sexual pull, but he was relentless. Knowing there was no escape, she stared down at him as he fed. Gavin wasn't turned off by her lactating. On the contrary, he seemed frenzied and hungrier than ever. As she watched, the place between her legs went liquid. When she couldn't take anymore, Lyla yanked his head back and covered his wet mouth with hers.

Gavin let her drop low enough for him to slide back inside. He fucked her hard, raising one thigh to go even deeper. Gavin wouldn't allow distance between them and accepted everything about her, even the things she didn't like about herself. How could she not love him?

Gavin's unrelenting thrusts pushed her over the edge. As her body milked him, Gavin came, gripping her ass and mashing their bodies together until he stopped pulsing inside of her. She panted against his naked, heaving chest and waited for her body to calm down.

"Okay?" he murmured.

"Yeah," she said lazily.

Gavin didn't move for a long time. When he finally disengaged, he carried her into the bathroom. He turned on the taps in the bathtub and shrugged out of his clothes. When the tub was full, he settled her in front of him. Lyla leaned back against his broad chest. They sat there with the occasional slosh of water echoing in the massive bathroom.

The charged energy around him had dimmed somewhat, but it would never vanish completely. It was a part of him.

Outside these walls, the world wasn't a beautiful place. It was dark, brutal and grim. The underworld was a place filled with untold horrors and people with no souls. Gavin had been taught not only how to survive in darkness, but to control it.

It had taken her being nearly gunned down while seven months pregnant for her to come to terms with the fact that the underworld needed a ruthless dictator at the hilt... and that man was Gavin. He spent the last four months reclaiming his territory. It was clear from Gavin's cold fury that he hadn't been able to locate Sadist, the man who claimed Gavin's title for almost two years. Sadist haunted Lyla's dreams, which were amplified with fear now that she had Nora.

"I miss having you beside me at night," he said and rested his face in her hair and inhaled. "It's been hell, baby."

"I miss you too."

"Nora's getting so big."

She smiled without opening her eyes. "She is."

His arms tightened around her. "You haven't been sleeping much."

She dropped her head back to see his face. "What do you mean?"

He tapped the watch on her wrist. "It has a heart

monitor. You barely get five hours a night and it's not because of Nora."

"Don't worry about it, Gavin."

"Why aren't you sleeping?"

She didn't answer. He cupped her cheek and ran his thumb over her bottom lip.

"Your panic attacks are becoming more frequent."

She scowled. "Blame Blade. He keeps springing surprise attacks on me throughout the day to see how I'll respond."

"It's a precaution."

In case she had to fight for her life. Again. "I know."

"You're becoming better than a decent shot."

His voice was warm with approval. She tilted her chin proudly.

"Yup *and* I can kick ass."

His mouth twitched. "You're cute."

She surveyed Gavin who was made of muscle. "Well, I can't kick ass like you, but I put two of your men down."

"Because you did a crotch shot."

Of course he knew that. "How often do you watch me on the surveillance cameras?"

"Enough."

She narrowed her eyes at him. "How much, Gavin?"

He kissed her forehead. "A lot."

"I can't believe you watched me this afternoon," she grouched.

"You should be happy I watched or I wouldn't be here right now." He cupped her breast and thumbed her nipple, making her jolt. "Why didn't you give me the green light if we could have sex?"

"You're busy."

"So?"

"You have better things to do."

His hand tightened on her sensitive breast. "Lyla, you're my first priority always."

"Giving me orgasms isn't a priority."

"It is to me." He dropped his forehead on hers. "I've been waiting to have you again. I jerked off watching you in my car, took care of business and came to you as soon as I could."

"That's romantic," she said dryly.

"You want romance?"

Lyla made a face. "Romance?" Their relationship had never been about flamboyant gestures or sweet words.

He looked offended. "You don't think I can do romance?"

"I don't need romance," she said.

Gavin eyed her narrowly. "I can give you romance."

She imagined him on his knees with a rose clamped between his teeth and began to laugh. Gavin didn't have a romantic bone in his body. When she ran from him, he blackmailed her into coming back. A year and a half later he gained her marriage vows by threatening to harm her cousin, Carmen. He was no prince charming. The thought of him trying to be romantic was ludicrous. It wasn't until she glanced at his face that she realized he had taken exception to her amusement.

"Gavin, it's not a big deal," she said, patting his

arm. He was a crime lord, not Romeo. "I never asked for romance."

He grasped her chin and glared down at her. "Was your ex romantic?"

"Jonathan?"

God, she hadn't thought of him in months. Jonathan, the IT consultant she left behind in Maine had been the definition of a gentleman. He was the sweetest man she had ever met and it wasn't an act. He wooed her with long drives along the coast, picnics on the beach and conversation. The memories slipping through her mind seemed like they were from another lifetime. A growl from Gavin had her gaze jumping back to him.

"What?" she asked.

"You're smiling."

"Oh."

"You're still smiling."

Lyla couldn't straighten out her lips, not when Gavin was giving her such a disgruntled look.

"*Was* he romantic?"

She shrugged.

"What does that mean?"

She threw her hands in the air. "Who cares if Jonathan was romantic?"

"I do."

"Well, it doesn't matter now, does it?"

"It does."

She rolled her eyes. "You are seriously one of the most primitive men I've ever met." She held up left hand and wriggled her ring finger. The blue diamond sparkled. "We're married and have a kid together."

"Was he romantic?"

Gavin was such a bullheaded ass. "Yes, he was."

He tensed and she realized she should have lied.

"Gavin, romance is nothing compared to—"

"I'll give you fucking romance."

He got out of the tub and she grit her teeth.

"Gavin, this is stupid," she said.

He hauled her out of the tub and toweled her dry.

"Gavin, you don't have to—"

He picked her up like a bride and carried her into the bedroom. He dropped her on the bed and braced himself on all fours over her.

"I want to be the one to give you everything," he stated.

She clasped his face between her hands. "You do give me everything."

"Except romance."

She jerked his head down and kissed him. He tried to pull away, but she wouldn't let him. She licked his bottom lip until he opened his mouth and slid her tongue inside. Her emotions, which had always been volatile whenever it revolved around him, flared. She poured her love into him so he could feel it.

Gavin shuddered and kissed her back. He kissed her with such force that she sank into the mattress. His hands moved over her body, reclaiming every inch for himself. She smiled against his mouth as he slid inside of her. He rocked himself deep and they both groaned.

"I live for you," he said.

Her heart thudded against her rib cage. "I know. You're risking your life for me."

"Since my life means nothing without you, it's not a hardship." His eyes bored into hers. "What do you want, Lyla?"

"I want to feel safe." It was the one thing he couldn't give her, not until Sadist was dead. It was the reason she couldn't sleep. When she slept, she had nightmares of the knife-wielding psycho. Her paranoia even leaked into her waking hours. A slamming door or tone of voice could send her drowning in flashbacks.

"I'm going to get him," Gavin said.

If there was a man who would find the fucker who haunted her nightmares, it was Gavin. "I know."

"I'm going to bring his head to you on a platter," he vowed.

She grinned. "Is that your idea of romance?"

He paused, chagrined. Lyla laughed and wrapped herself around him.

"Anyone can give me romance, but no one can give me what you do."

The monster inside of him that made him the most feared man in the underworld watched her with starving eyes.

"And what's that?"

"Real love."

He stopped moving. "Real love?"

"Any man handing out roses on the street can charm a woman. Any man can plan an elaborate proposal with jet planes spelling out the big question, but no one can promise to love you forever. No one can promise that they won't get divorced or be there for each other through thick and thin." She gave him a mock glare. "Do you promise to love me forever?"

"Yes."

No hesitation. Her heart warmed. She smiled as she clasped his face between her hands.

"What about a divorce?"

"Fuck no."

"You promise never to leave me?"

He leaned down and said against her lips, "Once this is over, you won't be able to get rid of me."

She didn't have to ask the last question because they had been through more than most couples went through in several lifetimes.

Gavin made love to her with a gentleness that brought tears to her eyes. He adored her. It was in every touch, every look. Gavin played with her, teasing until she clawed his back and cursed at him. Then he brought her to an orgasm so good that she did cry, holding onto him, absorbing the fact that he was strong, warm and alive. Sending Gavin back into the underworld made her sick with worry, but they had no other choice.

"I love you," he whispered.

She smiled with her eyes closed. Maybe Gavin wasn't what most people would call romantic, but he was *her* type of romantic and that's all that mattered.

He shifted to get out of bed and she clung, not wanting to let go of this moment.

"Not yet. Ten more minutes," she mumbled sleepily. She hadn't had a good night of sleep for four months. If he just lay with her for an hour...

"I'm not leaving."

One eye opened. "You aren't?"

"You think I can leave you now that I had you again?"

She beamed. "You're spending the night?" It was a night of romance and miracles.

"Yeah. I just need to check my phone."

Lyla flopped onto the pillows and listened to his voice as he spoke to someone in Spanish. She let the sound of his voice lull her and slipped into the first peaceful sleep she had in months.

CHAPTER TWO

Lyla

Lyla woke to the most beautiful sight in the world. Gavin sat up in bed with Nora on his lap. He spoke to his daughter who bounced excitedly, bright blue eyes shining as she responded to him. It made her stomach feel warm and squishy. This is what she always wanted. Seeing them together was her version of utopia. Gavin had been the one who insisted on kids and she was so happy he had.

Gavin nuzzled Nora who made a happy shrieking sound and wrapped her arms around his head. Beau pranced, wanting to play, but knowing that Gavin wouldn't allow him on the bed. Beau saw that her eyes were open and ran to her so she could smother him with kisses while he growled low in his throat in appreciation.

"Nora's trying to sit up," Lyla said.

Gavin gave his daughter an admonishing look. "Stop trying to grow up so fast!"

Nora wasn't intimidated by her father. She let out a happy gurgle and drooled. Lyla sat up, clutching the sheet to her bare chest.

"Da da da," Nora chanted as she bounced.

"Yes, I'm your daddy," Gavin said and brushed kisses over her face, "and he loves you so much."

Lyla's heart clenched. During the short stretches of time that Gavin was home, he doted on Nora. Carmen warned him that he was going to spoil her. The last time she said this, Gavin gave her a cool look.

"She deserves to be spoiled. She's mine."

Carmen threw up her hands, but Lyla saw her hiding a smirk. Carmen couldn't resist giving Gavin shit. They had an odd relationship, but it worked for them so Lyla didn't interfere.

"She's hungry," Gavin said.

Lyla sat up and reached for the baby. Gavin watched as Nora found her breast and latched on hungrily. Lyla flushed when she saw Gavin's heated gaze. She wasn't used to having him around for feedings.

"You shouldn't feel insecure about your body, especially about something natural like lactating. It made me hot to see you pregnant. Why would it be any different to see this?"

"I didn't think men would—"

His eyes narrowed. "You don't need to think about what other men want. You only need to think about me."

Lyla rolled her eyes. "Obviously I'm not thinking of anyone else. How could I?"

"Make sure it stays that way." He ran a hand down her face. "You slept good?"

"Like the dead."

"Feel good?"

She nodded.

"Good."

His hand ruffled through Nora's hair. In the

bright morning light, she saw a fresh cut on the back of his hand. She grabbed his hand to examine it and felt her stomach dip.

"Is this from a knife?" she asked.

"It's nothing, baby."

She stared at him as fear cascaded through her. "What happened?"

"It was nothing."

"I won't lose you," she whispered.

"You won't lose me."

"What if you're shot or—"

"I've survived much worse."

She bit her lip. "Gavin, if you can't find him, maybe—"

His expression tightened. "Don't, Lyla. I'm going to find him."

"But it's been four months. Maybe you killed him already and don't know it," she said hopefully even though she didn't believe it.

"He'll surface. He always does."

She ordered him back into the underworld. Guilt and worry lay heavily on her. She had become a paranoid recluse, only leaving the house to go to doctor's appointments. Thank God Carmen was here. Carmen didn't ask if she could move in. After Nora was born, she arrived with two suitcases and claimed a room. Surprisingly, Gavin didn't make a fuss about it. Carmen made her house arrest bearable.

"I know what I'm doing, Lyla. Don't worry about me."

"How can I not worry about you?" she snapped.

"I was raised in the underworld. I'm getting

close."

She tightened her hold on Nora. "You are?"

"I'm making people nervous. That's good." His eyes glittered. "I'm going to get him."

"I just want this to be over." It had been over two years since the attack that claimed Manny's life and left her scarred.

"It will be." Gavin sucked on her neck. "Coming home to you keeps me human."

She elbowed him. "Sex isn't the answer to everything!"

"Yes, it is. It reminds me how much I have to lose and that fucking isn't happening."

She waved a hand in his face and then dropped her eyes to Nora. "Watch your language, Gavin."

He grinned. "She's four months old."

"So?"

He shook his head. "I'm heading into the office. Janice and Alice have been asking about you and the baby. Do you want to come with me?"

Effectively distracted by the offer, her heart leapt with excitement while her belly iced with fear. "Is it safe to go out?"

"You're in my casino. Your security detail will be with you and you won't be left alone. Do you want to go?"

She hesitated only a moment before she said, "Yes, I'd like to go."

"We'll leave in two hours," Gavin said and headed for the bathroom.

Even while she felt safe in Gavin's fortress, lately she was beginning to feel the first stages of cabin fever. Before, she went out three to four times a week. Now, she left the house once a month.

Not only did Carmen help with Nora, she also trained with Lyla four times a week with a self-defense/mixed martial arts instructor and Blade who took them to a gun range on property. Carmen, who had been raised with an enforcer father and married into the Pyre clan understood what measures needed to be taken.

Lyla texted Carmen who responded immediately, saying she was down for the 'excursion.' Lyla scanned her messages and saw a text from her mother: *Please call. Really need to talk to you.* Lyla ignored the text. The last time she spoke to her mother was the day Nora was born. Her mother asked for money, of course. Traumatized by the attack at the field and Nora's birth, she hung up on her mother and ignored all messages and requests to talk since. Her father, a gambling addict, had fucked up again. It was nothing new. She was tired of cleaning up his shit.

Just as Nora finished eating, Gavin emerged from the shower. He took Nora so she could get ready. This felt so normal and domesticated. Lyla had an extra spring in her step as she applied makeup for the first time in months and donned a navy blue wrap dress. She added a white scarf to cover her scarred chest and a cover if she had to nurse Nora. She draped a coat over her arm and added stiletto boots.

She found Carmen in Nora's nursery with a bulging baby bag.

Carmen gave her a lascivious grin. "Did you get any sleep last night?"

Lyla smiled. "A little."

Carmen no longer looked like the Playboy bunny she had been when her husband was alive. It had been over two years since Carmen lost her husband. The crying spells waned and Carmen seemed to be adjusting to her new lot in life. She took out her breast implants, dyed her hair black and still managed to hook every man within a ten-foot radius. After wearing sweat pants for four months it was a shock to see Carmen looking like her old self. Today's ensemble was a nude skirt that hugged every curve of her body from waist to ankle and a white lace blouse. Carmen completed the look with white heels and large diamond stud earrings. The look was deceivingly demure, but an outright challenge to any man.

"You're asking for trouble," Lyla said with a grin.

Carmen beamed and posed with her hands on the stroller, looking like a seductive MILF. "I *love* trouble."

Carmen ruined her image by twerking in her tight skirt. Apparently, Carmen had been feeling the effects of cabin fever and had finally cracked.

"Okay, so you're dying for trouble. I get it. You already packed Nora's things?" Lyla asked.

Carmen gave a mock salute. "Yes, ma'am and I dressed Nora too. Let's get the hell out of here!"

Lyla laughed as Carmen wheeled everything towards the hallway. Blade, Lyla's bodyguard, efficiently folded the stroller and shouldered the baby bag.

"You're getting good at that, Blade. When are

you going to become a daddy?" Carmen asked as she sashayed past.

"When hell freezes over." Blade glanced at Lyla who had her arms crossed. "No offense. Babies aren't my thing."

"But Nora loves you," Lyla said.

"I like her well enough since she's my goddaughter," Blade said with a straight face, "but she needs a lot of everything and I don't have time for that."

Lyla patted him on the chest. There was a time when Blade scared the living daylights out of her, but those days were long gone. Blade took a bullet for her and was fast becoming part of the family, something he didn't seem thrilled with.

"Maybe when things calm down you can have your own life," Lyla said.

Blade's dubious expression clearly stated that he didn't believe there would ever be a time that they wouldn't need his services. When they walked into the kitchen, they found the cook finishing up fresh omelets.

"I miss coffee," Lyla said as she dug into her omelet.

"You can have some, can't you?" Carmen asked as she ate a banana.

"Not much and I want to load it with creamer, so it's best not to."

Her weird pregnancy cravings were gone, thank God, but she was still eating more than she used to. The workouts with her instructors and breastfeeding were burning off calories, but her body still needed more to produce milk. She was a bit self-conscious with the extra weight, but if Gavin didn't mind then why should she? She was a mother, after all, not a super model. Lyla jolted when Beau flopped at her feet. Lyla glanced down and received a baleful look from Beau who realized they were leaving him behind.

"I don't think daddy's going to let you in his casino," she said to him.

"I've been texting Alice," Carmen said.

Lyla looked up. "About what?"

"Some of her volunteer projects."

Alice, the Community Outreach Coordinator for the Pyre Foundation, was in charge of putting a good foot forward for Pyre Casinos. Last year Carmen and Lyla volunteered at a dog shelter, which is how Lyla ended up with Beau. Lyla enjoyed helping Alice, but after the last attack she retreated completely.

"Next week Alice has a volunteer day at a hospital. Gavin gave a generous donation to add a new wing."

Gavin walked in with Nora cradled in one arm. Lyla was momentarily sidetracked as she took in Gavin's slick appearance. He wore a crisp gray suit with a light blue shirt and silver tie. There was nothing hotter than a man with a baby.

Gavin raised a brow. "Ready?"

"Uh, yeah." She ignored the pool of desire in her belly. He took her twice last night. How the hell could she still be horny? She thought once they had Nora their libidos would slack off. Not so, apparently. "You didn't tell me you donated money to a hospital."

Nora's pacifier bounced as she yanked on her daddy's tie. Gavin didn't bother to snatch it from her chubby hands.

"It's a good cause." Gavin shifted his sleeve to glance at his watch. "Let's go."

Lyla bent down to kiss Beau and promised she would be back as soon as possible. On the way to the door, Lyla made sure the safety on her gun was on. Carrying a gun saved her life four months ago. She wouldn't be caught without it. She was sure Carmen was packing as well. The world they live in forced them to take extreme precautions.

They walked into the crisp morning. Lyla automatically glanced around to take in her guards. She didn't know what Gavin did to test what was left of his men and didn't want to know. All she knew was a quarter of their security went on the run and several of them disappeared after Gavin interrogated them.

Gavin placed Nora in the car seat and rode shotgun while Blade drove. Lyla scooted in beside Nora while Carmen sat on her other side.

"This is going to be the first time everyone sees her. You like her outfit?" Carmen asked.

Nora wore black leggings with a knit sweater with a cute heart design, matching boots and cap. Lyla brushed the back of her hand against Nora's cheek, which was toasty warm.

"She looks adorable," Lyla said.

"Of course she does. I bought her that," Carmen said proudly.

Lyla made faces at Nora, which made her giggle and reach for her. Lyla allowed Nora to mess up her hair before she pulled back and left her hand on her daughter's lap to play with. Lyla couldn't resist turning in her seat to look at the entourage of SUVs following them. It was normal to feel paranoid after what she had been through, right? Her eyes touched on the trunk. She had a vivid memory of lying back there, holding onto Beau, willing him to live after he had been shot.

Lyla took a deep breath and faced forward. She screwed her eyes shut and willed away the flashbacks, but they refused to be ignored. She could still hear the pop of gunfire as her guards turned on one another. Adrenaline flooded her body, which wanted her to go into fight or flight mode. Lyla sat back, closed her eyes and tried to calm down.

The flashbacks happened without warning. She had done everything in her power to avoid situations that would cause her anxiety, such as leaving the house. When she felt steady enough, she opened her eyes and saw Blade watching her in the rearview mirror. She looked away.

Gavin's fortress lay on the outskirts of the city, far from the prying eyes of society. The desert was an unforgiving place, much like the people who occupied it. Lyla had come to appreciate its starkness and take comfort in the isolation of their home.

Las Vegas was an oasis in the middle of the Mojave Desert. The lure of money and sex enticed millions to The Strip to try their luck since the 1930s. Lyla resisted the urge to cover Nora's eyes as they cruised down The Strip. Women with pasties on their breasts and skirts too short to cover their asses tried to make a quick buck by posing with nerdy tourists or preteen boys. Others dressed as popular characters while street performers tried to entertain the crowds.

Blade stopped in front of one of Gavin's casinos. Gavin unbuckled Nora from her car seat and carried her inside. Lyla shouldered the baby bag while Blade followed with the stroller. Despite her excitement about leaving the house, she was on edge and extremely tense. There were people everywhere and the blast of sound was overwhelming. The smell of smoke was heavy in the air and even though it wasn't even ten o'clock, cocktail waitresses held trays laden with liquor. There were no kids in sight, of course. Las Vegas wasn't child friendly, a point she tried to impress upon Manny when she was young and naive. However, Manny allowed her to create a black stallion statue instead of another naked figure for the gamblers to touch for luck.

They made their way through the casino to the employee area and executive offices. Gavin's employees stopped and stared at the sight of him with a baby. Several of the braver souls stepped forward to greet Nora who was fascinated by all the new faces. Gavin didn't offer Nora to any of the cooing women gathered around him. Gavin was a possessive bastard and didn't want to give his daughter to anyone for a second.

"Lyla!"

Lyla turned and saw Marcus approach. Before Gavin could interfere, his good-looking COO

29

kissed her on the cheek and wrapped her in a tight hug. Marcus had become dear to her in the short time she'd known him. Not only did he shoulder Gavin's workload, he was also unfailingly loyal, which he proved when Gavin was in jail for money laundering. Marcus was more aggressive in business than Vinny had ever been and was relentless in his ambition to expand the Pyre Empire. Marcus acted as if *he* was a Pyre and seemed determined to leave a brilliant legacy behind for the next generation.

"You're good?" Marcus asked seriously, cupping her cheek.

She loved that about Marcus. He could be cutthroat in business, but he was affectionate and treated her like a long lost sister. He didn't follow the rules of propriety where she was concerned, which drove Gavin insane.

"I'm good," she said.

He stood back and beamed. "You look great!"

She relaxed and her anxiety fell away. "Thank you."

"Where's my goddaughter?"

Gavin scowled as he broke through the ring of female employees around him. "I never made you Nora's godfather."

"You should," Marcus said, unperturbed by Gavin's surly attitude. He bent to catch Nora's attention. "Hi, baby, I'm Uncle Marcus." He held his hands out to her.

Gavin began to smirk, but that vanished when Nora reached for Marcus, a complete stranger. Gavin started to turn away. Marcus deftly snatched

Nora from her father who looked as if hell warmed over. Lyla wrapped her arm around Gavin's waist so he wouldn't harm Marcus who earned himself a bruised jaw in the past.

"Cool it," she said and tried to hide her smile.

"I don't like him touching you," Gavin growled.

How many times had she heard that since she met Marcus? It was obvious there was nothing romantic between them, but Gavin never failed to comment on it.

"He's like my brother."

They watched Marcus talk to Nora who was taken by his smooth voice and All-American good looks.

"We should make him her godfather," Lyla said and Gavin stiffened.

"Hell no."

"Why not? Look at him with her. I trust Marcus with Nora."

Gavin grunted. "I don't want him to think he's family."

"You trust him with your business and money, but not your family?"

Gavin didn't answer.

Marcus settled Nora on his hip and raked Carmen from head to heels while she spoke to a nightclub manager who was grinning like a fool. Marcus's normally expressive face revealed nothing of what he was thinking.

"Lyla, you're here!"

Alice, wearing purple slacks and an unflattering blouse with large flowers embraced Lyla and then backed away, clapping her hands. "You look great!

Where's the baby?"

Before Lyla could answer, Alice spotted Nora in Marcus's arms. She rushed over and talked to Nora who flapped her arms and smiled so wide that her pacifier dropped. Like Gavin, Marcus didn't relinquish his hold on Nora. Alice was disappointed, but she wasn't about to play tug of war with a baby or snap at her boss.

"He's hogging her," Alice complained and then bounced on her toes, eyes lighting up as she remembered something. "Are you able to volunteer at the hospital next week? Carmen said she'd talk to you about it."

"I'm not sure," Lyla said and felt Gavin fist his hand in the back of her coat.

"I'm on my way to a meeting with Janice to discuss the event. It's going to be our largest to date!" Alice eyed Gavin uncertainly, clearly uneasy about addressing him directly. "Are you coming, Mr. Pyre?"

"No," Gavin said shortly.

Alice didn't bother to hide her relief. It was clear she wasn't comfortable around her CEO. She turned back to Lyla. "You want to come to the meeting?"

Lyla looked up at Gavin. His jaw was locked. Clearly, he didn't want her out of his sight, but she was curious about the event and felt bad for not participating. Before Nora was born she had been extremely active in the Pyre Foundation and enjoyed volunteering.

"Lyla?" Alice prompted.

She went on tiptoe and kissed Gavin's bristly

jaw. "I'll be back." She glanced at Marcus who presented Nora to the casino workers as if she were his. "You'll keep an eye on Nora?"

"Of course. Blade," Gavin bit out and Blade materialized by her side, "bring her right back to me."

"Yes, sir," Blade said.

Lyla slipped away from Gavin, kissed Nora on the cheek and looked around for Carmen, but she was gone. Lyla tamped down her alarm. Carmen could take care of herself and she wasn't a target like her. Alice waved tentatively at Blade who regarded impassively in return. Four guards joined him.

"Did I miss something?" Alice asked out of the side of her mouth. "I thought we haven't seen you because of Nora. Is something else going on?"

"That's just Gavin being Gavin." Lyla didn't hesitate to put the blame on him.

Revealing anything about the attacks wasn't an option. Alice might keel over from the shock. Alice was a Utah native, a state known for its strict religion and conservative views. She never asked Alice what prompted her to come to Las Vegas, but she was glad to have her here. Alice was a beam of light in an otherwise dark city filled with greed and lust.

"You look great," Alice said admiringly as they walked through the casino.

"Thank you. I'm starting to feel... better."

Seeing Nora being fawned over by Marcus, Alice and the other employees made her feel as if she was a part of a community rather than a lone ranger. For the first time in months she wasn't worrying about Gavin in the underworld or Nora's future. She could live in the moment as she walked arm in arm with Alice through the casino, which was teeming with people.

"What are your plans today?" Alice asked.

"I'm not sure. Gavin said you and Janice have been asking about Nora so I thought we'd visit. Carmen came too, but I don't know where she's gone off to."

"Oh, I should have invited her to the meeting." Alice waved her hand. "Well, she's been involved from the beginning so she knows everything anyway."

Carmen had been in on the plans for the hospital event? How? She hadn't left the house.

Alice steered her into a conference room where Janice was holding court. Gavin's Public Relations Coordinator was a force to be reckoned with. Janice single handedly pulled Gavin's tattered image out of the trash after Gavin went to jail and Manny's grisly murder was splashed across the news. Between Alice and Janice, the Pyre name had become a beacon of hope in the communities that badly needed a benefactor.

"You're back!" Janice exclaimed, running forward in spiked heels and a tailored suit. She gave Lyla a fierce hug and then looked past Lyla to Blade, the only guard who entered the room. "Where's the baby?"

"With Gavin and Marcus," Lyla said.

Janice's eyes bugged. "You trust them with a baby?"

34

"I don't think I could pry her away from them. Gavin's obsessed and Marcus has elected himself her godfather."

"Blade, make yourself comfortable," Janice said, ever courteous, and led Lyla to the table.

Janice introduced her to six women who were managing this event and immediately began to outline the festivities. Gavin helped repair two wings of the hospital, which had been destroyed during a fire and made a sizable donation to build a new one. The hospital was celebrating the completion of the new wing, which Alice saw as an opportunity for the Pyre Foundation to reach out.

Alice spoke enthusiastically about the itinerary. It was clear that this had taken months to plan and the amount of people involved was staggering. Over one hundred Pyre employees were volunteering their time to pass out goodie bags and care baskets. Lyla was moved by the stories of the patients. Thanks to Carmen's connections, they had an impressive list of celebrities attending the event to draw the press. Lyla's brows shot up when she heard Kody Singer agreed to make a little girl's dying wish come true. Carmen was talking to her past fling?

Every person in the room possessed an abundance of love, caring and hope. It made the underworld seemed like an alternate universe. How could there be people with no souls on the same planet with someone like Alice who believed in the good in every human being? Just being in this room filled with compassionate, giving people made Lyla's fear and worry fade. The best way to combat the darkness was to get involved and be around people who were trying to make a positive difference in the world.

As the meeting concluded, Lyla was hugged and kissed on the cheek by the staff and volunteers. She had been alone for so long that the simple show of support made her eyes sting with tears. Alice and Janice stayed behind to ask about Nora and how she was doing as a new mother. Lyla hadn't been this relaxed in months and found herself wishing she could stay with them.

"So, are you coming to the event?" Alice asked.

"Yes!"

"Yay! I'm so glad. I've missed having you around."

"Is Gavin coming?" Janice asked archly.

"No. He has other things to see to," Lyla said.

Janice didn't push. Lyla wasn't sure how much Janice knew about the truth behind the rumors surrounding Gavin's involvement in criminal activities.

"No matter," Janice said briskly. "Gavin lets his money speak for him, which is what matters. He's done wonders for the community through the Pyre Foundation."

"We have to have a girl's day," Alice said.

"We should," Janice agreed. "Carmen and the three of us... and Nora, of course. I gotta run."

"Me too," Alice said after a harried glance at her Minnie Mouse watch.

"Love you, see you soon," Janice said and kissed Lyla on the cheek.

Alice copied her and both women disappeared

at a fast trot. Lyla looked at Blade who stood by the door during the meeting.

"Not a good idea," Blade said bluntly.

"It's a good cause. I want to help."

"Too many variables. Gavin won't allow it."

Her good mood was beaten back by cold, hard reality. She glared at Blade. "I can't lock myself in the house for the rest of my life. People need help."

"You can't help anyone if you're dead."

Lyla stepped up to Blade and pressed her gun against his middle. Blade didn't flinch. He just stared at her with cold, fathomless eyes.

"I am so sick of hiding from that bastard. If he comes for me, this time I'll be ready."

"You can't be prepared for everything."

Blade disarmed her so quickly she didn't have a chance to hang onto the gun. Her pistol thudded to the ground several feet away. Blade grabbed her arm and yanked hard. Lyla whirled and found herself in a chokehold. Even as panic tried to grab her by the throat, the lesson her self defense instructor drilled into her took over. Lyla kicked her stiletto boot up hard and fast as if she was going to kick her own ass and felt it connect with her target. Blade released her instantly and sank to his knees, hands over his crotch. He didn't make a sound as he knelt on the floor as if he was praying.

It had become a weekly ritual for Blade to surprise her at inopportune moments. The skirmishes were been unexpected and over quickly. Each time, she had responded correctly and today was no exception. It wasn't easy to endure these tests, though. It triggered memories of the other attacks. Lyla shuddered and tried to shake off the chill.

"Are you okay?" Lyla asked.

Blade growled, but didn't look up. Lyla fetched her pistol and put it in her purse. Lyla wiped sweat from her brow and brushed a hand over her scarf to make sure it covered her chest. Her hand brushed over the tip of a raised, ragged scar. She knew each and every mark by heart and could vividly recall the agony as Sadist inflicted the wounds, staring down at her with soulless black eyes. Lyla paced as she tried to suppress the memories. She turned on Blade who still hadn't moved.

"I guess that really works," she said.

If looks could kill, she would have perished. Blade's jaw flexed as he restrained himself. He rose slowly and took an experimental step before he waved his hand.

"Let's go," he said in a husky voice.

Lyla didn't need to be told twice. She walked out of the conference room and was confronted by the rest of her security detail. Two guards took the lead and two fell behind while Blade kept pace beside her. They walked along the outskirts of the casino.

"I'm ready, don't you think?" Lyla asked.

"Gavin won't let you attend. I'd just shoot you from afar and get it over with," Blade said, clearly still agitated from her crotch shot.

"But this guy likes to play." Her stomach pitched as memories of the past began to wash out her surroundings. "He could have shot Manny and I the first time, but he didn't. He drew it out. He wanted to torture Manny to teach him a lesson and he used his knife on me..."

Everything around her faded into nothingness. Memories of the day Manny was killed slammed into her. The elegant casino disappeared and she was once again in Manny's mansion, hands pinned behind her as she watched Manny being beat to death. Her body broke out in a cold sweat and she was flooded with terror. Someone grabbed her arm and she wrenched away.

"Don't touch me!" She backed up and tried to shake the visions away, but she could still hear the sound of bones breaking and the cruel laugh of the monster who systematically tore Manny to pieces.

"Lyla, it's okay, it's me."

Lyla came up against a wall, braced her hands on knees and tried to catch her breath. She clenched her teeth against the need to scream. She felt exposed and vulnerable with the guards watching, waiting for her to get a hold of herself. Lyla wished Alice or Janice was here to chase away her nightmares.

"Lyla, it's me," Blade said.

"G-give me a minute," she wheezed and placed a hand over her racing heart.

"It's all in your head."

Lyla raised her head and glared at Blade. "You think I don't know that?"

"This isn't the place to have a panic attack," he snapped impatiently.

Lyla was seriously considering shooting him when she heard one of her guards say, "Can I help you?"

"Morgan?"

Lyla straightened abruptly. Something about that voice snapped her out of her nightmare and into the present. It couldn't be... Lyla looked around Blade and came face to face with her past. Her body went cold with shock. Jonathan, the ex she left in Maine was standing less than eight feet from her.

CHAPTER THREE

Lyla

"Jonathan," she whispered.

Jonathan was just shy of six feet with light brown hair and eyes. He was clean-cut and approachable in khaki pants and a purple button up shirt. Jonathan had the softness of a man who didn't go to the gym and the paleness of someone who worked in front of a computer twelve hours a day. He hadn't changed a bit. Seeing him sent a spear of something sharp and painful zinging through her. It was as if Gavin's questions about romance conjured Jonathan out of thin air.

Memories of their first meeting tickled the back of her mind.

"Can I take you out to dinner?" he asked the first time he stepped up to her window at the bank.

"Sorry, no," she told him and tried to steer their conversation back on a professional level. "How do you want your bills?"

"Boyfriend?" Jonathan asked.

"No, I'm not looking for a relationship."

"Are you looking for a friend?"

She took in his awkward smile and nerdy appearance. It wasn't the first time she had been asked out, but it was the first time that line had been used and it hit her in the gut. She had been alone for so long and this guy exuded quiet strength and goodness. It was the lack of artifice in his clothing and smile. He wasn't playing a game.

Even though she wanted to say yes, she replied with, "Maybe some other time."

Jonathan didn't give up. For the next two months, he came in at least once a week and would wait until she was free, even if it was to withdraw ten dollars. Despite his persistence, he always kept the conversation light and never failed to make her smile. He always ended with a request to go out and she finally accepted. It was one of the best things she had ever done.

Her first everything had been Gavin. She didn't know anything else. Jonathan was a breath of fresh air. He lived modestly and had a normal nine to five. He filled her life with innocent movie dates and weekends exploring lighthouses along the coast. Their relationship morphed naturally. She kept waiting for something fucked up to surface, but it never had. Being with Jonathan restored her faith in humanity until Blade arrived and shattered her world.

"Morgan," Jonathan said and took a step forward.

He stopped when her guards blocked his way. Lyla drank him in. It was like seeing a ghost. She mourned the simple life she had in Maine and now it was in her face, rousing memories that made her feel as if she was in free fall.

"Morgan, are you all right?" Jonathan asked urgently.

"I'm..." She couldn't think. Her past life and lover were standing right there. She had been happy with him and now... Lyla was suddenly very aware of the layer of cold sweat on her skin, her scarred chest and the gun in her purse. What happened to the bank teller who dated Jonathan Huskin and lived an ordinary life on the East coast?

"We need to go," Blade said abruptly and grasped her arm.

When Blade fetched her from Maine, Jonathan had been on a business trip. That was a lucky coincidence for Jonathan since Blade had orders to kill him. Blade had never met Jonathan, but he wasn't slow on the uptake. Blade knew exactly who he was.

"What are you doing in Las Vegas? Who are these men?" Jonathan asked.

Her stomach rocked with regret and guilt. Jonathan was a great guy. She hadn't let herself think of him after she'd been forced to return to Gavin. Jonathan was the nice guy women regretted for the rest of their lives. He was gentle, caring and dependable. He coaxed her out of her fear and paranoia and into a healthy relationship that left her cautiously hopeful until Gavin ruthlessly took over again.

"Why did you leave, Morgan?" Jonathan asked.

The ache in his voice made her eyes sting with tears. After all this time he still cared.

Lyla opened her mouth, but no sound came out. Blade propelled her forward. She had no choice but to try to keep up with him.

"Morgan!" Jonathan kept his distance so her

guards wouldn't get physical with him. "What's going on? Who are these people?"

"We're her security detail," Blade said. "I'd back off if I were you."

"Why do you need security?"

Lyla closed her eyes against the sound of his voice, which roused nostalgia and happy memories that clashed with her recent panic attack. Her insides were a mishmash of emotion and turbulence.

"Morgan, tell me why you left," he begged.

Morgan. That name belonged to a woman who didn't exist. Lyla blinked back tears. Seeing Jonathan was just too much on top of everything else. "What are you doing here?"

"I'm here for a conference. Why do you need security? Did something happen? Are you all right?"

"She's married to the casino owner, Gavin Pyre," Blade said abruptly. "I'd watch my step if I were you."

Jonathan stopped in his tracks and disappeared from sight as Blade marched her along.

When Lyla discovered who Gavin was beneath the tailored suits, she left him. She got as far away from Gavin as possible and met Jonathan who could offer her the normal life she wanted. Jonathan loved her out of her trust issues and many hang-ups. Nothing dissuaded Jonathan. He became her rock and talked about moving to the suburbs, owning his own company and having her be a stay at home mom. That felt like a lifetime ago.

"There's no going back," Blade said.

Lyla glanced at him. "I know that."

"Then why do you look so devastated?"

Blade led her to Gavin's office and gave a perfunctory knock before he opened the door. Nora stood on Gavin's desk, hands braced against her father's chest as he conducted a business call on speakerphone. Blade closed the door behind her. Lyla stood there for a moment, trying to get herself together. Nora bounced excitedly and held out her hands. Lyla forced herself to move.

"Hold," Gavin said and pressed the mute button on the phone.

With one arm wrapped around their daughter, he grasped her by the chin and kissed her. Lyla was too rattled by Jonathan's appearance to respond. Gavin pulled back. She felt the heat of his gaze on her face, but didn't look up.

"Okay?" he asked.

"Yeah."

Lyla settled on Gavin's couch with Nora and shifted her scarf so she could breastfeed. Gavin resumed his call and paced as he talked on the phone.

Seeing Jonathan had shaken her to the core. Cozy memories of a life she forced herself to forget drifted through her mind. Jonathan was the first person to make her feel safe after she left Gavin. She'd begun to believe that she could have a future and some kind of normal in her life. If she stayed with Jonathan would they be married? Life with Jonathan would be smooth sailing. She wouldn't be scarred, responsible for killing at least two men or be dogged by panic attacks.

Her eyes latched on Gavin as he paced. Jonathan and Gavin couldn't be more different from one another. Gavin was dominant and possessed an aura of power and danger that was palpable. His role as the crime lord fed his natural tendency to control and manipulate things to his liking. Even as a teenager, she sensed something wild inside of Gavin and ignored it to her own cost. He was borderline psychotic, possessive and domineering, but he loved her and she loved him.

Gavin caught her staring and raised a brow. Lyla immediately shifted her gaze to Nora. She leaned down to draw in her sweet scent and wasn't prepared for the onslaught of sorrow. She had lost so many people—Manny, Vinny, her parents. Jonathan was a man she would trust with her life, but if he knew the real her he would run and never look back. Her heart squeezed painfully over things that could never be.

That note of hurt in his voice when he asked why she left made her feel like crap. The day Blade came for her was the first time Jonathan had gone on a business trip since they moved in together. Did Jonathan think she had been waiting for him to travel so she could leave him?

"Lyla?"

She jerked and saw Gavin watching her. Apparently, he had finished his call.

Gavin frowned. "What's wrong?"

She cleared her throat and adjusted Nora in her arms. "Nothing's wrong."

There was a long silence. She clenched her teeth and hoped she appeared serene rather than deeply troubled.

Lyla mentally bitch slapped herself. Jonathan was her past. There was no sense in wondering what could have been. This was her reality. She was married to Gavin Pyre and had a child with him. Her life would never be normal. She would have security guards, a gun and night terrors for the rest of her life. She couldn't get rid of her scars or change the fact that Gavin blackmailed her into leaving Jonathan and then coerced her into marriage by threatening Carmen's life. Gavin was who he was and she... She was now a part of him, good and bad.

"How did the meeting with Alice go?" Gavin asked.

Lyla placed Nora on her shoulder and rubbed her back. "It went well. Your donation for the hospital is very generous."

"It's a good cause." Gavin paused and then said, "I don't want you going to the event."

"I'm going," she said with more heat than she intended.

Gavin's brows drew together.

She tried to soften her tone. "Like you said, it's a good cause and they need as many hands as they can. I want to be a part of it."

"There will be other events."

Lyla tensed. "I want to go to this one."

"I said no, Lyla."

After the effort Alice, Janice and the employees exerted, the least she could do was show up. Besides, she needed to do something productive and be reminded that there were good people in the world, not only scum. Why spend another day pacing the house, waiting for bad news when she could be doing something that would make a difference?

"I'm going," Lyla said firmly.

There was a loaded silence in the soundproof office.

"You haven't left the house for months and now you want to volunteer at a hospital event to give him another shot?"

She didn't need clarification on who Gavin was referring to. "I'm not going to the mall, Gavin. I'm going to an event being hosted by *your* foundation."

"No."

No discussion, no elaboration. Just, *no*. The dictator telling her what she could and couldn't do. She ground her teeth.

"Blade will come with me. So will the other guards. I've been training—"

"You train in case of an emergency, *not* so you can attend parties."

"It's not a party!"

He slashed a hand through the air. "This isn't a discussion, Lyla. My answer's no."

"I already told Janice and Alice I would be there."

"I'll talk to them."

Lyla glared at him. "So I'm supposed to stay cooped up in the house forever?"

"Not forever, just until I find him."

"And when will that be?"

Gavin's eyes narrowed into slits. "What's gotten into you?"

"I need something to look forward to."

Her bottled up emotions churned inside of her—the four months without him, the need to be a part of something positive and after seeing Jonathan, the need to appear normal.

Nora fussed, making Lyla feel awful for raising her voice. She was still shaken from her panic attack and seeing Jonathan. She definitely wasn't up to the challenge of arguing with Gavin.

"You haven't complained about being confined," Gavin pointed out. "This morning you were scared to leave the house and now you want to attend a large public event?"

She closed her eyes and tried to rein in her temper. She didn't want to fight. "This is important to me."

"Like I said, there will be other events you can attend in the future. I'm through discussing this."

There was a short knock before Carmen poked her head in the office. "There you are."

Lyla was relieved by the interruption. She got to her feet and slung the baby bag over her shoulder. "I want to go for a walk."

Carmen looked between her and Gavin. "Sure."

Gavin didn't say anything as she walked out of the office. Blade eyed her suspiciously as she made her way through the employee hallway. Lyla placed Nora in the stroller and grit her teeth when Blade and the rest of her security detail surrounded them. Seeing Jonathan made her realize how fucked up her life was. Security guards, guns and the constant threat of violence—that was her reality. The woman Jonathan knew no longer existed.

"What's going on?" Carmen asked.

Lyla gripped the handles of the stroller and attempted to smile at the employees she recognized from other events.

"I just saw Jonathan," Lyla said through clenched teeth.

"Who?" Carmen asked.

"My ex."

"What ex?"

Lyla gave her a baleful look. Carmen's mouth sagged a little.

"Here? Did he see you?"

"Oh, yeah, he saw me."

"Does Gavin know?"

"No."

"What is he doing here?"

"He's here for a conference."

"You talked to him?" Carmen asked, scandalized.

"I was having a panic attack and he noticed me. Maybe that got his attention, I don't know." Lyla grimaced and shook her head. "He wanted to know why I left him."

"It's been, what, three years since you left? I can't believe he spoke to you. Most guys would have flipped you off."

"Jonathan's not like that."

"He's an IT consultant, right?"

"Right."

"What is that, by the way?"

"I don't know. He's obsessed with computers."

Carmen shook her head. "I can't imagine you with anyone besides Gavin."

When they turned toward the casino, Blade materialized at her side.

"What are you doing?" he asked.

"I want to go home."

Blade pulled out his phone. She had no doubt who he was calling. She resisted the urge to slap the phone out of his hand and decided her energy was put to better use keeping an eye out for Jonathan.

"Lyla wants to go home," Blade said and then handed the phone to her.

Lyla wanted to ignore the phone, but knew she wouldn't be able to leave without Gavin's consent, which grated on her nerves. Coming out today had definitely been a mistake. The measures Gavin took to ensure her safety now felt like a noose around her neck. Jonathan reminded her of a life that didn't require such strict rules.

Lyla took the phone from Blade. "Yes?"

"What's wrong with you?" Gavin growled.

"Nothing's wrong with me. I want to go home."

"You fight to go to the hospital event and when I tell you no for your own good, you want to leave?"

"I'm tired." It was the truth. The past two hours put her through the emotional wringer.

"You weren't tired before you went to that meeting with Alice and you weren't tired a minute ago when you argued with me."

God, he was such a bulldog. "I don't want to argue, I just want to go home."

"We'll talk when I come home."

That surprised her. "You're coming home tonight?"

"Yes." He sounded as if he was speaking through clenched teeth. "You welcomed me home last night and you're going to do the same tonight. If this meeting couldn't be put off, I'd force you to come back to the office and settle this now."

"There's nothing to settle. You said no and I'm supposed to do what you say, right?" She wasn't sure where the words were coming from, but they were coming out strong and full of attitude.

Out of the corner of her eye, she saw Carmen make a clawing motion. Clearly, she approved, but Blade shook his head in warning.

"You're going to pay for that," Gavin promised. "Give the phone to Blade."

Her mouth was a tad bit dry as she handed the phone to Blade who listened for a moment and then pocketed it. He led the way into the casino, which meant Gavin gave his permission for her to leave.

"Holy shit, Lyla. You're baiting him. I hope you can take the heat," Carmen said.

She wasn't trying to bait him. The last huge fight they had was when he forced her to marry him. To date, she had never won a fight, but she was too pissed off to care.

"Are you doing this purposely so he'll punish you?" Carmen drawled.

Lyla gave her a baleful look.

"Don't knock it till you've tried it."

Blade and the rest of her guards stopped just outside of the lobby. She listened with half an ear as Blade told the driver to bring the SUV around. Lyla searched the milling crowd for Jonathan.

"Do you see him?" Carmen asked in a low

undertone, eagerly scanning the crowd.

Was she that obvious? "No."

"Was he good in bed?"

After being dominated by Gavin in her teens, Jonathan's gentle lovemaking made her feel cherished and empowered. He let her lead and their time together had been filled with affection and laughter. She couldn't begin to compare fucking Gavin to making love with Jonathan. The experience couldn't be more different.

Carmen clearly picked up on her reticence because she tried to make it easier.

"Fine. Rate him on a scale of one through five."

"Four," Lyla said without thinking.

"Really? Impressive."

"He was..." She fumbled for words. "He was great. If you met him—"

Carmen gripped her arm. "You know that's not an option, right?"

Her words were an echo of Blade's. Lyla bristled, irritated. She looked pointedly down at Nora. "I know that."

"Okay. Because you sound like you're thinking... I don't know."

"I wasn't expecting to see him and then he was just *there*. It was like seeing Manny again." Lyla waved her hands. "It's the shock. Seeing him reminded me of my other life."

"Let's go," Blade interrupted.

They walked out to the car. Blade placed Nora in her car seat. He fumbled with the buckles and swore fluidly under his breath. When Lyla offered to help, he gave her a killing look that made her sit back with a shrug. Nora chattered excitedly and touched his face when Blade leaned forward to examine the tiny mechanisms. He froze, gave Nora a reproving glare that made no impact on the baby and checked the straps before he slammed the door.

As the SUV left Gavin's casino behind Lyla let out a long breath. God, she felt as if she spent all day away from home instead of only a couple of hours. She forgot how fast life moved. For four months she took a time out to learn to be a mother and refine her fighting skills so she could act accordingly in case of an emergency. One day out of the house and she became emotionally shipwrecked.

Lyla glanced at her cousin who had gotten all dolled up for today. "Sorry we didn't stay out long."

Carmen shrugged. "Don't worry about it. Today was a bust for me too."

"Where did you go?"

"I gambled a bit, won a thousand dollars and got hit on a lot."

"And?"

"Nothing."

"So why was today a bust?"

Carmen didn't reply. Lyla's intuition pinged.

"What happened with Marcus?"

"Nothing happened with him."

"Do you *want* something to happen with him?"

Carmen examined her nails. "No."

"Carmen."

"What?"

"You're gunning for him, aren't you?" Lyla was

relieved to focus on her cousin's love life instead of her own. "Wait, so he wanted you, you turned him down and now you're trying to get him to make a move again?"

Carmen looked irritated. "I never said that and I can get any man I want, thank you very much."

"And you want Marcus."

"I didn't say that."

"You don't have to. You won money, got hit on and still aren't happy."

Carmen tapped her nails together, a nervous habit she didn't exhibit often. "I don't know what I want."

"You don't have to figure it out today."

"I have to figure it out sometime. I can't live with you forever."

"Yes, you can."

Carmen snickered. "I'm sure that'll go over great with Gavin."

"He doesn't get a say," Lyla said sharply.

Carmen's brows rose. "Wow. You really did love your ex, didn't you? He got you all riled up."

How could she explain what Jonathan had been to her? She had been struggling to survive when he came along. He coaxed her out of the dark and just... loved her.

"He was so good to me. I never wanted to hurt him. I walked out with just a note."

"You love Gavin," Carmen said.

"I know that, but..."

"But what?"

"I don't know." She waved her hand. "It was just a shock to see him and it reminded me how fucked up my life is."

"It isn't fucked up. You have a baby and a man who loves you."

Lyla jerked her thumb at the line of SUVs behind them carrying the rest of her security.

"You have security, so what? You're rich."

"So are you. I don't see you with an entourage of hired guns."

Carmen shrugged. "You're high profile."

"I killed at least two men," Lyla whispered.

"They deserved it."

"Well, yes, but *still*."

Carmen slapped her thigh. "I can't believe you ran them over with a car. That is totally badass."

"It wasn't badass. I was desperate."

"I wish I could kill somebody."

"Carmen!"

"What?"

"You can't *want* to kill somebody!"

"I mean, kill somebody who *deserves* it, duh."

"You're crazy."

"No, I'm not. I grew up in the business and know how it works. Some people deserve to live and some don't. If you don't put the wild dogs in their place they spread rabies so we contain or eliminate it. Simple."

Carmen's father had been an enforcer so she grew up knowing what the Pyres did. Lyla hadn't. Everyone around her had a crooked view of the world, which is why she latched onto Jonathan. She didn't have to turn a blind eye to the things he did or twist her morals for those she loved.

"You were born to be a crime lord's wife," Lyla

observed quietly.

It made more sense for Carmen and Gavin to be together, but there was no attraction between them. Maybe it was true that opposites attract since Carmen had been with Vinny who was even-tempered and steady while Carmen was restless, manic and hyper.

"I was a crime lord's wife for less than a week."

Lyla saw the sheen of tears in her cousin's eyes and leaned against her. "Vinny was a good man."

"He was. No one can replace him."

"No," Lyla agreed, "but hopefully you have room in your heart to give a part of yourself to someone else."

"I don't think I have anything to give. I'm just horny."

The driver shifted restlessly. Lyla was glad they were pulling up to the fortress. She didn't need security guards offering to relieve Carmen's needs. Carmen deserved better than a quick fuck.

They walked into the house and collapsed in the living room. Nora laughed delightedly when Beau rushed to greet them and sniffed her madly.

"So, are you going to help at the hospital?" Carmen asked.

"Gavin said no."

"He's right," Carmen said, slipping off her heels and reclining on the couch like Cleopatra.

Lyla scowled at her cousin. "I can't stay in this house forever and this event sounds amazing. It's the largest effort yet. How come you didn't tell me you were rounding up celebrities to help with this?"

"I knew you'd want to help and Gavin would

kill me for suggesting it. But, since Alice got you fired up for it, that's not my fault."

"I want to be a part of this. I want to be around normal people for a day."

"I'm normal!"

"No, you aren't. You're as crooked as they come," Lyla said.

Carmen waved her hand. "Don't flatter me when I'm so horny."

Lyla sank into the cushions. "I want to be a part of this."

"Gavin hasn't found a lead on him yet?"

"No. How long is this going to last? One day I'm going to want to take Nora to a park and meet other kids. I might want to go shopping or visit your mom instead of making her drive all the way out here."

"Mom doesn't mind."

"That's not the point! We're *here* twenty-four seven. I keep waiting for another attack or a phone call telling me Gavin's hurt." Her hands clenched into fists. "I want to do something. I need to help and I want some kind of normal in my life. This isn't what I want for Nora."

"It won't always be this way and Gavin can handle himself."

"I know that, but he's still human. He bleeds and can be killed just as easily as someone else."

"I think of him as The Terminator," Carmen said. "He can go into any situation and come home without a scratch."

Lyla thought of the knife wound on the back of his hand. "He's human."

Carmen gave Nora big, smacking kisses. "I used to be so focused on going to the clubs. Now, this is my whole day and I'm good with it."

"We're getting old."

Carmen sniffed. "*You're* getting old. I'm just getting more fabulous."

"Whatever you say."

Carmen settled Nora on a blanket, turned on her belly and propped her chin on her hand. "Tell me about him."

"Who?"

"Your ex, hello!"

Lyla pictured him in her mind. "He's cute."

Carmen scrunched up her face. Lyla felt compelled to defend him.

"Jonathan's an average guy in every way. He's cute, polite, stable."

"Gavin would kick his ass," Carmen predicted.

"Of course he would. I don't think Jonathan knows how to throw a punch."

"If Gavin finds out about him, mention that. Maybe Gavin will let him live."

"Gavin can't get mad about Jonathan. We have a baby together."

"So?"

"So, I'm taken."

"That hasn't stopped Gavin from being a jealous psycho."

True. "He won't find out about Jonathan."

"You better hope not," Carmen said.

Lyla played with Nora and Beau while Carmen watched TV. When Nora and Carmen drifted off, Lyla carried the baby upstairs with Beau on her heels. Lyla activated the baby monitor, which gave her a view of the crib from her phone and walked outside. She wrapped her arms around herself as she paced around the pool.

Of course she didn't regret Nora or her marriage to Gavin. Despite the rocky dips in their relationships, they were meant for each other. She knew it in her bones, but that didn't stop her from realizing how much she changed since she left Jonathan. With Jonathan, she could be herself. With Gavin, she had to stand her ground against his much stronger personality and her moral compass no longer had a needle.

She changed after witnessing Manny's demise at the hands of the criminal underclass. Seeing Jonathan made her realize how far off the path she traveled. It forced her to look at her life and it was uncomfortable. She witnessed and experienced things Jonathan never would and that colored her world in shades of gray. Lyla hoped once they discovered Sadist's identity, she and Gavin could settle into some kind of normal. Until then, she would live under the suffocating security blanket Gavin provided.

Lyla went inside and stretched out on the couch across from Carmen. Even in sleep, her cousin looked photo-shoot ready. Lyla inwardly snorted and checked on Nora who was sucking her thumb with her other arm tossed over her head. Lyla listened to her daughter's quick breaths and shut her eyes.

CHAPTER FOUR

Lyla

"Lyla."

She opened her eyes. It took her a moment to realize she was stretched out on the couch in the living room. Gavin sat beside her, hand on her hip while his other held Nora.

"She's hungry and there isn't any bottles in the fridge," he said.

Lyla sat up, smoothed back her hair and smiled at Nora who drooled over Gavin's pristine slacks. She glanced at the couch where Carmen had been and found it empty. She yawned as she shifted her dress aside to nurse Nora.

"What time is it?"

"Four," Gavin said.

"That was a long nap."

Gavin said nothing. She looked up and found him watching her closely.

"What?" she asked.

"We argued today."

"I know."

"I'm doing this to keep you safe."

He wouldn't let up. She hadn't even been up for five minutes and he was already drilling her. No, she would never have a restful life with Gavin.

"You're donating so much money to a good cause and I want to help."

"There will be other events."

Lyla braced herself. "I want to go, Gavin."

A muscle ticked in his jaw. "You're pissing me off."

"Why?"

"You're being distant and bitchy."

Lyla said nothing.

"You're still doing it."

"I'm a human being. I have emotions. I can't ditch them as easily as you do."

He tensed. "There it is again. What the hell happened at that meeting with Alice?"

"This has nothing to do with Alice."

"Then what is it about?"

Nora made an urgent sound, clearly ill at ease by their heated voices. Lyla made comforting sounds and angled her body away from Gavin.

"We'll discuss this later," she said pointedly.

Gavin didn't move. She tensed, wondering if he was going to push the issue. He was on edge and capable of anything.

"This isn't over," he said and went to his office.

At the meeting with Alice and Janice the fear and worry lifted, giving her a glimpse of life outside the underworld. She wanted to be a part of it so badly that her eyes burned with tears. Couldn't she tiptoe into the light for a couple of hours without being shot at? How could she explain that she wanted to be around people who would fill her battered soul with light and goodness? She needed to live despite the dark cloud that had been hovering over them. How long would she have to live this way?

Lyla took a deep breath and tried to smile at Nora who was watching her with rapt attention. "Why is life so complicated, honey?"

Nora splayed her tiny hand on Lyla's cheek and regarded her seriously as if to say everything would be all right.

Lyla burped Nora and headed upstairs to bathe her. Carmen ambled in during Nora's bath.

"How's my goddaughter doing?" Carmen said to Nora who flapped her arms excitedly.

"I'm going to freak out when she starts walking and talking," Lyla said as Nora sat in the tub with only a hand braced against her back. Babies were amazing. They were intuitive, intelligent and observant. She loved watching Nora respond to her surroundings. She wanted Nora to be around people like Janice, Marcus and Alice, not locked up in this house.

"She's growing up fast, isn't she?" Carmen sighed. "I can't believe we were babies once." Carmen's eyes widened. "I can't imagine Gavin as a baby."

Lyla snickered as she imagined Gavin as a stern-faced baby. Carmen chattered to Nora who listened to every word with wide eyes. Carmen carried Nora to the nursery to change her. Lyla began to follow and came face to face with Gavin who blocked the doorway.

"Can you watch Nora, Carmen?" Gavin called.

"Sure," Carmen said from the nursery.

"I need to talk to Lyla."

Gavin closed the door. Lyla turned away from him and went back into the bathroom. She drained the tub and hung the damp towels.

"I watched the surveillance videos," Gavin said from behind her. "Blade said you had a panic attack, but he didn't mention that a man came up to you."

Lyla stilled. Gavin was too damn thorough.

"Did you know him? He followed you through the casino."

With a feeling of dread, she turned to him. "He's an old acquaintance."

Gavin regarded her through narrow hazel eyes. "Who is he?"

"Someone I used to know."

"Who?"

She realized with a sinking heart that Gavin wasn't going to let it go. "It doesn't matter."

"If it doesn't matter, why won't you tell me?"

"Because I don't want you to freak out."

He folded his arms across his broad chest. "I don't freak out."

She threw up her hands, completely over this fucked up day. "Fine, Hulk out, but I don't want to deal with it."

"Tell me."

"It was Jonathan."

Gavin's expression didn't change. "Jonathan?"

She could see it didn't register. "My ex."

Every inch of his body went rigid. His eyes took on a dangerous cast. "What the fuck is he doing here?"

"He's here for a conference."

He cocked his head. "You spoke to him?"

"He recognized me."

"And you spoke to him?"

"Yes."

"And you weren't going to tell me?"

"Nothing happened."

"Nothing happened," he repeated and the way he said it sent a ripple of alarm down her spine. "He's the reason you're fighting to go to the hospital and why you picked a fight with me twice today."

"Volunteering has nothing to do with Jonathan."

"Don't say that weak fuck's name in this house."

Lyla took a step back. "Are you serious?"

Gavin prowled towards her.

"Am I serious about hearing that the man you *lived with* and gave you *romance* saw you today?" He leaned down so their faces were only inches apart. "Am I serious about the fact that you weren't going to tell me? Fuck yes, I'm serious, Lyla. Deadly serious."

"What do you want me to say?" she challenged.

"I want to know how you felt when you saw him."

She blinked. "Felt?"

"Yes. *Felt.*"

"I was shocked. I never expected to see him again," she said.

"And?" he pressed.

"I felt... sad."

"Why?"

"He's a good man."

"A good man," Gavin repeated without inflection.

"Will you stop that? Geez." She ducked under his arm and paced away so she could breathe. "He asked why I left him and I..." She wrung her hands, looked up and realized she'd made a massive mistake.

"You don't owe him shit," Gavin snapped.

"You don't know him!"

"I don't need to. He's nothing."

"He *isn't* nothing." Her eyes pricked with tears. "Jonathan took care of me. He was my friend. I disappeared almost three years ago, but when he saw me today, the first thing he asked is if I was okay. If a woman left you high and dry, would you bother saying anything to her if you saw her again?"

"What the fuck are you talking about? I *did* that. You left me without a word and I looked for you for three years! Yes, I fucking know how it feels and I brought you back twice because you belong with me."

She rubbed her throbbing temples. "This is pointless." Gavin would never understand what Jonathan had done for her. She had been a lost, broken person after she left Las Vegas. She had been shattered by Gavin's betrayal and spent years alone because she was terrified to let anyone in. Jonathan healed her with his steadfast patience. He was a good man and an even better friend, one she had left behind.

"Do you love him?"

Gavin's question made her freeze. She turned

back and saw him watching her with a predatory stillness that screamed danger.

Gavin stirred her emotions into a tangled, seething frenzy. The love she had for him had the power to destroy her and it had in the past. What she felt for Jonathan paled in comparison. It was sweet, gentle and caring. Safe. That's how Jonathan made her feel. With Gavin, she had to constantly go to war. Was it no wonder she clung to Jonathan? Gavin scared the shit out of her.

She shook her head. "No, I don't love him."

Gavin stared at her for a long minute, almost as if he was weighing the truth in her answer before he held out a hand.

"Come here."

She saw the beast getting riled and couldn't find it in herself to care. It had been a shock to see Jonathan. It was normal to wonder about a different path. If Gavin had given her some fucking space, she would have worked all of this out on her own. Of course, Gavin didn't give her time and was determined to prod her open wound.

"Come here, Lyla."

"No. I want to shower."

"I need you," he said, his tone forceful and threatening instead of comforting and lover like.

"Later."

She turned from him and slipped out of her clothes. There was no sound from Gavin as she stepped into the shower. When she glanced back, she saw he was gone and breathed a sigh of relief. How the hell had this day gone so wrong? She got ready for the day with a spring in her step and now she wished she never left the bed.

It wasn't until she was wringing out her hair that a disturbing thought crossed her mind.

"Gavin!"

No answer. She slipped into her robe and dashed into the bedroom, which was empty. With a growing sense of panic, Lyla rushed downstairs and burst through the doors to his office. Gavin sat behind the desk, a phone to his ear.

"Don't you dare hurt him!" she shouted.

Gavin didn't move the phone from his ear. She rounded the desk and didn't stop until she was pressed against him.

"Don't, Gavin!"

Gavin stared at her for what seemed like an eternity before he said, "I'll call you back."

He set the phone on the desk, folded his hands across his middle and gave her his full attention. Every instinct she possessed told her to back away, but she stayed put.

"Who were you talking to?" she asked.

"I don't see why I should tell you since you clearly don't volunteer such information yourself," he said softly.

Lyla felt the hit and didn't acknowledge it. "Were you giving orders about Jonathan?"

He didn't answer, which confirmed her fears.

"Gavin, you can't—"

"I can do whatever I want," he interrupted silkily.

"But he didn't do anything—"

"He touched you."

"What?"

He rose from his seat. She couldn't stop herself from taking a step back. His control slipped enough for her to get a glimpse of his icy rage before his expression smoothed back into placid lines.

"He knows what it feels like to be inside of you," Gavin said quietly as he stalked her. "He knows what you taste like. That's why he ran after you today. He thought there was a chance to get you back even though you left him. He knows who you are now. He won't stop."

"Jonathan isn't like you," she said. "He's not going to blackmail me. He's a—"

"Good man?" Gavin said sharply. "Yes, we know I'm not that."

"This is ridiculous! You can't go after Jonathan because we used to be together."

It was clear from his expression that he didn't agree.

"How can you be so mad at him when you cheated on me with hundreds of women? I *saw* you fuck other women, yet you threaten the *one* man I've been with? How dare you!"

Gavin came at her in a rush. He pinned her against the wall and raised her so they were eye to eye.

"I told you about the other women. I didn't want my shit to touch you."

"It doesn't matter *why* you did it. You did and I have to live with those memories!"

"Why are you bringing this up?"

"You hate Jonathan enough to hurt him, but don't think I should feel the same way over the women you've taken?"

"Those women meant nothing to me," he said through clenched teeth. "I got off and didn't give a shit if they did. I never slept with them, never talked to them. I didn't use the same woman twice—"

Lyla slapped him across the face, shocking both of them. The awful silence made her heart race. She lowered her stinging hand and pushed against his chest.

"Let me go."

Gavin didn't move or speak.

"Back *off*, Gavin!"

He didn't move and she lost her temper. She struck out again, but this time he caught her hand. Gavin hauled her over his shoulder and carried her to the couch. He dropped and mounted her in a nanosecond and pinned both her hands above her head with one of his.

His hand collared her throat. "That part of your life is over."

"I know that."

"But it made you think about what you will never have, which is why you argued with me. You know I'm not a good man. I've done horrible things and will do more in the future."

His insight was scarily on point. Gavin was successful in business because he was a good judge of character and had a keen intuition that kept him a step ahead of everyone else. He had never practiced this talent on her before and it left her quiet and wary.

"You've paid a price for being mine." His hand left her throat and brushed over the scars on her chest. He undid her robe and stroked her stomach.

"I should have let you choose, but I couldn't. You belong with me."

"I'm not trying to get away from you, Gavin."

"You're holding back from me because of him," he said.

"I'm not! Listen to me!" She couldn't afford to be distracted by sex. "It was a shock to see him. I just needed time to think."

Gavin leaned down so their faces were less than six inches apart. "You don't need to think about him. You don't owe him anything. All you need to think about is me." He was poised over her like a beast ready to pounce. Dangerous emotions flickered through his eyes. "I need you."

"Gavin—" She let out a shriek as his fingers tunneled inside of her. She tried to scoot away from his fingers, but it was impossible with his heavy weight on top of her. He still had her wrists pinned above her head, leaving her body completely open to him.

"You feel this? This is all that matters," he said as she gasped and bucked beneath him. "Even if you begged me, I wouldn't let you go."

"I'm not going anywhere. Don't hurt Jona—"

"*Don't* say his name," Gavin growled against her cheek as his fingers played her expertly.

"Promise you won't hurt him," she demanded and closed her eyes to block out the pleasure so she could focus.

Gavin's fingers stopped moving and she opened her eyes. If she didn't trust him not to hurt her, she would have shrank away in fear.

"You're thinking of him while I'm making love

to you?"

"You're trying to distract me with sex!"

He kissed her with a desperation that ignited her. She arched into his hand and when he released her wrists, she clasped his face and kissed him back.

"I have to have you," he growled as his hand went to the front of his pants. "I have to make sure you're with me."

"I am with you."

"I won't stand for another man in your mind." He wedged his cock between her thighs, which were clamped together. "I can't have you questioning what we have."

"I don't, Gavin! Let me—"

She tried to spread her thighs, but he wouldn't allow it. She grasped handfuls of his shirt as he forged through her tight folds. They both moaned as he sank in to the hilt. He braced his hands on either side of her head as he thrust.

"Who do you belong to?" he growled.

"You."

"Who do you love?"

"You."

"Say my name."

"Gavin Pyre."

He moved faster and she held on tight.

"You wear my ring," he said through clenched teeth, eyes alight with possessiveness. "You bear my name and had my child. You'll never be his again."

She moved with him. "No, I won't. I'm yours."

He planted himself deep and she moaned.

"You won't speak to him again."

"Gavin, it was a freak thing—"

He cupped her chin. "Ever. You don't ever talk to him." He gave her a gentle kiss. "I love you too much. I need to know you love me back."

"I do," she said and moved with him. "I've given you everything."

"I need more," he said, burying his face in her hair. "I need everything. He can't have even a splinter of you. He's lucky he has fucking memories of you. If I could take that from him, I would."

"Gavin." She dug her nails into his ass. "Make me come."

Gavin fucked her hard until she exploded beneath him, breaking a nail as she clawed his back.

"Fuck, Lyla," Gavin groaned as he ground himself deep and came.

Lyla quivered as he rolled them on their sides. He tucked her against the back of the couch with his arm and leg tossed over hers. She brushed kisses over his face and ran her hand through his hair to soothe his beast. She suspected Gavin would be upset if he found out about her run in with Jonathan, but she never anticipated that Gavin would be upset enough to do bodily harm.

"I love you," she said against his mouth.

Gavin cupped her jaw and opened his eyes. Despite their recent passion, his face was still hard and implacable.

"You have nothing to worry about," she said. "It was nothing. I'll never see him again."

Gavin brushed his thumb over her lips.

"The girl he loved doesn't exist." She searched his eyes. "He doesn't even know my real name."

"You don't love him," Gavin said.

"No."

"You'll never leave me."

It wasn't a question, it was a demand.

"I promised you that before we had Nora."

"I need to hear it again. You didn't have a reason to leave me before."

"Gavin, I promise," she said.

He pressed against her as if he couldn't get close enough. His cock, which was still buried inside of her slid deeper.

"You know I'd do anything for you, right?" he murmured.

"I want to attend the hospital event," she said promptly.

Gavin cursed. "Lyla—"

"Seeing Jonathan," she began and squeezed him when she felt him stiffen, "made me realize how controlled my life is."

"There's a reason for that."

"I know, but for how long?"

"I can't allow you to put yourself in danger."

"Then come with me."

"I'm working."

"Just a few hours, Gavin. You can be there and so will Blade." She wanted him to feel the sense of community that she had in the meeting today. He gave generously, but didn't witness the difference he made in the community. He needed to step into the light so the underworld didn't consume him.

"I said no."

"Please."

She tried to lighten his mood by pouting outrageously. His eyes warmed fractionally. She lunged at him, kissing the hell out of him and pushing until he ended up beneath her. She rocked against him just because it felt so fucking good.

"Just let me go to this event and I swear I won't ask for anything else for the next six months," she begged.

"Lyla."

"I love Alice and the Make A Wish people are gonna be there. There's gonna be singing, games, dancing. Please, Gavin?"

He smacked her ass and she stopped moving.

A muscle jumped in his jaw. "You're a pain in my ass."

"Please."

"What about Nora?"

"I'll ask Aunt Isabel to watch her."

Gavin considered for a full minute. "I shouldn't let you go."

She sensed his capitulation and kissed the hell out of him to celebrate. She had *finally* won a fight! "You're the best husband!"

She rolled off of him and retied her robe. Gavin sat up and glared balefully at her.

"What?"

"Did you just manipulate me with your pussy?"

"Yes," she said smugly.

Gavin tucked himself away and towered over her. Lyla wasn't intimidated.

"You manipulate me with your cock so we're even," she said.

Gavin brought her against him and kissed her long and slow.

"I want you to be happy," he said.

Her breath caught in her throat. "I am happy. I just... I wish Sadist was dead and you were here with Nora and I. I don't like you being gone and..." Her hand brushed over the cut on his. "I'm worried all the time."

"Don't."

Oh, like it was that easy. "This hospital event is a day of joy," she explained. "It's about hope. I need that. That's why I want to go."

Gavin grunted. "Let's shower."

They walked out of the office and didn't run into anyone on their way upstairs. They showered together, both quiet and thoughtful. Gavin dressed in another suit, which meant he wouldn't be spending the night.

When they entered the dining room, they found Carmen feeding Nora a bottle, Beau at her feet. Carmen went into great detail about her gambling experience, which Lyla was grateful for since Gavin didn't say a word. Carmen shot her a loaded glance. Lyla shook her head in warning.

When Gavin rose from the table, Nora reached for him. He picked her up and headed to his office with Beau on his heels and closed the door.

"What was that about?" Carmen demanded.

"He found out about Jonathan."

Carmen's eyes bugged. "And you're still alive?"

"He didn't take it well."

"Of course he didn't. It's *Gavin*."

"I realize that."

Carmen glanced at the closed office. "He's not happy."

She sighed. "No, he isn't, but we'll get past this. Maybe the hospital event will cheer him up."

Carmen's eyes popped. "Gavin's going to let you go?"

"Yup."

"Damn, girl, you must be amazing in bed."

CHAPTER FIVE

Gavin

Gavin settled Nora on his lap as he typed on the computer. He was grateful for Nora's presence because she kept him from losing his shit. Claiming Lyla on the couch did nothing to purge the dark, tangled emotions pulsing in his chest.

The troubled, wistful expression on Lyla's face as she breastfed in his office bothered him all day. She hadn't been quick enough to smooth it off her face when she realized he was watching. He assumed Alice or Janice said something to upset her until he questioned Blade who mentioned that Lyla had an episode in the casino.

He watched Lyla's panic attack on the surveillance cameras earlier, but now that he knew the full context of what happened, he had to watch it again. He accessed the casino security cameras once more and enlarged the correct camera view. There was no way to isolate the audio, which pissed him off.

Gavin watched Lyla stumble to a stop. He had to switch to a different camera angle to witness a startling blankness settle over her face. Blade touched her arm and she recoiled as if she had been shot. Fear and loss claimed her features. Gavin's heartbeat accelerated with the need to react. Lyla backed up against the wall and braced her hands on her knees as she tried to catch her breath. Blade stood in front of her, obstructing Gavin's view.

A man stopped on the outskirts of Lyla's security detail. One of the guards noticed him before the others and held up a hand to stop his approach. He was going to get a raise. Gavin changed camera angles again as Lyla straightened and recognized the man. She looked as if she'd seen a ghost. Gavin leaned close to the screen so he could capture every nuance of Lyla's expression—shock, pain, regret. Her lips moved, forming the bastard's name.

Gavin stopped the video. He focused on Nora who smiled at him. Gavin rubbed his face against her soft skin and blew raspberries against her neck. She squealed delightedly and wrapped her arms around his head. He inhaled her innocence and it calmed the savage beast inside of him. He didn't care that she yanked his hair or drooled all over him. He would take whatever she gave him. Nora wasn't identical to the little girl in his dream, she was even better. He loved that Nora had her mother's silver blue eyes and couldn't deny that he was pleased that she inherited his black hair. He didn't question his need to brand Lyla and Nora. They were his.

When Gavin felt fortified enough he watched the rest of the video. It didn't matter that her ex wasn't handsome or a bodybuilder. Lyla wasn't a superficial person. She cared more about the substance of the person, which is why she left him the first time. His money, looks and lifestyle hadn't been enough to make her stay. It was obvious that the sight of this guy gutted her. She couldn't conceal her feelings, which is why the ex followed, trying to speak to her, believing he had a chance. Did he?

Gavin cradled Nora in one arm as he watched Blade propel Lyla through the casino. Blade hadn't told him about the ex because he wasn't a stupid man. Blade said Lyla had a panic attack and suggested Gavin talk to her. Blade left it up to Lyla to tell the truth.

The first time he watched the video he assumed the guy had mistaken Lyla for someone else. He hadn't been paying attention to Lyla's reaction since he assumed she was shaken by the panic attack, not the man. Now, he catalogued everything about the encounter. Lyla was clearly shaken and when the guy finally stopped his pursuit, he looked heartbroken. Welcome to the club, fucker. That's how he felt the first time Lyla left... and the second time. What had Blade said to make the ex stop dead in his tracks? Gavin wanted to know every word that was said, but it wouldn't cool his rage. He was already dangerously close to hunting the bastard down and making sure he didn't see the next sunrise. He could already imagine the warm, slow drip of the worthless bastard's blood on his hands. He should have sent Blade back to Maine to finish the job years ago.

Nora rubbed her face against his shoulder, bringing him back to himself. Lyla wouldn't leave him, but that look of remorse on her face made his soul feel as if it was being shredded. He had done everything possible to redeem himself for past sins, but now fear and panic were coursing through him. In the past, his only competition had been himself and now... Now, the only man on the planet she had feelings for had surfaced and caused Lyla to feel... what? What if she tried to leave him for the normal guy? She was crazy enough to do it. She was gnawing at the bit, trying to get out of the house. She wanted to volunteer at the hospital. Just the thought of her in a crowd made his palms sweaty with fear, but if he prevented her from going it would be another strike against him and he had enough of those already.

Gavin clicked on his email and read the report on Jonathan Huskin. Huskin was five foot ten, one hundred eighty pounds with brown hair and eyes. Graduated from Boston University with degrees in Computer Science, Business and Computer Engineering. He made eighty five thousand a year, paid his taxes and spent a lot of time traveling for work. He was the only child of Mark and Jackie Huskin who lived in Boston and were retired college professors. Had Lyla met his parents? Gavin sneered at the screen. This guy didn't even have a parking ticket. Huskin had never been in a car accident, arrested for public intoxication or been late on his fucking rent. He had no debt and made some investments that were doing fucking splendid.

If he killed the crime lord, he could give Lyla what she wanted. Every time he came home, he dreaded the inevitable question: *Any leads? Did you find him?* There was no trace of the fucker he called

Phantom. Why would this man scale an all out attack on his family, mutilate Rafael Vega and put twisted leaders in positions of power only to disappear when Gavin showed up to reclaim his title? It didn't make sense. He wanted to believe the crime lord was dead, but life never handed anything to him gift-wrapped. The Phantom was out there, biding his time. For what? For another chance at Lyla? Fuck that.

"Da, da, da," Nora chanted.

Gavin kissed his daughter on the forehead and walked out of the office. He could hear the distant murmur of Lyla and Carmen talking in the dining room. They spent everyday with one another and still managed to find shit to talk about. What the fuck?

Gavin climbed the stairs and headed to Nora's nursery with Beau on his heels. He sat in a rocking chair and settled Nora against his chest. She rubbed her face against his shirt and fussed a little. When he put his hand on her back, she calmed instantly. He rocked back and forth, staring straight ahead.

The fact that Lyla ordered him to go back into the underworld lifted a weight from his shoulders. It saved him from breaking his promise to her. Lyla knew he was a killer and still welcomed him home with open arms even though his hands were still wet from washing off the blood.

Gavin stroked a hand down Nora's small back. They were a family. They were happy, right? Uncertainty gnawed at him. The urge to dominate and control warred with his need to give her what she wanted. When Nora was asleep, he settled her in the crib. Beau got to his feet to greet someone. Gavin didn't need to turn to know who entered the room.

Lyla came to a stop beside him. "You have the magic touch."

His chest tightened. Sometimes he wondered if God designed him just for her. She made his life light up in color. Every smile, every touch made him crave more. He loved everything about her and couldn't imagine being without her. He wanted to ask about Huskin, but he didn't want to hear her answers. It didn't matter anyway. Lyla was his.

"I have to go," he said.

She took a deep breath and let it out. "I know."

He wanted to brand Lyla again, until he was certain there was no other man on her mind, but he had shit to do. He shouldn't have stayed last night or come home this evening, but dealing with Lyla was more important than the shit going down in the underworld.

Lyla stepped forward and wrapped her arms around him. "So the next time I need to get laid, should I call or text?"

"Both. Immediately."

She laughed as he leaned down and kissed her. He stroked her tongue with his and absorbed her taste, hoping it would tide him over until he could make time to come home again. When he raised his head, he was pleased when she rose on tiptoe to prolong the kiss.

"I love you," he said.

"Love you too. Hurry home to us," she said.

He gave her one last kiss before he walked out

of the nursery with the feel of her imprinted on his body.

When he walked out of the house, he strode towards his waiting car. He cast a glance over the small number of guards. With so many of his men turning traitor, he had to rebuild his army from the ground up and even brought in some retired talent from his father's time.

Gavin nodded to Barrett, a man in his late sixties who was built like a tank. Barrett knew the score. He had been an excellent asset in the past months as Gavin made his way through the underworld. Barrett stood by his side, cracking heads as if he hadn't retired fifteen years ago when he found out he fathered a child with a prostitute. Barrett hadn't lost his edge.

On their way to the Strip he made phone calls and checked his email. Marcus was the most efficient, annoying bastard on the planet. He kept Gavin apprised of every little detail of what was going on with the casinos. Gavin sifted through the information and made a mental note to talk to Marcus when his door opened.

Gavin nodded to the bellboys, valets and other staff. Three of his guards accompanied him into the hotel. His head of security for the casino waited just inside the door.

"Lance," Gavin said and inclined his head.

Lance handed over a room key. "Here it is, sir. Room forty two twenty one."

Gavin walked towards the elevator with his men on his heels. The doors opened to reveal Marcus who looked as perky and alert as he had this morning. He smiled at them.

"Twice in one day? This must be a record," Marcus said cheerfully and made no move to exit the elevator.

Gavin glared at his COO. How Marcus was aware of every move he made, he would never know. Gavin pressed the button for the forty-second floor and examined Marcus who wore his suit as if he had been born in it.

"What are you doing here, Marcus? It's almost midnight."

"I've taken up residence in one of the suites since there's always an emergency." Marcus messed with the handkerchief in his suit pocket. "There's a rumor that you're dead so I make sure I'm always around to squash the rumors."

Gavin couldn't care less about the rumors surrounding his absence. He had a mission and he wouldn't stop until it was completed. He had to admit that if it wasn't for Marcus's cooperation, there was no way he could spend as much time in the underworld as he was.

"When you're burnt out, let me know," Gavin said.

"Burnt out? I live for this," Marcus said, rocking on his heels with his hands in pockets.

"One day business won't be enough." He felt ancient and craggy beside Marcus who seemed full of life and optimism.

"I can't imagine that."

"Do you need my signature for something?" he growled as the elevator doors opened.

"No. I learned to forge that months ago."

Gavin gave him a sharp glance before he exited the elevator. A year ago a comment like that would have gotten Marcus a beating, but now he had bigger problems on his hands. Lyla was right. He trusted Marcus with his life and business, so why not trust him with Nora? If someone had the dogged determination to see things through, it was Marcus.

"You want to be Nora's godfather?" he ground out.

"What are you talking about? I *am* her godfather."

Gavin stopped in his tracks and fisted his hands at his sides so they wouldn't go around Marcus's throat. "You aren't."

"Of course I am."

Gavin bared his teeth and continued down the hallway with his guards and Marcus who seemed determined to tag along. If Marcus weren't so intelligent, he would have killed him months ago. He was a fucking know-it-all.

"Lyla looked amazing today, by the way," Marcus said casually.

He tensed. "Don't."

"And my goddaughter knew who I was. Remember, she even reached for me even though you were holding her—"

Gavin stepped into Marcus's space. "I haven't gone into the boxing ring for months and I'm due. You want to schedule an appointment?"

Marcus grinned at him. "Nah, I'm good."

"Motherfucker." Gavin continued down the hallway and ground his teeth when Marcus strolled by his side, whistling. "What do you want?"

"Nothing."

"I thought you had an endless list of shit to do."

"I took care of it."

"I can give you another list."

"No problem."

Too bad Marcus had the Pyre Casinos organized to the tee. Gavin dumped all his duties on Marcus four months ago. Aside from a few excellent questions, Marcus handled Gavin's workload with little effort and hadn't made a peep of protest.

"Remind me to give you a raise," he muttered.

"Already gave myself one."

Gavin would have taken exception to this, but he saw the room number he was looking for. He put the key card in the slot and walked in. The guards stayed outside as Marcus followed. Gavin surveyed the hotel room, which was tidy aside from a blazer tossed over the chair and the rumpled sheets on the bed.

Gavin slipped on gloves and glanced into the bathroom, which showed a toiletry kit hanging from the towel rack. A sleek suitcase perched on the luggage rack. Gavin opened it and quickly rifled through the contents. Either this guy was boring as hell or he was an undercover agent who had the most mundane set of props to bore anyone hoping to find anything interesting.

"You want to tell me why we're in a guest's room?" Marcus asked.

"No."

His tone didn't dissuade Marcus from remarking, "There doesn't appear to be anything out of the ordinary. Looks like a standard businessman." He nodded to the crisp shirts hanging in the closet. "He's probably here for a conference. Why are you interested in him?"

Gavin didn't answer. He opened the laptop on the desk and stuck a drive into it before pulling out his phone and pressing speed dial five. Z, his tech genius answered halfway through the first ring.

"Boss," Z said without preamble.

"Can you hack it?"

"Give me five minutes."

The laptop screen flickered as Z did his thing. Dozens of screens opened and closed at a rapid pace. Gavin turned from the laptop to find Marcus watching him closely.

"Business," Gavin said.

"Is that so?" Marcus didn't look convinced.

Perceptive motherfucker. He wasn't going to tell Marcus why he was hacking Huskin's laptop. To distract them both, he said, "The Monk deal?"

Marcus's face instantly cleared. "What about it?"

"Up the stakes by fifteen percent. He's a slimy bastard. Monk loves to back out at the last minute. Make him put his money where his mouth is."

Marcus's eyes were sharp. "Anything else?"

"I'm hoping to wrap up my business soon so don't penalize the construction company for the delays. It's normal and we're not in a hurry. As for the guy that slapped us with a penalty from the Nevada Gaming Control Board you mentioned in an email last week, I'll deal with him."

"Terry? I can handle him."

"He's dirty and he's gunning for us. I'll have a

chat with him and find out who his employer is."

"He was appointed to his position by the governor."

Gavin raised a brow. "Then I'll pay him a visit as well."

How the Phantom managed to do so much damage in so little time he would never know. What did the Phantom offer to recruit so many people? For the past four months, he worked his ass off and was no closer to discovering the Phantom's identity than he had been a year ago. His days were filled with paranoia, blood and violence. Uncovering the deals the Phantom made with the filth of the underworld made him sick. He thought he knew what evil was, but it was nothing compared to the twisted fucks he was currently dealing with.

"Anything else I should know?" Marcus asked.

Gavin glanced at the laptop and saw computer codes flashing across the screen. "The amenities for the homeowners are generous and well worth the fees. And Falkner designed the floor plans so I know it's the best use of style while still maintaining our signature and keeping it classy. Good job, Marcus."

"Wow. You really do read my emails."

"They do the trick when I need a nap. In the future don't write that formal shit. Get to the point. I don't have time to rifle through fifty emails a day."

Marcus nodded. "You got it."

His phone rang and he picked up. "Yeah?"

"There's a lot of security on this laptop. I'm going to need more time," Z said.

"Have you found anything interesting?"

"Am I looking for something in particular?"

"No."

There was a pause on the other end. He could feel Marcus watching him, probably trying to figure out what the hell was going on. The sane, civilized part of him knew that he had a dozen other things to do besides rifling through Huskin's shit, but he couldn't stop himself. He had to know everything there was to know about this guy.

"It looks like the laptop owner likes to write programs," Z reported.

Gavin frowned. "What type?"

"I'm not sure yet, sir."

"How much time do you need?"

"I don't know."

Gavin hung up and called one of his men. "Where is he?"

"At the Bellagio fountains."

"I'm on my way. Let me know if he makes a move." Gavin headed to the door and over his shoulder said, "When the files are uploaded to that drive, hand it to the guards outside."

"Where are you going?" Marcus called.

"Hunting."

Gavin strode down the hallway to the elevators. He made his way through the casino and inhaled clouds of cigarette smoke, cheap perfume and alcohol. A drunk stumbled into his path. Knowing that the man was making him richer allowed him to shove the man out of his way instead of killing him. His skin felt too tight for his body. The beast inside of him demanded blood. It took every ounce of control he possessed to walk calmly through the crowd, a demon amongst lambs.

The lights and noise along The Strip were as familiar to him as his own home. Gavin made his way to the Bellagio fountains where most of the tourists congregated to watch dancing water accompanied by music. Gavin spotted one of his men who turned his head to the left. Gavin followed his line of sight to a large German speaking family. A lone figure leaned against the stone wall, staring blindly at the show.

Gavin made his way to a spot adjacent to Huskin so he could examine the man who seduced Lyla into believing he was a good guy. Huskin looked like a nerd who played video games in his spare time. He was ordinary in every way from his brown hair and eyes to his facial features and build. He wasn't tall or short, fat or skinny. He was just... average. Huskin didn't seem aware of the crowd or the change in songs. He just stared blindly at the water, arms braced on the wall. The possibility that Huskin was remembering his time with Lyla made Gavin's hand edge towards his weapon. Only the fact that he could still taste her kept him from losing his shit.

The show ended and the crowd began to disperse. A man from the German family tapped Huskin on the shoulder. Following the German's exaggerated hand motions, Huskin nodded and took the man's camera to capture multiple shots of the family who kept switching positions. When the German thanked him profusely, Huskin smiled and waved as they walked away. Huskin appeared to be a nice guy, but everyone had a dark side. What was it about this guy that made Lyla feel something for him?

Huskin moved into the crowd and Gavin followed. Huskin didn't look around him at all the distractions Las Vegas had to offer. He was too deep in thought. Gavin stalked him for a block before he spied an alley. Gavin reached for his switchblade as Huskin drew near. Lyla reassured him that he had nothing to worry about, but he wouldn't take chances when it came to her. He would keep fucking up. It was inevitable. If she decided to leave him, he wouldn't allow her to have someone to run to. Fuck that.

Three men on the sidewalk created a rhythmic racket on tin buckets that was drawing a crowd. Huskin slowed, allowing Gavin to get close to him. He extended his hand to propel Huskin into the alley and paused when he saw it was already occupied. Two Mexicans stood in the entrance and they were both staring boldly at him. Gavin's instincts pinged a moment before one of them reached into his jacket. Fuck. Gavin didn't hesitate. He threw the switchblade and saw the man's head kick back. His partner's eyes bulged and he too reached into his jacket, but it was too late. Gavin barreled into him, shoving him out of the shadow of neon lights into darkness. The man shot wildly, narrowly missing Gavin's leg, which pissed him off.

The street performers banged away, drowning out the gunshot as Gavin slammed the gangster's head into the wall with all his strength. The man crumpled to the ground several feet from his partner who had Gavin's switchblade sticking out of his face. Gavin peered down at the bodies and noted the tattoos on their neck.

The underworld was calling.

Gavin texted his men about the bodies and strolled out of the alley. He paused a moment to pick Huskin out of the crowd, but he was gone. Fuck. An SUV pulled up to the curb. Gavin climbed into the passenger seat and glanced at his man.

"We're going for Santana," he said.

"You got it, boss."

Santana didn't know who he was messing with. He thought his drug operation was too big for anyone to touch him. He was wrong. Phantom let Santana into the city and his filth was spreading deep and fast. Gavin sent Santana a warning that he had taken back his throne and this was Santana's response—two men. What an insult. Santana had a reputation for being brutal in his home country, but Gavin had a reputation as well. He didn't care that he didn't have the manpower that Santana did. He was going to gut him... and tend to Huskin later.

CHAPTER SIX

Lyla

Lyla took aim and fired. The pistol bucked in her hand. The shock reverberated up her arm, but she held firm. She emptied the gun, reloaded and walked forward, firing with steady, focused precision. The ping of metal rang in her ears. She imagined that the metal plates were the scum of the underworld.

"Halt!"

Lyla flipped the safety on and holstered the gun in her shoulder holster. Blade walked up to her targets to check her accuracy. They had been at this for an hour and her shoulders were beginning to ache.

Blade walked back after examining her targets. "You're improving."

She raised a brow. "That's all you have to say?"

"I don't need you to turn into an assassin, I just need you to be accurate and stay alive," Blade said.

"Are we done?" she asked.

"We have one more exercise."

Even though she knew what was coming, her stomach iced with dread. Blade and two of her guards donned helmets with tinted face guards.

"You ready?" Blade asked in a muffled voice.

She nodded.

"Fight for your life," he said.

There was a moment of silence and then they lunged at her. Lyla whirled and ran as fast as she could across the massive backyard enclosed by a high wall. She wouldn't win in a physical altercation so running should always be her first option. The pool sparkled in the distance. Safety. If she reached the fortress, the game would end. She ignored the sound of heavy footfalls behind her and focused on the prize.

Arms wrapped around her middle and lifted her off her feet. Lyla went for the hands wrapped around her middle. She grabbed his middle finger and wrenched back savagely. The man shouted and began to teeter to the side. Lyla tossed her elbow back into his face. If he wasn't wearing the helmet she would have broken his nose. The guard released her and she sprinted for safety. The second guard tackled and then pinned her by sitting on her abdomen. Lyla thrust her hips up with all of her strength and felt her heart skip when she barely budged her opponent. Lyla improvised by grabbing the man by the balls and squeezing. The man yelped and dropped to the side. Lyla rolled, gained her feet and pulled her gun on the last man who held his hands up in surrender.

"Do you have to keep going for my balls?" the man on the ground wheezed.

"My instructor said I could yank them off," she said and holstered her weapon. "You got off easy."

"You may not always be able to use your gun," Blade warned, taking off his helmet and revealing

95

that he had been her last opponent.

"I know," she said and holstered the weapon.

She put her hands on hips and tried to catch her breath. No matter how much she trained, no matter what moves her instructor taught her, men were stronger. She had to fight dirty, there was no getting around it. This was always a sobering exercise because she knew how real the danger was.

"Good job," Blade said.

Lyla looked at the guard who had his hands over his crotch. "Sorry."

"Maybe we should wear padded suits if you're going to keep going for the goods," Blade said.

"You do that," Lyla puffed and jogged back to the house.

She entered through the kitchen and found Carmen at the table with Nora.

"That was good," Carmen said and held up a hand for a high five.

Lyla took a gulp of water and kissed Nora on the cheek.

"What did Blade say?" Carmen asked.

"I'm getting better."

"That's it?"

"I know," Lyla said as she plopped on a seat. "He's a hard ass."

"He always hangs back and watches how the guards attack so he can try something different on us," Carmen said.

"I swear, I keep looking around every corner because he keeps jumping me. Serves him right if I break something," Lyla muttered.

"Are you ready for tomorrow?"

"Yes!" She clapped her hands, beyond excited for the hospital event. "Your mom is excited to babysit."

"She loves babies and Nora in particular."

"How's she doing without you in the house? I know she was uneasy the first month you were here."

"She's getting along just fine. She sees her friends all the time and even asked if I'm moving out."

Lyla's eyes widened. "Wow. Are you?"

"I don't know. It doesn't make sense to buy a house just for me and I don't want to live in a condo. I think I'll stay with you or mom until I figure out what I want to do with my life." Carmen stared at Nora who played with her necklace. "I feel like I've been wandering around since Vinny died. Helping Alice with these events keeps me busy. My connections have finally come in handy."

"That's good."

"My schedule revolved around Vinny and now I don't know what to do." She drummed her nails on the table and bit her lip. "I feel like I can't move on with that fuck still on the lose."

Vinny had been Sadist's first victim. Sadist wasn't the one who pulled the trigger, but he called the hit. It had been a domino effect after that.

"That's understandable," Lyla said quietly.

Carmen rested her cheek on Nora's head and hugged her tight. "Maybe I'll have a munchkin myself. I want our kids to be close in age."

Lyla laughed. "Uh, I think you need a man for that."

"There's men everywhere," she said.

"I mean, a *good* man."

She shrugged. "I'm loaded. I don't need a man."

"Carmen."

"What?"

"What about your wild hairs?"

"What?"

"You always get a hair up your ass and take off to Africa on safari or some shit."

"You can take kids on safari."

Lyla held up a hand. "Please tell me you're kidding."

"Who wants to go on a trip?" Carmen waved Nora's hands in the air. "I do! I do!"

"I don't think so," Lyla said.

"I still have the RV," Carmen said and bobbed her brows.

"I enjoyed our time on the road."

"I did too. It was a good time out."

And now they were back in Las Vegas. She shook her head as she remembered the shotgun wedding and Gavin's bullying tactics to make her say her vows. He really was a psycho.

"Is Gavin coming to the event?"

"I hope so. Let me call him."

Lyla paced the living room as she dialed his number. On the fourth ring he answered.

"Lyla."

The sound of his voice felt like a caress. One thing was for sure. Her marriage would never be dull. Gavin was a lot to handle and his sexual appetite would always keep things interesting.

"Hi, baby. I wanted to ask about tomorrow."

"Tomorrow?" He sounded distracted.

Her heart sank. "The hospital event?" She tried to keep her voice light and airy.

There was a short pause and then, "You still want to go?"

"Yes." When he didn't respond she tagged on, "Please, Gavin."

He didn't speak.

"I want you to come," she said and then realized she had absolutely no idea what he was doing at that moment. He could be in a boardroom or standing over a body. "I mean, if you can make it, I'd like that."

Still no response. She stopped pacing and closed her eyes.

"I can't go?" she murmured.

"I'll be there in time."

She tossed her fist in the air and did a little jig. "Yay! You're the best. I'm going to call Alice."

"Okay."

She put a hand on her hip. "By the way, if you have time *after* the hospital, I'm due."

"Due for what?"

"For you."

A pause and then, "Then I'll be in you after the event."

She beamed and did another little jig. "I love you."

"The next time I'm home, do that dance for me," he said.

"What dance?"

"The one you're doing right now," he said and hung up.

She looked up at the camera in the living room and shook her head. Damn Gavin. Had he been watching her before she called or tapped in after he answered? He would always keep her on her toes.

Her phone rang in her hand. The screen read, Beatrice Dalton. Lyla pressed a button to make it go to voicemail and skipped into the kitchen.

"I'm going!" Lyla crowed.

"Awesome. I'll text mom about Nora."

"And I'm going to call Alice," Lyla said gleefully and stopped when her phone chimed from her mother's voicemail.

"Who's that?"

"My mom."

Carmen cocked her head. "You think she wants to see Nora?"

Lyla sighed. "That's what I want to think, but I don't think so."

Carmen shook her head. "Your dad is an ass."

"Yeah." She wished her mother would leave him. She would happily take her mother in, but that would never happen. Her mother would rather suffer with her father than get out of their toxic, hopeless marriage. Lyla couldn't be a part of it anymore. She had enough shit on her plate.

Lyla spun her phone on the table. "Am I being selfish by asking Gavin to go to this event?"

Deep down, she knew Gavin was right. The smart, *safe* thing to do was hide in the fortress until Gavin killed Sadist, but how long would that take? It had been four months of silence and she was ready to do something. She couldn't let another opportunity pass her by. Since her trip to the casino, she had been more restless than ever. She was nervous about leaving Nora, but that time would have come eventually.

"Wanting to attend an event that will help others isn't selfish," Carmen said. "Not every outing will end in blood. It's going to be okay, Lyla."

CHAPTER SEVEN

Lyla

Lyla took a deep breath as the SUV pulled up to the hospital, which was teeming with press, celebrities, volunteers, patients and medical staff. Gavin stood on the sidewalk and opened her door. He looked as polished as always in a navy suit and matching tie. He wore aviator glasses that concealed his mood. He helped her out of the car and turned to help Carmen as well. Carmen ran a hand over a blush colored gown that made her look deceptively sweet. She had turned into British royalty for the day. Lyla wore an army green dress she'd been wanting to wear for a while and black trench coat.

"The Pyre family is here!" Janice exclaimed, making her way through the crowd. "This is great! Gavin, do you want to do a speech?"

"No."

Janice didn't look surprised by his abrupt answer. "No problem. Alice is prepared. I'm so glad you decided to come."

Janice led them through the throng. A group of celebrities were taking pictures and talking to reporters. Carmen had definitely pulled together an eclectic and high profile group of celebrities. Up front was Bridgette Mackee, an actress who starred in a summer blockbuster, the brilliant and eccentric film director, Phoenix along with The Punisher, a UFC fighter.

Kody Singer spotted Carmen and abruptly left his interview to greet her. He smiled and grasped both of her hands as he talked. As Gavin pulled her through the crowd, Kody caught sight of him and took a hasty step back. Clearly, Kody hadn't forgotten the misunderstanding with Gavin during the opening night of Incognito. Kody pulled Lyla aside to ask about Carmen. Gavin took exception and choked him.

Lyla waved at Kody, but he averted his face. Lyla inwardly shrugged and squeezed Gavin's hand. "Okay?"

"Yeah," he said without looking at her.

Lyla ignored his clipped tone and focused on her hectic surroundings. Gavin shook hands with the celebrities, all of whom were staying at one of the Pyre Casinos. Gavin introduced her to those she didn't know and grudgingly obliged the press when they asked for pictures of them.

Gavin stepped away from her to take a call. From his body language, Lyla suspected something serious happened. Gavin's mouth was tight when he returned to her side. Everyone around her took a step back. She didn't ask what happened because he wouldn't tell her anyway.

Janice and the hospital director led the way to the new wing of the hospital. A bright red ribbon marked off the new wing. Alice walked up to the front of the crowd, beaming with pride.

"Thanks to the Pyre Foundation, we were able to build a new wing and restore two that were damaged by a fire. Let's give a round of applause to Gavin Pyre!" Alice announced.

Cheers sounded around them. Lyla smiled with pride at her husband who acknowledged the crowd with a curt nod.

"Mr. Pyre, will you do the honors?" Alice asked, holding out a massive pair of scissors.

Gavin stiffened by her side. Clearly, he didn't want to be in the limelight, but he stepped forward. He didn't pause for effect or look at the clicking cameras as he cut the ribbon. As applause rang out, Gavin handed the scissors back to Alice and resumed his position beside Lyla. She wanted to elbow him in the side, but didn't want to provoke him further. Gavin was making it clear that he had other things to do besides accompany her to this event.

"You can go," she said just loud enough for him to hear.

Gavin looked down at her. She didn't have to see his eyes to know that he was pissed. He had been tense from the moment she arrived. He cupped the back of her neck and squeezed. A warning. Lyla grit her teeth. This was the first time she had left Nora to go on an outing. It was a big day for her and she wouldn't let him ruin it. When Alice ran up to them, Lyla smiled at her.

"Come on, there's so much people to meet!" Alice exclaimed.

Lyla slipped out of Gavin's hold and went with Alice. She felt someone breathing down her neck and glanced back to see Blade on her heels. At the end of the corridor Gavin paced as he talked on the phone. Good riddance.

There were people everywhere. Volunteers handed out gift baskets and goodie bags to patients. On the basketball court, NBA star Michael Heatton helped patients shoot baskets. Lyla passed several rooms and saw the celebrities out in full force, taking group photos or sitting at the bedside of the recovering, sick or dying.

Lyla spotted Kody and Carmen in a little girl's room. Lyla knew from the meeting that meeting Kody was the cancer patient's dying wish. The wan girl perched on Kody's lap and beamed at the camera while her parents stood against the wall with tears in their eyes.

Alice grabbed two bouquets of sunflowers and handed one to Lyla.

"Let's go spread some sunshine," Alice said so enthusiastically that Lyla couldn't help but smile in response.

Lyla followed Alice who fearlessly walked into rooms to talk to patients young and old. Sometimes family or friends accompanied the patients. Once Blade scanned the occupants, he waited in the hallway.

Alice made everyone feel special. There was something about her spirit that lit up the room and made everyone believe that everything was going to be okay. These people were going through the worst time in their life. The Pyre Foundation was here to offer support, hope and make them feel that they weren't alone.

Many locals were aware of what the Pyre Foundation was doing in the community. Alice introduced Lyla who wasn't prepared for the patient's response. Even as she handed out sunflowers, the patient's showered her with gratitude and love. Lyla was overwhelmed. Alice proudly proclaimed that Gavin and Lyla were behind the funding for these events. Lyla listened to their hardships and tried to offer words of comfort and hope.

She didn't know how to respond when a patient clasped her hand and said, "You and your husband are doing God's work."

Alice was bursting with light. "She sure is, Maggie. I'll see you next week."

"Yes, child!" the old woman called as they walked out of her room.

"Next week?" Lyla asked.

"I visit hospitals in my spare time," Alice said as she marched Lyla down the hallway, stopping to direct several volunteers before she continued on.

"What spare time?" Lyla muttered.

"I know, right? It's important for me to remember that there are people much less fortunate than me. Hospitals are one of the loneliest places on earth. I like to bring a bit of sunshine."

"Where's Gavin?" she asked Blade as she paused in front of another room.

"Attending to business."

Lyla narrowed her eyes at Blade. "What's going on?"

"Nothing you need to worry about."

"He needs to meet these people."

"There's millions of people like this," Blade said. "Gavin is helping in his own way."

Blade's phone rang as Lyla walked into the next room. He stayed outside to take the call as Lyla spied an old man sitting up in bed reading a newspaper.

"Hello. How are you?" Lyla asked with a smile.

He narrowed his eyes. "You aren't a nurse, what are you doing in here?"

She was a bit taken aback by his rude tone, but she reminded herself that he was in pain and probably going through a lot. "Today we opened up a new wing of the hospital and we're spreading a little joy, one flower at a time."

She offered the flower.

"If you want to spread joy, there's something else you can do for me." He looked pointedly at his lap.

Lyla retracted the flower and gave him a tight smile. "I don't think *anyone* can help you with that."

He cackled. "You got some spunk. Maybe you're not a blonde bimbo after all."

It was a good thing she was the one who entered this room and not Alice. Alice would have blushed, encouraging the asshole to be even more outrageous and inappropriate. Remembering Alice's boundless optimism, she decided to ignore his awful first impression.

"How is your recovery going so far?" Lyla asked.

"Lousy. It's one fucking thing after another."

"What brought you in here in the first place?"

"A run in with an old acquaintance."

She frowned. "Meeting with an old friend made you sick?"

"I never said he was a friend."

The bathroom door behind her opened. She turned and saw a strange looking man with angular features, sunken cheekbones and protruding eyes. They widened comically when he spotted her. He was leaning heavily on a cane, which slipped, causing him to topple face first to the floor.

"Oh my gosh!"

She placed the flowers on the old man's bed and leaned down to help the man to his feet. It was an easy feat since the man appeared to be emaciated. Something tickled the back of her memory and then it hit her.

"You're Rafael's brother," she said. "We met at Lux."

Rafael's brother was dressed much the same as he had been the first time they met at a bar. That felt like a lifetime ago. He wore a button up shirt tucked into slacks. A thin belt circled his tiny waist. She picked up his black cane and held it out to him.

"Are you okay?" she asked and noticed that his hands were trembling. Too much coffee or nerves?

"You know my sons?" the old man asked.

"Sons?" she echoed and turned to face him. "Rafael's your son?"

"Was," the man said sourly. "He's dead."

She put a hand against her chest. "Oh, I'm sorry."

She didn't know much about Rafael other than the fact that he was good looking, Gavin loathed him and he ran a prostitution ring. She glanced at Rafael's brother who still had yet to say a thing. He didn't look like Rafael or his pervert father.

"Who are you?" the old man asked sharply.

"I'm Lyla. The Pyre Foundation is putting on an event today. I'm helping."

"Pyre?" the old man asked sharply.

"Yes, Pyre."

"What's your last name?"

She had been trying to avoid that tidbit. She lifted her chin. "Lyla Pyre."

The old man's expression became chillingly hostile. "You're Gavin's wife?"

Something about the way he said it made her hand inch towards the pocket in her purse holding her gun.

"You know Gavin?" she asked cautiously.

"He's the *acquaintance* that put me in here in the first place," the old man said. "He shot me in the shoulder and wrist." He held up his wrist so she could see an angry red scar on his otherwise pasty skin. "He doesn't care that I'm old, that sadistic fuck."

It was hard to feel sympathy for him after his perverted welcome. "Why'd Gavin shoot you?"

"Because he was pissed."

"So he shot you?"

"I pulled a gun on him, he dodged the bullet and I hit Steven instead." He nodded at his mute son with the cane.

This man tried to shoot Gavin when his back was turned? Lyla reached into her purse and closed her hand around her gun. This bastard could have killed Gavin. Of course, the one room Blade didn't check had to be occupied by Gavin's enemies. Did Steven and his father run the prostitution ring? Steven looked like a nerdy professor, not a part of the underworld. Steven didn't fit in with his family. No wonder he was so... odd.

"Who are you?" she asked.

"I'm Paul Vega." He waited for a reaction and when he didn't get one, he said, "I'm offended your husband didn't think to warn you away from us. Is he here?"

"Yes, he's on his way," she lied.

"That bastard has ice running through his veins." Paul shook his head and leaned back against his pillows. "He kills Santana two hours ago and then comes to an event his charity puts on. Fucking genius."

Lyla's tightened her hold on her gun.

"He poked the hornet's net on this one." Paul's eyes gleamed. "Santana's the biggest drug lord in Mexico. He set up shop here a couple of month's ago."

And Gavin killed him two hours ago? Her stomached clenched.

Paul tried to look innocent, but didn't pull it off. "I thought as his wife, you'd know such things."

"I don't need to know what's happening in the underworld."

"You're missing out." Paul inclined his head at Steven who was doing a great imitation of a statue. "He just started talking again."

"Excuse me?"

"Your husband broke Steven's jaw and

shattered his kneecap. He's had two surgeries and still has a fucking cane."

Lyla couldn't care less about Paul, but she didn't understand why Gavin would attack Steven. She turned to him. "Are you okay?"

Steven didn't answer. His face was still as a lake. When they were at the bar, Steven had been awkward when he offered to buy her a drink and now he was just... blank.

"Why did Gavin attack you?" she asked.

"Steven walked in after Pyre tried to choke me," Paul answered for Steven.

Reluctantly she turned back to Paul.

"Pyre gave what he thought was a fitting punishment when Steven tried to defend me." Paul snorted. "Look at him. He's no match for Pyre."

"When did this happen?"

"Six months ago, give or take," Paul said and winced as he shifted his thigh. "He still hasn't tracked down the new crime lord, huh?"

That surprised her. "You want to track down the crime lord who killed Manny?"

"I don't give a fuck about Manny," Paul spat. "I tried to kill him myself, but he had a sixth sense for a set up. Wily fucker."

Lyla tightened her grip on her purse and resisted the urge to beat him with it. "If that's so, why are you looking for the other crime lord?"

"He killed my son."

"He killed Rafael?" That rocked her world. Other than Manny, she didn't know Sadist made more hits.

"Rafael was killed a couple of days before

Manny."

"What makes you think it was the crime lord?"

"He likes knives," Paul said, eyes gleaming. "I hear you know something about that."

Her chest scars tingled. "And Gavin knows this?"

"Pyre thought Rafael had taken over. That's why he showed up in my office," Steven said.

"He shot you in your office?"

"That's Pyre for you."

Gavin did this when she was pregnant with Nora, she realized. "Did the crime lord kill anyone else besides Rafael and Manny?"

"There were a bunch of mutilated bodies that turned up around the city, but no one of note. I think he got a taste of blood and liked it," Paul said.

"What the fuck are you doing here, Vega?"

Blade walked into the room, pocketing his phone. His hand was on the butt of his gun. Steven held up one hand in surrender while Paul sneered.

"If it isn't the mighty Blade, Pyre's sidekick," Paul said.

"I'm Lyla's bodyguard now." Blade's eyes shifted between the two men and a glint of amusement lit his eyes. "Looks like you two had a run in with some sort of criminal. Someone I know?"

Paul bared his teeth. "I hope someone guts him."

Blade focused on Lyla. "Let's go."

Lyla didn't argue. She didn't say a thing to Paul or Steven as she walked out. She paused in the corridor and took a deep breath to fortify herself.

"What the hell were you doing?" Blade snapped.

She jolted. "What?"

"The Vega's are sick fucks."

"I didn't know that."

He shook his head. "If Gavin finds out they're here, he might finish them off. He isn't in a good mood."

"Is it because he killed that drug lord?"

Blade looked at her sharply and then glanced back at the hospital room. "Fucking Vega's."

"Did Gavin really kill him?"

Blade clasped his hands behind his back. "You should ask Gavin."

"Paul said Gavin is responsible for their injuries."

"You should talk to him about your concerns."

Lyla opened her mouth to argue when Alice ran towards her.

"Do you hear that?" Alice exclaimed.

She linked her arm through Lyla's and raced down the corridor as enthusiastically as a five-year-old. Lyla was glad she hadn't worn ridiculous heels like Carmen so she could keep up. On the lawn Mariah Gearthart sang acapella. Patients, visitors and medical staff opened windows or made their way outside so they could listen to her angelic voice. Alice led her to the front of the crowd and put her arm around an older woman and began to sway. Alice got the whole crowd going. Mariah sang several songs before she bowed. Everyone clapped and rushed forward to take pictures with her.

Somehow, Lyla ended up on the basketball court with the NBA star and was obliged to take a shot at the basket in front of a crowd of onlookers. Thankfully, she made the shot and settled on a bench on the outskirts of the crowd and watched the festivities with a smile on her face. She wished Nora were here. How would she be in a crowd? Would she cry or be fascinated by all the activity?

"Lyla."

Lyla glanced behind her. Her smile vanished. Jonathan wore a cap, sunglasses and high collared jacket. She faced forward and glanced around for Blade who was ten feet away, talking to another member of her security team. She gripped the edge of the stone bench as it hit her. Jonathan called her Lyla. He knew her real name.

"You shouldn't be here," she said, staring straight ahead.

"Because your husband is a mob boss?"

Lyla stiffened. Apparently, Jonathan had done his homework. But, if he believed the rumors about Gavin, why was here? "You don't know anything about my husband."

"Is your real name Morgan or Lyla?"

She didn't answer for a long minute and silently willed him to walk away. He didn't. She promised Gavin that she wouldn't talk to him, but she owed him her name at least. "Lyla."

"And you created a new identity when you left him? Is that it? Is that why you tried to warn me off?"

He was too perceptive for his own good. She wanted to turn around, but didn't dare. She felt

Blade's gaze on her. Jonathan stood back far enough that he was coasting beneath the radar. "What are you doing here?"

"I needed to see you."

"Why?"

"Because I need to know the truth."

"About what?"

"Why you called yourself Morgan, why you left."

"I can't talk about it. I think you should go." The answers to those questions didn't matter anymore.

"Are you afraid of him?"

"I'm not afraid of my husband, but you should be. If my husband sees you, he'll—" She broke off as Blade started towards her. "You better go."

"Problem?" Blade asked.

She turned casually and saw that Jonathan faded into the crowd. Lyla shook her head and got to her feet. "I'm hungry."

"There's a spread in the lobby."

Like the day at the casino, her day wasn't turning out exactly the way she imagined it. First the Vega's and now Jonathan. She grabbed a sandwich and bowl of fruit and settled on a settee in the lobby. Her guards settled around her. When Janice joined them, Blade moved one seat over to accommodate her.

"This is fantastic!" Janice said as she pocketed her phone.

"You and Alice have done an amazing job," Lyla agreed.

"I think she's trying to outwork me, but I won't

let her." Janice stole some fruits from Lyla's plate. "Who's watching the princess?"

"Carmen's mom."

"I still haven't seen Nora yet. When are we going to get together?"

"When are you and Alice free? You work around the clock."

"We'll figure out a day," Janice said and sipped from Lyla's drink.

"Can I get you something?" Blade asked.

"No, thank you," Janice said as she continued to pick at Lyla's food.

Lyla didn't have friends aside from Carmen because it was too dangerous, but as employees of Pyre Casinos, Janice and Alice fell into a different category. Janice and Alice went all out when they threw her baby gender party and baby shower. Lyla wished she could spend more time with them. Also, she wanted Nora to have aunts that doted on her.

Janice's phone rang. "We'll talk later, okay?" Janice rose and pulled out her phone. "Yes, this is Janice. How can I help you?"

Lyla watched Janice walk away and searched for Jonathan, but it was impossible to pick him out of the crowd. What did he hope to accomplish by researching her? Appearing at the event today was out of character for him. He wasn't one to pursue or obsess over something, but then again, he probably couldn't resist the mystery. If he really suspected that Gavin was a mob boss, he should have the sense to stay clear.

"Hey." Carmen took the seat Janice vacated and ate the rest of Lyla's food.

"Where's Kody?"

"Restroom."

Lyla gave Carmen a sharp glance, but she was too busy munching to notice. "You didn't go to the restroom with him, did you?"

Carmen gave her a very catlike stare. "Why would I do it in a bathroom when there's beds everywhere?"

Lyla blanched. "Please tell me you didn't."

Carmen crossed her legs. "Then I won't."

"Having fun?"

Carmen nodded. "Fun, draining, entertaining." Carmen got to her feet. "There's Kody. We're going to head out, okay?"

Lyla watched Carmen rush across the lobby towards Kody who had a foolish grin on his face. Lyla watched them leave with a heavy heart and continued to watch the crowd while she checked in with Aunt Isabel.

"Hey, honey!" Aunt Isabel said.

Lyla relaxed. "Hey, Aunty. How's it going?"

"We're having so much fun! She is adorable. I can't wait for all my friends to meet her. She's so much cuter than some of the babies I've been seeing."

Lyla laughed. "That's mean, Aunty."

"Telling the truth is a necessary evil, baby. Everything going good at the event?"

"It's great. So many people volunteered to help."

"That's good to hear. There's so little good to report these days."

"Yes. How's Nora? Did she cry?" Lyla bobbed

her foot nervously. It was the first time she had ever left Nora with someone and she couldn't enjoy herself fully. Of course, after all she had been through, it was a miracle that she left Nora at all.

"No, she's such a good baby. She's very loving. You're doing an excellent job, Lyla."

That warmed her heart. Aunt Isabel filled the space left by her own mother. All her parents cared about was each other. Nora didn't rank on their list of priorities unless she was a way to get back into Lyla's inner circle so they could ask for money. Aunt Isabel and Carmen were all she had and all she needed.

"I'll be home in an hour or two," Lyla said.

"Take your time. We're doing just fine."

"I love you. Thank you."

"No problem."

Lyla hung up and took a fortifying breath. Nora was safe and being smothered with love. She looked around the lobby and watched celebrities mingling with patients and their families. Spirits were high. Alice flitted from group to group to make sure everyone was having a great time. It was clear that this is what Alice was meant to do. It wasn't an act. It's who she was.

Gavin walked towards them. People gave him wary or curious looks as he passed. Despite the fact that Gavin killed a drug lord less than five hours ago, his suit didn't have any suspicious splotches and he was perfectly groomed. Gavin didn't appear to be worried, guilty or anxious about his recent activities. On the contrary, the only thing he was agitated about was her. He came to a stop in front of her and she got a whiff of his cologne. He smelled delicious. How the hell could he walk into the underworld smelling and looking like a million dollars? That would irritate the hell out of the criminal underclass for sure. Maybe he used his polished appearance to his advantage. No one who looked the way he did should possess the skills of an assassin.

"Time to go," Gavin said abruptly.

Lyla narrowed her eyes. "After lunch we're supposed to take a group shot on the lawn."

"You've been here long enough."

The director of the hospital approached, beaming. He inclined his head respectfully to Gavin.

"Mr. Pyre, you've done so much for our hospital. I hope you know how much we appreciate your contribution and all that you've done today."

The director held out his hand. Gavin hesitated a second before he took it.

"We're happy to help," Gavin said.

"And you," the director reached for her hand and she gave it, "you are a godsend."

Lyla raised her brows at Gavin before she smiled at the director. "You're so kind to remind my husband of that."

The director laughed and waved his hand. "Would you like a tour of the new wing?"

Gavin opened his mouth, but before he could answer, Lyla linked her arm through the director's.

"Yes, I would," she said and ignored Gavin's low growl.

The director blinked when Blade and four

guards rose. Lyla patted the director's arm.

"Precautions," Lyla said.

The director nodded hastily. "Yes, yes. I understand."

Gavin followed them to the elevator. The director kept up a steady stream of polite conversation. Gavin did nothing to engage. The director tossed him worried glances, probably worried that Gavin wasn't impressed by how they used his money. The director began to talk quickly and went into great detail about the state of the art equipment and innovative floor plan. It was interesting to walk through the corridors and peek into empty, pristine rooms, so far untouched by humanity. Lyla enjoyed the behind the scenes tour. The director pointed out the paintings on the wall that had been done by a local artist and led her into a hospital room, which had an aqua accent wall that made the room inviting and soothing rather than clinical and detached. Lyla walked up to the window and looked out at the shopping center across the street and the red mountains in the distance.

"This is beautiful," Lyla said.

The director went into great detail about the bed sheets, which were a higher thread count than they had ever been able to afford.

"The Pyre wing is going to be many people's home away from home."

"Pyre wing?"

"You didn't know it was being named after your family?"

Her family... "No, I didn't."

"We couldn't call it anything else," the director said jovially.

Gavin stood with his arms crossed in the middle of the corridor. Lyla went to him and gave him a hug.

"Let's go," Gavin said abruptly.

"But—" the director began.

"I have business to attend to." Gavin propelled Lyla down the corridor.

Lyla was dimly aware of the director talking to Blade and the other guards as they trailed behind them.

"Rude," she muttered.

"I have a lot to do today."

Lyla ground her back teeth. "Like what?"

"Don't worry about it."

What did he have to do now that he killed a drug lord? What was the next step? She opened her mouth and then closed it. Did she really want to know? Not really. If she knew what his agenda was for the day, she would get even less sleep than she already did.

Before they reached the elevator, the doors opened, revealing eight Mexicans. They were dressed in heavy jackets, jeans and too long shirts. What she could see of their skin was covered in tattoos.

Gavin halted, pulling her to an abrupt stop. She looked up and saw Gavin watching them intently. She looked back at the open elevator as the man in front smiled, showing a mouth full of silver teeth. Even as he reached into his jacket, a deafening bang sounded from beside her. The man's smile vanished as a hole appeared in the middle of his forehead. He staggered backward into two men who fell with him.

Gavin released her and squeezed off two more shots. A man clutched his chest. It looked as if a ripe tomato had been hurled at him. One of the cholos raised his gun and shot wildly. An agonized screamed sounded behind her. Even as she turned, Gavin ran forward.

CHAPTER EIGHT

Lyla

"Gavin!" Lyla screamed and took a step after him, only to stop in her tracks as she got a firsthand glimpse of Gavin in combat mode.

Gavin disarmed the man with the gun with a brutal chopping motion. Lyla heard something break and the man dropped to his knees with a scream. Gavin kicked him savagely in the face, toppling him backwards. Gavin turned to the next man and executed an uppercut punch. There was a sickening crunch as the man hit the wall. He crumpled to the ground and left a gruesome red smear behind. One of the gangbangers tried to run out of the elevator. Gavin hauled him back just as the elevator dinged and the doors closed, locking him into the enclosed space with three armed men.

"No!" she screamed.

"Lyla."

She turned and saw Blade on his knees beside the hospital director who lay in a pool of blood.

"No, no," she whispered, shaking her head. "What's going on? Who are they?"

"Santana's men." Blade rose, hand dripping with the director's blood. "He's gone."

"He's dead?" She couldn't comprehend it.

Everything happened so fucking fast. Not even two minutes ago, the director had been talking passionately about the new wing of the hospital and now he was a lifeless heap on the floor. "This can't be happening."

"It is." Blade pulled out his phone and speed dialed a number. "Z, access the hospital cameras. We're gonna need some interference." He hung up and looked at the other guards. "Two of you clean this up. The other two, follow me."

Blade grabbed her arm and led her back into the new wing. A ding stopped them both in their tracks. The elevator doors opened and Gavin appeared with bodies in disturbing positions at his feet. Even as Lyla took a step towards him, his head turned sharply to the left. The two guards standing over the director went down on one knee and cleared their guns even as shots were fired down the hallway.

"Fuck, let's go," Blade snapped.

Gavin pulled the fire alarm. Lights flashed and a deafening blare echoed down the corridor. Her guards threw open the door that led to the emergency exit stairs. As Blade propelled her into the stairwell, she looked back and saw Gavin cut a man's throat with a knife and then toss it into another man's face. Men were converging on him like ants. None of the cholos seemed to care that she and her guards were getting away. They were here for Gavin.

"We can—" she began, not wanting to leave him.

"Gavin can take care of himself. He can't focus with you around. We gotta get you out of here,"

Blade said.

The stairwell was filled with people. Blade and the guards holstered their weapons as they climbed down three flights of stairs. Lyla focused on putting one foot in front of the other. She wanted to fight by Gavin's side, but she knew Blade was right. Her combat skills were sloppy and amateur compared to Gavin's. He could hold his own.

The confusion and panic of those around her amplified her own fear. The edges of her vision darkened with memories just waiting to latch onto her and send her spiraling into waking nightmares. It was happening again. Another battle, another tragedy, another scene with bloody bodies in her wake.

Blade grabbed her arm in a painful grip as they entered the lobby, which was a hubbub of chaos. Patients in hospital beds and wheelchairs were everywhere. Medical personnel struggled to be heard over the blaring alarm. They yelled for help to get the patients onto the front lawn. Alice and Janice were in the midst of the fray, directing people outside.

Lyla took a step towards them, but Blade squeezed her. "We have to get out of here."

"But I can—"

"No. My job is to get you safe. We don't know how many more there are."

She could barely keep up with his fast clip. The guards pressed in close and she struggled to keep her shit together. Of course, the day of the hospital event had to be the same day Gavin killed a drug lord.

They walked through the deserted emergency room and left the hospital behind as they crossed to the parking garage. Blade pulled out his phone and talked to the driver's.

"Lyla!"

Jonathan jogged towards them. She was torn between hugging him in relief or screaming at him to stay away from her.

"Are you all right? What's going on?" Jonathan asked.

"Jonathan, you should leave," she said as they entered the ground level of the parking garage.

"Is there a fire?"

One of her guards reached into his jacket.

Lyla grabbed his arm. "No!"

"We don't have time for this," Blade hissed.

"Don't!" she warned her guard who dropped his hand from his weapon. "Go, Jonathan."

Squealing tires sounded as two SUVs whipped around a corner and stopped in front of them. Blade reached for her arm and then shoved her to the ground. Bullets ricocheted against the bulletproof car. Lyla reached into her purse and grabbed her gun as she rolled and knocked Jonathan off his feet.

"Get down!" she yelled as she took in her surroundings.

Cholos used parked cars for cover. Her guards scrambled to do the same.

"Get in the fucking car!" Blade shouted at her.

Lyla army crawled towards the SUV and tried to block out the noise. One of her guards dropped with an agonized yell. Lyla raised her head and raised her gun.

"Lyla, *go!*" Blade shouted with such urgency that she resumed her slow progress to the SUV.

She made it to the back door and reached for the handle. A bullet sparked against metal less than six inches from her hand. She dropped and the driver's door opened.

"Get in!" the driver shouted as he covered her.

Lyla shot up, opened the door and dove onto the back seat. She slammed the door and heard the ping of bullets bouncing off the car. Lyla sat up, tossed her purse and flipped the safety off her gun. There were men everywhere. Her guards were pinned. She couldn't run the cholos over. There were too many obstacles and they were in an enclosed space with lots of hiding spots. Her eyes fell on Jonathan who was on the ground, hands over his head. He was a sitting duck.

Lyla cracked open the door and shouted his name. Jonathan dropped one hand and looked in her direction. He couldn't see her through the tinted window so she stuck her hand out and gestured for him to come. To her relief, he began to crawl towards her. She couldn't watch him bleed out in front of her. When Jonathan was right below the door, she tossed it open and covered him. Jonathan leapt in and slammed the door.

"What's happening?" Jonathan shouted and ducked as bullets bounced off the window.

"Get her out of here!" Blade roared at her driver.

Even as the guard backed into his seat, a cholo rushed out from behind a car. Lyla heard the click of an empty chamber as her guard ran out of bullets.

The man shot him at point blank range and stuck his ugly face in the SUV. Lyla pulled the trigger. The man staggered back, face a bloody mess. Lyla crawled over the console and slammed the driver's door before she fumbled with the seat settings and locked the doors.

"What's going on?" Jonathan shouted from the back seat.

"Didn't I tell you to stay away from me?" Lyla shouted back.

She looked in the rearview mirror and breathed a sigh of relief as Blade and the three remaining guards got into the SUV behind her. Blade honked and jabbed his finger at her. Lyla didn't hesitate. She jammed her foot on the gas pedal and careened towards the exit. She caught a glimpse of the front lawn of the hospital flooded with people before she whipped onto the highway and passed a squad of police cars.

Lyla set the gun in the cup holder and clutched the steering wheel with shaking hands. A perfect day ruined by the fucking underworld and it's fucking politics. The hospital director, a good man, was dead. Hundreds of sick and terrified people were now milling on the hospital grounds, waiting for word on an imaginary fire and who knew if the gunfight between the gang and Gavin would spill into the rest of the hospital.

"Lyla."

She looked at Jonathan in the rearview mirror. His hair was disheveled and he was pale with shock.

"What's going on?" Jonathan whispered.

"You should have gone on with your life and forgotten about me," she said.

"You have a gun." His voice was faint with shock. "And you know how to use it."

Damn right she did. She trained to know how to kill and that's what she'd done. Her hands flexed on the wheel. Just like the last time, she didn't feel an ounce of remorse. If anything, she wanted to turn around and do more damage. Her chest burned with rage. Those fuckers. They didn't care about innocent bystanders. They opened fire anytime, anywhere.

The sound of her phone ringing filled the car. "Pass my purse!"

Jonathan tossed it on the console. Lyla dug through her purse as she navigated the freeway and kept an eye out for cops. She glanced at her phone, which showed Blade's name.

"Are you hurt?" Blade asked when she answered.

"No."

"Good. Drive home."

"Okay. Any word from Gavin?"

"No. I have men driving from the compound to you. I'm going back to help. Are you going to be okay?"

Her heart clenched. "You think he's...?"

"Don't borrow trouble. Get home, you hear me?"

"Yes," she said and hung up.

"This has to do with your husband being a crime boss, doesn't it?" Jonathan asked.

Lyla clenched her teeth and glanced at her ex

who had no idea how close he came to death today. "Where are you staying?"

"Lyla, talk to me."

"About what?" she demanded fiercely.

"About what's happening."

"It's safer if you don't know. You can't tell anyone what you saw today. I have to drop you off somewhere safe. Where should I take you?"

"I'm staying at Pyre Casino."

She wanted to strangle him. "You need to leave as soon as possible."

"Why?"

"My husband will freak when he finds out you were at the event today. How could you be so foolish?"

"I heard that your husband's foundation was putting it on and thought you might be here. I extended my stay, hoping we could talk."

"Talk about what?" she shouted, pounding the wheel with her fist. "What you saw today, that's my life now, Jonathan."

"How can you say that and think I won't ask more questions?"

"I can't take you to the Strip," she said to herself and took the next exit off the freeway.

"Where are you taking me?"

"Check out of your room by phone, don't go back for anything. You might be on someone's radar now..." She shook her head as she cruised down the highway, searching for a nondescript accommodation for him. Her phone rang and she snatched it to see Blade's name on the screen again. "Yes?"

"Where the fuck are you going?" Blade barked. "I told you to go home. You're veering off course."

"I need to get him somewhere safe."

There was a sharp silence. "You have him in the car with you? I was hoping he'd been shot so I wouldn't have to do it."

"Damn it, Blade. He doesn't know!"

"Fuck, Lyla. You're putting yourself at risk for him. I can't let you do that."

"I'll check him into a hotel and leave, I promise."

"I'm turning around."

"No! Help Gavin!"

"You're my first responsibility. Gavin would have my head if anything happened to you."

"I'll do this and go home."

Blade hung up. She cursed and turned into a motel. She put the gun in her purse and looked at Jonathan. "Let's go."

Jonathan slid out of the backseat and walked beside her. "What's going on?"

"They're coming for me. You need to check in and lay low."

"But—"

"I need a single room," Lyla told the bored front desk clerk.

"How many nights?" the girl asked without looking up from her cell phone.

"One," she said and glared Jonathan into silence.

Jonathan had to leave tomorrow. If Gavin didn't come for him, the Santana's gang members might. She had to impress upon him how fucking serious this was.

Lyla checked him in under a false name and paid with cash. She grabbed the key and rode the elevator up to the second floor.

"Lyla, I don't understand what—"

"You don't need to understand." Lyla located his room, unlocked the door and pushed him inside. She jabbed a finger in his face. "I'm not the girl you knew. You can never see me again, got it?"

Lyla turned away and wasn't prepared when he gripped her arm and dragged her into the room. He slammed the door, which bounced open from the force he used. Lyla's mouth dropped. Jonathan manhandling her was just as shocking as a gun battle in a hospital.

Jonathan braced his hands on her shoulders. "I spent the past three years wondering what happened to you. Now that I've found you again, you think I can walk away, knowing you're in danger?"

She opened her mouth, but no sound emerged.

"It's me," he whispered.

She swallowed hard. "I know."

The familiar scent of his cologne surrounded her. She gripped handfuls of his shirt as reaction set in. Another battle, another time pulling the trigger. Fuck. Her eyes filled with tears.

He clasped her face between shaking hands. "Talk to me, Lyla."

"I have to go. You have to forget what you saw today. My husband will kill you if he finds out about this. Use your computer skills to disappear."

"Did you leave me because of him?"

"Jonathan, don't."

"Did he do something to make you leave? I reported you missing. I was obsessed with the thought that you'd been kidnapped, but the cops couldn't find anything. I've been going crazy and then I see you in the casino and... You think I can just move on with my life without knowing what happened? You knew I loved you. I would do anything for you."

She stared into his tortured eyes and her heart twisted with regret. "I'm so sorry, Jonathan. I never meant to hurt you and... I'm not that woman anymore. You should forget we ever knew each other. It's over."

"Who are you?"

"I need to go."

He didn't release her. "Please, give me something."

She stared at him and saw the confusion and frustration bubbling beneath the surface. She never should have gotten involved with him. She always knew there was a possibility Gavin would find her and she moved in with Jonathan anyway. He didn't belong in her world. Her world was dark, dirty and perilous. He had a future and the possibility of a happily ever after.

"I love my husband," she said.

He closed his eyes as if her words physically hurt him. She felt a resounding pang in her breast. She had been trying to spare him this, but there was no getting around it.

"I can't tell you about his business because I don't know much about it. You need to let me go, Jonathan, for your own good."

He stared at her. "You've changed."

She tilted her chin. She wasn't going to apologize.

"You killed a man today." His eyes searched hers and softened slightly. "But you're still the girl I knew. I don't care what you call yourself. You still feel something for me. I can see it in your eyes. You saved my life today."

"You saved mine," she said and felt the prick of tears.

He gripped her arms. "Are you in trouble? Do you need to get away from your husband? I can make you disappear."

"I should have made sure Blade took care of you after I located her in Maine."

Lyla whirled and saw Gavin standing in the doorway. His suit was splattered with blood, but he was standing without assistance, which meant the blood wasn't his. Her burst of happiness and relief disappeared as he raised a gun.

"Time to rectify my mistake," Gavin said in a quiet voice that scared the crap out of her.

Lyla stepped in front of Jonathan and spread her arms wide so Gavin wouldn't get a clear shot. "Gavin, don't!"

"Get out of my way or I'll prolong his death," Gavin said softly.

Lyla set her teeth. She had been through a bloodbath today and wouldn't allow him to create another. "Jonathan's going to leave. I'll never see him again."

"You promised you wouldn't talk to him again."

"I didn't ask him to come, Gavin!"

"Move, Lyla."

He shifted to get a clear shot and she went on tiptoes to cover Jonathan, "Gavin, stop!"

He holstered the gun and pulled out a knife already stained with red. Gavin advanced with lethal intent. She knew what he was capable of. Jonathan didn't have a chance in hell. Lyla's heart threatened to beat out of her chest. This was spiraling out of control.

"He's done nothing wrong," she said.

"He touched what's mine and he's trying to take you from me."

She took two steps forward with a hand up. "I'm not going to leave with him. I told him I love you."

Gavin shoved her to the side. Lyla pivoted as Gavin raised the knife for a killing strike.

"Gavin, *no!*"

Fear gave her the speed she needed. She launched herself at Jonathan, causing him to stagger back as she wrapped herself around him, shielding him with her body. She closed her eyes and waited for the blow, but nothing happened. She raised her head and looked behind her. Her skin prickled as she looked into Gavin's eyes, which were incandescent with rage.

"Release him," Gavin said.

"Gavin, please!"

"Blade," Gavin bit out.

Blade advanced into the room and ripped her away from Jonathan. She clutched at Jonathan with desperate hands, pulling him with her. Blade squeezed her wrists, causing her fingers to contract and release him.

"No, Gavin, don't!" The scream came from her gut. "Please don't! He hasn't done anything wrong!"

"Get her out of here," Gavin said.

Blade lifted her into the air and she fought savagely, all to no avail. She caught a glimpse of Gavin advancing towards Jonathan who wasn't going to raise a hand to defend himself. She couldn't let Gavin wipe Jonathan off the face of the earth. The only crime Jonathan committed was befriending a woman who belonged to Gavin Pyre.

"Gavin, you kill him, I'll leave you!"

Blade froze. For a moment, she wasn't sure if Gavin heard her and then he turned slowly. His face had been wiped of all emotion. Blood dripped from the knife that had already seen unspeakable horrors today. The room was so quiet, Lyla swore she could hear the drops hit the carpet.

"You're choosing him over me?" Gavin asked.

"He's done nothing wrong," she said, breathing hard. She shoved against Blade who dropped her. She walked up to Gavin, eyes never leaving him for a second. Gavin was capable of taking on six men at once. One move and Jonathan would be lost to her forever. "Don't do it, Gavin."

His stillness scared the shit out of her. She stopped a foot away and tentatively reached out. Her fingertips wrapped around the hand that held the knife. His skin felt like warm iron beneath her fingertips.

"Please," she whispered, "don't do this."

Gold eyes bored into hers. His energy pulsed in

the air, raising the hair on the nape of her neck. The promise of violence swirled around him.

"He'll leave and we'll never see him again," she promised. "I'm not going to run away with him."

"You promised you would never leave me," Gavin said.

"I can't let you kill him."

"Because you love him?"

"No, because this isn't right."

Gavin's hand flashed out and gripped her chin. "He wants you. He loves you. I can't allow him to live, Lyla."

"You can," she insisted as terrified tears coursed down her cheeks. "You have to."

Her hand trembled as she cupped his face. When he didn't move, she stroked. She was very aware of their audience and how precarious the situation was. Anything could incite Gavin to attack.

"Please," she whispered.

Lyla took a risk and moved in closer. The breast of his suit was stiff with blood, but she didn't care. She wrapped herself around him, silently pleading with him not to do this.

Gavin's hand touched her hair and a moment later he picked her up. Lyla collapsed against him and shuddered in relief.

"Thank you," she whispered.

Gavin carried her out of the room. Over his shoulder, she saw Jonathan sag to his hands and knees. Now, he knew all of his suspicions about her husband were correct. Gavin wasn't civilized or rational. He was a crime lord who did whatever he wanted. Jonathan was lucky to be breathing.

Lyla lost sight of him as Gavin strode down the corridor. Blade and two guards followed.

"You won't kill him?" she whispered.

Gavin didn't look at her.

"Gavin?" She stiffened when she realized he was going to come back and finish the job later. "Gavin, promise me!"

No response.

She shoved against his shoulders. "Gavin, you can't—"

Gavin slammed her against the wall, knocking the breath out of her and raised the knife she didn't realize he was still holding. He pressed the slick blade against her cheek and she stopped breathing.

"Do you want me to bleed him dry in front of you?"

Her heart stopped. "No."

"Then don't fight me."

The monster that lurked inside of him was in control now. Her husband was nowhere in sight. She was very aware of cold steel pressing against her cheek and his charged body caging her in.

"You betrayed me," Gavin hissed.

He tipped his head back and let out an angry roar before he brought the knife down. Lyla screamed and raised her hands to protect herself as the knife sank into the wall six inches from her head.

She felt a whoosh of air as Gavin's body disappeared. Lyla lowered her arms and saw Blade standing in front of her, facing off with Gavin.

"Get out of my way."

"I'll take her home and give you some time," Blade said calmly.

Gavin bared his teeth. "Get the fuck out of my way, Blade."

Blade reached into his pocket and pulled out a syringe. Blade sedated Gavin several times after Manny was murdered. It was clear Blade thought he needed another dose.

Gavin stepped up to his second in command. "Are you threatening me?"

The guards took a reflexive step back, but Blade didn't budge.

"It's my job to keep her safe, even from you," Blade said.

He was putting his life on the line by defying his employer. Lyla opened her mouth to intervene, but she was too late. Gavin snatched the needle and plunged it into Blade's neck. Blade flinched, but otherwise, didn't try to protect himself. Gavin emptied the syringe and Blade dropped to the floor.

"No one comes between me and Lyla," Gavin said.

He stalked towards her. She tensed to make a run for it and blinked when Blade shot to his feet and put Gavin in a chokehold from behind. He produced another syringe and before Gavin could react, deployed it into his neck. Instantly, Gavin swayed.

"You fucker," Gavin wheezed.

"I have to save you from yourself," Blade said grimly as Gavin dropped face first on the carpet and didn't move.

She and Blade stared at one another.

"Call the elevator," he ordered.

Lyla nodded, stumbled towards the button and pressed it. Blade pulled the knife out of the wall, handed it to one of the wary guards and hefted Gavin over one shoulder. The elevator arrived with a merry bing and they all got in.

CHAPTER NINE

Lyla

Lyla stood in the corner of the elevator, staring at Gavin draped over Blade's shoulder. How Blade was able to handle his weight was a mystery. The guards stood as far away from Blade as possible, as if they expected Gavin to wake and kill them.

She shook from head to toe. Gavin almost killed her. He was inches from—

The elevator opened on the ground floor. Blade dug in Gavin's pocket and tossed one of the guards a set of keys. The guard instantly jogged towards Gavin's Aston Martin while Blade dropped Gavin in the trunk of the SUV as if he was a piece of luggage. He closed the back and pointed at Lyla.

"Get in," he barked as he rode shotgun.

The driver floored it. Lyla hastily belted herself in as the SUV careened out of the lot. She glanced in the trunk and saw Gavin roll from his back to his front.

"Marcus, it's Blade. Expect some visitors," Blade said on his phone. "Yeah, Gavin and Lyla are fine. We're taking them home. Expect Gavin to be absent from work for a while. Who? Carmen? Yeah, she left before the shooting. I don't know who with. Some fucking actor or some shit. I gotta go."

Lyla closed her eyes and willed this day away. She was physically and emotionally maxed out. All she wanted was to lay in a quiet, dark room with her baby and pretend the outside world didn't exist. No matter which way she turned, disaster was inevitable.

Blade spoke rapid, furious Spanish on the phone. Lyla understood enough to realize he was filling in for Gavin, speaking to his men who were in clean up and contain mode. They would erase or disturb surveillance cameras at the hospital and parking garage and even the hotel where Jonathan was. Gavin had the power to erase a person's identity and could kill in plain sight without being caught.

Lyla looked back at his large, lifeless body and shivered. When he woke, there would be hell to pay. Not only would she have to answer for Jonathan, she was the reason he had to be sedated. Didn't he realize the difference between justice, self-defense and outright murder? Lyla clutched the door handle because she needed something to hold onto. How could her life go so wrong in so little time?

When they pulled up to the mansion Lyla opened the front door and was greeted by Beau who barked and licked her hand. She smoothed a hand over his head and then looked past him to Aunt Isabel who had Nora on her lap. Nora babbled excitedly when she saw her.

"How was your day, dear?" Aunt Isabel asked.

Before Lyla could think of a response, the

guards walked in with Gavin. Aunt Isabel's face went ashen with fear. She leapt to her feet.

"Is he hurt?" Aunt Isabel asked.

"Sedated," Lyla said and took Nora from her.

Aunt Isabel opened her mouth and then shut it. As the widow of a former enforcer, she knew not to ask.

"Where's Carmen?" Aunt Isabel asked.

"She went out with Kody Singer."

"The actor?"

"Yes."

Lyla held Nora close and kissed her on the forehead. The smell of baby powder clashed horribly with the stench of cold sweat and dried blood.

"Here." Lyla handed Nora back to her aunt. "I need to see to Gavin." She looked up the stairs, but the guards were nowhere to be found. "Where'd they go?"

Aunt Isabel pointed and her stomach clenched. Lyla headed towards the basement. She had been here twice in her life. The first was to witness Gavin beat a traitor to death and the second was to find her father tied to a chair, also beaten to a bloody pulp by Gavin Pyre. Lyla felt a sense of déjà vu as her damp hands slid over the iron railings. Unforgiving fluorescent lights revealed a concrete room with suspicious splotches on the floor and Gavin sprawled on a cot with a thin mattress. The guards nodded to her as they passed.

Blade stripped off Gavin's bloody jacket, revealing his double shoulder gun holster and guns in his waistband. Blade lifted Gavin's pants leg to reveal two more guns and his empty knife sheath. Blade removed Gavin's shoes and socks and investigated them thoroughly.

"In his shoe?" Lyla asked skeptically.

Blade held up a thin switchblade. "Gavin's always prepared."

"No kidding." She wrapped her arms around herself as she watched Blade systematically disarm Gavin, even taking his belt. "What was in the first syringe?"

"Water."

"You knew he would use it on you."

"I suspected."

"You know him well," she said and swallowed. "Do you think he would have...?" She couldn't finish her sentence.

"I don't know."

"You don't know and sedated him anyway?"

"All I know is you can make him do anything." He fixed her with a piercing expression. "You should have let Gavin kill him."

"I can't—"

"He's a dead man walking. Gavin *will* kill him. There's no getting around that."

"I can't let him kill Jonathan. He didn't do anything wrong."

Blade shook his head. "You're not in Kansas, Dorothy. You're in the underworld where men mark their women by carving or tattooing their initials on her face. I'm surprised Gavin hasn't pressed you to do it."

Lyla stared at him. "Tattoo my face?"

Blade shrugged. "Tattoo something. It doesn't

have to be your face."

"Gavin's not a thug."

"Don't kid yourself. Gavin survives in the underworld because he's as ruthless and cruel as they are. He understands them because he *is* them. He just has money, power and a legit company to run."

Lyla ran a finger down Gavin's rigid, menacing face. "What are you going to do when he wakes up?"

"See how he reacts."

"You know he's going to be pissed."

"Yes."

"Locking him up is going to make it worse, don't you think?"

Blade flipped the switchblade thoughtfully with one hand. "You didn't see him after Manny died."

Lyla watched the switchblade tumble through the air before Blade caught it and wove it through his fingers. Blade never took his eyes from Gavin.

"Gavin hasn't been himself since Vinny and Manny were killed. He's on a hair-trigger. He calmed down once he got a ring on your finger and got you pregnant, but what you did today..." He shook his head. "It would push any man over the edge."

"I can't let him kill Jonathan!" Lyla shouted.

Blade wasn't impressed by her outburst. "Gavin demands unwavering loyalty from everyone he does business with. Why should you be the exception?"

Her mouth dropped. "I am loyal to him! What are you talking about?"

"You chose your ex over Gavin."

"Not letting Gavin kill him was choosing him over Gavin? That doesn't make sense!"

Blade shrugged. "When he wakes, you're the one who has to face him. You have about four hours to figure out how you want to handle him."

He walked out of the basement, leaving Gavin barefoot in slacks and shirt. Lyla knelt beside the bed and looked at her husband. Even unconscious and unarmed, he was a scary bastard. They had been through too much for this to break them. How could she make him understand that she wasn't in love with Jonathan? She had feelings for him, of course, but she wasn't going to leave Gavin for him. Killing Jonathan because of Gavin's insecurities was crossing the line. She accepted that he killed, but she couldn't let him do this.

"I love you," she whispered before she left the basement. She had four hours before he woke and all hell broke loose...

Aunt Isabel stood in front of the TV, which played live footage of the chaos at the hospital. Lyla paused behind her aunt as a reporter spoke.

"The fire alarm activated. No one is quite sure why. Some witnesses say they heard gunshots, but so far the police have not been available to confirm or deny that there was a shooting incident. It's going to take a while for everyone to be accounted for, but right now, all seems to be well. The Pyre Foundation was here today with several celebrities spreading a little joy and hope." The reporter turned to Janice who stepped forward with her million dollar smile. "Janice here is one of the organizers for this event. Can you tell us what happened here today, Janice?"

"I didn't hear any shots fired or see anything suspicious," Janice said. "When the fire alarm went off, we all pitched in to make sure everyone got out safely."

The reporter nodded. "And can you tell us about this event you had today?"

"Of course," Janice said.

Despite the events of the past hour, Lyla's lips curved a little. Janice always managed to spin everything into a positive light for the Pyre Foundation's image.

When would they find the hospital coordinator's body? He was dead, along with some of her security and a bunch of gang members. Did Gavin have cops in his employ that would cover up the incident? The parking garage was far enough away from the hospital that the isolated incident had gone unnoticed, but what happened when everyone found their cars decorated by bullets?

"Lyla, are you okay?" Aunt Isabel asked.

"Yes."

Aunt Isabel hugged her tight. Lyla felt tears fill her eyes, but refused to let them fall. Aunt Isabel pulled back and braced her hands on Lyla's shoulders. Lyla hoped she didn't look as lost as she felt.

"You've been through so much, honey," Aunt Isabel said quietly. "We all have."

Lyla nodded and blinked rapidly.

"Trust Gavin to take care of it," she advised.

Lyla gave her a shaky smile. "I'll try."

"That's my girl."

The front door burst open and Carmen rushed in with her shoes in hand, hair a mess. She skidded to a stop when she saw Lyla and her mother.

"Why the fuck aren't you answering your phone?" Carmen shouted.

Lyla pulled her phone out of her pocket and saw that it had a blank screen. "Oh, it's dead."

Carmen pressed a hand against her chest and sagged against the back of the couch. "You bitch. I hate you."

Lyla hugged her cousin who dropped her shoes and held on tight. Beau butted his head against Carmen in welcome. Carmen pet him, but didn't release Lyla.

"Where's Gavin?" Carmen asked in a muffled voice.

"In the basement."

"What? Why?"

Lyla moved her eyes to Aunt Isabel who was watching the news. Carmen gave Lyla a tight squeeze before she released her.

"We were at a restaurant and they had the news on. I got in touch with Alice and Janice, but neither of them knew what happened to you and I..." Carmen blinked back tears. "I fucking hate this. Every time I leave you alone, shit goes down." She lowered her voice. "*Was* there a shooting?"

"Yes." Lyla picked up Nora and cuddled her baby close before remembering that she was covered in only God knew what. "I'm going to give Nora a bath."

Aunt Isabel nodded. "We'll be here if you need us."

Carmen collapsed on the couch and cuddled against her mother who pulled her close. She was glad Aunt Isabel was here, but wished she could cuddle up to her own mother.

Lyla paused in the doorway of the master suite and walked on tiptoes to the bed. She reached beneath the nightstand and quietly pulled the gun from its hiding place. She methodically checked the room with Nora on her hip and relaxed when she found that they were alone. She attended the event to restore her faith in humanity. All she had gained was another healthy dose of paranoia and fear.

Lyla bathed with Nora and then settled on the bed to breastfeed. God, she had nearly been gunned down *again*. Would this ever stop? Lyla saw her dead phone on the nightstand. She balanced Nora as she plugged it in to charge. The screen flickered to life. A series of beeps, rings and chirps sounded. Lyla thumbed through her phone and saw several texts from Janice, Alice and Carmen. She listened to two frantic voicemails from Carmen and deleted one from her mother before she could hear the first word.

The bedroom door opened. She reached for her gun, only to stop short when she saw Carmen who changed out of her tailored dress. Face bare of makeup and dressed in yoga pants, Carmen crawled on the bed and sat cross-legged in front of Lyla.

"Spill," Carmen demanded.

"Where's Aunt Isabel?"

"She went home. She got out of this life and didn't want to be around for whatever happens next."

"She's a smart woman," Lyla said.

"The news obviously doesn't know what the fuck went down."

Lyla draped Nora on her shoulder to burp her. "After you left with Kody, the hospital director gave Gavin and I a tour of the new wing. When we were about to leave, the elevator was filled with gangbangers. Gavin started blasting away and pulled the fire alarm when he realized there were more of them than he thought. Gavin killed a drug lord this morning and then came to the hospital event. Those guys were his men."

Carmen made a rolling motion with her hand. "Go on."

"They were gunning for Gavin so Blade got me out of there. In the parking garage, we got jumped. Jonathan was there."

"Who?"

Lyla clenched her teeth. "Jonathan, my ex."

Carmen frowned. "What was he doing there?"

"He wanted to talk to me."

Carmen held up a hand. "Oh hell no! You talked to him?"

"He followed us to the parking garage and nearly got shot. I drove him to a hotel when I found out he was staying in a Pyre Casino. I told him to forget he ever knew me. He was worried about me. He said he could help me disappear and what's when Gavin showed up."

Carmen's mouth dropped open. Nora burped and Lyla set her daughter in her lap.

"Gavin tried to kill him. I stopped him."

Carmen's mouth stayed open.

"Blade sedated Gavin because he..." Lyla swallowed hard as she remembered the murderous expression on Gavin's face. "He was out of control. He slammed his knife into the wall this close to my face." Lyla held up a hand to show her and shivered.

Carmen put both hands over her face and groaned. "Shit, Lyla."

"Yeah."

She dropped her hands. "You have to let that guy go."

"I have."

She leaned forward. "No. I mean *let him go*, as in, let Gavin do what he's gonna do."

"What?"

"Lyla, Gavin's a psycho."

"No, he isn't," she said hastily.

Carmen gave her a put upon look. Lyla remembered the look on his face as he approached Jonathan and sighed.

"He's... not normal."

"He's fucking unhinged, okay? Jesus, you're acting like Gavin's a pussycat. He isn't. He's a straight up killer and he'll do whatever it takes to get what he wants, comprende?"

"Why are you telling me this?"

"Because you don't get who Gavin is. He's going to kill your little ex and he's going to make him suffer."

"Jonathan didn't do anything wrong!" she said for what felt like the tenth time.

"In your eyes. Gavin won't let you feel an iota of affection for any other man. Gavin's the most possessive psycho I know and that's saying something!"

"Carmen, he can't kill Jonathan."

"He will."

"I won't let him," Lyla said fiercely.

Carmen stared at her for a pregnant moment and then sighed. "There she is."

"Who?"

"My cousin from California."

"What?"

"You can take the girl from the beaches, but you can't take the idealism out of the woman."

"Idealism? You think trying to save an innocent man is idealistic?"

"It's unrealistic when your husband is Gavin Pyre. This guy isn't innocent. He showed up at this event. Why? Because he wants you. That makes him guilty as fuck and that's why Gavin's going to take him out. If your ex knew who Gavin was, he should have stayed away."

"He thought I was in danger. He was worried about me."

Carmen made the sound of a buzzer when you answered wrong on a game show. "Two strikes. Now he's out."

Lyla glared at her cousin. This is why she needed to get out of the house. Carmen and Blade believed it was perfectly acceptable for Gavin to kill anyone he wanted. "Gavin can let him live."

"He can?"

"After what happened, I can guarantee I'll never see Jonathan again."

Carmen shook her head. "You don't get it.

Gavin won't let you have split loyalties."

There it was again. Loyalties. "I am loyal to Gavin. Jealousy and possessiveness aren't justifications for committing murder!"

"Lyla, you live in the underworld! Gavin doesn't need justifications, he just needs cause. He's blown guys heads off for not responding fast enough to a question. Having you defend another man made him lose his motherfucking mind! Can't you see that?"

"I won't let him do this. We've been through so much," Lyla said as she brushed a hand through Nora's hair. "This is small in comparison."

"You being with another man in a hotel room doesn't sound small."

"It wasn't like that!"

Carmen rolled her eyes. "How the hell could you get yourself in so much trouble in so little time?"

Lyla threw up her hands. "I've been with only two men in my life and I have to stop one from killing the other. My life is fucked up."

"That's your fault. You chose Gavin knowing what kind of man he is."

She wanted to argue, but decided it was a moot point. "One of the cholos killed the hospital director. Was that on the news?"

Carmen sobered. "No."

Her head throbbed so she stretched out on the bed. Beau jumped up, circled twice and settled with his eyes on her.

"How'd it go with Kody?" she asked, desperate for mundane conversation.

"He asked me to go to Europe with him."

Panic flooded her. She didn't want to be alone, but Carmen deserved to have a life. "What did you say?"

"I told him I'd think about it." Carmen gave her a discerning look. "But you know I'm not looking for commitment."

Lyla tried to hide her relief. "I know."

"And how can I even think about going when you're neck deep in this shit?"

Lyla rubbed her face against the pillow and cuddled Nora close. "It's a mess."

"When is Gavin going to wake up?"

"In two or three hours."

"And what are you going to do?"

"Make him promise not to touch Jonathan."

Carmen stared at her. "You can't be serious."

"What else can I do?"

"Let Gavin do what he's gonna do and hope it's over quickly."

"I can't do that."

"Lyla, Gavin grew up in the underworld. He doesn't have morals."

"I can't let him kill Jonathan."

Carmen sighed. "Let me take Nora and let you catch some z's."

"Are you sure?" Lyla asked as her eyes closed.

"Yeah. You're going to need your strength to face Gavin after he's been sedated."

Carmen bounced Nora on her hip as she walked to the door. "Your mama's crazy, baby girl. This world isn't for the faint of heart. Did I tell you about the time I watched my dad blow this guy's brains out? I think I was seven."

"Carmen!" Lyla groaned.

"Nora needs to know these things."

"At four months?"

"The earlier the better. Her dad's Gavin fucking Pyre. She's going to know how to shoot a gun before she's eight years old."

Lyla burrowed into the covers and moaned when her phone rang, but after a quick look at the screen she answered, "Hey, Alice."

"Oh my God! Are you okay?"

"I'm fine. Are you?"

"Yes. Did you leave before the shooting?"

"During. Blade got me out."

"And he's okay as well?"

"Yes."

Alice let out a breath. "Janice and I have been worried sick. It's madness here."

"Has anyone been hurt?" she asked, clutching the phone, waiting for the inevitable discovery of the hospital director.

"I'm not sure. We're still trying to account for everyone. I wanted to make sure you were okay. Your phone was off earlier."

"I know. My battery died. I'm sorry." She hesitated. "Is there anything I can do?"

"No. You coming today was great. I just hate that something like this had to ruin it. I have to go. Thanks for everything you did. It meant a lot to me."

Before Lyla could respond, Alice hung up. Lyla dropped her face on the comforter. If she hadn't come, none of this would've happened.

CHAPTER TEN

Lyla

"Lyla."

A hand shook her shoulder. Lyla grunted and blinked at Blade.

"What?" She felt as if she had been drugged. Her mind was suspended in no man's land.

"Gavin's awake."

That brought her back to reality with an unpleasant jolt. Images of the director covered in blood, the cholos and Gavin swinging a knife at her slid through her mind in rapid succession. Lyla sat up and grabbed the lapels of her robe, which were gaping open. Blade was too busy typing on his phone to notice.

"How long has he been up?" Lyla asked.

"Half an hour."

"He's been up that long and you only woke me up now?" She scooted off the bed and headed to the closet.

"He stopped trying to break down the door ten minutes ago."

"He tried to break down an iron door?"

"Yeah. He nearly fucking did it. You calling him The Hulk isn't far off the mark. I'm seen him do crazy shit when he wants to."

"Is he asking for me?"

"He hasn't said a thing since he woke up."

Lyla grabbed the first set of clothes she got her hands on—a pair of sweat pants and a shirt with a big heart on the front. Blade headed to the door the moment she emerged from the closet.

"Wait. I want to know what's going on," she said.

"With what?"

Lyla stared at him. "The hospital incident."

"What about it?"

Was he being deliberately obtuse? "The hospital director was killed. You're not going to be able to cover that up, are you?"

"The cops suspect gang activity, but it's hard for them to get confirmation since the surveillance cameras were damaged. We took care of our bodies, left the gang members there and made it look like they turned on each other." Blade jerked his head at the door. "Come. Let's get you to Gavin."

Lyla's hands became damp with sweat as she followed him. It had been a while since she had to handle an out of control Gavin and she wasn't sure she was up to the challenge.

"I'll be watching on the surveillance camera in case you need help," Blade said when they reached the basement.

Lyla glared at him. "You're making me more nervous."

"Just prepping you, Dorothy."

"Asshole," she muttered.

When she didn't reach for the handle Blade leaned against the wall and put his hands in his pockets.

"Do you really think he'd kill me?" she whispered.

"No," Blade said. "Hurt you, yes. You're his weak spot, his Achilles' heel. No matter how you look at it, you chose another man over Gavin today. After taking care of business at the hospital, he tracked you to the hotel and found you with another man who offered to make you disappear. Of course Gavin's going to kill him. Then you made matters worse by touching him and pleading for his life. Gavin won't share you."

"I'm not asking him to!"

Blade shrugged. "Gavin has his own set of rules. You live in his world, you live by them. Period."

Lyla grit her teeth. He was her husband and she should be able to talk to him. She could make him understand, right?

"The longer you make him wait, the worse it will be," Blade said.

"You're the one who drugged him!"

"You weren't in any state to handle him."

"I know," she muttered. "Thanks." But now she had to deal with Gavin's wrath, which she could only imagine was worse than it had been in the hotel. Lyla stared at the door and made no move to open it.

"I'll come with you," Blade decided.

She couldn't hide her relief. "Okay."

Lyla eased the heavy door open and glimpsed the dented side of it before she stepped onto the landing. She peered down the stairs, but couldn't see the rest of the room from this angle. Her heart pounded in her ears as she waited for Gavin to appear, but he didn't. Fuck.

Lyla started down. She felt as if she were walking to her doom rather than to talk to her husband. Of course, in most American households, husbands weren't sedated or locked in basements to stop them from going on killing sprees. She allowed Gavin to go back into the underworld to destroy Sadist, not kill anyone he felt like. They had so much bigger problems than her ex who was in love with a woman who didn't exist.

Halfway down the steps she saw Gavin in front of the cot. He stood on the outskirt of the circle of fluorescent lights. His eyes were a burning copper that didn't bode well for her. He looked as if he had been shipwrecked. His shirt was unbuttoned and splattered with blood and his slacks were shredded at the knee, probably from trying to break the door down. Lyla made it to the bottom and stopped with her hand on the rail.

"Are you okay?" she asked.

Gavin didn't move or speak. She was dimly aware of Blade standing behind her. On the surface Gavin looked composed, but the air crackled with his energy, which was dark and vicious.

"Changed loyalties, have you, Blade?" Gavin asked.

"My loyalty is to both of you. I did what I thought was best."

"If you hadn't already bled for her, I'd shoot you." A muscle ticked in Gavin's jaw. "Get the fuck out of here, Blade, and turn off the cameras."

Lyla stiffened and turned to see Blade assessing Gavin closely. Blade caught her nervous glance, nodded and then left. Lyla listened to the sound of him climbing the stairs and flinched when she heard the door shut, locking her in the basement with her husband.

"Did you come here to plead for his life?" Gavin asked.

"Yes."

"Don't bother." Gavin prowled in the shadows. "Why were you with him in the hotel room?"

"He got caught in the crossfire when we were ambushed in the parking garage. I couldn't leave him there so I dropped him off at the hotel."

"You promised not to talk to him." His unemotional voice made her skin prickle with alarm.

"I didn't know he was going to be there."

"You saw him before the attack, didn't you?"

Her heart sank. "Yes."

"What did he want?"

There was only one reason for Jonathan's appearance and they both knew it. In her eyes, it didn't matter why. Jonathan wanted nothing to do with her *now* so what he said prior to the attack didn't matter. "He wanted closure."

"Is that right? And how did he think he was going to accomplish that?"

"He just wanted to know the truth."

"And what did you tell him?"

"To move on and forget he ever met me."

"Didn't you warn him what I'd do to him?"

She shivered. "Yes."

"And he still took the risk. He knew the consequences for trespassing, Lyla."

"He doesn't understand your world—"

"*Our* world."

He closed in on her and her body locked against the need to run. Gavin was a natural predator. Fleeing would only make things worse.

"You fucked up today," Gavin said.

"So did you." The feeling of being hunted pissed her off. She shouldn't be afraid of her husband, but she was. The polished veneer was what most people saw, but she knew about the beast beneath the pretty exterior. "You could have killed me."

"If I didn't love you so much, I would."

Her breath whooshed out of her. "What?"

"I told you why I never committed fully the first time," Gavin said as he backed her against the wall and planted both hands on either side of her head. "I didn't want anyone to have such power over me."

His will was so strong that she could feel it pressing in on her, willing her to submit.

"You have the power to save me," he said quietly and rubbed his thumb over her bottom lip. "And the power to destroy me." His eyes met hers. "Today, you destroyed me. You threatened to leave me for him."

"Gavin, I couldn't let you—"

His thumb slid into her mouth. Her lips closed reflexively before she tried to turn her head away.

"Gavin," she garbled as his thumb slid deeper. What the fuck was he doing?

"Suck," he ordered.

"We have to—"

He leaned down so their faces were inches apart. "Do it, Lyla."

Her mouth watered as she held his feral gaze. He was on the precipice. One wrong move and he would lose it. Since his hand was in her face, she saw that his knuckles were swollen and ripped from God knew what. She raised her hands and felt him tense until she gripped his wrist. She brushed her finger over the cuts and then did as he asked. She sucked.

"I was so desperate to keep you safe, to get you away from those fuckers. I tracked you to that hotel, unsure why you were there and then I hear him say he can make you disappear." The fingers resting against her jaw tensed. "There's something you don't understand about me, something you never did. When it comes to you, I'll do whatever it takes to have you with me. I'll steal you from another man, blackmail your father or threaten someone's life to bind you to me." His eyes met hers. "Or kill a man for coveting what has always been mine."

She pulled back. "Gavin—"

He replaced his thumb with his pointer and middle finger and sank them deep so she stopped trying to talk. His fingers skittered over her tongue and thrust slowly in and out of her mouth. Lyla shifted restlessly. Why the fuck was this turning her on? And how could she be turned on when she should be pleading for Jonathan's life?

"I'm not the kind of man you want to fall in love with you," Gavin said quietly, eyes fixed on her mouth. "Men like me, when we find a reason to live, we hang on too tight. I know men who have killed their wives because they can't handle how she makes them feel."

Lyla dug her nails into his chest and felt his muscles tense in reaction.

"I never understood that feeling until today," he said.

"Gavin—"

He wrapped one hand around her neck and pulled her away from the wall. He walked her backwards until the back of her knees hit the cot. The narrowing of his eyes gave her a split second of warning before he whirled her around and bent her over. Her hands landed on the thin mattress. Gavin yanked her sweat pants down and trailed rough, calloused fingers over her bare ass. Goosebumps rose over her body.

"What are you doing?" she demanded and tried to wriggle away.

"Don't move," he ordered.

"Gavin—"

"Don't talk."

Gavin placed his hips firmly against her ass and rocked as he bent over her. She could feel his cock pressed firmly between her cheeks. When he lapped the back of her neck with his tongue, she shifted restlessly.

"This isn't right," she said through clenched teeth.

Gavin worked the two fingers she had been sucking into her damp heat. Her mouth dropped open at the pleasure/pain. When his fingers curled, her back arched and she went on tiptoes, calves burning.

"If this is wrong, why are you wet?"

He rested his slick thumb against her asshole and she jerked, but that fucking mammoth hand on her back kept her bent over and at his mercy. She sucked in a breath as his thumb penetrated. She wriggled her ass to dislodge him, but he wasn't deterred. He withdrew his thumb to replace it with the slick fingers from her pussy.

"Gavin, we need to talk."

Lyla bucked forward as he laved the dimples above her ass.

"We're done talking."

She felt the head of his cock. Alarmed, she reached back to splay her hand on his rock hard stomach to slow him down. He gripped her waist and impaled her on him. Lyla let out a strangled shriek.

"That's it, baby girl. Let me in."

"I-I don't think I can take—"

"You don't have a choice."

He pulled back before imbedding himself fully. Lyla screamed. Gavin collared her throat with one hand and her breast with the other and bowed her upwards.

"Gavin," she gasped.

"You bring out the best and worst in me." His bristly jaw scraped her soft cheek. "A man like me can't have a weakness like you, but I do. Some think because I'm married and have a kid that it's made me soft, but being with you has made me more dangerous than ever."

She dug her nails into his arm as he began to

fuck her ass.

"I've already thought of ten ways to kill him," he said through gritted teeth.

Lyla tried to pull away. "Gavin!"

He didn't miss a beat, he kept thrusting nice and slow. "Strangling him would make me happiest. Up close and personal."

"Gavin, please—"

"I'm going to kill him. Nothing will stop me. I'm going to bathe myself in his blood until it's cold so I know he's really fucking gone."

He pumped his hips hard enough to make her scream and then he bent her over again. His hand kneaded her breast before it skated down her abdomen to her clit. He grabbed her hair and wrenched her head to the side so he could kiss her. When he pulled back, she saw his eyes were filled with rage and lust.

"You think you've tamed me? You're not even close. You can't control me."

There were no inhibitions, no rules. It was just her and Gavin and nothing else mattered. His hand sank into her hair and pulled as he thrust home. Gavin fucked her ass as if he owned it, which he did. Lyla climaxed, screaming and clawing the mattress. Gavin made her feel like a savage. He growled like a wild animal as he came, grinding himself against her before he pulled out abruptly.

Lyla collapsed on the mattress, panting. Gavin zipped up his pants and turned to her. His climax hadn't cooled his temper. If anything, he looked angrier. Her heart sank.

"If I didn't love you so much, I never would

have stepped down from my position and my father and Vinny would still be alive."

Lyla felt as if he punched her in the stomach.

"If we didn't have Nora, I'd lock you in here," he continued.

The pleasure he evoked from her body was replaced with despair. Lyla wanted to curl up in a ball. Instead, she whispered, "I gave up a normal life to be with you."

Gavin said nothing. He stared at her as if she were something distasteful.

"You force me into your world, but I'm *not* a part of it and I will not bow down to it." She lifted her chin. "I had to change. I understand that sometimes, people need to die. I don't have to agree with what you do or how you do it, but I trust that you know what's required, but in this... There's a difference between killing a thug in the underworld and murdering a man who thinks he's in love with a woman who doesn't love him back."

Tears burned her eyes. She rose, very aware of her throbbing behind, his seed leaking out of her and the way he tensed as she took a step towards him. She searched for the right words and willed him to understand.

"I trust you to do what needs to be done in the underworld. I trust that you won't lose yourself, that you won't cheat on me. I trust that you'll find that fucker and you'll avenge Manny and Vinny. I've changed since I watched Manny die, but I haven't changed so much that I can ignore the fact that you're killing an innocent man." She held up a hand when he opened his mouth. "He. Is. Innocent. He dated a woman he thought was single. Period. He was nice to a woman who had no one and there are too few people like him in the world. What I felt for him can't compare to what I feel for you." She searched his eyes, looking for recognition or acceptance. "You married me and told me that you would do whatever it took to make me love you again. I love you, but if you do this, you'll break me, break us."

She reached out and even as fear coursed through her, she stroked a hand down Gavin's imposing face.

"I love you," she said.

No reaction from Gavin. The predator weighed every word out of her mouth.

"You can't erase my memories by killing him. We've been through too much to let Jonathan rip us apart. If you do this, you'll destroy us."

She waited for a full minute for him to say something, but he remained silent. He was a living, breathing statue of a man who wouldn't yield. As the silence stretched, she realized his silence was her answer. She dropped her hand as a tear coursed down her cheek.

"Nothing I say will make a difference, will it?" she whispered.

"No."

She averted her eyes and walked towards the stairs. When she reached the door, she banged on it hard enough to make her hand ache. A guard opened the door and she walked out with Gavin on her heels.

Lyla walked towards the kitchen and let herself

into the backyard. She welcomed the hard slap of cold air and paced across the cold tiles to a lounge chair. The last hint of light faded from the sky. She settled on a chair and stared blindly into the lit pool until it became a blur as tears gathered in her eyes.

Nothing had changed. Gavin would do whatever he wanted despite how she felt. She was as scared, pissed and helpless, as she had been when Gavin went back into the underworld when Vinny was killed.

She looked up at the blanket of black sky above her. There was no bird flying overhead or shooting star to signal that all would be well. This was the real world where good didn't always overcome evil.

The back door opened. She wiped at her eyes and saw Blade coming towards her with a trench coat. She accepted the coat and wrapped it around her to ward off the cold.

"You're in one piece," Blade observed.

"Doesn't feel like it," she mumbled.

"You'll get past this."

"Why is it always me that has to get over it and not him?"

"Because he's a badass motherfucker."

"So?"

"So... no one can stop him when he wants something."

"My life is always going to be like this, isn't it?"

"Like what?"

"There's always going to be an emergency and I'll have to make decisions that will tear me up inside."

"You'll get used to it."

She wiped away a tear. "And if I don't want to?"

"You already know the answer to that," Blade said and headed inside.

Lyla blew out a shaky breath and wrapped her arms around herself. Life was hard. Life as a crime lord's wife was even harder. She wished Manny was here. A tear she couldn't contain slipped down her cheek. *If I didn't love you so much, I never would have stepped down from my position and my father and Vinny would still be alive.* That fucking killed her. Gavin was right. If he hadn't stepped down for her, Sadist wouldn't have made a play to become the crime lord. Vinny wouldn't have volunteered to take his place and Manny would be traveling the world or browsing through antique shops if it wasn't for her. The cost of her and Gavin being together was astronomical... and they were still paying.

She turned her head when she saw movement out of the corner of her eye. Gavin stood in the shadows. He came forward, the clip of his shoes loud in the hushed silence. He looked every inch the wealthy businessman and not a man with murder on his mind. He looked as flawless and untouchable as James Bond in his tailored suit, hands in pockets, expression nonchalant. In contrast, she felt as if she was on the verge of falling into a chasm from which there would be no return.

Gavin stopped in front of her. She couldn't meet his eyes, not when he looked at her as if he hated her. There was nothing more to say. He would do what he wanted and there was nothing she could do to stop him. She felt so goddamn helpless. She thought the days of not being in control of her destiny were a thing of the past. Apparently not. Everyone sided with Gavin and thought it was his right to take Jonathan's life. She didn't agree. If he killed Jonathan, would she leave him?

The silence stretched. What did he want? His presence fanned the throbbing pain in her chest. Gavin was tearing her apart, but that was nothing new. She was always the one that had to conform, not him. No matter what she said or did, he wouldn't change, so where did that leave her? Was this the beginning of the end for them?

She jolted when a calloused hand cupped her chin. Gavin tilted her face up. She kept her eyes closed. A tear leaked out of her left eye. She hoped it was too dark for him to see, but his thumb brushed it away before it could travel halfway down her face. Her breath hitched as another tear escaped. She wasn't prepared for the gentle kiss he pressed against her lips.

Lyla opened her eyes, but he was already on his way back to the house. "Gavin."

He didn't stop. He walked back into the house and disappeared from sight.

CHAPTER ELEVEN

Gavin

Santana's brother trembled like a plucked bow as Gavin held his head at an angle guaranteed to end his miserable existence. Santana's men scattered after Gavin executed their leader. Gavin thought he bought enough time to attend the hospital function and come back to finish gutting Santana's operation. Seeing those cholos in the elevator with Santana's brand on their neck sent a spear of ice-cold terror through his body when he realized that he had put Lyla at risk.

"How did you know to send men to the hospital? Are you tracking me?" Gavin bit out.

Santana's brother's mouth flopped open and closed like a fish. Gavin bent his head a fraction more and he squealed like a stuck pig.

"How did you know?" Gavin bellowed.

"I-I got a call."

"From who?"

"Stark."

Everything in him went on alert. "Eli Stark?"

"Si. He's an informant, sells information. He gave the location of hospital."

"What else?" Gavin asked.

"That's it, I swear."

Gavin broke his neck, rose and stared down at the body without really seeing it. Eli Stark. This wasn't the first time he heard whispers of Stark, but it was going to be the last. Once, he considered Stark a loyal associate, but that changed after Stark's mother had been brutally attacked. Stark blamed him for not protecting her, which gave him motive. Selling information to a Mexican drug lord? It didn't sound like Stark, but people changed. After his mother was attacked, Stark quit his position as detective and went on a bloody rampage to avenge his mother before he fell off the map. Well, it was time to draw him out of hiding.

Gavin dug through Santana's brother's pockets and found condoms, drugs and a cell phone. He used the dead man's thumb to unlock the phone and debated whether to cut it off for future use, but changed the passcode instead. He scrolled through recent calls, most of which were unavailable.

He dialed his tech genius from the phone. "Z, it's me. I need you to tap into this phone and unblock some numbers."

Z didn't ask questions. "Give me ten minutes."

"And locate Eli Stark's mother."

A pause. "Sir?"

"I don't know her name. She went into a coma almost three years ago."

"I'll find out," Z said.

Gavin pocketed the phone and glanced around the room. The blood-splattered walls reflected how he felt on the inside. Bodies littered the ground around him. It took him less than two hours to track Santana's brother to a set of cabins on the outskirts of the city.

Santana was a sick fuck. Gavin made sure to clear out the child prostitutes they discovered earlier this morning. Gavin didn't feel a lick of remorse for drawing out Santana's death since he found the fucker molesting a baby. If he let the justice system do their thing Santana would get several life sentences and live off taxpayer's money, reading books and educating himself about the legal system to see how he could get out. Or, he would join one of the gangs in prison and claim the lives of too many prison guards who were just trying to make an honest living. Fuck that. He knew Santana's brother would retaliate, but he hadn't expected them to stage a public attack that cost four of his men's lives and put Lyla and too many others at risk. Stupid fucker.

He was high on rage and feeling especially savage. The lethal fury racing through his veins hadn't dissipated as he slay anyone who crossed his path. The fight with Lyla made him crazed. He couldn't fault Blade for drugging him today. What he felt this afternoon when he walked into that hotel room was inexplicable. Blade had done his job and prevented him from doing something unforgivable to his wife. In the basement he lost control. He wanted to hurt her, to punish her. Lyla would lie to protect this guy, which showed how deep her feelings for Huskin ran. He wouldn't allow it. Lyla was supposed to heal him, not break him. Hearing her cry and plead for another man's life made him feel homicidal.

Gavin reloaded his gun and walked outside to

see if there was more work to do. Unfortunately, his men had already taken care of everything. Those that thought they were safe in these cabins were now strewn across the sand. His men knew the drill and were already loading the bodies into the SUV to be transported to be buried in the desert where they would never be found.

A man at his feet moaned. Gavin looked down and saw that the man had been shot twice in the gut, a painful way to die. When he saw Gavin, his eyes bulged and he made urgent, terrified noises. Gavin crouched as the man tried to edge away. Gavin pulled out his knife and yanked the man's head to the side to examine Santana's brand—a skull tattoo with the number twenty four in roman numerals on his throat.

"I'm gonna need this," Gavin said, tapping the tattoo with the tip of his knife.

The man tried to push his hand away. Gavin restrained him with ease and got to work. By the time his phone rang, the man was dead and he held a dripping slice of skin with Santana's brand on it. He grabbed a switchblade and pinned the piece of skin on the outside of the cabin. If more men tried to take refuge in these cabins, they would know he wasn't far behind.

"Yeah?" Gavin said into the phone.

"I unscrambled the numbers. What are you looking for?" Z asked.

"An incoming call that came in at around nine or ten this morning." An hour or two before the attack.

"There was a call at ten oh one. It's a prepaid

174

phone, not registered to anyone."

"Give me the number." Gavin wrote the number on the wall in blood. "Got it."

"The caller was at the hospital that was attacked when he made the call."

Gavin closed his eyes to rein in his beast. "And which hospital is Stark's mother at?" He waited, but already had a sneaking suspicion that he knew the answer.

"Same hospital. She's on the fourth floor."

Was it just by chance that Stark had been visiting his mother at the same hospital where they were having an event? "I'm gonna make a call, try to pinpoint his location."

"Will do, sir."

"How is everything with the surveillance tapes?"

"Scrambled."

"Good work."

Gavin hung up with Z and glanced at the bloody numbers as he plugged them into his phone. As the phone began to ring, he walked back into the silent cabin so the caller wouldn't hear the groans of the dying.

The line picked up, but no one spoke. The silence stretched.

"This is Gavin Pyre."

He thought he heard an indrawn breath on the other end, but couldn't be sure.

"You fucked up today. I'm coming for you."

The line went dead. Gavin stood in the middle of the cabin for a moment to get his bearings. There was a fine trembling in the hand holding the phone.

Gavin called Z. "Did you get his location?"

"He's at the hospital."

Adrenaline fizzled in his veins. The monster inside of him roared with the need to end this fucker. He swallowed his need to mutilate the dead bodies and washed his hands before he walked outside. He slid into his car and didn't have to signal for a group of men to follow. Six men stopped what they were doing and loaded into an SUV.

Gavin headed back to the city. There was a firestorm taking place inside of him. Fury burned a hole in his gut. When he was gutting Santana this morning, the man claimed he didn't know the identity of the Phantom. Gavin figured he was telling the truth since he started Santana's death by cutting his fingers one by one. If Eli Stark was part of this mess, he might be the key to finding the Phantom once and for all.

Gavin strode into the hospital with his men following at a discreet distance. The lobby was filled with cops, reporters, medical staff and concerned family members who were still trying to figure out what happened this morning.

Gavin took the elevator to the fourth floor. As he strode through the corridor, he approached two cops. Their hands edged towards their weapons. Every cop in the state recognized his face. The dirty ones knew exactly what he was capable of while the other half suspected and dreamed of being the one to bag him. Too bad they had never been able to pin shit on him until the money laundering charge. He had been at such a low point that he hadn't acted swiftly enough and had to serve time or let them dig deeper and possibly find evidence of first-degree murder since he hadn't been in his right mind at the time. Gavin looked them boldly in the eye, daring them to do something. They didn't.

He glanced into rooms as he passed. Most patients were asleep. Some family members eyed him suspiciously, but he was gone before they could ask what he wanted. Hospital staff rushed through the halls despite the late hour.

Gavin opened a door without knocking and leaned in, expecting to see a sleeping patient. Paul Vega sat up in bed, papers scattered over his sheets and a laptop on his tray table. He looked over the top of his glasses at Gavin. The light from the screen illuminated the hatred in his eyes, which he didn't bother to conceal.

Gavin stared at him. What the fuck? The fact that his lifelong enemy was a patient at this hospital was too convenient. Was this the only fucking hospital in the city?

"Fuck off, Pyre," Paul growled.

Gavin glanced back at his men. "Find Stark's mother. Two of you stay with her. The other two sweep the hospital floors and see if you can locate Stark."

Gavin stepped in and closed the door behind him. "What are you doing here, Paul?"

"What the fuck does it look like? I have pneumonia." He took off his glasses and glared at Gavin as he advanced across the room. "You're not allowed in here."

"I'm allowed anywhere. No place is off limits. I

177

thought after I fucked you up in your office, you'd realize that."

It was true that Vega looked like shit, but his frail appearance didn't mean he wasn't dangerous.

"I have a lot of work to do, Pyre."

Gavin stopped beside the bed. "Restful day?"

"No thanks to you," he said sourly. "You must have a death wish to kill Santana. You stirred up a hornet's nest and don't have the manpower you're going to need."

In his youth he endured many of Paul's futile attempts to wrench the title from his father. Despite the fact that his father and now he had thrashed Paul soundly, Vega still didn't respect his authority, which made his fingers itch for his knife. When he asked his father why he didn't just kill Paul, his father said, "Better the devil you know."

"You're losing your hold on the city, Pyre," Paul said quietly. "Why don't you just give it up?"

"Give it up to who?"

Paul gathered his papers and began to stack them, rapping them on the tray table to straighten them out. He was nervous. Gavin eased closer and saw his body tense.

"You know something, Paul?" he asked and made sure his voice was light and pleasant.

Paul studied his papers as if the information on it were more important than their conversation. "I'm too busy running my practice to delve into the underworld."

"Yet you knew I got Santana. How?"

"I have my sources."

"You're lying to me, Vega," Gavin said.

"I don't owe you shit. You told me you'd find the crime lord who murdered Rafael and you haven't."

"I will."

Paul scoffed. "He's too powerful. You're in over your head. He's giving us—"

Paul stopped, but it was too late.

"You're joining the man who murdered your son?" Gavin asked.

Paul bared his teeth in a snarl. "I either join or end up like Manny. He's rewarded me, offered me more than you fuckers ever did." Spit flew as his emotions got the better of him and rage made him reckless. "How many can you kill? You think your name will protect you? You have nowhere to turn. Manny and Vinny are gone and he's already carved up that pretty wife of yours. Who's next?"

Gavin wasn't aware that his body moved. He didn't hear the laptop and papers crash to the floor when he wrapped his hand around Paul's throat or notice Paul's hand scrabbling over his suit. He wasn't aware of anything until he saw Paul's glazed eyes staring up at him. He was dead. The fact that he didn't remember strangling Paul to death should have alarmed him. It didn't. One less enemy was a plus in his book.

The door opened. Gavin whirled and saw Steven Vega in the doorway, leaning on a cane. Before Steven could do more than register that there was a man standing over his father's bed, Gavin had him pinned to the wall. Steven Vega's eyes were wild with panic as Gavin squeezed his skinny neck. Steven wriggled like a fish on a hook with tears in his eyes. He was so pathetic that Gavin's beast retreated in disgust.

Gavin tossed Steven on the ground. He landed on all fours and cowered.

"Your father's dead," Gavin said.

For a moment Steven didn't seem to hear him and then his head snapped up. He stared at Gavin and then struggled to his feet and limped to his father's bed. Steven's hands hovered over his father's face.

"He sided with the man who took my place," Gavin said. "You know anything about that?"

Steven shook his head without looking away from his father. A tear slid down his cheek.

"I should kill you," Gavin said.

Steven's thin body went rigid.

"If you're smart, you'll stick to the courtrooms and not get involved in the underworld like Rafael and your father." He paused and added, "If you don't, you'll meet the same fate. You understand me?"

Steven didn't move.

"Yes or no?"

"Y-yes," Steven whispered.

Gavin walked into the hallway and saw one of his men standing outside of a room. He approached and told his man about Paul Vega. His guard immediately set off to take care of the paperwork and whatever else was needed.

Gavin walked into Maureen Stark's hospital room. A lone sunflower perched in a vase on the table. Gavin gripped the bedrail and leaned down to examine her. She had a shock of white hair, was on the heavy side and bore no resemblance to Eli.

It had been nearly three years since Eli's mother went into a coma, yet he hadn't pulled the plug. The bloody trail he left in the wake of her attack was proof that he had feelings for her, but his unwillingness to let her go revealed his depth of devotion and love. The hospital bills were hefty and backing up fast. Is that why Stark betrayed him?

Images of his own mother passed through his mind. She was soft-spoken, gentle, and affectionate. He thought of Lyla and Nora and turned away from the bed. His guards were watching him, waiting for orders.

A crime lord couldn't afford to have a heart.

"Get rid of her," Gavin said as he walked past them and left Maureen Stark behind.

CHAPTER TWELVE

Lyla

Lyla sat on the floor with her back against the couch as Nora lay on her back and played with her toys. Beau sat beside her. She absently scratched his back as she tried to make up her mind. She glanced at her watch and then around the room before she typed in Jonathan's number. He could have changed it in the past two years, but... She dialed and put the phone to her ear. The phone rang four times. She wasn't sure whether to be relieved or worried and then...

"Hello?"

Lyla let out a long breath. "Jonathan?"

"Lyla, are you okay?" he asked immediately.

She dropped her face into her hand. She wasn't sure what she was. "Yes, I'm okay. Are you?"

"I'm back in Maine."

"You still live in the same place?"

"Of course."

She bit her lip. "Jonathan, you can't stay there. I tried to talk to him, but..."

"No one can control him. That's why that guy tranquilized him."

Lyla froze. "You saw?"

"Yes. You're in danger, Lyla."

He had no idea. "So are you. I'm so sorry—"

"I shouldn't have interfered in your life. You left me for my own good. I realize that now."

"I don't know what he's going to do, Jonathan."

"Did he hurt you?" he asked sharply.

"No."

"Don't worry about me. I can take care of myself."

"How?" she snapped and then her spine snapped as she sat up straight. "You're not going to go to the cops, are you?"

"Would that do any good?"

"Probably not."

"Then I'll handle it."

Her gut clenched. "I want you to keep in touch with me. I have to make sure..."

"Make sure I'm breathing?"

"Call me everyday, morning and night."

"I don't think that's a good idea."

"I don't care!"

"Lyla, calm down."

"How can you be so cavalier about this? You saw him yesterday."

"I did." A pause and then, "I'm worried about you."

"You should be more worried about yourself."

"I never imagined you were hiding something like this." He sighed. "That's life. Sometimes you're stupid enough to fall for a girl who used to date a crime boss. That's the luck of the draw."

"This isn't a joke."

"I know," he said, sounding more sober. "I'll be in touch."

"Call me when you go to work and when you come home."

"Isn't he monitoring your phone?"

He had in the past. It's why she hesitated to call Jonathan, but she couldn't handle the suspense of not knowing whether he was alive or not. "He has more important things to do."

"If you say so."

"Call me when you get off work," she ordered.

"Yes, ma'am. Stay safe, Lyla."

"You too."

Lyla hung up and dropped her face between her knees and took long breaths. Jonathan was still alive. She hadn't been able to sleep after Gavin left. How could she after the things he said in the basement?

The front door opened and her head rose. She straightened when Marcus appeared. She rose, alarmed.

"Is something wrong?" she asked as he strode towards her.

Marcus didn't stop until he wrapped his arms around her. She was stunned and then she hugged him back.

"Marcus, you're scaring me," she said.

He pulled back and set his hands on her shoulders. His eyes were troubled.

"I know what happened at the hospital yesterday," he said.

"Oh."

Of course he did. How could Gavin be MIA at Pyre Casinos without Marcus's cooperation? It surprised her, though. Marcus seemed too strait laced to know everything that Gavin did on the side. Apparently, even Marcus wasn't what he seemed.

"Are you all right?" He pulled back and scanned her.

"Yes, I'm fine. Is that why you came?"

"Yeah, Blade briefed me and I just wanted to make sure you're okay."

That was beyond sweet. After what happened yesterday, his concern was like a balm on her raw nerves. Fighting for her life had become a regular occurrence, but Marcus treated her like a fragile flower and she liked it.

"I'm okay. You're so sweet for coming out here."

"Of course," Marcus said simply as if his arrival was nothing out of the ordinary. "Blade said Carmen left the hospital before the shooting started?"

"Yes."

"And she's safe?"

"Uh, yeah. Did you want to—?" She pointed upstairs, but he shook his head.

"No, I just wanted to make sure everyone was fine."

He looked down at Nora who screamed in delight at nothing in particular. He knelt beside her in his flawless suit and grinned at her.

"You're a happy girl, aren't you?" Marcus asked and Nora's eyes lit up. "You're going to drive your daddy crazy, okay? I'll teach you how."

The front door opened again and Lyla tensed, expecting to see Gavin and was stunned when Alice and Janice waltzed in.

"Oh my gosh!" Alice shouted and rushed forward.

She hugged Lyla and rocked her from side to side while she babbled fervent apologies.

"I'm so sorry! What are the chances that some gangsters would choose to come into that hospital to battle during our event? I'm sure Mr. Pyre is furious. I'm scared to check my emails. He can't fire me over this, can he? I heard the authorities still don't know why the gang members were there, but there were *two* incidents, one in the new Pyre wing and one in the parking garage." Alice pulled back and scanned Lyla. "Are you hurt? Are you okay? Do you need to talk to someone?"

"No, I'm okay." Their arrival was like a breath of fresh air, clearing out the doom and gloom hanging over the fortress.

"Are you sure?" Alice insisted. "Sometimes people can be traumatized by the sound of gunshots or what could have happened."

If Alice only knew... "I think I'm going to be fine."

Alice squeezed her arms and stepped back, only to notice Marcus holding Nora. Worry disappeared from Alice's face. She hopped and clapped her hands.

"I never got to hold her the other day. Oh my God, she's adorable! Give her to me, Marcus!"

Janice came forward and also gave her a hug. "I'm so sorry about yesterday. Although it was truly unfortunate, we got even more positive publicity for the Pyre Foundation so..." Janice bobbed her hands as if they were scales. "No one was seriously injured except for the hospital director. Did you hear?"

Lyla suppressed a vivid image of the director lying in a pool of his own blood. "Yes, I did." Lyla felt as if there was a hole burning in her chest. Knowing the cause of the shooting and playing dumb was absolute hell.

"From the amount of damage done, the cops are shocked that only one innocent was killed in the crossfire."

How many of Gavin's men had been killed? Lyla jumped when Nora shrieked as Alice blew raspberries on her neck. Beau decided the crowd was too much for him and trotted out to the backyard.

Lyla surveyed the small group in her living room. "Coffee?"

"Yes!" all three of them said at once.

Happy for the company, she headed to the kitchen and was trailed by all of them.

"When did you leave the hospital?" Lyla asked.

"Around ten last night. We stopped here on our way to work," Janice said.

Their level of commitment was unheard of. "You stayed there until ten? Didn't you get there yesterday at six?"

"Yes, but the hospital staff and patients were all frazzled," Alice said. "Everyone's scared and confused. We couldn't leave."

Lyla swallowed her guilt as she handed out cups of steaming coffee. Janice and Marcus talked about some business function coming up while Alice bobbed around the kitchen with an ecstatic Nora.

Alice looked paler than normal, but still happy. How the heck could she look this awake after dealing with a crisis?

"What's your next project?" Lyla asked.

Alice's eyes lit up. "I'm teaming up with a dog shelter and a school to have a play day."

Lyla's heart lightened. "Oh my gosh. I want to help."

Out of the corner of her eye, she saw Marcus's head turn in her direction, but she ignored him. Marcus had never been one to hover around her like Blade, but it seemed this shooting had shaken him.

"It's going to be great," Alice said. "We're inviting parents to join as well. We're hoping to have a bunch of adoptions out of this."

An image of kids running with dogs in a field lightened the heavy weight on her chest. She would like nothing more than to be a part of it, but once again, she would have to sit out not only for her own safety, but for others as well.

Beau came through the doggy door and planted himself at Alice's feet, staring up at Nora.

"I'm glad to see Beau's bonding with Nora," Alice commented.

"He's obsessed with her," Lyla said.

"Why shouldn't he be? She's adorable!"

Alice baby talked to Beau who wasn't impressed. His ears twitched in her direction, but his tail didn't wag. Alice didn't seem to mind Beau's subtle rejection.

"I'm so happy Beau found a home with you and Mr. Pyre. If I didn't work so much, I'd get a pet myself. One day I will."

"Well, good morning," Janice drawled.

Lyla turned and saw Carmen standing in the doorway in a red silk robe and Hello Kitty slippers. Her eyes were bleary from sleep and she appeared perplexed by the company. Lyla didn't blame her. The last time they had this much people in the house was during Nora's baby shower. It had been a hollow tomb ever since.

"What's going on?" Carmen asked and made a beeline for the coffee pot.

"We're stopping by to make sure you and Lyla are okay after yesterday," Janice said and then examined her red nails. "Although I thought I saw you leave with Kody Singer before everything went haywire."

"Yeah," Carmen yawned and noticed Marcus for the first time. "What are you doing here?"

"Good morning, Carmen," Marcus said politely.

"She's not a morning person," Lyla said and shot Carmen a chiding look.

"Well, I'm off," Marcus said, setting his cup in the sink and kissing Lyla's temple. "Let me know if you need anything."

"Thanks, Marcus," she said as he kissed Nora and headed out.

"You made Marcus her godfather?" Alice asked.

"Yes. Nora has two godfathers, Marcus and Blade," Lyla said.

"And I'm her only godmother," Carmen said as she hopped up on the counter to drink her coffee.

"Your bodyguard is her godfather?" Alice asked.

"He'd take a bullet for Nora." And already had for her.

"Anything happen with Kody?" Janice asked Carmen as she glanced at her watch. "Usually celebrities are difficult, but he was really sweet and prompt. You add gorgeous on top of that, I couldn't ask for more."

"I want something a little more than looks and the ability to be somewhere on time," Carmen drawled. "We were at a restaurant when we saw the news. I came right home."

"Are you gonna see him again?" Alice asked.

"I don't know." Carmen looked extremely bored with the conversation.

"I think she should date Marcus," Lyla blurted.

Carmen jolted, nearly spilling coffee on herself. "Lyla!"

"You and Marcus?" Alice asked excitedly.

Carmen glared at Lyla. "Marcus and I are nothing."

"Do you want to be something?" Janice asked with a raised brow.

Carmen hesitated and Janice pulled out her phone.

"What are you doing?" Carmen demanded.

"I'm checking his schedule."

"I don't want him!"

Janice narrowed her eyes at Carmen. "I think thou doth protest too much."

Carmen crossed her arms and glared at them.

"I love Marcus," Lyla said.

"He's a fair boss," Alice said earnestly. "Mr. Pyre is..." She flushed when she looked at Lyla and then shook her head wildly. "I mean, Marcus is great."

"Gavin's not mean to you, is he?" Lyla asked.

Alice threaded her fingers together. "No. He's just..."

"Yes?"

"Scary." She waved her hands. "I mean, he's intimidating."

"He is," Lyla agreed with a nod.

Alice blinked. "He's your husband and you think he's intimidating?"

"He can be." Alice only knew Gavin in the civilized business world. If she knew how Gavin was at home or in the underworld, she would faint.

"Marcus needs a woman in his life," Janice said encouragingly to Carmen who had her lips compressed into a straight line. "He works too much and if I'm saying that, it's pretty bad."

"I don't need you guys to hook me up with Marcus. If I want him, I'll have him," Carmen growled.

Janice glanced at her watch again. "Alice, we have to roll."

Alice nuzzled Nora. "I'll see you soon, pretty girl."

There were hugs and kisses all around and then they were gone.

"What was that?" Carmen asked.

"What normal feels like," Lyla said as she settled on a chair to feed Nora.

"No, I mean about Marcus."

Lyla eyed her frazzled cousin. "There's something between you two."

"There isn't," Carmen grouched and peered into the cupboard closest to her. "Why are you up so early anyway?"

"Couldn't sleep."

Carmen found a box of graham crackers and munched. "What's the latest drama?"

Lyla glanced around, but saw no sign of Blade. "I called Jonathan."

"Lyla, you didn't!"

"He's alive!"

Carmen shook her head. "Not for long."

"Don't say that."

"Fine." Carmen demolished a square and reached for another. "But you know I'm right."

Blade walked into the kitchen. "After Nora goes down for her nap, I'll meet you two in the weight room."

Carmen gave him a baleful glare. "Go away, Satan."

"Your trainer isn't coming today so I'm filling in," Blade went on.

"Don't you think we deserve a day off?" Carmen snapped, waving her graham cracker.

"No," Blade said simply and walked out.

"When we spar today, I'm so going for his balls," Carmen said.

CHAPTER THIRTEEN

Gavin

Gavin walked through the apartment Lyla once lived in with Huskin. The apartment was a fusion of traditional and modern, but he didn't see the appeal. He looked out the window at Portland, Maine. It was just after midnight and there was no movement in the neighborhood. A private car waited across the street for him while two cars at either end of the block held men watching for Huskin. What was the nerd doing out so late at night? If he were smart, he would heed Lyla's advice and run.

Gavin turned from the uninspiring view and paced through the apartment, shoes clicking on the hardwood floors. Huskin's office was predictably geeky with comic books and Star Wars posters on the wall. He had a three screen computer set up and gadgets Gavin couldn't begin to identify. Gavin tried to imagine Lyla in this environment, but he couldn't imagine her anywhere but where she was—with him, where she belonged.

Gavin hesitated in the doorway leading to the bedroom, but forced himself to enter. There was nothing out of the ordinary. Like Huskin's hotel room, it verged on boring. He was grateful since any hint of Lyla's sex life with this guy was only going to make him draw out his death.

Gavin focused on a photograph on the nightstand. A Lyla he didn't recognize smiled shyly at the camera. She looked incredibly young in a hoodie with Huskin wrapped around her. There was a lighthouse in the background along with the choppy sea. She was the one who'd taken the photograph since Huskin's arms were around her waist. Gavin closed his eyes as a deluge of pain cascaded through him. Only Lyla could do this to him. No other person on the planet had this much power over him. He remembered her indignation about the women he'd been with. What she didn't understand is he fucked those women without emotion. She loved another man. No comparison. He put the picture frame down and walked out of the bedroom. He didn't look around for any more photographs because he couldn't take it. He settled in an armchair facing the door and waited.

How did men handle seeing their women with someone else? Gavin sat forward, elbows resting on his knees, hands folded as if he was praying. He took a deep breath and let it out slowly when everything in him wanted to destroy this tidy apartment and turn it into the mess he was becoming. Did Huskin have more photographs of her? Naked photographs? Gavin's chest expanded with the need to roar, but he choked his demon and tried to stuff it back into the dark depths. Wrecking Huskin's apartment would do nothing to assuage his need for retribution. He needed Huskin to accomplish that feat.

Gavin closed his eyes as his head throbbed. He

couldn't afford to sleep longer than two or three hours at a time, not with Santana's men on the loose and the underworld revolting. The longest stretch he was unconscious in months was when Blade sedated him. Fuck. There were people to hunt, question and possibly torture for information, yet here he was in Maine, waiting for Huskin to walk through that door so he could rip out the dagger twisting in his heart.

An image of Lyla's silver blue eyes filled with tears flashed in front of him. *I love you, but if you do this, you'll break me, break us*. He wasn't noble. He wasn't the idiot in the movies who let the woman walk away with the better guy. Fuck that. He would murder any man she thought could make her happy or give her a better life. Even after all these years, Lyla underestimated what he was capable of. He had always known that he didn't deserve her, but he wasn't going to give her the opportunity to find the right guy. Lyla made that decision herself by leaving and she fucking found him—Mr. Boring with his nine to five and safe little life. What did Huskin say to her before the attack at the hospital? What was said in the hotel room before he overheard Huskin saying he could make her disappear? Lyla did an excellent job evading him for three years. He didn't need her to have a connection with a man who could make her disappear forever. Just the thought of coming home to an empty house without Lyla and Nora made him insane.

He thought they were through being on opposing sides of an issue where neither of them would compromise. First, it had been his position as crime lord, which she had changed her stance on. Now, she was asking him not to kill a man who wanted to save her from *him*. A normal man would feel jealousy, ignore it and be satisfied with the fact that she wore his ring, bore his child and said she loved him. He wasn't that logical or evolved. Lyla left him twice and for very good reasons. Even now, any psychologist or sane friend (thank God Carmen grew up in his world and didn't encourage Lyla to leave him again) would tell Lyla to take Nora and run. He wouldn't allow it. Lyla would get past this. She had to because he wasn't going to deviate from his course. Huskin had to die and she had no choice.

Huskin lived a safe existence free of the evil he walked through everyday. Z sent him a recording of Lyla's conversation with Huskin this morning. She didn't think he had time to monitor her? Was she fucking crazy? Lyla didn't comprehend the depth of his obsession with her. She tried her damnedest to warn Huskin that his life was in danger, but Huskin wasn't concerned. Even through the recording, Gavin could feel the tension between them of things left unsaid and unfinished. Hearing the easiness between Lyla and her ex made his insides feel as if acid was eating away at his organs. She *dared* call her ex. He didn't know how to handle her rebellion. His first instinct was to lock her in the basement. An echo of his father's voice slipped through his mind, *The way to make a woman stay isn't by abusing her. It's by loving her so much that she can't imagine being without you.* Fuck. He couldn't love Lyla more than he already did. His parents didn't have the relationship that he and Lyla did. He couldn't control her. She left him *twice*. His mother never left his father, she supported him no matter what.

His phone buzzed in his pocket. He pulled it out and read the text. Finally. He couldn't bear to sit here any longer with his thoughts. He was a man of quick decisions and actions—except when it came to Lyla. She turned him into an indecisive, raving lunatic. If he didn't love her so much, he'd hate her for her influence over him.

Gavin heard approaching footsteps, the jingle of keys and then the door opened. Jonathan flipped the light switch, placed his messenger bag on the stand beside the door and turned. There was no surprise or fear on his face, just weary acceptance.

When Gavin entered the apartment, he searched for a security system and found none, which he thought was odd at the time, but he was too focused on his mission to ponder it. How could Huskin possibly know that he was here? Or, had he been expecting him?

Gavin's demon began to salivate, eager for the kill. He could shoot Huskin, but that would be over too quickly. He could break his neck—no, he could *start* their session by breaking his fingers, digit by digit since those hands knew what Lyla's skin felt like. On that thought, he should slice off his dick for daring to trespass. Maybe he could—

"No gun?" Huskin asked.

Gavin moved his jacket just enough for Huskin to get a look at a real gun, not the ones he probably saw on video games. "You aren't surprised to see me."

Huskin shrugged. "You would have killed me in that hotel room if Lyla didn't make such a scene. I knew sooner or later you'd finish the job."

Huskin's phone rang. Gavin waited to see what he would do. Huskin eyed him for a moment before he slowly reached into his pocket.

"It's Lyla," Huskin said.

Every muscle in his body tensed, but he kept his face expressionless. Fuck it. He was going to lock her up in the basement, blister her ass and then fuck her until she came to her senses. He didn't care what dad said. Calling another man? No. *Fuck* no. The tips of his fingers twitched with the need to grab his gun and finish this guy. He was a nobody yet Lyla's loyalty to him made Huskin Gavin's worst nightmare. Huskin's hand moved towards the phone and Gavin's moved to his gun. Huskin pressed a button and Lyla's voice filled the room.

"Jonathan, you nearly gave me a heart attack! You got off work hours ago! Why've you been ignoring my calls?"

"Sorry, I was working late," Huskin answered.

"Oh my God. You aren't taking me seriously, are you?" Lyla snapped.

"I am," Huskin said, eyes fixed on Gavin.

"You aren't. You don't know what he'll do to you."

"I think I do," Huskin replied.

The sound of a baby crying filled the room, short-circuiting Gavin's killing haze. Nora. Fuck he missed his baby girl. Why was she crying? He hated that sound with a passion. He would never be able to ignore her cries if he was in the vicinity. Thank fuck she wasn't a fussy baby. The sound of his daughter in distress ripped at him.

Huskin nabbed his attention when he staggered as if he had been shot. He leaned against the closed apartment door with an anguished expression.

"You have a child with him?" Huskin whispered.

There was a long pause on the other end. "Yes. A daughter."

Huskin dropped his head into his hand and didn't speak.

"I thought I told you," Lyla said.

"No, you didn't."

Even Huskin knew having a child changed everything. It was the reason he impregnated Lyla as quickly as possible. He wasn't just Lyla's husband, he was the father of her child and that made them a family. Huskin clearly grasped that Lyla would have to leave her husband *and* child to be with him, which wouldn't happen. *That's right, motherfucker, she's all mine.*

"I told you, I love my husband. I'm married and I have a daughter."

Her desolate tone made his gut tighten. He hurt her, but he couldn't stop, not when she was focused on keeping Huskin alive.

"I have to go," Huskin said hoarsely.

"I'm sorry, Jonathan."

"Bye, Lyla."

Huskin hung up and looked at Gavin with a suspicious sheen to his eyes.

"What are you doing here?" Huskin snapped.

Gavin blinked. He couldn't believe this little shit. He had thirteen weapons on his person, not counting his bare hands, which could do more damage than people believed.

"What?" he asked, daring Huskin to speak to him in that tone again.

"You have her. What the hell do you care about me for?"

The killing rage shattered as Huskin's words penetrated. Lyla was his and she wouldn't leave him for Huskin. He didn't like loose ends or the fact that Lyla had history with another man, but that couldn't be helped. The only thing that would alter her love would be to hurt a man who clearly had no chance with her.

Huskin pushed himself away from the door, set his phone on the counter and slumped on a kitchen stool. "You want to kill me on principle, don't you?"

Perceptive bastard.

Huskin met his gaze boldly. "I've read a lot about you. From what I saw in the hotel room, it must be true."

Gavin said nothing.

"The media insinuated that you're involved in organized crime. I know you've been to jail and your father was murdered." Huskin paused for input, but continued when Gavin merely watched him. "When I met Lyla I couldn't understand why such a beautiful woman couldn't look me in the eye."

Gavin stirred, but forced himself to stay still. He

had been trained to control his heartbeat to fool lie detectors and lay in wait for his prey for days. Huskin was clearly suicidal. He'd be damned if he showed Huskin that the bastard hit a nerve.

"I figured she had been abused by her family or," Huskin inclined his head, "by a boyfriend."

Gavin leaned forward slightly. Huskin's tone was cool and clinical, but the insults were anything but.

"It took me months to gain her trust, but she never told me who she was running from. It was you. That's why she got a new identity and started a new life."

Gavin rose. If Huskin wanted to die, he would do it up close and personal as he had been fantasizing about. Huskin was calm personified, as if he was fine with meeting his maker right here and now. It was unnatural. Even those who worshipped the devil didn't want to be in hell with him.

"She's changed," Huskin stated and ran his hand over the countertop absently. "The way she walks and talks... The woman I knew wasn't capable of telling someone off, much less killing a man."

Blade recounted Lyla's latest kill to him. Knowing that she could handle herself in an emergency allowed him to focus on his shit. He was damn proud she was his wife.

"What have you done to her?" Huskin asked.

Gavin advanced slowly. "The world we live in demands that we adapt, so we do."

"Your world? Meaning the criminal world?"

Gavin stopped a few paces away from Huskin.

"You're better off not knowing."

They eyed one another in silence. The air pulsed with accusations and charged emotions.

Huskin shrugged one shoulder. "I guess I should warn you that you're being recorded."

Gavin raised a brow. "Why are you warning me?"

"Because you have to tell someone they're being recorded before the evidence can be used in a court of law."

Fuck. The nerd pulled a fast one on him.

"I'm glad you didn't destroy that picture on my nightstand. It's the only copy I have," Huskin said.

He was impressed and intrigued despite himself. He was always informed about the latest technology and whatever Jonathan was using was something he had never heard of. "You knew I was here. Why didn't you call the cops?"

"Curiosity. You didn't wreck the place and you didn't have the gun pointing at the door when I came upstairs. Besides, if I don't counter my command in the system, whatever the cameras record in the next three hours will be sent to the police. Lyla would be free to live her life with you in prison for first degree murder." Huskin tapped the screen of his cell phone. "Even if you look like you're in control, I know differently. The system is picking up your vitals. Your heart rate has stabilized, but it's still elevated."

Huskin was too strait-laced to make up stories, which could only mean that he had access to an extremely sophisticated security system. He reflected on Huskin's office of tech gadgets and made the mental leap.

"You created it didn't you?"

Huskin hesitated and then admitted, "After Morg—I mean, *Lyla*, disappeared, I couldn't stand not knowing what happened. It didn't make sense for her to leave. I was obsessed with the thought that she had been kidnapped. I called in the cops, but had no proof. Creating a sophisticated, undetectable security system has become a hobby of mine."

Gavin didn't like the fact that Lyla was behind Huskin's creation, but he was a businessman and a paranoid one as well. "How many cameras do you have?"

"Enough."

Huskin may be naive, but he had a backbone. This shouldn't have pleased Gavin, but it did. "Quit your day job. I'll be your investor, but I get first dibs."

Huskin blinked. "You have to be kidding me."

"I run casinos, among other things. You don't want to be an IT consultant for the rest of your life, do you?"

"You're not going to kill me?"

"Who said I was going to kill you?"

"You're armed."

"You can never be too careful."

"I'm not going to be part of the mafia," Huskin said staunchly.

Gavin's mouth curved despite himself. Huskin was a self-righteous little thing. He appreciated Huskin's candor. It wasn't often that he met someone with morals and standards. Meeting someone like Huskin reminded him there was a world beyond the criminal underworld and Las Vegas. To balance out the evil he faced every day, there had to be light in the world. For him, that was Lyla. Jonathan was also a representative of the good that very few possessed. He could almost understand Huskin's appeal for Lyla. Huskin was his antithesis. Gavin had to comfort himself with the fact that Huskin would never again have the pleasure of being buried inside his wife.

His phone rang. Gavin pulled it out of his pocket. Lyla. He couldn't afford to speak to her in Huskin's presence. Huskin hadn't revealed his presence to her, but he didn't want to push Huskin more than he had already. It was clear that Huskin loved Lyla, enough to sacrifice his life so she could be free. It was romantic and idiotic. How would Lyla respond if she found out that her nerd was willing to put it all on the line for her? Did she already know and that's why she fought so hard for Huskin? Huskin was intelligent. He couldn't match Gavin physically, so he fought in his own way— with intelligence and technology. Little surprised him, but Huskin managed to do the impossible.

Huskin regarded him steadily as he tapped his fingers on the countertop. "You're going to hurt her."

Gavin said nothing.

"You're out of control."

"You're alive, aren't you?"

Huskin shook his head. "What does she see in you? It can't be your money or looks."

"Lyla and I have history."

"I always knew she was too good for me." Even as Gavin nodded, Huskin added, "And she's too good for you too."

Fuck. Gavin resisted the urge to laugh. "She is, but I'm not letting her go."

"You live in a dangerous world. You could get her killed."

He didn't need a fucking lecture from Lyla's ex, but he could see that the guy was genuinely worried. Heartbreak was written all over his face. Gavin decided to do something nice for the first time in his life and give the poor schmuck some reassurance. "I have something important to take care of before I get out of."

Huskin gave him a derisive look. "How do I know that's true?"

"Because it's Lyla's ultimatum."

Huskin examined him keenly. "That's why you're letting me live. She said she'd leave you if you killed me."

Fucking smart bastard. "Lyla wouldn't leave me."

"Are you sure?"

The desire to be nice fled as quickly as it came. "Don't push me, Huskin."

"I'm not going to let you invest in my security system."

"You need an investor, especially since your mother has pancreatic cancer and you're thinking about moving back to Boston to help."

Huskin froze. "How do you know that?"

"I have a tech guy named Z. He'll contact you."

"I won't be forced into this!" Huskin got to his

feet, jaw set.

Gavin raised a brow. "You know I run casinos. My investment will be legitimate with papers and lawyers involved."

"I can handle this myself."

"How can you when you have a full-time job and a mother who doesn't have much time?" He paused for emphasis and twisted the knife. "Lyla's in danger."

Huskin's brows bunched together. "I know that. Because of *you*!"

"You know my father was murdered."

"Yes."

"Lyla was with him that day."

Something flickered in Huskin's eyes.

"She was stabbed eight times. I nearly lost her."

Huskin sank back on his stool as if his legs were too weak to hold him up.

"The killer is still on the loose. That's why I'm in the underworld, to finish this. He attacked Lyla for the second time four months ago when she was seven months pregnant."

"What the hell are you doing here?" Huskin snapped. "You need to catch him."

"He's smart and careful and sends out troops while he cowers in the dark."

"Maybe I can..." Huskin's voice died out and he glared. "I'm not doing this for you, Pyre, I'm doing it for Lyla!"

Gavin nodded gravely. "I know. Your security system could be handy not only in my casinos, but in our home."

Huskin didn't speak for several minutes. Gavin

waited patiently.

Huskin sighed. "I'll give notice tomorrow."

"I'll have my lawyer contact you."

"I won't be a part of the mafia."

Gavin started towards the door. "Who said I was part of the mafia?"

Huskin cursed under his breath and then stood. "Why aren't you asking me to destroy the tape of what we just talked about? Aren't you afraid I'll talk to the cops?"

"No."

"How can you be so sure?"

Gavin paused with his hand on the door. "Because I know what kind of man you are."

Huskin frowned.

"I know why Lyla trusts you." The knowledge still felt like someone was carving up his insides, but he understood why Lyla fought for Huskin's life. He was a good person and there were too few in the world. "You're an honorable man. You'd never do anything to hurt her."

Huskin said nothing. His pain filled the room. Gavin opened the door so he could take a breath of fresh air. He knew what Huskin was going through. They were in love with the same woman and they both lost her at some point. Unlucky for Huskin, he wasn't an honorable man. He would fight and kill to keep Lyla by his side. This time, he didn't have to.

"Move to Boston to be with your mother," he ordered and then softened the blow by adding, "I lost my dad. I know what it feels like. You should be there when it happens."

Huskin took a deep breath and nodded.

"I'll have Z contact you," Gavin said and closed the door.

Gavin walked out of the building and approached his private car. A guard got out of the passenger seat and opened the door for him.

"Clean up, sir?" he asked.

"No," Gavin said as he got into the backseat.

"No?"

Gavin met his startled gaze. "No need for cleanup."

The guard inclined his head. "Yes, sir."

As the car left Huskin's apartment behind, he called Z.

"Sir?" Z answered wearily.

"A man named Jonathan Huskin has developed a sophisticated security system I want you to take a look at."

Z sounded a bit more awake as he answered, "Sure."

"Let me know what you think of his program and assess his skills. If he's good, you may have a partner."

"I'll get right on it, sir."

Gavin hung up and made a few phone calls before they reached the runway. He boarded his plane and accepted a glass of water and popped aspirin as his men took their seats. His phone began to ring. He glanced at the unavailable number on the screen and answered, "Pyre."

"Where's my mother?"

He hadn't talked to Eli Stark in years, but he still recognized his voice. It took less than a day for Stark to realize his mother was MIA.

"So you finally decided to return my call," Gavin said.

"You called me?"

"I did the talking while you played possum last night. I told you that you fucked up."

"What are you talking about? I haven't talked to you in years. I'm a free agent."

"Cut the crap, Stark. Santana's brother ratted you out. I know you were feeding Santana information."

His men fell silent once they heard Stark's name. They all knew Gavin wanted his head.

"I don't know jack shit about this," Stark said.

"This isn't the first time your name's come up."

"I'm not involved in anything to do with Santana."

"How are you paying for your mother's medical bills?"

A pause and then, "That's none of your fucking business. Give her back to me."

"Who's the crime lord?"

"I don't know. I'm not working with him."

"How much does it cost to make you talk?"

"I don't know who he is." Eli sounded as if he was speaking through clenched teeth.

"Call me when you determine a price." Maybe Stark would be good for something before he gutted him.

"Did you—?" Eli's voice was thick with rage. "If I find out you killed my mother, Gavin, I'll end you."

"Not if I end you first," Gavin said as he hung up.

His men waited for orders, but dispersed when he didn't give any.

Once upon a time he would have trusted Stark with his life and now, very soon, he would kill a man he once considered a friend. It wasn't the first time and it wouldn't be the last.

Gavin eyed his men as the engines revved. He was ninety percent certain the men in his employ were loyal, but there was always a chance that he had a rat in the bunch. He couldn't get Paul Vega's words out of his head. *How many can you kill? You think your name will protect you? You have nowhere to turn.* Like Paul, people were hedging their bets on him or Phantom. The fact that Phantom was still alive and made successful hits on his family hurt his reputation and made him look weak. Men like Stark would sell him out in a heartbeat. He didn't know who he could trust. Aside from torturing and killing every man in the underworld, the only way to solidify his claim to the title was execute Phantom publicly.

The Phantom had to be someone he knew. No outsider could roll into Las Vegas and take the underworld from him. The Phantom slipped into the underworld too easily. It had to be someone who was already established. When he bowed out and Vinny took his place, the Phantom saw his chance and took it by calling the hit on his cousin before going after his father to win over the bloodthirsty underworld. Gavin couldn't trust any of his former contacts. Like Paul, they had been bribed in some way. Fuck, Paul joined up with the man who carved up his son. It was unbelievable. He had no backup and no one to turn to...

"Tell the pilot to head to New York," Gavin ordered his men.

"You got it, boss."

Gavin pulled out his phone and tapped into the surveillance cameras at home. Their master suite was dark. He could barely make out Lyla beneath the covers. He still wasn't sure how he wanted to deal with her. He switched to another camera and saw Blade prowl through the hallway. He paused in front of Lyla's closed door before he went into the nursery to check on Nora. He stood over the crib for a minute before he pet Beau and then went downstairs. Blade was the only man he trusted implicitly, which is why he was Lyla's shadow. He wasn't sure how Blade would react if he tried to give him another job.

All was quiet at home. He was too close to New York not to stop by for a short visit. His battles in Las Vegas could be delayed a few hours.

CHAPTER FOURTEEN

Gavin

Two hours later Gavin stepped out of a taxi in front of a townhouse. Memories of his childhood and teenage years skipped through his mind. Gavin was dimly aware of slamming doors as his men joined him. Gavin started towards the townhouse that belonged to the Romans, one of four families that ran New York's underworld. It had been a second home to him as a child. Before his hand touched the front gate, three men in suits and trench coats stepped onto the front steps. Gavin opened the gate and approached, even as one guard raised his hand in warning.

"Hold it right there," the guard began.

"Mr. Pyre?" An older guard pushed the younger man aside and gave him a respectful nod. "It's been a long time."

"Yes, it has," Gavin said. "Are they here?"

"They are, sir. Are they expecting you?"

"No."

"Let me escort you."

"Thank you." Gavin passed the younger guard who took a step back now that he knew his identity.

Gavin stepped into the townhouse, which was warm and smelled of fresh cookies. A gleaming wooden staircase led to upper and lower floors. The townhouse was five stories tall. A grand chandelier lit the entrance hall. There was a hushed quality to the richly furnished home despite the fact that it was milling with security.

A large painting framed in gold caught his attention. Gavin walked towards it and was dimly aware of the older guard requesting that his men wait in the formal sitting room. Gavin gave his permission with an absent nod and surveyed the family portrait of the Roman family. A severe Italian-Spanish man in unrelieved black sat beside an English woman with a sunny smile and brilliant green eyes. A little girl with dark brown curls and her mother's eyes was held possessively close on her father's lap. Three boys stood behind their parents and sister. Roque, the oldest, looked to be in his early twenties and took after his father with broad shoulders, black hair and his mother's eyes. The second brother, Raul, was in his late teens and had a lean figure and keen hazel eyes. The third brother, Angel, had pale blue eyes and olive toned skin.

The last time Gavin had been here was to attend Marco and Margaret Romans' funeral. His father stayed in New York for months to console the younger children and help Roque establish himself as the new head of the Roman clan.

"This way, Mr. Pyre."

The guard led him downstairs. Gavin glimpsed New York's skyline from the large windows on the second floor. Guards in flawless suits were openly armed and eyed him suspiciously, but didn't stop their progress to the basement. Two guards were posted in front of the basement door. The guard accompanying him spoke to them in a low voice. They pounded their fist three times on the door before they inclined their heads and backed away.

Hip-hop music assaulted his ears as he stepped into the basement, which had the look of a high-end club. There was a bar against one wall along with a round table for poker. Gavin's shoes sank into the lush black carpet. Strippers who danced without a care in the world occupied two silver poles. Raul, the second Roman brother, sat on a black leather couch in a three-piece suit. He ignored the strippers and stared intently at his laptop screen while he sipped wine. Raul turned his head and when he saw Gavin, shot to his feet, startling one of the strippers who slid a foot down the pole before she caught herself.

"Jesus Christ!"

Raul set his glass down and spread his arms wide. Even as he embraced Gavin hard enough to make him grunt, there was a thump and shriek behind one of two closed doors. Over Raul's shoulder, Gavin saw the door open. Angel appeared, wearing nothing but a pair of black boxers with a gun in his hand. The man before him was far from the teenager in the portrait. When Angel spotted Gavin, a broad smile spread over his face.

"Son of a bitch!"

Raul stepped back and Angel took his place. Angel hugged Gavin and then kissed him on both cheeks. Gavin raised a brow at his cousins who couldn't be more different if they tried. Raul was the businessman in the Roman family. His tailored suit, slick hair and glass of wine encapsulated who he was—cultured, sophisticated, controlled. Angel in his boxers with lipstick smears on his body was just as telling. Angel was the rebellious youngest brother, a party animal and playboy. Gavin saw movement in the room Angel vacated. Four naked women slipped on lingerie.

"Why didn't you tell us you were coming?" Raul asked.

"Impulse trip. I had business in Maine."

"Come, come," Raul said and waved a hand at Angel. "Make him something, would you?"

"What do you want to drink, Gavin?" Angel walked to the bar and stuffed the gun in the back of his boxers.

"Whiskey. Neat."

Raul sat and grabbed his glass of wine. "How long has it been, cousin?"

"Too long," Gavin said and took the glass Angel handed him. "A lot has changed."

Angel settled on the couch with a glass of clear liquid and didn't acknowledge the woman who settled on his lap. "No kidding."

"Your basement's changed," Gavin said as the women vacated the room they occupied with Angel and sauntered forward. He sized them up and wasn't surprised to see that they all possessed perfect bodies, flawless features and greedy eyes.

"I persuaded Raul and Roque to liven the place up a bit," Angel said and waved a hand to encompass the decadent man cave. "We come here to unwind and try the talent." He nodded approvingly at the prostitute grinding on his crotch. "You game, Gavin?"

"No, I'm married," Gavin said and ignored the woman who sat beside him, so close he could feel her body heat and the fragrance of her perfume, which was tainted by Angel's cologne.

"I heard that," Raul said. "We didn't get a wedding invitation."

"Shotgun wedding," Gavin said and glanced at the prostitute as she placed a hand on his upper thigh. "I'm married."

"Your wifey isn't here," the woman purred and arched her back to show off her fake breasts covered in pink glitter, which she pressed against his arm. Her hand sank into his hair as she leaned into him, hooking one leg over his. "What she doesn't know can't hurt her, can it?"

She grabbed his cock and he lost it. He grabbed her hand and flipped it back. The prostitute fell off the couch and dropped to her knees so he wouldn't break her wrist. The strippers on the poles stopped twirling and the other women lounging nearby edged back slowly.

"I'm *married*, you understand now?" Gavin asked.

The prostitute nodded fervently, eyes wide and terrified. She looked towards Angel whose total focus was on Gavin. Her whimpers of pain filled the room as the music paused between tracks. Gavin forced her to stay on her knees for a full minute before he let her go. She collapsed face first on the carpet and then scooted away, cradling her sprained wrist.

Angel smacked the ass of the prostitute frozen solid on his lap. "Looks like my cousin's not in the mood. Why don't you all clear out?"

The women didn't hesitate. They ran to the door. In their haste to vacate the room, they forgot to saunter. Angel grabbed a remote and turned off the music.

"I'm glad you didn't break her hand," Angel said, spreading his legs wide as he downed the rest of his drink. "She's talented. Of course, she doesn't need her hand to do her work, but it speeds up the process so she can take more men in one night."

Before Gavin could respond to that Raul interjected, "So there's married and *married*. I'm guessing you're the latter."

Gavin nodded. "My wife is everything to me."

Angel stared at him. "You're a fucking legend. I can't believe you're monogamous. You fucked around more than all of us combined."

"Lyla's different."

"I gotta meet her," Angel said and then eyed him. "You never returned our calls."

Gavin inclined his head. "I know. I'm couldn't handle them at the time."

"We couldn't make it to the funerals because of business," Raul said.

"I got your cards."

"What did you do to the fucker who did in Uncle Manny?" Angel asked.

It always came back to that. Gavin felt the familiar slap of rage and sipped whiskey to cool himself down. Denying himself the pleasure of ripping Huskin limb from limb, the interaction with Eli Stark and the fact that he had no leads on the Phantom left him feeling edgy and violent. Whiskey traveled through his body and settled in his gut, taking away the unrelenting burn.

"That's why I'm here."

"Why?"

"I haven't caught him yet."

There was a sharp silence. His cousins stared at him as if he materialized out of thin air.

Raul scooted to the edge of his seat and raised a hand. "What do you mean, you haven't caught him yet?"

"This guy is a fucking ghost."

Gavin couldn't sit still. He rose and refilled his glass. Retribution in their world was brutal, swift and done back ten fold. All of them would rip the world apart in the name of vengeance, but in the end Lyla had been more important to him. He hunted her when he got out of prison instead of the man who claimed the title. That cost him. Now, he was trying to reclaim an underworld that was complete chaos and run by a faceless, sadistic killer.

"This guy took over the underworld long enough to fuck up the whole city. It's going to take years to clean up the filth he unleashed. He's too smart to reveal his identity to anyone."

"What do you need?" Raul asked.

The pressure on his chest eased. Ever since Vinny died, he felt something missing. Vinny had always been at his side. Gavin didn't question his loyalty, as he'd had to question every other person in his life. There was no replacement for family.

This feud with the Phantom had been going on long enough. It had been an impulse to visit his cousins and his intuition hadn't steered him wrong. Even though they hadn't seen each other in nearly a decade, family was family and they would aid him in whatever he needed.

"I need a man at my back I can trust until this is over," Gavin said.

Raul and Angel looked at one another for a heartbeat and then Angel inclined his head.

"Angel will go with you," Raul said.

Gavin nodded. "After I kill the Phantom, I want out."

Once more the Roman brothers looked at one another and then back at him.

"Why?" Angel asked.

"My wife's suffered enough. I promised her I would kill this guy and get out."

Silence reined.

"After I kill the Phantom, I want to hand over the underworld to a replacement that I can teach while I'm still in to see if he can hack it."

Angel leaned forward. All signs of the ladies man vanished. His pale blue eyes were narrow and intense. "You want to give up your title?"

"Yes."

"And you need someone to take over?"

"It's not that easy. The city is in turmoil and the fucker's I've kept under lock and key are now causing public shootings and kidnappings when they feel like it."

Angel leaned back and rested his arms along the back of the couch. "I'll do it."

Raul turned his head sharply. "Angel."

"You have everything under control here," Angel said. "Roque's coming out of the joint soon and then what? I'll be third in command and with you two at the top, I'll never see any action. What's happening in Vegas sounds like my kind of party."

Gavin considered Angel who was several years younger than him. The three Roman brothers had grown up in the family business as he had. Angel was the youngest and most reckless. He wasn't sure what his cousin had been up to in the past decade, but if he was going to hand the city to someone, there was no one better than family.

"Roque will have my head if I let you go off to Vegas and become a crime lord on your own without backup," Raul said.

"I'll be there," Gavin said and his throat tightened. "I tried to hand the underworld over to Vinny and they gunned him down. It won't be easy. They're like wild animals. One mistake and you're dead."

Angel's eyes gleamed. "Now you're trying to turn me on. When do we leave?"

"Are you sure?"

Angel smiled as innocently as a toddler. "You can't stop me now that you've issued a challenge like that. When do we leave?"

"Whenever. My plane is on standby."

"Your own plane. Fuck." Angel strolled towards a phone in the corner of the room and spoke quickly in Italian.

"Can he handle it?" Gavin asked Raul in low tones.

"Yes," Raul said succinctly. "I'm the businessman, Angel's the enforcer. I keep the books clean and Angel makes sure we don't get fucked over. We had trouble when Roque went to prison, but Angel put a stop to that and he was just out of high school. Don't underestimate him. We haven't had any trouble for three years and he's getting restless. I have to drown him in women and find all kinds of things to keep him busy. I was worried he would take off before Roque got out and try to take over another city."

"Take over?" Walking into another crime lord's territory was suicidal.

"Angel wouldn't hesitate to kill anyone if it meant having some action." Raul sighed and drained his glass. "If we didn't already have control of the largest city in the United States, Angel would have gone there and tried to conquer it."

"Sounds like he needs a hobby," Gavin said mildly and wondered how his cousin would react to the mayhem going down in Sin City.

"People underestimate Angel because he's young and too pretty for his own good. Your city sounds like Angel's type of playground."

Angel hung up the phone and settled on the couch with his legs crossed. "Viva Las Vegas. Fuck *yes*. This is turning out to be an interesting night."

"I need to kill this fucker. He's been playing me for years and it's going to stop. I have a family now and I can't put them at risk. Besides, I have enough on my plate with my partner wanting to expand Pyre Casinos."

Angel shook his head. "I can't imagine you

married with a kid."

"Believe it."

"Family is everything. If you want out, you need someone to take over who knows how to run it and who won't lose themselves in the filth." Raul looked at Angel who was grinning like a maniac. "Don't think I'm not going to keep tabs on you."

"You do that." Angel got to his feet. "Gav, you have to say hi to Luci. She'll kill you if she finds out you were here and didn't see her."

"I don't want to wake her," Gavin said and glanced at his watch. It was three in the morning.

"Tonight's family night so I came over. She was messing around in the kitchen an hour ago," Raul said.

Gavin noted the way the guards looked to Angel, not Raul when they walked out of the basement. Raul had always been more reserved than Roque and Angel. He was the steadfast brother and the voice of reason. As they started up the stairs with Angel conversing with the guards, Gavin walked alongside Raul.

"How's Roque doing?" Gavin asked.

"He's alive," Raul said with a shrug. "He gets out of prison next year. When he gets out, he'll take his place and I'm going to take a vacation in the Bahamas."

Gavin shook his head. "I was in for a year. I don't know how Roque's handled being in for seven."

"After Roque gets out and takes his title *and* after the Bahamas, I'm going to pay you a visit. I want to see your wife and kid," Raul said.

"You should. You've shouldered the load for a long time."

"Same as you." Raul shook his head. "I don't know how you and Roque do it. If it wasn't for Angel, I would have let the underworld go a long time ago."

Gavin shrugged. "It's in our blood, just as it was in our father's."

The Roman family had their fair share of heartaches and betrayal. It went hand in hand with being a part of the underworld. They all paid a price for being crime lords. Gavin couldn't imagine Roque being imprisoned for eight years. Every criminal in prison would be gunning for him. How many men did Roque murder in seven years to stay alive? If Roque was a force to be reckoned with before, New York would shudder in terror when he was released.

They reached the third floor. Angel slammed open the door that led into a massive kitchen, which had all the latest appliances. A beautiful woman with dreamy green eyes and waist length dark brown curls stood in front of the kitchen island scraping cookies onto a large platter.

"You can't be done already!" she complained. "There were six women. I should have another hour at least! You need to work on your stamina, Angel."

Angel grabbed a cookie, took a savage bite and tapped her nose. "I'm going to Sin City, princess!"

Luciana frowned at her brother and didn't seem bothered by the fact that he wore only his underwear or that his skin was covered in hickeys, bite marks and lipstick.

"What are you talking about? Are those girls still here? I want them to try my almond cookies."

"I'll take one of those," Gavin said as he stepped into the kitchen.

Angel ducked as his sister tossed the metal spatula and hurled herself at Gavin as if she were eight years old.

"Gavin!" she screamed.

Gavin couldn't stop himself from smiling as he caught Luciana and whirled her around as if she were still a kid instead of a full grown adult. Luciana shrieked in delight and kissed him on both cheeks.

"What are you doing here? Do you want some cookies?" she asked.

"Yes, I would," he said and set her down.

Luciana rushed to the platter and used tongs to put two cookies on a dainty plate that felt as sturdy as construction paper in his hand.

"Would you like a cup of tea?" Luciana asked.

Gavin suppressed a flinch. "No, thank you."

Luciana pushed him onto a stool and propped her chin on her fists. "What are you doing here, Gavin?"

"I need help." Gavin took a bite of the warm cookie and almost closed his eyes as the taste awakened a sweet tooth he didn't know he possessed. "Fuck me."

"*You* need help?" Luciana sounded shocked.

"I'm human," Gavin said with a shrug.

"Which is *why*," Angel said deliberately to get his sister's attention, "I'm going with him."

Luciana's eyes bounced from Gavin to Angel

and then to Raul who poured himself a cup of tea.

"You're going to *Las Vegas*? What? I want to go too!"

"The situation isn't good, Luci," Gavin said and reached for more cookies.

"You're going to leave me with *Raul*?" Luciana said indignantly.

Raul scowled. "What's wrong with that?"

"You never come home and you don't let me do anything! At least Angel takes me dancing once a week."

Angel grinned at her. "I'm sure Raul will take you to the office to show you his accounting skills."

Luciana's eyes widened in horror. Gavin stiffened when she focused those hypnotizing green eyes on him.

"Gavin, can I come too?"

Raul and Angel tensed, but they didn't try to interfere. He was leery of accepting Angel's help after what happened to Vinny, but he trusted Raul's judgment. If Raul said Angel could do it, he believed him. But there was no way in hell he would toss Luciana into the mix.

"It's too dangerous," he said and took another cookie.

"But Angel's going!"

Gavin wasn't used to having anyone argue with him aside from Lyla. Emotional outbursts weren't his scene.

"I have a gun and I know how to use it," Angel said loftily and leaned against the wall, looking like a Hispanic version of James Dean.

Luciana grabbed a knife from the chopping

block and hurled it at Angel. The knife imbedded into the wall three inches above his head. Angel raised a brow at Luciana while Raul glared at his sister.

"What did I tell you two about playing with knives?" Raul snapped.

"I'm an excellent shot," Luciana said hotly. "I can take care of myself. And don't you dare lecture me about guns. You know I'm just as good as you, Angel."

No one who knew about the Roman's reputation would be able to imagine them gathered in a kitchen at three in the morning arguing while drinking tea and eating warm almond cookies like a normal family. The appliances in the kitchen changed, but the feeling of belonging and warmth hadn't. Gavin rummaged in the fridge for milk as Raul and Luciana began to shout at one another.

"Gavin's searching for Uncle Manny and Vinny's killer, Luci. This is serious shit. And after, he's going to step down," Raul said.

Luciana's eyes popped. "Step down? And who's going to take—*Angel*? You? No!"

Angel's expression softened. "You know I've been wanting to do my own thing for a while now."

"B-but," Luciana's eyes filled with tears, "it's so sudden! When are you leaving?"

"Tonight."

As a tear slipped down her cheek, Angel pushed off the wall and hugged her. He whispered in her ear as she cried. If anyone paid a high price for being a Roman besides Roque, it was Luciana. She had been twelve when her parents were murdered and witnessed the whole thing. Her brothers were understandably overprotective and her life was much more restricted than Lyla's.

Gavin was forcefully reminded of Nora as she watched Angel console his sister. How would he react when Nora wanted to go off on her own? Would he refuse or accompany her? What if she wanted to go to college in another city? It sent a chill down his spine. He shook away the disturbing thought. He would deal with it when the time came... or lock Nora in the basement until she saw things his way.

"When can I visit?" Luciana asked as she wiped away her tears.

"As soon as it's over," Gavin assured her.

"You promise?"

"Yes. I'll send for you and then you can meet my wife and daughter."

"You have a daughter?" Luciana marched towards him and thumped his chest with surprising force. "And you haven't sent me pictures? What the hell is wrong with you?"

Gavin didn't know how to react. He noticed Raul hiding a grin behind his teacup. Dainty bastard.

"I've been busy killing people," he said.

"That's not a good excuse," Luciana snapped and put her hands on hips. "Your daughter's the first of the new generation. She needs to know her extended family."

Her words warmed him. This is why he came. For too long he had gone without family, without support. He isolated himself after Vinny and his father's death instead of reaching out. Just being in the Roman household with his cousins made him feel as if he had an army around him. Their support gave him hope that this nightmare would be over soon.

A maid wearing a uniform that looked as if she worked in a high-end resort walked into the kitchen and inclined her head.

"Your bag's are ready, Mr. Roman," she said.

"Thank you." Angel went to his suitcase and opened it up to reveal an impeccable packing job. Angel ruined it by rummaging through until he found jeans, a white shirt and leather jacket. While he changed in the middle of the kitchen Gavin answered Luciana's questions about Lyla and Nora.

His phone rang. When he saw Z's name, he picked up immediately. "News?"

"Boss," Z hesitated and then finished in a rush, "something went down at your place."

All the warm feelings in his chest were doused by icy dread.

"I noticed a disturbance on the surveillance cameras and tried to call Blade, but his phone had a busy signal. I tried several guards and no one picked up. I just got the cameras back online. I think there was an attack at the front gate. Looks like something rammed into it and there's a fire on the south side of the property the men are putting out. I don't see any dead bodies. I can see men on the property, but I can't get through to anyone. I can only watch the live feed and try to figure out what's going on," Z said in a rush.

Even as he opened his mouth to ask about Lyla,

Z launched into another hurried explanation.

"I checked the house cameras. The rooms are empty. I don't see your wife, Blade, the baby, nothing. I tried to review the footage, but it's been fucked with. I don't know what happened. All phones are out of order. Your wife's watch isn't working either. I can't track her. I'm trying to get in touch with the guys and bring everything back online."

"Let me know what you got as soon as you have it," he rapped out and hung up.

He pulled up the surveillance cameras on his phone and flipped from angle to angle, his heart accelerating with every empty room he saw. If there was a hit on the house, Blade would have gotten Lyla out. That was a safety precaution after his father's house had been infiltrated. Blade would take her to a safe house and stay there until he made contact.

Gavin called Lyla's phone and received a busy signal. Same with Blade. Knowing he left Lyla open to another attack made him feel like a worthless bastard. If he hadn't left to kill Huskin, he would be there right now, not on the other side of the continent.

"Gavin?" Luciana asked tentatively.

He looked up and saw his cousins watching. "There was a hit at the house. Someone fucked with the cameras and no one can call in or out. Blade and my wife are gone."

Luci shoved Angel. "Go on. Get out of here." She launched herself at Gavin and gave him a fierce hug before she pulled back, green eyes narrowed.

"Make this motherfucker pay, Gavin. Kill him slowly."

He kissed her and turned to Raul who clapped him on the back.

"Anything you need, Gavin, you call," Raul said and hugged his brother. "Give the Vegas underworld our love, brother."

Angel showed his teeth. "Of course."

"And let us know when this fucker's buried. We'll pull out our best wine and toast Uncle Manny and Vinny."

Gavin walked out of the townhouse, chilled to the bone. He was thousands of miles away while his wife once again went through hell. She had to be alive. He wouldn't allow himself to think of any other outcome. Any hint of an attack would prompt Blade to get her the fuck out. He had to believe that or go insane.

CHAPTER FIFTEEN

Lyla

Lyla sat up, mouth open on a soundless scream and thrashed wildly. Something heavy thudded to the ground, jolting her out of nightmare. The only sound in the room was her harsh breathing. There was enough moonlight coming through the bedroom window to see that she was safe at home. It was just a dream.

Lyla flopped back on the pillows and bit back a sob. The nightmare was a mix of new and old horrors. She relived Manny being tortured by Sadist and felt the knife dig into her skin at the same time that she heard Nora scream, which jolted her awake.

She fumbled for the lamp and realized that's what she knocked to the floor. She slipped her gun into the back of her leggings and tiptoed into the nursery. The sound of Nora's even breathing made her weak with relief. She stood there for several minutes before she went down the hall to Carmen's room. She slipped beneath the covers, her back to Carmen who lay flat on her back. Lyla took a deep breath and tried to calm herself.

"Lyla?" Carmen rolled over and tossed an arm over her waist and felt the gun. "You okay?"

"Bad dream."

Carmen grunted. "Must have been a bad one."

Even now, she could recall the sound of crunching bone and the ominous silence when Manny stopped screaming. She shuddered. "It was."

Carmen squeezed her. "It'll be okay."

How many times had Carmen said that since Manny was murdered? When would it be okay? She was so tired of being afraid. Sadist dominated her real life and her dreams. It was unbearable. If she had a crack at Sadist, she wouldn't hesitate. No matter how much she built him up in her mind, he could bleed and therefore die. She had to remember that.

Her body begged for sleep, but her mind wouldn't cooperate. She tried the breathing technique, but after fifteen minutes she gave into her body's compulsion to move. Lyla threw back the covers and Carmen moaned.

"What are you doing?"

"Sorry. I'm going to get something from the kitchen."

"What time is it?" Carmen asked hoarsely.

Lyla glanced at the clock. "Midnight."

"I'll come too."

"You don't have to."

"I know, bitch, but you need me."

Carmen slipped into a silk Chinese robe with a dragon on each breast. She belted it with a yawn and slipped into two fluffy pink clouds that masqueraded as house slippers. Carmen carried her phone and checked on Nora through the video monitor as they passed.

"What was the dream about?" Carmen asked as they started downstairs.

"Same old."

"Sadist?"

"Yeah."

"The only way you can exorcise that fuck is to watch him die. Maybe Gavin can mount his head on the wall after. Then you can throw darts at him anytime you want."

Lyla paused in the entrance of the kitchen, dumbstruck by the imagery. "That does hold some appeal. Damn, I'm going to the dark side."

"You never had a choice. Besides, it's better on the dark side. You do what you want and don't have to spend your time feeling guilty. You want something? Go get it. No if, ands or buts. Besides, knowing Sadist is dead would make *me* feel better." Carmen dug around in the cupboards and came up with cocoa packets and a bag of colorful marshmallows. "Maybe after he's dead I'll know what to do next."

Lyla tossed a kettle popcorn packet in the microwave and tried to shrug off the images that clung to her memory. How did her mind conjure up Sadist's voice so perfectly? That mocking, sweet voice that should have belonged to a nice man, but instead belonged to a monster.

Carmen handed her a cup with a mound of heart and star marshmallows.

"I think I need some cocoa with my marshmallows," Lyla said dryly.

"You have to eat the marshmallows to get to the cocoa," Carmen said and popped one into her mouth. "Come on, they're good for you."

"I'm going to tell Nora not to believe a thing you say."

Lyla ate a green marshmallow. She felt as if she were thirteen again. Who knew that she would be married to a crime lord, have a child with him and still be eating popcorn and marshmallows with Carmen as if they were still innocent preteens?

"It's good, right?" Carmen asked.

"Yes. This is how I should end all shitty days." Lyla shook popcorn into a bowl. "I'm so sick of this. I want all of this to be over. I want Gavin home, I want Sadist dead, I want Jonathan alive."

"Two out of three isn't bad."

Lyla glared at her. "I need all three."

"You can handle two out of three."

"Jonathan has to live."

"Girl," Carmen drawled, "just take what you can get. Before you saw Jonathan at the casino, you totally forgot he existed."

"Yes, but I believed he was in Maine, doing his thing. It's a different story if my psycho husband murders him!"

"I can't believe you didn't tell him you had a kid."

Lyla flinched. Carmen had been there when she made her last call to Jonathan. Hearing the devastation in his voice brought tears to her eyes. She kept hurting him and didn't know how to stop. "I thought I told him!"

"Well, you didn't," Carmen said heartlessly.

"Every time I see him, I'm in a state of shock. Fucking give me a break. I didn't do it on purpose."

Carmen munched on marshmallows. "Who knew your life would become a soap opera? A love triangle, a psychotic murderer and a husband who worships the ground you walk on."

"Gavin doesn't worship the ground I walk on." *If I didn't love you so much, I'd kill you.* She hadn't been able to get his words out of her head.

"Gavin would do anything for you." When Lyla opened her mouth, Carmen waved her hands. "If Jonathan was an asshole, Gavin killing him would be so romantic!"

"But he's *not* an asshole!"

Carmen sighed theatrically and ate a pink marshmallow. "I know. So sad."

"Every time I think Gavin and I are on the same page, he does something to make me question if our lives will always be like this."

"Sorry to break it to you, babe, but once a crime lord, always a crime lord. Even if Gavin gets out of the underworld, which is debatable, he'll never *really* be out. You know that."

Blade walked into the kitchen and glared at them. "What are you two doing up?"

"You want popcorn?" Carmen extended the popcorn bowl, which had marshmallows in it too.

Blade's lip curled. "No."

"Your loss," Carmen said and munched away.

"Have you heard from Gavin?" Lyla asked.

"No," Blade said.

She called Gavin after she spoke to Jonathan. Even if he was mad, she wanted to hear his voice. He didn't pick up. What had she expected?

"Do you know if he's in Las Vegas?" she asked.

Blade gave her a direct look. "I don't keep tabs on the boss."

"Would you tell me if you knew he went to Maine?"

"No."

She glared at him. "If Gavin told you to kill Jonathan, would you?"

"Yes."

No hesitation.

"Why?" she demanded.

"Because whatever it takes for Gavin to do his job is worth it," Blade said.

"What the hell does that mean?"

Blade's phone rang before he could answer. He glanced at the screen, frowned and said, "What?" He listened for a moment and glanced at Lyla.

Her heart skipped. "What?"

"Your dad's here," Blade said.

It took her a second to register. "Now?"

"Yes. He's at the gate. He's been beaten pretty badly."

She didn't give a fuck. "I don't want to see him." Whoever beat him had a good reason, she was sure. The last time she saw her father was the day of Carmen's father's funeral. She threatened to shoot her father if she heard him slander Manny in the future. Seeing her father *so* wasn't what she needed right now.

"He says he needs to talk to you. It's urgent," Blade said.

"You know how I feel about him," Lyla snapped. She had been avoiding her parents months before Nora was born. How dare her father show up here out of the blue? Of course Gavin wasn't here to kick her father's ass.

"I know he's a bastard, but he says it's an emergency."

"A money emergency," Lyla sneered.

"I want to be sure," Blade said and gave orders to allow her father on the property.

She should have taken sleeping pills. Blade would have had a hell of a time trying to wake her up for this awful confrontation. Just the thought of having to face her father made her stomach churn with anger, hurt and dread. For most of her life she played the obedient daughter even after she moved out of her family home. A large portion of the allowance Gavin granted her, she gave to her father to support his gambling habit. Gavin blackmailed her into leaving Jonathan by threatening to kill her father who stole half a million while in his employ. Sacrificing her life for her father made no difference to him. It wasn't until she had been nearly killed and witnessed Manny's murder that her attitude towards her father changed. Life was too short to spend it around someone who didn't love or respect you.

Blade walked out of the kitchen. Lyla made herself busy to buy time. Carmen skipped out of the kitchen with the popcorn bowl in the crook of one arm. She was wide awake now and thrived on drama, unlike her.

"Where is she?"

Her father's shout stoked the maelstrom of emotions in her. This was *her* house, not his. He didn't think she might be asleep at midnight or that she might be exhausted because she had a four month old? No, he arrived in the middle of the night, beat up and shouting. Yes, that was Pat Dalton.

Lyla stalked out of the kitchen. Her father had, indeed, been severely beaten. It wasn't the first time she had seen him in this state. Gavin had the honors of dealing out a much deserved punishment, which made no impact on her father. Lyla didn't feel an iota of sympathy since she was sure this was a warning from a loan shark.

Pat Dalton looked as if he walked through a slaughterhouse. His clothes, which she belatedly realized were originally a beige pajama set, had been tie dyed with bloody splatters. His face was swollen and battered, but his injuries didn't match the amount of blood saturating his clothes since he was standing without assistance. His crucifix, which he shouldn't be allowed to wear was covered in crusty red flakes. She stopped several feet away and caught a whiff of the metallic stench that clung to him.

"What do you want?" she asked, not in the mood for his shit.

His muddy brown eyes, normally filled with disdain or jealousy now held an enraged terror that grasped her attention more effectively than a shout. A premonition caused her to glance around the room, but her mother was nowhere to be found.

A sense of urgency grabbed her by the throat. "What happened? Where is she?"

"She's gone."

"What do you mean, gone?" Panic slammed

into her with the force of a freight train. "Where is she? Whose blood is this?"

Hands encrusted with rivulets of dried blood flexed at his sides. "They took her."

Lyla's world rocked on its axis.

"Who took her?" Blade barked in a no nonsense tone that made Pat jerk.

He ran trembling hands over his chest as if to make sure he was still intact. "I-I was sleeping. I woke up when these men pulled me out of bed. They were wearing masks and began to beat me. I could hear Beatrice screaming. There were at least four men. One of them hit me here." He touched his temple where he had a lump the size of a golf ball. "I must have passed out. When I woke up, the house was ransacked and she was gone."

"You owe someone?" Blade barked.

Before Pat could answer, Lyla lunged for him. Blade yanked her backwards and wrapped an arm around her.

"Lyla, get a hold of yourself!"

"What did you do now?" Lyla shouted at her father.

Pat took a step towards her, the cords on his neck sticking out. "What have *I* done? What have *you* done?"

That penetrated enough for her to go very still. "What?"

"I have a real job. We're barely making ends meet. I don't have the money to gamble. My nose is clean. There's no reason for someone to take your mother unless it has to do with you." Pat jabbed his burgundy colored finger at her. "*You* and *Pyre* are

239

up to God knows what."

She couldn't be responsible for her mother's disappearance, could she? "Then why has she been calling me?"

"She wants to meet your kid, why else?"

Guilt threatened to choke her. "W-when I had Nora, she asked for money."

"We had a rough patch, but we pulled through, no thanks to you."

The way Pat looked at her as if he would love nothing more than to squeeze the life out of her made her body erupt with goose bumps.

"All your mother wanted was to meet her grandkid and now she's—she's—"

"Why didn't you call 911?" Blade asked her father.

Pat's hands fisted at his sides. For a second, Lyla thought he wasn't going to answer. Before she could scream at him, Blade released her and backhanded her father with a casual ruthlessness that told everyone without words that he was going to get answers by any means necessary. It happened so fast that no one had time to react. Her father's mouth sagged as he stared at Blade with a hand pressed against his face.

"If you want your wife to be found alive, stop fucking with us and answer the question. This isn't a pissing contest," Blade said in a no nonsense rumble. "What makes you think Gavin has anything to do with the break in and your wife's abduction?"

Her father reached into his pocket and pulled out a post it note, also splattered with blood. In beautiful, elegant scrawl the note said, *Tell Lyla I'll see her soon.*

There was a loud roaring in her ears. That sick fucker had her mother... No. *No!* This couldn't be happening.

"Gavin will get her back, Lyla," Carmen said.

Lyla opened her mouth, but no sound came out. All the calls and texts from her mother she ignored since Nora's birth came back to haunt her. Lyla had issues with her mother because of her father, but Beatrice *was* her mother. The thought of her in Sadist's hands made her ill.

"You better not be lying, Uncle Pat," Carmen spat. "If Gavin doesn't kill you, I will."

"Why would I lie about this? Beatrice is missing!" Pat shouted.

There was a crushing weight on her chest. Sadist was still fucking with them. Now he branched out from the Pyre family to hers. Why? What was the point? The fact that her father was here and her mother wasn't scared her shitless. Sadist knew that her mother was her weak spot. How could he know that?

Carmen smacked the screen of her phone. "What the fuck?"

"What?" Lyla asked numbly.

"My phone doesn't have service."

Blade pulled out his own phone. He jabbed his finger at the screen, held it to his ear and then cursed. "Fuck."

Lyla walked to a landline phone and picked it up. There was no dial tone. She stared at Blade and Carmen who watched her expectantly. She shook her head. A muscle jumped in Blade's jaw. He

241

opened his mouth just as a faint popping sound came from outside.

CHAPTER SIXTEEN

Lyla

"Get away from the window!" Blade shouted and shoved Carmen to the ground.

"What is it?" Lyla asked, even though she knew.

"Gunfire."

"It's him." Sadist was here to finish it. Lyla pulled out her gun and rose.

"Get Nora," Blade ordered. "We don't have enough men to hold them off."

Her daughter's name snapped her out of the red haze of fury.

Blade shoved her towards the stairs and pulled out his gun. "Hurry!"

Carmen barreled towards her. "Come on, Lyla."

Lyla whirled and ran upstairs with Carmen on her heels. There was a loud boom that made the windows shudder. What the fuck? Did they bring bombs? It was happening all over again. Sadist was here. Her worst nightmare was coming true. Sadist was launching an all out attack. He was here to finish them off. Where the *fuck* was Gavin?

Beau stood in front of the crib, tail standing at attention, growling low in his throat.

"I'll get Nora. You have a leash for Beau?"

Carmen asked, digging through the drawers and coming up with a baby carrier.

"Yeah. Come, boy," Lyla said and dashed into her bedroom.

She snatched Beau's leash and a bag of guns and ammo before stuffing her bare feet into a pair of sneakers. Lyla quickly clipped the leash to Beau and went down on her knees to meet his eyes. His ears flicked from side to side as he listened to the commotion outside.

Lyla gripped Beau's face and looked into his alert eyes. "Stay with me, okay? Stay with mommy. You're going to be okay."

She dashed into the hallway and saw Carmen with Nora strapped to her chest and a baby bag slung over one shoulder. Their eyes met for a moment before they moved towards the stairs.

"Let's go!" Blade roared.

They rushed downstairs as Pat tried to scuttle under the couch. Blade hauled him up and shoved him towards the wine cellar.

"Where are you taking me?" her father shouted.

"We're getting out of here," Blade said.

"What? How—?"

Blade placed his gun against her father's temple. "Do what I say or die. I don't have time for this shit."

Pat glanced at her before he held his hands up and allowed Blade to propel him forward. Blade punched in the code for the wine cellar and they rushed down the wide steps. Blade closed the door. The silence put them all on edge.

"What the fuck is going on?" Pat asked again.

No one answered because they all knew what was happening. Carmen swayed as she cradled Nora's neck. Her baby was still blissfully asleep. Thank God Nora could sleep through a gun battle.

The wine cellar was a small room with three walls full of wine bottles. Lyla had only been here a handful of times, but she knew what to do. She went to the third shelf and pulled off eight bottles before she saw the square panel. She tapped it and typed in her code before she realized Gavin might have changed it since he told her seven years ago. The panel flashed green and then it swung inward. Lyla was so relieved, her eyes stung with tears. She shot to her feet and pushed the wall open.

"There's a way out?" Pat asked, astonished.

He tried to go first, but Blade hauled him back and nodded to Carmen and Lyla. Lyla stepped forward. Two lights at ground level lit up as Beau edged forward, sniffing madly. A dark tunnel stretched out in front of them. The darkness was so dense that she took a step back and bumped into Carmen. Blade and her father forced Lyla forward. More lights flared.

"Lyla, lead the way," Blade said.

Beau eagerly started forward and pulled Lyla after him.

"Still no phone service," Blade reported from the rear. "Let's roll."

Lights welcomed them into the hollow tunnel made of rock and stone and then faded back into darkness when they passed. Nora fussed, but they couldn't stop. Lyla focused on putting one step in front of the other and felt naked without her phone, a flashlight or adequate clothing. The cold penetrated easily through the large weave of her oversized sweater and leggings. Carmen hadn't changed out of her robe or house slippers and had to be freezing.

The tunnel seemed endless and the feeling of being safe began to fade. Where the hell were they going? The sound of her father wheezing came from behind her. It seemed like a half hour passed before the tunnel opened up into a cave with a dirt floor. Four ATVs waited for them. By mutual accord, Blade and her father climbed onto one. Lyla forced Beau onto the floor in front of her and took Nora from Carmen who got into the driver's seat.

"Gavin doesn't leave anything to chance, does he?" Carmen asked as she turned the key in the ignition.

"No." She only wished he could have foreseen that Sadist would strike again. Fuck, four months of radio silence and now this.

Blade took off on a narrow dirt path with only the headlights of the ATV for light. It was like an awful Disneyland ride. They hit ruts that made Lyla clamp her legs around Beau and hang onto Nora for dear life. They climbed steep inclines and then rushed down slopes. Dirt gave way to sand and they continued on. The fact that Gavin carved an escape route through the mountains was unbelievable. The sheer planning and work that must have gone into this was mind-blowing.

Blade braked in front of a small fleet of SUVs in a cave. Beau scrambled out of the ATV while Lyla stepped out with Nora. The SUVs pointed at a wall that seemed to be made of solid rock. Blade pulled out his phone.

"Any luck?" Carmen asked.

"No service, but that's not surprising since we're in the middle of nowhere." Blade jerked his chin at Lyla. "Gavin should be able to track her through her watch."

"Where are we going?" Carmen asked.

"Safe house in Arizona," Blade said.

"Can't we stay here?" Pat asked.

"No. The protocol is to head to a safe house so that's where we'll go. Get in the car."

Blade got into the driver's seat and her father took shotgun. Carmen lifted the back so Beau could jump in. Lyla slid onto the backseat and huddled into the corner to breastfeed Nora who calmed instantly. Lyla stroked her daughter's face as the fake wall of rock lifted, showing an endless expanse of desert highlighted by a half moon.

Blade messed with the GPS, which only showed a snowy screen.

"Fuck," Blade swore.

"Do you know where you're going without directions?" Lyla asked.

"Yeah."

Blade navigated through the desert without lights. They were in the middle of nowhere without a road in sight. Her teeth rattled as the SUV handled the off road terrain with ease. How could Blade possibly know where they were? Lyla swallowed her questions. She trusted Blade with her life so she'd let him take the lead.

Lyla felt nothing. She was past fear or anger.

Sadist would never stop. Lyla looked down at Nora and could see just a hint of her face by the moonlight coming in from the window. Nora's eyes were open and moving around the dark interior of the car. She blinked and clutched at Lyla as the SUV dipped into holes. Lyla held her close and noticed that Carmen managed to put a cap and socks on her daughter despite the chaos.

Carmen leaned between the two front seats, her face tight with exhaustion and worry. Lyla looked down and saw that her once pink house slippers were now brown and filthy.

"What's going on?" Pat asked.

The tension in the car ratcheted up to a screaming pitch. This war had been going on under her father's nose for years. Despite the fact that Manny had been murdered, Gavin went to jail and she had gone missing, her father hadn't asked questions until now. Lyla thought of her mother and squeezed her eyes shut. She would get her mother back.

"Someone has it out for the Pyres," Blade said finally. "It's the same guy that killed Manny."

Her father tried to turn in his seat and encountered Carmen. "So it *is* your fault!" he shouted.

Lyla clenched her teeth as guilt raked her insides.

Carmen got in her father's face. "You've never been a father to Lyla. As far as I'm concerned, you should be happy we didn't leave you there to die."

"You've always been a disrespectful bitch—"

Blade's fist flashed out. A moment later Pat

slammed into the window. The sound startled Nora who began to cry. Lyla cuddled her daughter to her chest as Blade continued to drive.

"I don't like you." Blade's voice held no inflection, which made his delivery all the more effective. "You're a lazy, shady fuck who has no respect for anyone. You're all mouth and can't back up your shit. You were all for Lyla being with Gavin as long as she gave you money to gamble. Far as I can see, Gavin should have killed you when he caught you stealing. That's the price you pay for taking what isn't yours. Only the fact that Gavin loves your daughter has kept you alive, yet you treat her as if she's trash."

They all leaned to the left as the tire dipped into a hole.

"I don't like you," Blade said again. "And I don't care who you think you are. Right now you're not in control, you don't call the shots and you have no rights. I hear anything I don't like coming out of your mouth, I'll put us all out of our misery and put a bullet through your head before I dump your body in the middle of the desert. Shut your trap or I do it for you. We clear?"

Not a peep from her father. Lyla dropped her head back as it throbbed with the beginning pangs of a tension headache. Holy fuck. One innocent trip to the casino started a chain of events that couldn't be stopped. Where was Gavin? Hopefully, he already knew what happened and was able to track her through the GPS imbedded in her watch. What if he was in trouble too? No, she couldn't think that way. It would drive her crazy and she had to keep her head.

They were in the middle of nowhere. It put her on edge. She peered out of the window, waiting for a car to appear out of the darkness. She hoped they didn't get through the guards to the house. What if they touched Manny's urn? Lyla closed her eyes and fought tears. She should have taken him.

She lurched forward as the SUV slid onto pavement. Blade spun sharply and slammed on the gas.

"How long will it take to get to this safe house?" Carmen asked.

"Two hours," Blade said.

"I know about the one in Utah," Lyla ventured, desperate to talk about anything but the cloud of doom hanging over them. "How many safe houses does he have?"

"Half a dozen. The one in Arizona is one of the closest and I know how to get there." He tapped the unresponsive GPS. "I don't know what the fuck is going on with this shit."

Carmen pulled out her phone. "Still no service."

Nora sat on her lap and burped loudly. Beau leaned over to make sure she was all right and waffled in Lyla's hair. She reached back and scratched him under his chin.

"You're such a good boy," she praised.

"Yes you were," Carmen agreed and kissed his cheek.

"Get some sleep," Blade advised.

"How?" Lyla asked as she bounced Nora on her lap.

"We don't know what else that fucker has in

store for us tonight. You should rest while you can."

Lyla dropped her face on Nora's chest and inhaled. Sadist wouldn't get her baby. Lyla dropped the seat and crawled in the back of the SUV with Beau and found some blankets. She placed Nora on her back and watched her baby kick and wave her arms. Beau lay beside her with his head on his paws.

Thoughts of her mom in Sadist's hands chilled her to the bone. Sadist didn't keep his victims... Lyla squeezed her eyes shut. She watched Manny die. God wouldn't be cruel enough to take her mother too, could he? Helpless despair filled her chest, drowning her. Why did Sadist hate her so much? It had just been chance that she was at Manny's house that day, but now he was striking out at her family. That was personal. What fueled this monster?

Lyla tucked Nora against her body and breathed in her scent. The world could fall around her, but she would do whatever she had to for her daughter. She fought to bring Nora into this world and she would pay whatever cost to keep her here. Her thoughts turned to Gavin and her chest burned with fury. If he was in Maine and therefore leaving them vulnerable to an attack, she would never forgive him.

***

"Lyla."

She opened her eyes and found herself curled

protectively around Nora who was asleep. Beau was gone and there was a harsh chill coming in through the open doors of the SUV. Lyla sat up and saw the back of the SUV was open. Carmen reached for the baby and hustled into the darkness.

Lyla felt worse than she had before she slept. Her mind was sluggish and unfocused. Lyla scooted out of the SUV and landed on coarse sand. Lyla looked around. A small cabin sat at the base of a canyon in the shape of a horseshoe. Jagged peaks seemed to touch the starry sky. Lyla walked around the SUV and saw that the safe house was at the top of a steep incline. Just on the horizon was the faint glow of city lights. Lyla wished they were in the city, not in the middle of nowhere with no one around for miles.

Lyla walked towards the cabin, which was set deep enough into the canyon that no one would see the lights. She stepped onto the worn, creaking porch and heard Blade cursing.

"What is it?" she asked.

"Still no reception. I've been checking every fifteen minutes since we got on the road," Blade snapped and stuffed his phone in his pocket. "Did they bug our phones? What the fuck?"

The house had one bedroom and was sparsely furnished with wooden chairs and not much else. Carmen came out of the bedroom with a blanket wrapped around her and Nora. Pat sat at a small dining table, face buried in his hands.

Lyla used the facilities and splashed water on her face to wash away the grogginess and grime. The bathroom had one set of towels and toilet paper, but nothing else. She looked at herself in the dingy mirror. The woman looking back at her possessed dull, defeated eyes.

Lyla trudged into the kitchen and opened the cupboards, which were empty. The house had electricity, but no rations, not even drinking water. Lyla wasn't about to drink from the rusty tap. She went into the bedroom where Carmen huddled on a twin bed with Nora.

"I changed her diaper and put on the warmest clothes she has," Carmen said through chattering teeth.

Beau passed by Lyla, sniffing the floor excitedly.

"I'm going to talk to Blade," Lyla said.

Her father sat at the table, staring intently at his phone. Blade's punch gave him a fresh set of bruises on his cheek. He looked like a walking dead person. She wished he would wash up.

She walked outside and saw Blade standing at the top of the hill, looking out over the desert.

"What are we going to do?" she asked.

"Most of the safe houses are near cities where we can pick up supplies." Blade jerked his head at the city lights. "How do you want to do this?"

Lyla blinked. Blade was asking for her advice? "What?"

"I'm not going to leave you here if you're not comfortable."

She wasn't 'comfortable' with any of this, but they had no choice.

"I need you all to stay calm. My instinct says you should be safe here. I need to go to the city to call Gavin. He needs to know where we are. We could have gone to several safe houses and this is one of the oldest." Blade glanced back at the house. "I would take Pat with me, but he doesn't have extra clothes and I can't afford to have him draw attention since he's covered in blood. Can you handle him?"

"Yes. Carmen will stay with me."

"I'll take Beau so he won't distract you if your dad acts up."

Blade whistled and Beau came out on the front porch. When Blade opened the door, Beau hopped into the passenger seat. Lyla fetched the bag of ammo she brought along and slung it over one shoulder. She and Blade faced one another.

"Thanks for getting us out of there," she said.

"It's my job to keep you safe."

Lyla went with her gut and wrapped her arms around him. Life was too fucking short. She was exhausted, terrified and hovered on the verge of despair and heartbreak. Blade was one of her people and she wanted him to know that. Blade didn't hug her back. He felt like a marble statue. That didn't stop her from giving him a hard squeeze before she drew away.

"Tell Gavin that I'm going to kick his ass when I see him again." She would do worse than that if she survived.

Blade glanced at the bag slung over her shoulder. "Are you sure you can handle Pat?"

"Yes."

"I'll be back as soon as I can."

Blade got into the car. She caught a glimpse of

Beau's doggy face as Blade drove away. Blade was indestructible like Gavin and her biggest defense... and he was leaving them to make contact with Gavin. She took her phone for granted. She also took Gavin for granted and now... Now everything was up in the air. She had no idea if her mother was dead or alive, the fate of the guards at her home was or what horrors the sunrise would bring. Her life had become a series of tragedies and trials. Where was her happily ever after?

"Lyla?"

She turned to see her father on the steps. "Yeah?"

"Where's Blade?"

"He went into the city to make contact with Gavin."

"He left us here?" he shouted.

Lyla tightened her hold on the bag of bullets. She wasn't in the mood for her father's belligerent attitude, which returned as soon as Blade left. Her father's face went purple with rage. After looking into the masked eyes of a killer and facing certain death numerous times, her father's tantrums were a walk in the park. She eyed him objectively as he huffed and puffed as if he had the ability to turn into the Hulk.

"Where is your husband?" he demanded as if he had every right to know.

Lyla walked up the steps and had every intention of ignoring him until he grabbed her arm and jerked her to a halt.

"Where is he?"

Lyla wrenched her arm out of his grasp. "*Don't*

touch me."

"So he's back to his old tricks, huh?" He sneered. "He gets you pregnant and then takes off and lets you deal with his mess?"

"You don't know anything about my life. Shut up and stay put."

Lyla walked into the house. Carmen was trying to entertain Nora who was awake and extremely fussy.

"Blade went into the city to call Gavin," Lyla reported as she sat on the edge of the bed and took Nora and began to breastfeed again.

Carmen stretched out with her head pillowed on her arm. "Smart."

"So it's just us for now."

All her training was to prepare her for this moment—a moment she never thought would come again. The fact that she had company made things worse, somehow, because there was more at stake than just her. Carmen and Nora were here and they were integral to her life. If she lost either of them... Where the *fuck* was Gavin? If he was in Maine—

"This is awful," Carmen said.

Lyla focused on her. "What do you mean?"

Carmen tugged the blanket around her. "The waiting to see what happens next."

Lyla brushed her finger over Nora's cheek and was relieved to find it warm to the touch. "It's a game to him."

"Sick fucker. What's the most painful way to die? That's how he should go."

She thought of her mother and squeezed her eyes shut as a flood of emotion filled her. Why take

256

her mother? What did he want with her?

"Lyla, she's going to be okay."

Her vision was blurry when she opened her eyes. She blinked rapidly.

"She'll pull through, just like you did," Carmen said.

Lyla blew out a shaky breath. "I hope so."

The sound of rapid footsteps made her stand. She looked through the open doorway at her father who walked from one end of the room to another, twisting his hands together and muttering to himself. Of course, he didn't bother to keep guard. He was probably thinking of more shit to heap on her shoulders. She settled on the edge of the bed and saw Carmen's eyes flutter shut as exhaustion took her.

Lyla sat quietly and tried to calm her whirling, chaotic thoughts. When Nora drifted off, Lyla set her beside Carmen who tucked her close. Lyla cleaned up in the bathroom and splashed her face once more. She was so weary, she felt sick, but she couldn't rest until Blade came back. What if Blade couldn't get in touch with Gavin?

When she exited the bathroom, her father's muttering seemed even more frenzied. He didn't seem to be aware of her presence. Was he finally reacting to mom's kidnapping? She tried to catch what he was saying, but it was too low and jumbled for her to understand.

Lyla cracked open the front door and listened. There was absolutely no sound aside from her father's faint footfalls. She held her gun at her side as she walked out on the porch and then down the steps. She had another gun in her bag. She thought of tucking both into her leggings, but that was stupid. Maybe she should get a belt with a double gun holster. She would look like a woman from the Wild West with a gun on each hip. That's how she felt—as if she was part of a world where there were no rules and no safe place. In the underworld, one could never be too prepared.

The faint glow of the city was a beacon in the distance. The desert stretched out before them, covered in cacti, shrubs and trees. There was no road, which would make Blade's progress slow and arduous. She wrapped her arms around herself as the cold penetrated. She closed her eyes and focused on calming her breathing. She was alive and Nora was safe. She couldn't do anything for her mother at the moment. All she could do was stand here and wait for something to happen. Her fighter instincts were elevated. Even when her hand went numb, she refused to tuck the gun away. Everything in her screamed out a warning. Sadist was always one step ahead. How many times would she escape before she ran out of luck?

When her face was numb from the cold and there was no sign of a car, she walked into the cabin, which was only fractionally warmer. She walked into the kitchen and was debating whether to drink from the tap when she realized that her father wasn't in the living room. The bathroom was empty and the bedroom door was partially closed. Lyla swung it open and had a split second to take in the scene. Her father stood over a sleeping Carmen and Nora. The bag of ammo was open and her father had her second gun in his hand.

A loud blast ripped through the room, startling Carmen and Nora awake. Lyla wasn't aware of the fact that she still held her gun or that she pulled the trigger. Her father's body jerked like a puppet on a string as a bullet sliced through him. The gun he held fell with a dull thud. Nora began to cry and kick frantically as her grandfather fell to his knees beside the bed with his blood staining the wooden floor.

CHAPTER SEVENTEEN

Lyla

"Lyla, what—?" Carmen sat up, eyes wide with horror.

Lyla braced herself against the doorjamb as her legs trembled. She just shot her father who would have killed his granddaughter in cold blood.

"Lyla?"

Carmen's voice roused her from her horrified stupor. Carmen stood on the opposite side of the bed, Nora clasped to her chest, face ghost white.

"Get her out of here," Lyla whispered.

"What happened? Why would he—?"

"Carmen, go."

Her mind was a blank slate of rage and denial. She vowed that Nora wouldn't be exposed to this lifestyle, yet her grandfather had been shot less than a foot from her at four months old. She had questions for him and she couldn't do it with Carmen and Nora present.

Carmen's eyes locked on hers before she nodded abruptly and left with Nora. The sound of Nora's screams faded as Carmen moved into the kitchen, leaving Lyla with her father. Lyla forced herself to move forward until she stood in front of Pat who pressed a hand to the wound in the middle of his chest. The bullet went clean through.

"Why?" she whispered.

"I had to," he said through clenched teeth.

"You had to kill your granddaughter?"

Lyla felt as if she were having an out of body experience. Surely, this wasn't real. Maybe she was having a waking nightmare. She watched blood gush through his fingers with detached fascination.

"Tell me why," Lyla whispered.

He glared at her. "Fuck you, Lyla."

His phone flashed in the pocket of his bloody pajamas, catching her attention. Even as her father tried to reach for it, she knocked his hand away and held it up.

A text from a blocked number flashed across the screen: *Fifteen minutes out.*

His phone had service. Lyla stared at her father as everything coalesced in her mind and the blood in her veins turned to ice. "You're working with him?"

"I don't know what you're talking about," he puffed.

Something erupted inside of her. Lyla kicked her father right over his bullet wound. He fell flat on his back with a tortured yell she didn't hear over the roaring in her head. The taste of betrayal permeated her mouth. She raised the gun as she stood over him.

"Tell me the truth about mom." When he didn't answer fast enough, she pulled the trigger. He writhed beneath her, clearly in agony, but she felt nothing. "Talk." She didn't have time.

Fifteen minutes.

"They have her."

"Why should I believe you?"

Although his eyes were dilated with pain, hatred gave him the strength to spit, "They raped her in front of me. One right after the other."

The hand holding the gun wavered. She felt as if she had been kicked in the stomach.

"They told me if I wanted to see my wife again that I would go to your house." His body shook as if he were receiving tiny electrical shocks. "It was supposed to end there. They didn't know there was an escape route. There's a bug in my phone that disrupts electronics, which is why the phones don't have service."

"You should have told me this from the beginning! We could have done something."

Her father's sneer was a weak imitation of his normal disdain. "Why? You think *Gavin* can solve this? He can't. His shit has leaked into *my* life and now your mom... Now she's..."

"Why kill Nora?" she asked, but there was no reply. He was gone.

Lyla jumped when the phone chimed, a reminder of the unread text. She tapped the text message and pulled up the exchange of messages from the blocked number.

We're tracking you. Any sign of Pyre?

No, her father replied.

Where are they traveling to?

A safe house in Arizona.

Are they able to use their phones?

No.

There was a long lag and then her father said,

Blade left to go to the city.

Good. Save us time. Take care of the brat. Don't kill your daughter. He wants her.

There were no more messages from her father.

Fifteen minutes out.

Lyla swallowed bile and knelt beside the bag of ammo in the corner. She grabbed her second gun and stuffed bullets and magazines into her pockets. She didn't look at her father as she walked out of the bedroom. Carmen was in the kitchen with Nora strapped to her chest.

"Lyla?"

"They're on their way." She stared at her daughter who cried pitifully. Like them, Nora was overtired, scared and confused. They were in the middle of nowhere with no backup and Sadist's men on the way. Terror threatened to obliterate her icy composure. This was it. She could feel the walls closing in around them.

"Sadist?" Carmen whispered his name. "He's coming?"

Lyla held up the phone. "They've been tracking us."

"Is Uncle Pat...?"

"He's dead." The words fell from numb lips. "We have to get out of here."

"And go where?"

"We can't be in the house when they get here. We have to make a run for it."

Carmen opened her mouth to argue and then closed it. "Okay."

They ran onto the porch and down the steps. Lyla cautiously approached the incline and searches the desert landscape. She didn't see any headlights or hear the sound of an approaching vehicle, but she knew they were out there. Fifteen minutes. Fuck.

Lyla rounded the house and started after Carmen and Nora. The canyon loomed around them, protecting and trapping them. Was there a way through? A cave they could hide in? They wove around cactus that towered six feet high, waist high shrubs and creepy looking trees without canopies. There were scorpions, snakes and God knew what else out here, but they had no choice. The moon cast enough light for them to avoid being impaled by the spines of the overgrown, wild cactus.

Lyla skidded to a halt as the phone vibrated in her pocket.

Why are you on the move?

Lyla held the phone away from her as if it turned into a snake. How could she be so stupid? Of course they were tracking the phone. Her first instinct was to toss it as far as she could. The other part of her knew that the key to finding her mother and possibly the identity of Sadist was in this piece of evidence.

"Hold up," Lyla called. "I'm going to call Blade."

"*Run* and call him!" Carmen retorted.

"They're tracking the phone."

Carmen stopped in her tracks. "Call him and toss it, Lyla."

Lyla dialed Blade's number and promised she would thank him for forcing her to memorize it. Her heart thudded in her ears as the phone began to ring.

She glanced back the way they had come and was surprised at how much ground they covered, but they were nowhere near the base of the canyon, their only hope for cover. Just when she was afraid that the call would go to voicemail, he picked up.

"Who is this?"

"Blade, it's me." Lyla clutched the phone with both hands.

"Lyla? Whose phone is this?"

Her throat closed up.

"Lyla?"

"He's dead."

"What? Who?"

"My dad. I shot him. He was going to kill Nora."

"Fuck."

"You need to come back, Blade. They're coming. They should be here any minute. My dad's phone was interfering with the signal. They've been tracking us the whole time."

"Get out of the house."

"I am. We're heading toward the canyon."

"I spoke to Gavin. He's in New York. I'm on my way back."

The ice in her veins spread to her heart. Gavin was miles away. By the time he got here it would all be over. She was truly alone with Carmen and her daughter in the middle of nowhere with a team of trained killers about to arrive any minute.

"He said they gang raped my mom in front of him."

The words burst out of her mouth before she realized she was going to say anything. She ignored

Carmen's horrified gasp.

"He has her, Blade, and he wants me too. They told my dad to kill Nora and take me."

"Lyla, run."

"What about mom?"

"Lyla, you're my first priority. You find a place to hide and I'll find you."

"But the phone—"

"Get rid of it. Hide. Stay alive until I get there."

Blade hung up. Lyla stared at the screen as another text appeared: *Did you take care of the kid?*

Lyla gripped the phone so hard, she was surprised it didn't shatter in her grasp. Lyla turned off the phone, put it in her pocket and stared at the edge of the ridge.

"Come on, Lyla," Carmen said, her voice sharp and urgent.

"Go, Carmen."

Carmen stomped back to her with a mewling Nora. "What the hell are you doing? Lyla, we're sitting ducks out here."

"We should split up. They're going to find Pat's body and realize we're on foot. They won't kill me, but they have orders to kill both of you. You have to go, Carmen."

"Lyla, don't do this to me."

"Carmen, promise me you'll take care of her."

"Lyla, *no*."

"Promise me!"

Carmen grabbed her arm and tried to pull her along. "We're going to stay together!"

Lyla twisted out of Carmen's hold and pressed kisses over her daughter's face. Nora wailed pitifully and gripped Lyla's clothing. The placid remoteness that allowed her to think began to fracture as she gently unfurled Nora's tiny fingers and stepped back.

"Go, Carmen."

"I'm not going without you!"

"They're going to find us quick, especially with Nora crying," she said above her daughter's howls.

Carmen's terror was easy to read even in the dim light.

"You run and don't stop, Carmen."

"Please," Carmen whispered, shaking her head as tears streamed down her face. "Please don't leave me."

"I'll hold them off until Blade comes and distract them if I have to. Here." She tucked the second gun into the pocket of Carmen's robe. "Go."

"Lyla, you can't do this to me."

"I love you. Now, *go!*"

They stared at one another. For a moment, she thought Carmen wouldn't go.

"If you get one fucking scratch on you, I'll kill you," Carmen hissed before she whirled and ran as fast as she could towards the mountains. The blanket from the house streamed behind her like a cape.

Lyla circled around the house so she would see them arrive. She replaced the bullets in her magazine. Eight bullets. Eight tries to defend herself before she had to reload. She crouched behind a mesquite tree. Most of the landscape had only spotty coverage so they lucked out in this location.

Lyla found a spot about thirty feet from the house. From this angle she could see the front porch and the ridge where they would appear. She went on tiptoes to search for Carmen, but there was no discernible movement and the only audible sound was her own ragged breaths.

Lyla took a deep breath and let it out. She could do this. She had to. No Gavin, Blade, security guards or Beau. It was just her, a gun and her wits.

Sadist had her mother gang raped. The walls around her heart shuddered under the weight of guilt, sorrow and rage that savaged her insides. Sadist killed Manny, kidnapped her mother and manipulated her father into murdering his grandchild. Lyla refused to look at the house, as if that would erase what she'd done. This had to be a dream. If this were real, she would be scared out of her mind. Instead, she felt nothing but the bite of fury and an icy coldness that obliterated all thought. She welcomed it because whatever came next, she couldn't afford to have a conscience. The need to retaliate was a drum beat in her blood. For the first time in her life, she understood what drove Gavin when Vinny and his father were murdered. She didn't feel like a person, more like a machine with a mission and purpose—survive, protect, and kill if necessary.

Time passed. She didn't feel the cold. She didn't feel anything. The environment was unforgiving—just like her. These men belonged to Sadist. They were monsters who carried out orders to murder children. She wouldn't go with them. She would die before she allowed them to take her to

Sadist. Did he personally want to dismember her while she was alive? Fuck that. If anyone was spilling blood it would be her. What morals she had shriveled up and died in the house along with her father. No matter what the cost, she would protect her own. Neither Carmen nor Nora would die here. She wouldn't allow it.

Lyla scanned the landscape once more and then dropped into a crouch when she heard an approaching vehicle. Lyla was eerily calm. Headlights pierced the darkness and a minute later two SUVs pulled in front of the house. Doors opened and men stepped out, guns drawn. She slowed her breathing as if that would conceal her better. She was too far away to hear what they were saying but the rumble of their voices carried in the quiet.

Two men from each SUV approached the house. She watched as they kicked the door down and walked in. Within seconds, they reappeared. They walked to the SUV and reported their findings to their comrades. Two more men exited the SUV, guns drawn. Eight men. They wore some kind of black on black ensemble. She couldn't make out features, but listened to the rumble of their voices as they came up with a plan. In short order, the SUVs rounded the house with four men flanking them on foot. They headed towards the canyon, which sent a spear of unease through her until she saw that the SUVs were going to have a hell of a time finding a path between the massive cactus, mesquite trees and prickly shrubs.

Lyla focused on the two men who stayed

behind. Lookouts. They knew Blade would make his way back at some point and would alert the others if he approached. She couldn't let that happen.

"You think the daughter did it?" one man asked the other.

"Her or the smoking hot cousin."

There was a pause. Her muscles ached as she moved slowly in a half crouch and closed the distance between them. She was about twenty feet away, close enough to see that the men were Hispanic and in good shape. She didn't dare go any closer since there wasn't anything higher than waist high shrubs to hide behind.

"Must have been the daughter. Pyre married her for a reason. Word is she's building up quite a tally. She killed some boys during the last two runs." He elbowed his comrade. "You think he'll let us try the daughter?"

The other man shrugged. "Sounds like he wants her for something special."

He grabbed his crotch. "I'll bet. The mother wasn't bad. Took her twice before she passed out."

Lyla stopped breathing. He had a nice smile, couldn't be over thirty and looked like a decent guy, but the words coming out of his mouth told the real story. This man raped her mother?

"You think she's still alive?"

"If she is, she won't be for long," the other said as he pulled out a cigarette.

"If she's still at the compound, I'll do her again before he buries her. I can't believe these mental bitches went on foot."

Lyla began to raise her gun, but froze when he walked in her direction to look around the house to watch the progress of the search party. Headlights pierced the darkness while the men yelled to one another as they spread out. Lyla took her eyes off her quarry as worry pierced through the dull roaring in her head. Nora. Carmen. She prayed Carmen found a good hiding spot and managed to calm Nora. She should be following the search party to create a diversion to give Carmen time, but she wouldn't last long without backup. Blade was their only hope of getting out of this alive and these two men were going to prevent that.

"They couldn't have gone far." The cigarette bobbed in his mouth. "You got a light?"

"No."

"You think the dead guy has one?"

"He's in his fucking pajamas."

"You think there's something in the kitchen?"

"No."

"One sec."

The man abandoned his post and jogged towards the house, leaving Lyla alone with the man who raped her mother. He was less than ten feet away and had no idea of her presence. She glanced at the search party. Would they hear the gunshot? The rapist jerked his head around and she heard it, the sound of an approaching vehicle.

He reached into his pocket for his phone. Lyla sprang up and his head snapped around. Their eyes met for one heart stopping moment before she pulled the trigger. His head kicked back, black droplets spraying everywhere before his body dropped.

"What the—?"

Lyla swung the gun around and shot the second man in the doorway. He staggered back as she got him in the chest. Blade crested over the ridge and barreled around the house. The search party fired at the SUV.

With their attention on Blade, Lyla used the commotion to run towards the canyon to find Carmen and Nora. There was a pained scream as Blade took a leaf out of her book and ran over a man. Three down, five to go. The enemy vehicles were trying to turn around to face the threat and not having much luck since the wild vegetation boxed them in.

"Hey, there she is!"

A man spotted her and she immediately dropped to all fours. Car engines roared, men shouted and bullets flew. Lyla heard a bark. She lifted her head in time to see Beau leap out of the SUV window and launch himself at a man who fell backwards with an agonized cry. Fuck it. Lyla focused on the bigmouth who noticed her. She popped up and pulled the trigger. The first shot nicked his shoulder, but the second put him down.

"What the fuck?" someone shouted.

Lyla focused on one of the SUVs that was trying to battle a cactus. The driver seemed to have given in for the moment. He had a high powered rifle balanced on his open window and was blasting Blade's windshield, which wouldn't hold up for long. Lyla used her last three bullets and the deafening blasts ceased. Lyla pulled a full magazine out of her pocket and slammed it in before she followed the sound of Beau's growls. She put the bastard out of his misery and nudged Beau away from the body.

"Beau, come," Lyla ordered.

Blade rammed into the driver's side of the second SUV with enough force to tip the SUV on its side. Blade slid out of the SUV and ran to the upended vehicle. Three shots and then silence descended.

Seven down. One left. Where was he?

"Lyla!" Blade rounded the SUV, chest heaving. "You all right?"

"Yes. I split up with Carmen and Nora."

"Where?"

Lyla pointed in the general direction she saw Carmen run. "There's one guy left."

"Fuck." Blade raced back to his SUV and whistled for Beau.

Lyla went to the SUV with the driver who slumped half out of the open window. She made sure there were no surprises in the back seat before she took the wheel and followed Blade as he flattened shrubs. Lyla ignored the blood on the steering wheel and seat. Her entire being focused on any movement over the suddenly quiet, still desert landscape.

Out of the corner of her eye, she saw a flash accompanied by a popping sound. Lyla's heart dropped to her toes. She wrenched the steering wheel to the left and plowed over everything in her path. Branches reached into the open window and scratched her arm and cheek. Lyla didn't notice.

She slammed the SUV to a halt when it couldn't go any further and ran as fast as could, dodging through the monstrous cactus.

She rounded a tree and tripped over a body. "No!"

"Lyla."

She raised her head and saw Carmen with Nora strapped to her chest, gun in hand. Lyla squeezed her eyes shut as relief cascaded through her in a heady wave that left her lightheaded.

"Are you hurt?" Blade asked.

Carmen walked forward as if she were sleepwalking and didn't answer. Blade took a bawling Nora from Carmen who did nothing to stop him.

"She's freezing. Come on, we don't have much time," Blade said and rushed back to the car with Nora.

Carmen helped Lyla to her feet. They stared at one another for a long moment.

"Okay?" Lyla asked.

Carmen nodded.

"Stupid bitches."

Lyla looked down at the man at their feet. How he could be bleeding to death and smirking at them was beyond her. She had been close to death herself and it wasn't anything to joke about.

"He won't stop coming," the man said through clenched teeth. "He's going to destroy Pyre."

"Who is he?" Lyla demanded.

His eyelids fluttered as he tried to stay conscious. "No one knows who he is. He isn't stupid."

"Where's the compound where they're holding my mom?"

He raised his dirty finger, stuck it in his mouth and hummed. Lyla's stomach turned over.

"She was great, by the way."

Lyla slammed her foot on his chest and heard something break. *"Where is she?"*

Blood trickled out of his mouth as he convulsed. Lyla dropped to her knees, grabbed handfuls of his jacket and shook him.

"Where?"

"You're too late," he said before his body went lax.

Lyla dropped him and knelt on the desert floor as emotions consumed her.

"Lyla?" Carmen whispered.

Lyla rose, took the gun from her and started back to the cars. Her mind was a blank slate as she opened the door to the second SUV, got in and slammed her foot on the gas. She heard Blade yell her name as she wrenched the SUV around and started back towards the cabin.

Lyla slapped her hand on the GPS built into the dashboard. A map of their routes appeared on the screen. There was one location the SUV kept returning to, a large red dot in the middle of Las Vegas. Lyla set the course as she passed the safe house and started down the ridge. Her rearview mirror showed Blade's flashing headlights far behind her. She didn't stop. She couldn't.

When the SUV skidded onto the highway, the first hint of the coming sun brightened the sky. Lyla stared blearily at the bloody sunrise, which seemed appropriate after the night she had. Her body was coiled so tightly, she felt as if she might shatter.

Lyla drove with such single-minded intensity that she didn't realize Blade caught up to her until he tried to run her off the road. Lyla jerked the wheel to avoid him. Blade's window was down and he was more furious than she had ever seen him. He shouted at her, which was pointless since her windows were rolled up. He jabbed his finger at her and held up his cell phone.

Lyla slammed her foot on the gas even as she reached in her pocket for the forgotten cell phone she picked off her father. She turned it on and immediately saw Blade's number on the screen. Apparently, there was enough distance between them for him to have a signal. She had less than twenty minutes between her current location and this fucking compound. She wouldn't let anyone stop her.

"Pull over," Blade ordered.

The lump of ice in her chest where her heart used to be weighed a ton. "No."

"What the fuck are you doing?"

"They have my mom."

"We have men working on it."

"They have her at the compound."

"I don't give a fuck where they have her. Pull over, Lyla."

"Fuck you, Blade. I'm getting her. The GPS tracks all their routes. There's one place they keep going back to. It's their compound. I know it. You want this to stop? Send as many men to this address." She rattled it off and merged onto a freeway. "I'll be there in nineteen minutes, with or without backup."

"Gavin said—"

The ice splintered.

"Fuck Gavin!" she shrieked and slammed her hand on the steering wheel. Emotions threatened to break her in half. She clenched her teeth to stuff it back in. She didn't have time for a breakdown. That would come later when her mother was safe. "I'm tired of waiting for other people to take care of me. I can do that my fucking self. This is my mom. I got her into this, I'm getting her out. You want to help? Call the guys, get them there."

"Lyla," Blade's voice was controlled once more. "Let me—"

"Get them there, Blade."

Lyla hung up. She was done playing this game. It had to end now. Sadist wasn't allowed to claim the one parent she had left.

The phone rang. Gavin's number showed up on the screen. She barely resisted the urge to toss it out the window. She turned the phone off instead. Fuck him. Blade mentioned that he was in New York, which was too close to Maine for her peace of mind. If he went after Jonathan, therefore leaving her to deal with this shit on her own she would never forgive him.

The GPS led her past downtown Las Vegas. At a stoplight, a pedestrian passing in front did a double take. Lyla couldn't begin to imagine what she looked like. For the first time, she looked at her hands, which were rust colored with dried blood. She didn't have to look down at her sweater and tights to know they didn't fare much better.

When the light turned green, Lyla slammed her foot on the accelerator. The compound was in the middle of a block of abandoned warehouses. Lyla's senses prickled with an odd sense of déjà vu. Two thugs kidnapped and held her in a warehouse years ago. She had been unconscious when they brought her in and too distraught to notice when she left. Everything in her screamed that this was the same place. A glimpse of Blade's SUV in the rearview mirror stabbed at her icy determination. Nora and Carmen couldn't be here.

The sight of a group of vehicles made her heart slam into her throat until one of the doors opened and she saw Barrett, an older guard who Gavin had put in charge of security at home. He was alive. Lyla lowered the window as he came around to her door. She couldn't read anything from his implacable expression. He took in her bloody appearance without batting an eye.

"We can take it from here," Barrett said.

She tightened her hands on the wheel. "No. I'm going in."

Blade appeared at her window and brushed Barrett aside. The vehicle with Carmen, Beau and Nora sped away. Her grip on the steering wheel eased slightly. At least they were safe.

"Lyla—" Blade began.

"We're wasting time," Lyla said impatiently. "I'm not leaving until I see her alive."

"You don't want to see this," Blade said.

"Yes, I do." It couldn't be worse than killing her own father. She didn't need anyone to shield her from Sadist's work. She had firsthand experience and it was *her* mother. It was her duty to be here. When she caught up to Sadist, she would pay him back tenfold.

"Gavin's gonna—"

"Gavin isn't here," she snapped. "We're wasting time."

Blade examined her. She could feel him debating whether he should get physical with her.

Lyla looked straight into his merciless black eyes. "Don't."

Blade shook his head. "Fuck. You don't move from my side, got it?" He turned to Barrett. "How many men do you have?"

"Thirty. More on the way."

"It'll be too late by then," Blade said.

"Blade, Gavin's gonna—" Barrett began.

"I got her. She can hold her own. You focus on directing the men." Blade slid into the passenger side and looked at Lyla. "Let's roll."

Barrett didn't look happy about the situation, but he jogged back to his SUV. Lyla started through the maze of warehouses.

"I have to do this," Lyla said.

"I know."

Blade said nothing more as he reloaded both their guns and watched the screen as Lyla navigated around car piles and garbage. When she was a block away, Blade told her to stop. She obediently parked. Blade slid out and spoke to the men who armed up and put on earpieces.

Mom had to be here. The past six hours began to hit her all at once. Lyla rested her face on the steering wheel, took a deep breath and gagged when she smelled the stink of the driver's dried blood and guts. She sat back, rolled down the window and took deep breaths of fresh air. Exhaustion threatened to drag her under.

"Lyla?"

She opened her eyes and saw Blade standing at her window.

"Okay?" he asked.

"Yes." It was almost over.

"Here."

He held up a man's jacket with a zip up the front. Lyla stepped out of the car and nearly crumpled. She grit her teeth as she forced her quaking legs to support her. She couldn't lose her head now, not when she was so close. Blade stared at the warehouse as she stripped off her stiff, filthy sweater and slipped into the jacket. Her shredded leggings showed scrapes and dried blood from her run in the desert. Lyla zipped the jacket and wrapped her arms around herself for warmth.

The echo of gunfire reached her. She started towards the sound, but Blade caught her arm, pulling her to a halt.

"They're clearing the way," Blade said and tapped his earpiece.

"I need to—"

"Lyla, we could be outnumbered ten to one. Just wait. You're not invincible. You're no help to your mom if you're dead."

She grabbed her gun and stuffed two magazines into her pocket. Her mind was a spinning whirlpool of fragmented thoughts and images. The sounds of the battle taking place in the warehouse beckoned to her. Violence and death—they were becoming her constant companions. An image of her father's body flashed through her mind. She closed her eyes and waited for the stabbing pain in her chest to recede.

"I guess target practice came in handy."

She opened her eyes to find Blade watching her.

"You did good," he said.

The price of admission into the underworld was blood and she had spilled more than her fair share. No matter what she did, the underworld kept dragging her back.

"Look at me."

She focused on Blade who looked disgustingly capable. His hand rested on the butt of his gun and his clothes, while soiled, weren't ripped and covered in blood as hers was. His eyes, while bloodshot, were alert and clear.

"Carmen told me everything. You did what you had to," he said.

She couldn't take a full breath. She felt as if there were glass shards in her chest.

"You were everything I could have hoped," Blade continued as she tried to hold herself together. "You were cool under pressure and executed with the precision of a professional. You didn't let emotions get in the way. You did good, Lyla."

She dug her fingernails into her palms.

"It's either you or them. I'm damn glad it was them." He stepped close and cupped her chin in his hand. "You hear me? You did the right thing."

"I did the right thing by killing my father?"

"It's either that or have Nora and Carmen dead before sunrise."

Her throat swelled. She dropped her face forward until it hit Blade's chest. She tried desperately to contain the maelstrom inside of her. If she let loose, she wasn't sure she could put herself back together again. Blade slid his hand into her tangled hair and said nothing. She grabbed a fistful of his jacket and clenched her teeth against the need to scream.

When Blade stiffened, she looked up and saw that he had one hand cupped over his earpiece. A muscle leapt in his jaw.

"Copy," Blade said and looked down at her. "Let us take care of this."

"Is she alive?"

Blade hesitated and her heart stopped.

"It isn't pretty. She needs to go to the hospital. Let them bring her—"

Lyla ran towards the warehouse with her gun in hand. The door was being manned by one of Gavin's men. He held up a hand as she approached, but after a glance behind her, he stepped aside.

Although the exterior of the warehouse looked like a rust bucket the interior was brand new. The warehouse towered three stories high. High windows let in light from every angle. On the first floor were three rooms with the doors wide open. She glimpsed drugs in one room and money in another, but her eyes were on the second floor where a group of men gathered in front of a set of rooms.

"Lyla, you don't want to see this," Blade said from behind her.

"She's up there?"

"Lyla—"

She ran towards the iron staircase and ignored bodies littered over the steps. Nothing penetrated the urgency rushing through her. She needed to see her mother to make sure she was okay. When she reached the second landing, Barrett stepped forward, face grave.

"Mrs. Pyre, you don't want to—" he began.

"Let me pass," she snapped.

The men didn't move, so she shoved her way through their ranks and stopped in the doorway. Lyla took one look into the room and felt her world disintegrate. She screamed, a sound filled with rage and despair. No. *No.* This had to be a nightmare.

"Lyla."

Blade gripped her shoulder and tried to pull her backwards.

"No!" Lyla ripped free and passed three naked dead men to reach her mother who was bound by wrist and ankles to the four posts of a bed. The mattress was saturated with her mother's blood. Her mother had been whipped and beaten so severely that the only feature she recognized were her mom's platinum locks. Lyla's shaking hands hovered a foot over her mother. No part of her had been left untouched. It looked as if her mother had been mauled by a wild animal. There were deep slashes across her face and abdomen. Her hanging skin glistened with cum and blood.

"Mom?" Her stomach lurched as she used the

sleeve of the jacket to wipe slime and blood from her mother's face. "Mom?" She tugged on the restraints. "Get these off her."

No one moved.

"Get them off her!"

Four men rushed forward and quickly cut the restraints. One guard shrugged out of his jacket and tossed it over her body.

"Mom? Can you hear me?" She placed one hand over her mother's lips and one on her chest. Her chest moved a tiny fraction at the same time that Lyla felt a small puff of air on her palm.

"She's alive!"

Blade picked her mother up as gently as possible. Her mother didn't make a peep as Blade started towards the door, rapping out orders. Lyla turned to follow, but stopped when she tripped over one of the naked men sprawled on the floor. Her mother had been in this state and they—. She pulled out her gun and emptied the magazine into his body, which shuddered from the impact. She reloaded, walked to the next man and repeated the process until all three men were bullet filled piñatas. She wasn't sure she had a heart anymore. She didn't feel anything.

Lyla started towards the door, but a flash of red caught her eye. She looked up and saw a camera with a red light over the doorway. Lyla didn't ask for permission. She snatched the gun from the nearest man's belt. The guards backed up as she aimed at the camera and shattered it with one shot. She slapped the gun against the guard's chest and walked out of the room. Gavin's men gave way as she walked down the staircase like an automaton.

Blade had her mother in the back seat of the SUV. Lyla cradled her mother's head on her lap and stroked her hair, which was caked with blood and other stuff she wouldn't let herself examine.

"I'm sorry, Mom," she whispered. "I'm so sorry."

CHAPTER EIGHTEEN

Lyla

Lyla stared down at her mother who lay in a hospital bed in the ICU. Her body was wrapped in bandages and a machine was helping her breathe.

Their entrance to the emergency room caused a sensation. Her mother was whisked away and Lyla had been forced to be treated as well. They cleaned the wounds on her legs, arms and face while asking questions about her mother and why she was covered in blood. Blade said something about a camping accident and she nodded since the doctor seemed to need some kind of confirmation from her. As for her mother, Blade concocted a story about hiring a private investigator that was looking into her disappearance and located her in this state. The doctors said the police would have to be contacted. This should have scared her, but she felt nothing. After her latest near death experience, being questioned by cops didn't rouse a hint of anxiety.

The doctor's litany of her mother's injuries played over and over in her mind.

"Your mother's injuries are traumatic. She's lost a lot of blood. She's had several strokes due to someone choking her. She has multiple head fractures as well as a broken ankle, broken shoulder..."

The doctor continued, but she couldn't hear over the white noise. Seeing her mother in the warehouse had been bad enough, but knowing the extent of the physical trauma made her entire being recoil.

"She's in a coma," the doctor said clinically. "It's amazing she survived such a brutal attack. I hope the cops can find the monster who did this."

Lyla dropped into a chair beside the hospital bed. She hesitated as she reached for her mother's hand, which had chunks of flesh missing from it. Three of five fingers were in braces. The men hadn't left anything untouched. Lyla kissed her mother's palm, right over a deep gash.

"I'm sorry." Her voice sounded as dead as she felt.

Their history faded into nothingness. This woman was her mother, her flesh and blood. She couldn't bear to look at her mother's face because it was so gruesome. Her mother didn't deserve this. The dam that kept her from losing her mind since the attack crumbled. Lyla rested her mother's hand on the bed, buried her face against the sheets and sobbed her heart out.

There was no getting around it. This was her fault. Because of her connection to Gavin, her parents had been dragged into the underworld with her. She would have paid any price to save her mom from this.

The only sound in the room was the heart monitor, which increased her anxiety. Any moment now, she expected to hear the sound of her mother's heart flat lining. How could her mother recover from this? She trembled with the need to retaliate, to lash out at someone. She felt as if she were balancing on the edge of a cliff. A gust of wind could tip her over into a black hole where she'd never emerge. Her mother's life hung in the balance. She felt this way when Manny was murdered—helpless, horrified and enraged. A scream built in her throat. The doctor said they had to 'work' on her mother as if she was a car they had to put together.

"Lyla."

She lifted her head as Gavin walked into the room. He looked as slick and untouched as always. In comparison, she felt as if she had been skinned alive—raw, dirty, violated and vicious. Lyla stood and backed away as he approached.

"Stay back," she said hoarsely.

He didn't stop.

"Don't you *dare* come close to me. Look at her!" Lyla pointed at her mother. "Look at her!"

Gavin's eyes flicked to her mother. His expression hardened and then came back to her.

"I'll never forgive you for this," she whispered.

Gavin reached for her. She knocked his hand away. That didn't deter him.

"I don't want you touching me!" She didn't want anyone touching her, not when her soul felt so savaged and raw. "You said you would protect us! I told you not to go and you *left*—"

Gavin hauled her into his arms. She fought him as if he was Sadist. She completely lost it, scratching, biting, and screaming. Her breath whooshed out of her as Gavin pinned her to the floor. She was blinded by tears of grief and rage. She trusted him to take care of her and he betrayed her.

"I hate you!" she screamed. "I'll never forgive you for this!"

Lyla was dimly aware of shouting medical staff and then Blade was there, shoving Gavin aside. Lyla lurched up and latched onto him. She was splintering into a million pieces. She couldn't stop shaking and she needed to hold onto someone who had never let her down.

"Lyla."

Blade smoothed her hair back before he rose with her in his arms. He moved swiftly. She buried her face against his chest, screwed her eyes shut and tried to hold onto her violent emotions.

"Drug me," she whispered.

Blade's step faltered. "What?"

"Sedate me."

"You sure?"

"Do it. I-I can't take anymore."

"Lyla."

She clutched him like a child who needed reassurance and comfort. She buried her face in his chest and screamed as the tears came. The horror of the past seven hours barreled into her, leaving her devastated.

She felt a pinch in her neck as Blade applied the needle. A blessed numbness spread over her shattered soul, swept away her sorrow and replaced it with nothingness.

**

When Lyla woke, she felt as if she had been run over by a truck. She was flat on her back in a soft bed and didn't have the strength to move her limbs. Every inch of her body ached and her mind was a complete blank. There was no sense of time or space and she wasn't concerned. Sleep threatened to pull her back under. She closed her eyes and bent her foot in a mini stretch. The stab of pain caught her off guard. She shifted her legs, which scratched against the fine sheets like sandpaper and then it all came flooding back.

Lyla shot up in bed and couldn't stop her gut-wrenching scream. It didn't take longer than ten seconds for a door to her left to burst open. Blade appeared in the doorway with his gun. She was home in the master suite she shared with Gavin. After the cabin in the middle of the desert and the grisly warehouse, the rich cream colors and luxurious setting seemed all wrong.

"Is it safe?" she asked.

"Yes. They attacked the front gate and tossed an explosive on property, but they didn't penetrate when they realized there was another way out," Blade said.

"How long have I been out?" She tried to throw back the duvet, but that feat seemed to be too much for her weary body.

"Six hours. You should sleep longer."

"I need to see my mother."

"There's nothing you can do for her, Lyla,"

290

Blade said.

Her heart stopped. "She's—?"

"Your mother's alive, but her state hasn't improved."

"I should be there."

"We have men guarding her. They'll let us know of any changes."

Lyla opened her mouth to argue, but stopped when Carmen appeared with Nora on her hip. Carmen rushed forward, set Nora on Lyla's lap and dropped her face into Lyla's hair. Beau leapt up on the bed, nudged her with his wet nose and settled beside her with a huff.

"I thought I was going to lose you," Carmen whispered, voice thick with tears. "Don't you ever scare me like that again."

Nora smiled up at Lyla, unfazed by her near death experience. Even as Lyla's trembling hand ran down Nora's cheek, the baby nuzzled Lyla's chest, clearly seeking a meal. Lyla physically recoiled.

"What is it?" Carmen asked, raising her head.

Lyla glanced at Blade who was already in the process of closing the door. She raised Nora away from her chest and kissed her on the cheek.

"Did Nora eat?"

"Yeah, I gave her cereal. Why?"

"She's acting like she's hungry."

"She probably wants to bond with you. She's been a little stressy. Besides, your boobs must be full."

The moment Nora nuzzled her, her breasts filled with milk, but her heart was racing. Last night she turned a corner. Her father was the first of five men to die by her hand. Every shot pushed her closer to a precipice from where there would be no return. What she witnessed in the warehouse shoved her over the edge into a straight up killer with no conscience or morals. Even now, something dark and twisted inside of her demanded retribution.

Nora grinned at her, making her heart squeeze with a wild rush of emotions. She wanted to cuddle her daughter, but memories of what she'd done kept her from holding Nora too close. She didn't want to infect her baby with... her. Having Nora breastfeed from her suddenly felt abhorrent. A normal person would be horrified that they killed their own parent, but she felt nothing. Was it because she was in shock or really felt nothing? Maybe she was morphing into a sociopath.

"Lyla? What's going on?" Carmen asked.

She hugged Nora close. "Thank you for taking care of her when I was..." Going off the rails, killing people and shooting the dead bodies of her mother's rapists. Her throat closed up. "Thank you."

Carmen shot to her feet and smacked Lyla upside the head. "Don't you ever do that to me again, bitch!"

Lyla blinked. "What?"

"You tell me to take Nora and run while you sacrifice yourself? Do you know what that did to me? I could hear gunshots going off and I thought—I thought—" Carmen paced and waved both hands in front of her face as tears poured down her cheeks. "I didn't know what was happening. I was trying to keep Nora quiet and that guy found us."

Carmen paused to savagely kick Beau's doggy bed before she resumed her frantic pacing. Beau, Lyla and Nora watched avidly. Carmen planted her feet and did a Peter Pan pose.

"I shot him." Carmen sounded half defiant, half proud of herself.

"I know," Lyla said.

Carmen sniffed. "He was my first."

"I know."

Carmen let out a gut-wrenching scream and punched her fist in the air. A second later she bizarrely stomped the ground with one foot as if she were trying to put out a fire.

"I got him! That should teach him to mess with a woman with a baby! That motherfucker! He was calling me like a dog, 'Here slutty, slutty.'" Carmen made a gun with her thumb and pointer finger. "I got him, Lyla. I did it."

"You did good."

Carmen took a deep, fortifying breath. Her bravado faded to reveal the vulnerability and terror she tried to conceal. She fell to her knees beside the bed.

"How did you do it?" she whispered.

"Do what?"

"How did you have the—" Carmen made fists with both hands and shook them in Lyla's face, "*cojones* to tell us to run? To go back and face those men by yourself..." Carmen covered her face with both hands and moaned. "I can't do that ever again. I can't."

"I'm sorry," Lyla said.

Carmen grasped her hand and squeezed with her eyes shimmering with tears. "Aunty Beatrice?"

Lyla's throat closed up. Carmen rose and wrapped her arms around Lyla. She took a deep, shuddering breath and the tears spilled over.

"Carmen, I think there's something wrong with me," Lyla whispered as Carmen's cotton candy scent engulfed her.

"Why?"

"My mind went blank and I just... I just—"

Carmen pulled back to give her a fierce look. "You became a fucking badass." She held one hand to her chest and waved one in the air as if she was in church. "I mean, Lyla, you took out five professionals. I heard what they did to your mom at that warehouse... and what you did too."

Lyla couldn't breathe. She set Nora on the bed, went to the window and threw back the curtains. Guards milled on the property. There was no sign of the attack that sent them fleeing through the underground tunnels. If she hadn't heard the sound of gunfire taking place or the bomb, she wouldn't believe there'd been an attack on the fortress.

"Lyla?"

She turned and saw Carmen watching her with Nora on her hip. Lyla ran her hands over her face and saw that although she wore a clean nightgown, she was still covered in... stuff.

"I need a shower," Lyla said and headed towards the bathroom.

"What are you going to do?" Carmen asked as she settled on the vanity bench with Nora.

"What do you mean?" Lyla called as she stepped under the spray and vigorously began to scrub herself. She wondered how many people's blood she had on her skin.

"Blade told me you saw Gavin at the hospital."

She didn't want to talk about Gavin. She was so fucking angry at him. He risked their relationship because he couldn't stand that she had been with another man. Gavin's blind jealousy resulted in this—a fuck up of epic proportions. Had Sadist known that Gavin wasn't in Las Vegas and that's why he scaled this attack? If Jonathan was dead, what was she going to do about Gavin?

"Gavin must have gone through hell, trying to come home when all this crap was going down," Carmen continued.

Lyla stepped out of the shower and examined her reflection. She didn't look any different, although her eyes seemed a shade darker. Was that possible? Her skin was paler than normal, which was expected. The woman looking back at her had bloodshot eyes and an impassive expression that concealed the turmoil going on inside of her.

"This has to end," Lyla whispered.

"Yes," Carmen agreed and kissed Nora. "Gavin is probably slaying everyone in his path, trying to find out who Sadist is."

"Did you undress me?" Lyla asked suddenly.

"Of course. Blade isn't going to do it. He wants to keep his head on his shoulders."

"The phone was in my pocket—"

"Blade gave it to Gavin."

She blew out a breath. Sadist didn't trust

anyone, which is how he survived this long, but he was human and could make a mistake. She hoped they would find something on the phone that would identify him. He wore a mask the day Manny was murdered even though he never intended there to be a witness. Sadist was intelligent, cautious and cruel—a dangerous combination.

"What are you doing?" Carmen asked as Lyla slipped on jeans.

"I have to see Mom."

"You're going out again?" Carmen asked indignantly. "Lyla, it's not safe."

"You didn't see what mom went through, Carmen. I can't leave her there alone. I owe her more than that." She focused on Nora who was chewing on Carmen's shirt. "Can you stay here and watch her?"

"Lyla, you took on those guys at the cabin, your dad and then went on a rampage to find your mom. You need to eat and chill."

"I don't have time to chill." Lyla slipped on a shoulder holster and put her leather jacket over it. She slipped ammo and a magazine into her purse and went into the bathroom to fix her hair, which was wet, limp and in her face.

"Lyla, let Gavin do what he does best. You're putting yourself at risk—"

Lyla slashed her hand through the air. "Mom's in the hospital because of me. If I wasn't with Gavin, this wouldn't have happened in the first place. If it was your mother, would you leave her there alone?"

Carmen sighed. "You're running on fumes,

Lyla."

"I'll sleep when I'm dead."

"Not funny."

Lyla grasped Carmen's face between both hands and rested her forehead against her cousin's. "I need you here with Nora. You're the only one I trust to carry this out. I could do what I had to at the cabin because I knew you would protect Nora with your last breath. I need you to do this for me."

Carmen sniffled. "I'm supposed to be the protector, not you."

Lyla's lips twitched into a small smile. "Once all of this is over, I'll let you take the lead again." She kissed Carmen and then Nora. "I'll be back."

Lyla yanked open the bedroom door and came face to face with Blade. His eyes flicked over her.

"You're armed," he said.

"I'm going back to the hospital."

"Lyla, you're exhausted. Maybe you should—"

Lyla ignored him and marched down the hallway, down the stairs and out the front door. Her attention fixed on Gavin's silver Bugatti, which rounded the drive. Her heart slammed against her chest. She had only a fuzzy memory of what went down between her and Gavin in the ICU, but it hadn't been pretty. The sight of him made her lightheaded with rage. He not only sacrificed the future of their relationship by going after Jonathan, he had put all of them at risk and this was the result. She would never forgive him.

Before Lyla could decide what to do, the Bugatti stopped and a man unfolded from the driver's seat. It wasn't Gavin. He was gorgeous and looked fresh off the cover of Bad Boy magazine. He was tall and lean and wore a black tee with jeans and a thick leather belt riding low on his waist. He gave her a brilliant smile as he strode towards her. Lyla glanced at the guards who were watching their interaction closely, but nobody made a move to stop him.

Before she could move back, he grasped her shoulders and kissed her on both cheeks. Lyla had been treated to the gesture before by Manny, but she was nonplussed by it coming from a stranger.

"I'm Angel," he announced as if that was supposed to mean something to her.

An apt name for a man with a face like that. "Hi. Who are you?"

"I'm family."

"Excuse me?"

Angel looked her over. "Where are you going?"

"Who are you?"

"Where are you going?" he repeated.

"To the hospital."

Angel nodded. "Your mother?"

She stepped away from him. "Seriously, who are you?"

"Angel Roman."

She froze. Everyone knew about the notorious Roman family from New York. She heard about the Pyres connection to the Romans, but had never met any of them until now. "You're visiting?"

"Something like that," Angel said with a smile she didn't trust.

The door opened behind her and Blade appeared.

"Angel," Blade said, voice tight.

"Old man," Angel acknowledged and jerked his thumb at the Bugatti. "Want a ride? I'm testing out Gavin's car to see what I want to buy."

"I'll take her," Blade interjected and gestured to the guards to bring a car around.

"We'll meet you there," Angel said and draped an arm over her shoulders.

"Angel—" Blade began.

Angel turned his head. All signs of the affable bad boy vanished. His eyes were cold and sinister.

"I know who she is. You think I'd let anything happen to her?" Angel asked.

Blade said nothing.

"We'll meet you there," Angel said firmly and led her to the Bugatti.

Lyla glanced at Angel as he climbed into the driver's seat and revved the engine. An SUV pulled in behind them and Blade got behind the wheel.

"We always have driver's," Angel said conversationally as he peeled out of the driveway and barreled towards the gates. "This car is *nice*. What car do you drive?"

"Don't drive," she said faintly as they passed through the gates with inches to spare. "Blade usually drives."

"Maybe when this is all over you can," Angel said easily as he shifted gears and put on mirrored shades.

Silence fell. She didn't feel like talking, especially to someone she didn't know. She looked out at the desert, which passed in a blur thanks to Angel. He may not drive often, but he handled the car with the efficiency of a racecar driver.

"Gavin's going to fix this."

Lyla tensed, but didn't look at him.

"He came to New York, said he wanted to step down because you've paid too high a price for his role. We heard what happened to Uncle Manny and Vinny, but we weren't able to come out for the funerals. Shit's been tense in the city. We thought everything here was taken care of until Gavin showed up and told us about this fucker."

Something clicked. "You're taking his spot?"

"Yeah."

She turned her head. "You don't know what you're taking on."

He glanced at her. "You know who I am."

"Yes."

"Then you know I was born and bred for this."

"Gavin was too."

"Gavin would do it for the rest of his life, but you want out so he'll give you that. Gavin's fully capable of doing this until the end of time." He shifted gears and then said, "You didn't grow up in the life. I get it and hearing what you went through, what you're still going through, I don't blame you."

"You said Gavin went to New York?" she asked quietly.

"Yeah."

"Do you know if he went anywhere else?"

Out of the corner of her eye, she saw him glance at her.

"What do you mean?"

"Do you know if he stopped anywhere else besides New York?"

"He mentioned something about Maine, I think. Why?"

Confirmation, even though she hadn't needed any. Lyla's heart felt like a stone in her chest.

"Gavin's checking on the leads from the warehouse, phone and the GPS on the vehicle you drove. He asked me to watch over you," Angel said.

"I didn't ask where Gavin is."

"I know. I'm telling you."

She fisted her hands in her lap.

"Heard you screaming this morning." When Lyla said nothing he added, "Saw Blade bring you out, drug you. Heard the state your mom's in, don't fucking blame you."

The city loomed in the distance. She wanted to tell Angel to shut the fuck up, but had a feeling he would ignore her order.

"Heard your dad swung the other way and you killed him... and a bunch of others."

Lyla closed her eyes to stop herself from attacking him.

"You may not be born in our world, Lyla, but you're handling yourself just fine."

"Shut up," she whispered.

"You did what you had to. Life sucks and you're still here, breathing and protecting what's yours. There's no shame in that."

Silence descended and she thanked her lucky stars. She focused on keeping her mind blank as Angel navigated through the city to the hospital. He parked the Bugatti. Before he could turn off the car, Blade slid into the slot beside them. Lyla started towards the hospital and was brought to a halt by

Angel who snatched her hand and laced their fingers together.

"What the hell are you doing?" she snapped and tried to tug her hand away.

"You're shaking."

She hadn't noticed until he pointed it out. "That doesn't mean you need to hold my hand."

"Doesn't hurt." He eyed her disgruntled face and grinned. "You're cute."

"I'm not used to strange men holding my hand."

"We're family."

"How, exactly?"

"Gavin and I are first cousins."

Oh, shit. That was a little too close for comfort. "I don't need you to hold my hand. I'm fine."

He squeezed her hand. "You're not fine. Let me take care of you."

"Why do you care?" She didn't expect a bloodthirsty Roman to be the handholding type.

"When something happens to one of us, it happens to all of us."

"I'm not family."

"You are now. You're Gavin's, which means you're mine too."

She blinked. "Excuse me?"

"You're mine," he stated baldly. "Someone fucks with you, they fuck with me. You and Gavin have been without family for too long."

Lyla was so distracted by Angel's primitive views that it almost distracted her from what she was about to walk into. Lyla went up to the ICU desk and when she gave her mother's name, received a wary glance. She wasn't sure if it was

302

because of the nature of her mother's injuries, because the nurse heard about her freak out this morning or because of the host of men around her.

"We're limiting Beatrice Dalton's visitors," the nurse said, eyeing their group.

"I understand," Lyla said.

"We'll wait here," Angel said and kissed her cheek.

Lyla stared at him. She didn't know what to make of him. He was blunt, affectionate and annoying. She glanced at Blade before she followed the nurse to her mother's room.

"No changes," the nurse said.

Even though she knew what to expect, the sight of her mother's bandaged body with tubes coming out of her still hit her like a ton of bricks. She stopped in the doorway, unable to get her legs to move.

When she composed herself, she sat by her mother's side and cradled her hand. She stared at her mother's swollen eyelids and willed them to twitch or better yet, open. Nothing. Lyla rested her aching head on the edge of the bed and breathed. Her mother was all she had left. She had to live.

The beeping monitor and the sound of all the machines got on her nerves. She tried to ignore them but the longer she sat there, the worse it got. She hated seeing all the tubes and needles and found herself reaching for the IV to rip it out of her mother's arm before she jerked away. She was turning into a fucking psycho. Was she trying to kill her own mother? She forced herself to leave.

When she left the ICU she found Blade, Angel

303

and the rest of the guards in the hallway. Angel moved forward and took her hand again.

"Good. I'm starving," he said. "You hungry?"

"Hungry?"

"Yeah. Let's see what they have in the cafeteria. How's your mom?"

"Same," Lyla said numbly and looked down at their clasped hands. She was holding hands with a member of the Roman family, one of the most ruthless and notorious crime families in America.

Angel noticed her glance and shrugged.

"It's a habit you'll have to get used to. I'm always taking Luci out and you have to keep a hold on her or she'll disappear."

"Luci?"

"My sister."

"How old is she?" she asked, trying to imagine Angel escorting a young girl around New York City.

"Twenty-five."

Lyla was outraged. "You have to hold onto your twenty-five year old sister?"

"You don't know Luci. She could get into trouble at a library."

"Do you hold your brother's hands too?" she asked snidely, offended on Luci's behalf.

"Only when they're drunk," Angel said without missing a beat.

"Do you always hold women's hands?"

"Only the ones I don't want to lose track of."

"And you're not married?"

"I have wild oats to sow, baby."

"You just said family means everything, blah

304

blah."

"Yeah, but that doesn't mean *I* have to get married. I'm happy with nieces and nephews... and cousins. Lots of cousins. I'm built to protect, that's my job."

Although she wasn't hungry, Angel grabbed a salad and sandwich and settled with her at one of the tables.

"Eat," he said before he bit into his pizza.

When she glared at him, he grabbed her fork and stabbed greens and a piece of chicken. Clearly, he intended to feed her. She snatched the fork and took a bite. When she didn't go back for another bite, Angel took the fork and did the same process.

"I can feed myself!" she snapped.

"Then do so," he said.

"No wonder you've never married. No woman would put up with your bullshit," she muttered.

"It's not bullshit. I'm taking care of you."

"It's not your job to take care of me."

"Of course it is," he said.

Lyla looked at Blade. "I can't pass on these genes. I'm not having anymore kids."

"Don't count on it," Angel muttered.

Lyla didn't realize she'd reached for her sandwich until she swallowed the first bite. She glared at Angel who snickered. "You're annoying."

"So I've heard. By the by, Luci wants to visit when Gavin guts this motherfucker."

"Luci?" Blade echoed.

Angel looked up. "Yeah."

"She's coming to Las Vegas?" Blade asked sharply.

305

"When it's safe," Angel said.

Lyla raised her brows. "You know her?"

"Met her a long time ago," Blade said.

Angel's expression tightened. "Yes, a very long time ago."

She looked between them. "When?"

Blade glanced at Angel and then down at her food. "Finish your food and I'll tell you."

Angel held Blade's gaze for a long moment before he demolished his hospital food. Obviously, Blade had a history with the Romans. Not surprising, really, but she had the feeling it wasn't going to be a happy story. Nevertheless, she wanted to hear it. She ate as much as she could before she sat back. Blade took her tray and dumped it and signaled to the other guards who were already on their feet.

They walked out of the cafeteria and she asked, "So, what's the story?"

When Blade didn't speak, she glanced up and saw him looking down the corridor. She followed his gaze and halted when she saw Gavin striding towards her. He wore a black suit and crimson tie. Her stomach rebelled at the sight of him.

CHAPTER NINETEEN

Lyla

Lyla whirled, but found her way blocked by Angel and the other guards.

"Get out of my way!" she bellowed.

No one moved. She reached into her jacket for her gun. Blade disarmed her and took the second gun for good measure. Before she could snatch a weapon from one of them, a hard hand whirled her around and the next thing she knew, she was dangling over Gavin's shoulder.

"Let me go!" she shouted.

She wasn't up to a confrontation and she had nothing to say to him. She pounded his back and cursed when her hand hit one of his guns. That was going to leave a bruise.

She heard Angel laughing and braced her hands on Gavin's back to raise her head to give him a dirty look. Blade watched them with his arms crossed over his chest.

"Do something!" she snapped.

Blade shook his head at her before Gavin turned a corner and she lost sight of them. Lyla was about to scream her head off when Gavin slammed into an empty hospital room. The only light came through tiny slats in the blinds.

"Gavin, don't you dare—" she began, but lost her breath when he dropped her on the bed with enough force to stun her.

Gavin straddled her and yanked off his tie.

"What the fuck do you think you're—" she began, but was silenced by a hand over her mouth.

Lyla tried to bite and claw, but Gavin easily overpowered her. His tie replaced his hand. He pinned her arms to her sides using his thighs. Lyla had never been more enraged in her life. She surged beneath him and silently vowed to make his life a living hell.

The second she could wriggle a hand free, she did so and went for his eyes. Gavin grabbed her hand and lifted it over her head. Something cold and hard wrapped around her wrist. She tugged, realized she was handcuffed to the bedrail and screamed into his tie. Gavin bound her other hand just as quickly.

"You motherfucker!" Lyla seethed through the gag.

Gavin splayed his body over hers, subduing her kicking legs easily. He gripped her jaw when she tried to head butt him and leaned down, close enough to see the determination burning in his eyes.

"You aren't allowed to hate me," he said quietly.

Lyla glared at him. She could do whatever the fuck she wanted. He couldn't control her emotions.

Gavin surveyed her rebellious face and then kissed her over the gag. She jerked her head back. He wasn't perturbed. He kissed the curve of her jaw, the line of her throat and then slid down to her chest. Lyla stiffened as he unbuttoned her shirt.

"I really like the bras with these front clasps," Gavin said conversationally as he undid hers.

Lyla grit her teeth as he licked her nipple and then sucked one into his mouth. Lyla yanked on her cuffs, which fucking hurt. She tried to twist away without success. His hand stroked her belly as he played with her breasts as if they were in their bedroom at home and he had all the time in the world. She saw a shadow pass the window and began to struggle again.

Gavin flicked her nipple with his tongue and she jumped. He released one breast and moved to the other. Lyla hung onto the bedrails as she tried to contain her body's reaction to his ministrations. He thought he could distract her with sex? He was sorely mistaken.

Minutes passed and her toes curled in her boots. Fucking Gavin. The sound of his suckling filled the room. She trembled beneath him. The fucker knew every sweet spot she had and was trying to drive her crazy.

Gavin unexpectedly buried his face between her breasts and clutched her to him. He took a deep breath and then another before his grip eased. He looked up and caught her gaze.

"Blade told me what happened. *Everything* that happened," he said gravely. "I'm sorry."

She didn't want to hear that from him. Sorry wouldn't erase the fresh blood on her hands or her mother lying comatose in ICU.

"I know you blame me for what happened with your parents."

Lyla erupted beneath him. Gavin straddled her middle and gripped her face with both hands. She had no choice but to meet his gaze. Any semblance of cool control was gone. Gavin's eyes were seething and he was breathing hard, as if he was trying to hold something back.

"I'll take the blame for your mom, but I refuse to feel guilty about your father. If you didn't kill him, I *would*," he hissed. "And nothing you said could stop me from making him suffer for even thinking of betraying you. Thank *fuck* you had the courage to do it, baby girl, or I would be kneeling by your grave right now. I wouldn't survive that."

Lyla closed her eyes against a surge of tears.

"I know you want time." A pause and then, "When have I ever given you that?"

Lyla opened her eyes and glared through the tears.

"You don't need time, you need me, Lyla." He shook his head, kissed both breasts and then slid down her body to her belly. "And I need you."

He unzipped her jeans and began to peel them off. Lyla spread her thighs in a vain attempt to keep her jeans on. Gavin cupped her pussy and she automatically clamped her thighs together, allowing him to yank them off. Fucker. A group of nurses paused outside of the room and she panicked. She kicked him in the shoulder and jerked her head at the silhouettes. He barely spared them a glance, caught her ankle during the next kick and bent her leg up and wide.

"Gavin, don't!" Lyla hissed, which sounded unintelligible even to her own ears.

Gavin settled between her thighs and kissed her over her black lace underwear. She jerked and then tried to jam her heel into the back of his head with no luck. Gavin rested his face against her inner thigh and laughed softly, which made her renew her efforts to kill her husband.

"You should know, you fighting me is only making me want you more," he said softly.

Lyla yanked hard on the cuffs, which clanged loudly.

"I like your bite." He nipped her sensitive skin. "And you like mine."

Arrogant motherfucker. She wished she was bone dry... but she wasn't. Her stupid body was ready for him.

"Blade told me you took out four trained men and then used dead men for target practice in the warehouse. I never imagined you like this, but I like it." He ripped off her underwear and ignored her muffled swearing. "No, I *love* it. You protect what's yours at any cost. You're my equal, baby girl, my badass. *Mine*."

Gavin put his mouth on her. She tried not to react, but it was impossible. Gavin went deep and ate her out as if she was the rarest delicacy on the planet. She panted through the gag and didn't even have the option of trying to brain him by clamping his head between her thighs since he had them splayed wide.

It took her less than five minutes not to give a fuck about the crowd in the hallway. She forgot why she was in the hospital, how Gavin fucked up and about her desert hunt. All that mattered was

311

what Gavin could give her—sweet oblivion.

"Gavin," she moaned.

His finger dipped into her pussy and then trailed to her ass. His finger explored and then circled teasingly. Lyla didn't hesitate. She rocked back on his finger and took it up her ass. Gavin groaned as if he was the one being tortured and raised his head.

"I can't," he hissed.

He sat up, unzipped his slacks and planted himself deep with one thrust. There was no finesse or teasing now. He was breathing hard and his hands cupped her ass so he could go as deep as possible. Her hands strained against the cuffs while her body undulated against him.

"I need this," Gavin said hoarsely and buried his face in her hair. "I need to make sure you're with me."

She was with him, all right. She was so with him that if she wasn't cuffed, she would be clawing the hell out of his back and commanding him to fuck her hard.

"I can't do this again, Lyla. My heart can't take it," Gavin said as he rocked inside of her. "This needs to end. Now."

She couldn't agree more.

He lifted her legs over his shoulder and he was hitting that spot—but not hard enough!

"Gavin!" she shouted and found him watching her.

"You're beautiful."

She milked his shaft with her inner muscles. His eyes narrowed and he stopped his teasing, soft rhythm that wasn't taking her over the edge.

"You want me?" he growled.

She nodded and then glared for good measure.

"Then that's what you'll get," he said and slammed home.

Lyla hung onto the handrails as Gavin did what he did best. She was glad for the gag since it muffled her moans. Gavin hit that spot and she erupted. Gavin rode her through it and then tucked his head beside hers on the pillow as he pounded her into the bed until he came with her name on his lips.

Lyla floated. She didn't have a care in the world. She was cock drunk and liking it. Nothing existed outside of this room.

Gavin lifted his head. His expression was too severe for her liking.

"Now, you're going to listen," Gavin said.

She stared at him. Couldn't this wait?

"I went to Maine to kill Huskin."

Lyla stiffened. Drowsy weightlessness was replaced by cold, hard reality. Gavin, who was still inside of her, rocked, sending pleasurable zaps through her still sensitive body.

"You know what kind of man I am," Gavin said, eyes boring into hers. "I'm not the schmuck who will stand aside while another man who has history with my wife makes a play. No man is allowed to touch you. No man is allowed to come between us. You don't protect another man from me. Huskin overstepped. He knows the rumors about me and still made a play for you, one he knew could mean his life. He made that decision."

Gavin brushed his hand down her cheek. He

was watching her closely.

"You understand?" he asked.

Grudgingly, she nodded and felt him relax a little. He kissed her brow and continued to shift inside of her as if he wanted to keep her ready for another round.

"You don't choose another man over me, Lyla."

She glared at him. She *wasn't*! As if he could read her thoughts, his eyes narrowed and he leaned in closer.

"You did. I'm your first priority, not some ex you haven't seen in years, even if he has a heart of gold," Gavin sneered. "I was raised to take what I want and destroy anybody in my way." His hands smoothed down her sides. "I don't take chances with you."

"But—"

Gavin clamped his hand over the gag. "Hush, baby girl."

Lyla glared at him.

"I get it," he said.

Get what?

"I get why you were with him." He burrowed deeper inside of her so that her mouth fell open on a gasp. "You wanted sweet and normal, baby girl, but you aren't. You never were. You were pretending. What you had with him, not real. You feel this?"

He rocked inside of her. Her toes curled and her moan filled the room.

"This is what I'm fighting for, what I'll die for. You were made for me. Maybe I'm not what you wanted, but I'm what you need." He kissed away a tear at the corner of her eye. "You should have told him about Nora from the start."

Lyla jerked. How could he know that?

"Knowing you had a kid made a difference to him. Why do you think I insisted on getting you pregnant? It matters, having a baby together. It binds you irrevocably to me. Even he gets that." Gavin tugged on her earlobe with his teeth. "You think I don't have time to listen to your phone calls? You're wrong. Everything that concerns you is my top priority. Don't ever make the mistake of thinking you come second to anything."

He began to move with more purpose.

"Huskin's resourceful and now an employee of mine."

She couldn't believe it.

"He created a sophisticated security system designed to send evidence to another source within hours of my crime." Gavin tucked his head beside hers and muttered, "Fucker's too smart for his own good."

"Gavin," she huffed.

He nuzzled her sweetly while his body drove her nuts.

"Being thousands of miles away when you needed me..." His voice changed, became rougher. "Worst feeling in the world knowing I left you open for that sadistic fuck to—"

There was an anguished note in his voice. She raised her hand to touch him, but it was still bound.

"I fucked up. I'll take whatever you want to throw at me. You shouldn't have been put in a position to do the things you had to do." Gavin raised his head and looked down at her. "But thank fuck you did. I'm going to make the Phantom suffer. I'm going to bring you his head so you know it's really over." He brushed his thumb over her bottom lip. "Do you hate me, baby?"

Of course she didn't hate him, but she wasn't happy about being gagged, handcuffed and fucked in a hospital room. He was insane. He didn't give a fuck what anyone thought and there was no stopping him when he wanted something. She glared at him and gave him nothing.

Gavin squeezed her breast and then reached into his jacket pocket and pulled out a key.

"I like seeing you cuffed and gagged," he mused as he released one hand. "We need to do this more often."

Lyla yanked the gag down. "Get off, Gavin!"

He kissed her cheek when she turned her face away. "Still mad?"

"I'm going to be mad at you for eternity!"

"Eternity's a long time," he said as he released her other hand, which she immediately used to brace on his shoulders to keep space between them. This was a spectacular fail since he gave her his weight and her bridge collapsed.

"Fucking heavy ass brute," she huffed.

"I told you when we married to punish me," Gavin said as he rolled so she was on top and then manipulated the bed controls so they were in a sitting position. "Give me your best shot, Lyla." One hand went to her clit. "And I'll give you mine."

"Gavin, you can't—"

Her head kicked back as he simultaneously pinched her clit, bit her neck and slammed balls deep into her.

"I can do anything I want," he growled against her skin. "I'm going to do whatever it takes to have you with me."

"You're such—" she panted and stopped when he did something amazing with his cock. Against her will, her arms went around him.

"Such what?" Gavin crooned into her sweat soaked hair as he controlled her movements with his hands on her ass.

"You're—you—you fuck—" She couldn't string a sentence together, much less think of a decent insult when he was pleasuring her.

"This is how I need you, desperate for me."

Lyla was dimly aware of the mechanical whirr of the bed as it switched positions. She braced her hands on either side of his head as the bed flattened and caught a glimpse of his hungry expression before he sank a hand into her hair and pulled her down until their lips collided. He banded a hand around her waist to keep her in place as he fucked her. Gavin drank in her moans, pleas and whimpers and demanded more. She ripped the sheets from the bed as she climaxed, wrapped herself around him and hung on for dear life. Gavin planted himself deep and came while brushing kisses over her face.

"You don't play fair," she whispered.

He didn't answer as he ran his hands over her naked body while he was still fully clothed. She laid her cheek on his chest and listened to his rapid heartbeat as her tremors ebbed.

"I was so scared," she whispered.

Gavin's hands stilled.

317

"I told Carmen to run with Nora. All I had was one gun, eight bullets. I hid and waited." She let out a shuddering breath and Gavin's hands began to move again, stroking and soothing. "I heard them talking about fucking mom. I killed them."

She could still feel the gun bucking in her hand and the chill of the desert pressing on her.

"I went... cold. I didn't care who they were. I just pulled the trigger." She let out a long breath. "All I could think about was what they were doing to her." Lyla swallowed hard. "I shot dead bodies."

"Would it make you feel better to know I've done the same?"

"You have?"

"They're good target practice."

She raised her head. "Are you serious?"

"Lyla, no matter what you do, I've already done it."

"That shouldn't make me feel better, but it does. Do you have any leads?"

Gavin's energy, which had lessened considerably after two orgasms, flooded the room. The hairs on the nape of her neck rose.

"Not yet, but I'll get him, Lyla."

"He's playing us." Cold fury poured through her. She couldn't stop it. She dug her nails into his chest and felt his muscles flex in response. "I want his head, Gavin. Whatever it takes, you do it."

Gavin kissed her hard and deep and then drew away with his chest heaving.

"You were made for me," Gavin murmured. "Do you still hate me?"

She thumped him on the shoulder and slid off

him. Her legs weren't quite steady when they hit the floor. "I'll think about it."

She swiped up her jeans and was thankful for the connecting bathroom so she could wash up. She looked thoroughly fucked. Her cheeks were flushed, hair a tangled mess, lips swollen and eyes glazed with satisfaction. Damn Gavin.

He came into the bathroom, looking disgustingly slick. His suit was a bit rumpled, but he appeared just as composed as he had when he brought her in here.

"I'm leaving Blade, Angel and eight guards," Gavin said, running a hand through his hair. "I have two men watching Carmen's mother just in case."

Lyla nodded and turned to face him. "Angel tells me he's going to take your place."

Gavin said nothing.

"He's... interesting."

"You'll get used to him."

"Can he do it?" she asked, thinking of Vinny.

"He's from New York."

"Meaning?"

"Meaning he won't let anyone fuck with him." He caged her against the sink. "You okay?"

She nodded.

He cupped her face. "I'm sorry."

She blinked back tears. "It's done. Go get him."

He kissed her and then led her out of the hospital room. Blade and Angel were talking in the hallway. They turned when the door opened.

"Did you kiss and make up?" Angel asked with a lascivious grin.

"You're annoying," Lyla snapped.

"Lyla!"

She looked down the corridor and saw Marcus rushing towards her. When he reached for her, Angel blocked his way.

"Who are you?" Angel asked aggressively.

Marcus stopped and looked Angel up and down before he asked, "Who are you?"

"Angel Roman."

Marcus glanced at Gavin before he held out a hand. "Marcus. We've never met. I usually deal with Raul."

"Raul's the businessman," Angel acknowledged and shook his hand.

Marcus walked around Angel and engulfed Lyla in a tight hug. "How are you, honey?"

"You let him touch your wife?" Angel snapped at Gavin.

"Lyla won't let me kill him and he makes me a lot of money," Gavin said.

"Still, he isn't family," Angel muttered.

Lyla rolled her eyes at the Neanderthals and pulled back to give Marcus a tremulous smile. "What are you doing here?"

"Gavin told me what happened. Are you all right?"

"I'm okay."

"Carmen?"

"Good. She's home with Nora."

Marcus cupped her face. "Be safe, damn it."

"I will."

Marcus kissed her on the cheek. "I have to get back, but I had to see you." He looked to Gavin. "Let me know when it's over."

Gavin nodded. "I will. Now, get back to the casino. The cops are all over us."

Marcus nodded and left without another word.

"He's a ballsy bastard, isn't he?" Angel muttered.

"He's great," Lyla said defensively.

"You can't touch men like that outside of the family. It's indecent."

Lyla's mouth sagged. "What did you just say?"

"Gav, you can't let her—"

"Since when did a hug equal giving a guy head?" Lyla snapped.

"We don't let our women—" Angel began.

"Not the time." Gavin cupped her face and kissed her one last time. "I love you. Stay with Blade and Angel."

"Where are you going?" she asked.

"Hunting."

With that, he walked away, leaving her with mixed emotions.

"Can you walk?" Angel asked with false concern.

Blade elbowed Angel with enough force to make him gasp for air and sink to one knee. Lyla tipped her nose in the air and walked back to the ICU. When she sat by her mother's side and took her hand again, she felt more human and a lot less like a ticking time bomb.

Gavin would find Sadist and kill him. She had to keep that front and center in her mind so she wouldn't go crazy. Despite the fact that Sadist always seemed to be five steps ahead, she had to remember that he was human and could bleed... and therefore die.

Lyla looked up as two nurses walked in. Lyla released her mother's hand and took a step back so they could do what they needed to. She watched the nurse check her mother's drip and noticed that her hand was shaking. Too much caffeine?

"Mrs. Pyre," the other nurse said, drawing her attention. "Are you doing all right?"

"As well as can be under the circumstances," Lyla said.

"Do the police have any leads?"

She felt something tight grip her heart. "No."

The second nurse rummaged in the cart beside the bed. Obviously not finding what she was looking for, she moved towards another cart in the corner.

"I haven't seen a case this bad in years," the first nurse said and squeezed Lyla's arm. "I'm so sorry."

"Thank you," Lyla said and was dimly aware of the second nurse moving behind her.

"We're going to do everything we can for your mother, okay?"

"Okay—" Lyla began and then hissed when something pricked her neck. She recognized the feeling since Blade sedated her only a couple of hours ago. She reached up to pull the syringe out, but before she could her legs gave out and she crashed to the floor.

"Hurry up, get her on the gurney. We'll wheel her out under a sheet and then—" the nurse said and then everything went black.

CHAPTER TWENTY

Lyla

Lyla woke feeling like her arms were going to fall off. She moaned and realized several things simultaneously. She was on her knees on cold, hard concrete. She was also blindfolded, gagged and her hands were bound behind her. It took a full minute for her to think past the pounding in her head. She scooted backwards to ease the tension on her shoulders. Her hands hit cold stone and skated down to discover that the chain shackling her wrists together behind her back were threaded through a metal circle at the base of the wall. The length of chain allowed her to rest on her knees, but not enough to stand.

Lyla rested her back against the wall, but this did nothing to alleviate her cramping muscles. Memories of the nurses passed through her mind. She bared her teeth as rage beat back the fear. If those nurses hurt her mother, she would gut them herself.

Lyla shifted restlessly and heard the clink of a chain, which seemed unnaturally loud in the enclosed space. Unlike the cuffs Gavin used on her earlier, the metal shackles on her wrist were at least three inches thick and no joke. Her watch with the

GPS was gone and so was her wedding ring. She was still in her jeans and button up top, but her leather jacket and shoulder holster was gone.

The sound of an agonizing scream reached her ears followed by another. Her heart leapt. Was this Sadist's torture chamber? Her mouth watered as bile rose. She swallowed with difficulty since the gag was so tight that her mouth couldn't close. Her lips ached. She tried to shift the gag out of her mouth by rubbing it against her shoulder. When her neck cramped, she straightened abruptly and let out an infuriated scream.

Fuck Sadist! If he was going to kill her, get it over with! Even as her emotions raged, an image of Nora appeared in her mind. She yanked savagely against the chain. Fuck. Nora... Nora needed her. So did Gavin. Oh, Gavin. He was going to Hulk out. And Carmen was going to freak out. She should have chilled at home like Carmen said, but no, she had to sit by her mother's bedside and now here she was in... wherever the fuck she was.

She wasn't sure if seconds, minutes or hours passed. Her shoulders burned, went numb and then came to life with a dozen needles stabbing into her, making her moan in pain. She tried to work the gag free without success. She went through every emotion possible, yanking at the chains and growling like a wild animal when rage obliterated all thought and then giving into tears of helpless rage and then despair.

Lyla heard the jingle of keys and thought she was hallucinating. Then, she heard the squeak of a doorknob and felt a slight gust of wind as the door swung open. Through the blindfold, she saw the faintest hint of light. She balled her hands into fists and waited for whatever came next. Would he stab her to death? Beat the crap out of her or just slit her throat?

She breathed heavily through her nose as she waited. And waited. The screams she heard earlier were loud and piercing now that the door was open. Lyla's heart pounded with dread and fear. She scooted back and then stiffened when the door closed and she was thrown back into complete darkness. What the fuck?

There was no sound in the room. Was a guard checking on her? Someone had the wrong room? She didn't hear the scrape of a key in the lock. Dizzy with fear, she waited for something to happen. Long minutes passed. She shivered and then moaned as a shaft of pain shot through her arms.

"Lyla."

The soft voice came out of the darkness right in front of her. Lyla screamed and reared back so hard that she collided with the wall. It was him, Sadist. She would never forget that voice. Her body erupted with goose bumps and she completely lost her shit. She fought against the chains, desperate to get away from him. Two years passed since this monster murdered Manny and carved her up. There was no one to save her, just like last time. This was it. This was the end.

"It's been too long," Sadist crooned.

Lyla faced the direction his voice emanated from and screamed at him. If she weren't bound, she would claw his eyes out and try to kill him with her teeth.

"I must say, I like seeing you like this."

Of course he did. He was a sick fuck.

"You know, Lyla, you're quite fascinating. You have nine lives. You're my only victim who survived. The cuts I made were fatal and yet, here you are."

Oh, God, he sounded closer. She imagined he had a knife held in front of him that she could impale herself on if she was stupid enough to try to attack him with her arms bound behind her. She tried to get away from him, but there was nowhere to go. She willed the wall to swallow her. She couldn't be at the mercy of this man twice. God wasn't that cruel, was he?

"Imagine my surprise when I bribe Gavin's guards to kill you and even pregnant you survive. What are the odds?"

The touch of a smooth hand against her cheek made her stomach revolt. She edged away, but the stupid chains kept her in place. The touch came again, a finger stroking down her cheek and then her neck.

"You're so beautiful. Everyone sees what you want them to see, but I know better."

He grabbed the front of her shirt and pulled. Buttons popped off and then rolled across the floor. She scooted back, which did nothing to deter him. He ran his hands over her raised chest scars and hummed in the back of his throat. Her stomach heaved and she resolutely swallowed. Oh, God. What was he doing?

"You bear my mark, Lyla. What does Pyre think of that? I hope he thinks of me every time he touches you. The almighty Gavin Pyre brought to his knees by little old me."

Sadist chuckled. She was lightheaded with rage. This monster killed Manny, stabbed her and was responsible for the brutal rape of her mother. He was right here, inches from her and she could do nothing.

"I heard you killed your father." A pause and then, "That's something you and I have in common, killing a family member, but they deserved it, right? You've become quite heartless, Lyla. I *like* it."

His hand collared her throat and brushed over her fluttering pulse. She tried to evade his touch with no luck. She was powerless to do anything and he knew it.

"Such fire. What happened to the sweet innocent who pleaded for Manny Pyre's life?" Even as her breath caught in her throat, he continued, "You still don't know who I am, do you? I always wondered if you would figure it out, but you never noticed me. I thought you were different at first, but you turned out to be like every other woman. I hate women. I'm sure you've put that together already. I've never met one who wasn't focused on the bottom line. My mom sold me to my dad for two thousand bucks and my dad abused the hell out of me, trying to turn me into a tough guy like Gavin. What dad never realized is I don't have to be a tough guy like Gavin. I can be my own type of man and that's even more powerful. I'll never be able to kill Gavin, but I know someone who can."

She felt a thrill of fear when she heard the hiss of a zipper. One hand slid through her hair and over her bruised lips.

"I approached your father. He was in deep, of course. He was about to lose his house and was ripe for the picking since he hates Gavin. Who doesn't? He's a rich, macho asshole who thinks the world should bow at his feet. He collects more enemies than anyone I know, but too many still fear him. So, they're here tonight to watch the crime lord take his final bow."

His hand traced her chest scars with frightening familiarity.

"Your father sold you and your daughter to me for five hundred thousand. We took your mother for insurance and raped her in front of him so he knew the score. I never intended to let either of them live. First you survive my blade and now your mother. It's quite... aggravating."

When she screamed her fury at him, he tapped her nose reprovingly.

"Tonight is my finale, the end of the Pyre Empire and the beginning of my reign. Lucifer will lure Gavin here after I'm done with you. Lucifer's the only one who can take Gavin and he has a score to settle with him. I need Gavin's end to be public so there's no mistaking who's in control now. Too bad you won't be able to watch, but I promised Lucifer I'd give him a show in return for ending Gavin."

He sank a hand into her hair and gripped as he pressed his cheek to hers and inhaled deeply. His skin shouldn't be soft, smooth and warm. No human could be this evil. Lyla tried to knock him off balance, but the fucking chain kept her anchored and harmless. Fuck!

"Are you ready to give everyone a show?" A cold finger traveled over the scar inches from her heart. His breath hitched. "Lucifer taught me how to kill, how to prolong a death and how to make people respect you. You have to do it with *flair*. Gavin's good at that, but then again, so am I."

His voice was uneven. Her heartbeat slowed as if his voice was poison. Her body felt heavy with dread and hopelessness. This is how she would die, with Sadist's voice in her ears.

"Unfortunately, Lucifer says I'm not allowed to touch you until everyone's present to enjoy it. Shame. I'm going to enjoy this, Lyla. I always finish what I start, which means I'm paying your daughter a visit tomorrow."

His hand gripped her hair and yanked back savagely. He groaned and then she felt a string of something wet and warm splatter over her face. She retched and tried to turn her face away, but Sadist kept her still until he was done. He panted as he examined his handiwork and then shoved her so she fell on her side on the floor.

"That's for my father," he said.

There was no sound of retreating footsteps, but she felt a draft when the door opened. She saw a flash of light through the blindfold and the sound of torturous screams before the door closed, enclosing her in hell.

CHAPTER TWENTY-ONE

Gavin

Gavin blasted the woman's head off and allowed the warm spray of blood to splash over him. He waited for a flicker of satisfaction, but he felt absolutely nothing.

The nurse who had taken Lyla from him did this as a favor for her crack head boyfriend who worked for Marcel, a gangbanger Gavin had never heard of. Both nurses, the crack head boyfriend and Marcel lay at his feet. None of them had shit for him, which meant they were pawns being used by a higher up. It had to be Phantom. The thought of Lyla back in his grasp made his insides contract. He held up Lyla's wedding ring and watch, which the nurse intended to pawn.

"What now?" Angel asked.

He called on every contact he had. Everyone's phones were off. No one was at home, in their office or on the Strip. They were just... gone. Something was going down tonight. He sensed it with every fiber of his being. He had no leads, no one to hunt. Nothing.

His phone rang. He reached into his pocket, eyed the unavailable number and put it to his ear.

"Gavin."

It took him a moment to place the voice. When he did, something close to fear shot through his system. "Lucifer."

The man on the other end chuckled. "I'm flattered you recognize my voice."

It had been years, but no one forgot the sound of the devil's voice. Angel and Blade were watching him, but they didn't ask questions, they waited patiently.

"I have something you want," Lucifer said.

Every hair on the nape of his neck stood up.

"I'll be waiting for you."

Lucifer hung up. Gavin slowly lowered the phone and took a deep breath.

Blade's hands balled into fists at his side. "Lucifer's involved in this shit?"

"So it seems."

"Who's Lucifer?" Angel asked.

"I need to go home," Gavin said and snatched the keys for the Bugatti out of Angel's pocket.

"What the fuck? You're going to get changed when you know where we have to go?" Angel asked.

"Lucifer won't start until we get there. He likes an audience." Gavin glanced at Blade. "Burn the fucking house down."

Gavin got into the Bugatti and tore out of the neighborhood. In his rearview mirror he saw the flicker of flames.

Nine hours ago Angel forced his way into the ICU and found Lyla missing. It took too fucking long for them to figure out what happened and hunt these fuckers down. When he got the call about

Lyla missing, Blade had a syringe ready, but Gavin's wrath was ice cold. He couldn't afford to lose his shit.

Gavin pulled up to his home. The guards that came towards the car froze when he emerged looking like an extra from Kill Bill. He walked into the house and took the stairs two at a time. He stripped off his suit, showered and redressed. When he was done he slipped on brass knuckles and strapped on a collection of knives. He walked out of the bedroom and hesitated only a moment before he entered the nursery.

Carmen sat in the rocking chair with Nora in the crook of her arm. Carmen's expression was ravaged with worry and fear. Bloodshot eyes flicked to him when he entered. She rose.

"Did you find her?" Carmen whispered.

"I got a call from Lucifer."

He didn't need to say more. Carmen understood. All the blood drained out of her face.

"Lyla's in Hell?"

Gavin didn't answer. He didn't allow himself to wonder what they'd done to her because that would shatter his control and he couldn't go into Hell with anything but a clear head. He had to believe she was there, alive and whole. Any other alternative was unacceptable. He took Nora from Carmen. His daughter blinked up at him with Lyla's eyes. The edges of his control began to fray. He had to suppress the killing haze. Not yet. He buried his face against his daughter for a moment and drank her in.

This would end tonight. If Lyla didn't return,

neither would he.

"Gavin," Carmen whispered.

He clenched his teeth to hold back the rage building in his throat. His hands shook as he held Nora. He looked down at her as she kicked his chest and waved her arms. She looked up at him with such trust and innocence. *I'll bring Mom back.* He said it silently because he wasn't capable of speaking. He tipped Nora against his chest and took a deep breath, the first in what felt like hours.

"Gavin." Carmen's baby blue eyes shimmered with tears. "Bring her back."

He nodded and handed Nora over. "Take care of her."

Her fear clouded the air. "Gavin."

"No matter what happens, you take care of Nora," he ordered.

Tears began to fall. "Gavin."

"Promise me," he snapped.

"Gavin, you can't do this to me."

"Promise me, Carmen."

Carmen grabbed a handful of his shirt and yanked. He obliged and took a step forward. He and Carmen had a long and complicated history. They loved with an abandonment one never recovered from and they loved the same people, Vinny and Lyla. They'd both lost Vinny. He'd be fucking damned if he lost Lyla and he saw the same fire in Carmen's eyes. If Carmen didn't have Nora to care for, she would come with him. He had no doubt Carmen would spill blood if it meant getting her cousin back.

"You bring Lyla back to me," Carmen hissed as

tears spilled down her cheeks. "And you make that motherfucker *pay*."

He nodded and she released him.

"You got this, Gavin."

"You armed?" he asked, even though there was a host of men on property.

Carmen lifted her sweater to show a gold gun in the waistband of her pants. He nodded and turned away from her.

"Be safe, Gavin," she called after him.

He walked away and blocked out the sound of Nora fussing. Angel and Blade were waiting in the driveway. Gavin glanced at his men who looked uneasy. It was clear Blade told them their destination.

"Good luck, boss," Barrett said and several others echoed it.

Gavin nodded and slid into the passenger seat of the SUV. Blade floored it. No one spoke as Blade zoomed towards the neon lights of the city.

"I called Marcus, told him if this goes bad, he becomes CEO," Blade said.

Gavin nodded and glanced at Angel in the backseat. "You don't have to come."

"Don't, Gav."

"You don't know what this is."

"Then why don't you explain it to me since Blade hasn't said shit. Who's Lucifer? You think he's the one who did in Uncle Manny?"

"No, it wasn't Lucifer." He was sure of it. Lucifer didn't wear masks. He *wanted* people to know about his kills.

"So Lucifer is *helping* the guy who did in Uncle

Manny," Angel surmised.

"Looks that way."

"And this Lucifer is a big shot in the underworld?"

"Not in the underworld."

"Then where?"

"In Hell."

"Hell?"

"Hell is a Death Club."

"A what?"

"An underground fight club gladiator style where only one opponent lives. No guns allowed. It's also a brothel and slave trade hub."

Angel leaned between the two front seats. "And this is all under the radar?"

"Yes."

"An underground fight club, huh?"

"The brothel is for hardcore customers. It's common for the whores to die on the job," Blade said. "And who knows what else goes on there."

"Why would Lucifer want Lyla or work with the guy who did in Uncle Manny?" Angel asked.

"Because he has a score to settle with Gavin," Blade said. "He beat him once, but Gavin broke the rules and Lucifer's never forgiven him for it."

"How'd you break the rules?"

"Only one opponent survives," Gavin said. "I didn't kill him."

"Why not?"

"Because I didn't want to run Hell."

A pause and then, "So what did you do?"

"I knocked him out and left. Haven't been back since. Lyla's the only reason I'd go back to Hell and Lucifer knows it."

"So you think Lucifer kidnapped Lyla so you two can duel to the death?" Angel asked.

"I don't know." He had a feeling Phantom was involved. Lucifer wasn't the kidnapping type.

"How long ago has it been since you beat him?"

"Five years ago." The day after Lyla left him the first time.

"Whose side is Lucifer on?"

"No one's." Gavin rubbed his thumb against the brass knuckles, which had done damage in his youth. "In Hell anything goes. The people that go to a place like this are killers looking for the kind of entertainment they can't get anywhere else." He thought of Lyla being in a place like that and closed his eyes. Lucifer wouldn't do anything to her yet.

"How come you never told me about Hell? Fuck. This place sounds like my type of Disneyland."

"You might want to call Raul," Blade said.

"No need. We're all coming out of this alive and with Lyla," Angel said.

Blade bypassed the glittering Strip and turned onto a dingy street with broken streetlights, dirty liquor stores and abandoned buildings. Blade pulled into the parking lot of a nude bar. The sign out front wasn't lit and there were only two other cars in the vicinity.

"No one's here," Angel said.

"There's lots of ways into Hell. This is one of them," Blade said. "There's a locked compartment under your seat. Stash your gun there."

Gavin didn't take his eyes from the shabby

building, which had no windows.

"You have a knife?" Blade asked Angel.

"Of course."

"Good. You're going to need it," Blade said as they stepped into the bar.

Death and depression clung to the walls of this place. He could taste it in his mouth. The dancers moved with a sluggishness that said they were high on something. The men lounging in the dark corners didn't move or speak. The beat of music struck a dark chord in him. The type of people who were drawn to this place had no hope or souls. These men didn't care whether they lived or died. Once you entered Hell, your life was on the line. Many entered, few left breathing.

Gavin ignored the dancers, patrons and bartender who watched him weave between the tables. He walked through an open door beside the stage. The light here wasn't much better. He walked down a hallway with rotting planks and into the dressing room of the dancers who were doing drugs and completely oblivious to their presence. He turned into the walk in closet, which was filled with the shit strippers wore before they bared it all. He pushed on the wall of hooker shoes and it swung open.

"Holy fuck. We don't have shit like this in New York. We have to step it up," Angel murmured.

Gavin led the way down the narrow, creaking staircase and approached a group of men guarding a black metal door. They were smoking and playing poker. One man looked up and surveyed them with one eye. The empty socket of his other was on full display.

"We got Vegas royalty here, boys," he drawled.

The men threw down their cards and started patting him down.

"You fighting?" one of the men asked.

Gavin didn't answer because it went without saying. They spied his brass knuckles and admired his knives before they moved onto Blade.

"That you, Blade? It's been a while, hasn't it?" One Eye stepped to the side so he could see Angel. "Who are you, pretty boy?"

"This is my cousin, Angel," Gavin said.

One Eye grinned, showing that he had three teeth left.

"We make demons out of angels here." One Eye suddenly narrowed his eyes. "Your cousin?" He looked more sharply at Angel. "You a Roman?"

Angel nodded and One Eye elbowed his friend. "Roque's brother."

"You know my brother?" Angel asked.

"Everyone knows your brother. He stepped into the arena several times. Those were nights to remember."

"They're clean," the other man announced.

"Lucifer expecting you?" One Eye asked Gavin.

"Yes."

"I have a feeling tonight's gonna be entertaining, boys." His eye roved over the three of them and nodded. "*Very* entertaining."

One Eye opened the door and gave them a mocking bowed as they passed.

"Welcome to Hell, my brothers."

Gavin walked into Hell and heard Angel suck in

a breath. Hell was a two-story amphitheater with wide staircases that led down to the sandy Pit, which saw more action than the Colosseum. Nearly every seat in the arena was taken. The only sound in Hell was the sound of metal clashing as the men in the Pit fought with swords, rousing Gavin's beast.

Gavin turned to the bar and scattered tables where men watched the action on the screens instead of in the bloodthirsty crowd where their throats could be cut. Gavin focused on a man drinking Coke, lounging at a table with a crossword puzzle in front of him. The giant man watched the TV screen as idly as if he were watching a commercial. He snorted in disgust when one of the fighters was decapitated. He twirled a pen between two fingers and scanned the crowd. When he saw Gavin, the pen stopped moving and a wide smile curved his mouth. Lucifer's Polynesian, Russian and Swedish blood made him into a monster of a man. Despite his size and reputation, he managed to appear as unthreatening as a California surfer, but Gavin knew better. Lucifer knew every method on earth to kill a man. Gavin resisted the compulsion to grab his knife as they approached.

"I never thought I'd see the day that you lost control of the underworld," Lucifer said in greeting.

"I want my wife," Gavin said.

Lucifer waved a hand with red nail polish. "I heard you were partial to your wife, but I didn't believe it. What makes her different from any other?"

He wasn't going to have this conversation with him. "Give her to me."

Lucifer ignored his order and steepled his hands in front of him, fingers touching at the tip, perfectly aligned. "A friend of mine came to me with a generous offer. He offered to share the experience of torturing your wife in the Pit using his considerable skills and then summon you for the rematch I've been waiting for."

Blade and Angel crowded him, ready to restrain him if need be, but Gavin's demon was in control and it wasn't easily baited, not with Lyla's life at stake.

"This is generous of my friend," Lucifer continued blithely, "but you and I go way back, Gavin, and I want a fair fight. I want you clearheaded, not distracted because you see your wife in pieces."

"I have no interest in ruling Hell," Gavin said.

Lucifer's eyes danced with excitement. "So sure you'll beat me?"

"Yes." He had no choice but to win. He wouldn't think of any other outcome.

Lucifer waved a hand. "Come now, Gavin. I think you'll come to appreciate Hell as much as I do. My friend can run the underworld and you, Hell. I'm sure you two can see eye to eye if you put your hostilities aside."

"No," Gavin said.

"Was what he did so bad? He set you free, Gavin."

"What the fuck are you talking about?"

"After he murdered your father, you went on a rampage. I'm impressed you managed to hide that many bodies. That's *you*, your true self, the one your father knew you would become. That's why he put you in the Pit at twelve."

Gavin felt Angel's glance and ignored it.

"You and I are one and the same." Lucifer licked his lips. "We need violence the way other people need sex."

"What I need is my wife."

Lucifer snorted in disgust. "Your obsession with this one woman is unhealthy."

"Is she alive?" Blade asked.

Lucifer's eyes flicked to him and narrowed. "Going soft, Blade?

"Is she?" Angel demanded.

"You Romans, so family oriented," Lucifer mocked. "What are you doing here, Angel?"

"You know me?"

"Of course. You've built up quite a reputation in New York."

"Then you'll be happy to hear that Angel's going to take my place in the underworld," Gavin said. "So your *friend* is out of the running."

Lucifer rarely poked his head out of Hell, but if he chose to, he could make Angel's rule of the underworld hell on earth.

"A Roman in Sin City?" Lucifer mused with a cruel smile. "What about New York?"

"Raul can handle it and Roque will be out soon. I need a challenge," Angel said.

Lucifer chuckled. "You came to the right place. These two," he jerked his head at Gavin, "have torn the underworld apart."

"I didn't start this war," Gavin said quietly.

"Are you sure?"

"Yes."

There was an agonizing scream from the Pit and a cheer from the crowd.

Lucifer stacked his feet on the chair opposite and considered him. "The reason my friend came to me is because he needs you to die publicly and he can't match you. He's been saving you for me. A gift, if you will. Tonight's the finale."

Lucifer didn't blink his soulless eyes. He was like a snake, waiting for the perfect moment to strike.

"Word on the street is that you're going soft, Gavin. You step down as crime lord for some *woman* and now the city is in shambles. Every enemy you ever made is here tonight to watch you lose your throne."

"What do you want, Lucifer?" Gavin asked.

"I told you, a fair fight."

"That isn't it." He was certain of it.

Lucifer loved games, especially one with high stakes. It was no coincidence that Lucifer called him before Lyla was brought into the Pit. Lucifer wanted something bad enough to double-cross his *friend*.

Lucifer spread his hands. "What else could I possibly want?"

Gavin had no fucking clue what a man like Lucifer could want from him. "You tell me."

Lucifer said nothing for a long minute. In the Pit, there was the sound of a cracking whip and a piercing scream.

"You and I both know there's very little in life that interests me," Lucifer drawled. "Everything is so fleeting." He gestured to the TV screen as a whip sliced a man's face open. "Tonight, I would enjoy my friend's show and I could fight you, but then it's over like that." He snapped his fingers. "And then I'm bored again."

It took every ounce of Gavin's control not to grab Lucifer by the throat and throttle him. Gavin didn't have time for Lucifer's sociopathic ramblings, but he held all the cards. Lucifer held the key to two things Gavin needed: Lyla and the Phantom's identity. Fuck.

"I'm looking for an arrangement with more longevity," Lucifer said.

Gavin ignored the chill that ran down his spine. "Which is?"

"I've always had a soft spot for you, Gavin. We have a lot in common. We were both raised in Hell. You part time, of course. I can't deny that I'm happy to see you home. This is where you belong."

There was no point in arguing with Lucifer so he said nothing. Angel and Blade were very still on either side of him. They were all waiting for the axe to fall.

"I call you into Hell and you walk in as if you own the place in a fucking suit, knowing that alone is enough to make men want your head," Lucifer grinned. "Fuck. I have your wife, your Achilles heel, and you come in stone cold. He wanted you on your knees, but you'll never give in." Lucifer shook his head. "Fuck, Gavin, I've missed sparring with you."

"What do you want, Lucifer?"

"What do you think about being my sidekick?"

Gavin's beast slipped the chain. He leaned forward. Wood crackled beneath his hands as he sank brass knuckles an inch into the table. "Not gonna happen. What do you want, Lucifer?"

Lucifer drummed his fingers. "For starters, I want a good show."

"A good show," Gavin repeated flatly. Lucifer's idea of a show was to watch someone dismember a body piece by piece.

"My friend and I go way back," Lucifer drawled. "Not as far back as you and I, but still... He keeps in touch and brings me gifts, unlike you."

Gavin couldn't imagine what kind of 'gifts' Lucifer enjoyed. Lucifer had been born in Hell and had seen and done things that made Gavin's stomach churn.

Blade stepped forward. "You want a show?"

Lucifer's eyes glinted with bloodlust. "Always."

"Then we'll give you one," Blade decreed. "All of us will fight."

Lucifer eyed them each in turn, weighing what he knew of their combat skills.

"I want more," Lucifer said and his focus shifted back to Gavin. "Why did you stop coming to Hell?"

"What?"

"You used to come once a month. You took on as many men as you could in an hour and then left, calm as you please. Then one night you show up, challenge me, beat me, don't kill me and never return. What changed?"

Lucifer may not have normal emotions like compassion or fear, but he possessed a healthy dose of curiosity. Although Lucifer wore an indifferent expression, his eyes were focused and intense.

"I found a reason to live." Like the women he used, Hell was another outlet. When Lyla left, it changed everything. He didn't realize he loved her until she disappeared. Finding out what happened to her became an obsession, a drive that overrode his destructive demon. The fight with Lucifer was the last time he indulged himself and then he went cold until he got her back.

Lucifer's lip curled into a sneer. "And you *live* for your wife?"

Blade shifted. "Lyla's special."

"There's no such thing as a special woman."

"You must have heard about her body count. It's pretty impressive."

Lucifer waved a hand. "She ran over some guys with a car and shot a couple of morons. Big deal."

"She killed her father."

Lucifer's attention sharpened. "Her father?"

His sudden interest made Gavin tense. Blade was trying to negotiate for Lyla's life by playing on Lucifer's fondness for the violently unique, but Gavin had a feeling this could backfire in a bad way.

"Her father sold her out. Lyla found him about to murder her kid. She shot him, no hesitation."

Lucifer looked at Gavin. "You have a kid?"

"A daughter," Gavin said grudgingly.

Lucifer's expression was thoughtful as he asked, "What else?"

"Lyla unloaded a clip each into three men who raped her mother. She has nine kills and she just started. Who knows what she'll do in the years to come?"

Lucifer looked unduly impressed. Graphic images of what Gavin could do to Lucifer danced through his mind. He forced himself to look away and saw Angel staring at Lucifer as if they'd uncovered the devil. Gavin understood the feeling. Dad brought him here to teach him a lesson—about real evil and how little those in Hell cared for life.

"Can you imagine how their daughter will turn out?" Blade continued. "Between Gavin and Lyla, she's going to be a monster."

Gavin glared at Blade. What the fuck was he doing?

"They could have more kids," Blade went on. "Do you know what havoc they'll wreak? They could be regular patrons here."

Lucifer held up a hand. "Okay, okay. Fuck." Lucifer downed the last of his Coke as if it was a shot and got to his feet. "I have conditions."

Gavin shifted restlessly. Blade gripped his arm and squeezed.

"First, I'm coming with," Lucifer declared.

Blade nodded.

"Two, I meet them once a year."

Gavin stiffened. "Meet who?"

"Lyla and your kid."

Gavin started towards Lucifer, but Angel and Blade held him back.

"What for?" Angel asked.

"To hear about their kills," Lucifer said as if that should be obvious.

"What if Lyla doesn't kill anyone else?" Blade

asked.

"If she's as interesting as you say, that shouldn't be a problem."

"Why do you want to see the kid?"

Lucifer had a peculiar expression on his face. "I've never been a part of a kid's life."

"For good reason," Angel muttered.

Lucifer frowned. "I could teach her. With their blood in her veins, she has to be a fighter. It would be... interesting."

Gavin lunged for him, but Blade and Angel held firm.

Lucifer frowned at him. "Don't you want your daughter to be prepared?"

"For what?" Gavin asked through clenched teeth. Adrenaline pumped through his body. The sounds of another battle in the Pit made him yearn to feel the clash of steel and give Lucifer the fight he hungered for.

"Your daughter will be hunted all her life," Lucifer said and Gavin stilled. "Your family has generations upon generations of enemies. Even if you step down, it'll never stop. Once you're in, you can't get out." Lucifer spread his arms wide. "I can teach her how to be invincible. She's a girl so..." Lucifer tapped his chin. "I can teach her how to use her brain and not her strength. Even if she turned into a weight lifter, she couldn't best a man that way. She has to think dirty. Pluck out eyes, rip off dicks. That kind of thing."

Lucifer was definitely insane, but there was something strange going on. It was almost as if Lucifer was feeling *paternal*. Angel shuddered and

Gavin made up his mind.

"Fine."

Lucifer stopped listing all the ways Nora could kill with her bare hands. "Huh?"

"You can teach Nora when I think she's ready to know that shit," Gavin said. Hopefully Lucifer was murdered before that time came. If not, he would take care of Lucifer himself.

"What about annual visits?" Lucifer asked.

"No."

Lucifer crossed his arms. "Then the deal's off."

"Fuck. Fine. It'll be supervised."

Lucifer pointed at all of them. "You all fight tonight, right? I want three deaths per man, so nine deaths minimum. I want them bloody."

Gavin would drop as many bodies as he had to. "Deal."

"I want *bloody*, bloody, got it?" Lucifer snapped.

"The faster you give me my wife, the faster you get your fight," Gavin snapped back.

Lucifer held out a hand. Angel and Blade released him. When Gavin went to shake his hand, Lucifer withdrew.

"Maybe you and I can spar occasionally?" Lucifer asked.

"Two seconds or the deal's off," Gavin barked.

Lucifer quickly took his hand and shook. "Okay, *fine*. Geez."

"Take me to my wife."

Lucifer went to the bar and grabbed another Coke before he waved a hand, indicating that they follow him. Hallways led out of the arena into the brothel and whatever other salacious activities Hell offered. Lucifer turned down one of the dimly lit hallways, which led to a red elevator. Lucifer pressed the down button and turned to Gavin.

"You know, there hasn't been a kid in Hell since you and I?" Lucifer asked as he popped the top of his soda.

"For good reason," Gavin said. "Our father's were the only ones fucked up enough to have us fight to the death before we were teenagers."

Once more, he felt Angel's glance, but didn't return it.

Lucifer shrugged. "It's kept us alive."

The elevator arrived. They all stood behind Lucifer with their hands on weapons as the elevator traveled down two floors. The elevator opened to reveal a hallway with red walls and carpet. Moans, squeaking beds, screaming and snapping whips echoed down the corridor.

Lucifer walked up to the first room and opened the door. Gavin shoved him aside, expecting to see Lyla. Instead, he found a man fucking a woman chained to the wall. There was blood everywhere. Whether it was his or hers, Gavin didn't know or care. He slammed the door and turned on Lucifer who was opening the next door, exposing a woman stomping on a man's dick. The woman looked up.

"Carry on. Wrong room," Lucifer called and shut the door.

"What the fuck are you doing?" Gavin growled.

"I don't know where she is. She's here somewhere."

Gavin reached for Lucifer, but Blade stepped

between them.

"How many rooms are there?" Blade asked Lucifer.

"Sixty six."

"If you're fucking with me—" Gavin began.

"I'm not," Lucifer said crisply. "They should be coming for her any minute now."

Blade and Angel ran through the hallway, opening and closing doors. Gavin slammed Lucifer against the wall and grabbed him by the throat. When he began to apply pressure, Lucifer did nothing to stop him. On the contrary, he looked delighted.

"You're trying to change your stripes, Gavin, but you can't deny what's inside of you."

"What the fuck are you talking about?"

"You're a junkie like me, but it's not for drugs. No, it's for violence." Lucifer's voice was hoarse from Gavin's grip. "By unleashing his true self, he freed yours too."

Gavin tossed him to the side. Lucifer was too quick to fall on the floor like Gavin wanted him to. He took one step and pivoted with perfect balance.

"You try so hard to deny your desires, Gavin. It's a crime."

"Fucking find my wife," Gavin snarled.

Lucifer opened another door, revealing a man with a drill about to do primitive surgery on a woman who splayed on the bed looking blissed. Lucifer gave the fucked up couple a thumbs up and closed the door.

"Stop!" Blade shouted.

At the end of the corridor a man held a limp

woman draped over his shoulder. It took only a second for Gavin to recognize Lyla's distinctive blonde hair. He started forward even as the man turned, revealing Eli Stark's profile.

CHAPTER TWENTY-TWO

Lyla

The sound of the door opening roused her. She raised her head, but of course she couldn't see through the blindfold. The faintest hint of light penetrated through the material. Terror flooded her. Lyla erupted, straining at the chains. Her wrists protested, but she couldn't stop. No, she would fight to the death.

"Stop."

It wasn't Sadist's voice, but it could be one of his cronies who would take her to the 'show.' Lyla screamed into the gag.

"I'm not going to hurt you," the gravely voice said.

She didn't believe him for a moment.

"Stop fighting. I'm going to get you out."

That penetrated. Lyla paused and felt the brush of fingers on her face. She jerked back, nearly braining herself on the wall in her haste to avoid his touch.

"That fucker," he said and then, "hold still."

The chains went taut and she resisted the impulse to fight like an animal. Then, the chains loosened and she fell face first into the concrete. Her arms trembled as her muscles protested being in such an awkward position for so long. Lyla bit back a whimper and tried to lever herself up, but her arms were useless.

Two hands tucked under her armpits and pulled her into a sitting position. She had no balance and began to tip to the side. The man cursed and clamped a hand on her shoulder to keep her upright. Cramps wracked through her and she moaned.

"Are you hurt?" he asked.

A goon fetching her for the 'show' wouldn't care that she was hurt, right? A kernel of hope flared and she shook her head since he still hadn't taken off the gag. She desperately wanted to see who he was, but her arms were limp noodles at her sides.

"We don't have time," the man said impatiently.

A hard grip forced her to her feet. She moaned again as needles shot through her legs. This was temporary because a broad shoulder rammed into her stomach and she was suddenly airborne. He gripped the back of her thighs and began to move. Her arms hung down, bouncing against his ass as he walked. She twitched her fingers and sucked in a breath. Fuck that hurt. Her head spun as her white knight (or was it new captor) turned left and then right. The muffled sounds she'd been hearing through the door were now on full blast. Screams and moans assaulted her ears. If she had the strength, she would have covered her ears. God, what was this place?

"Stop!"

Lyla's stomach lurched as the man carrying her came to an abrupt halt and turned, making her dizzy and nauseous. The man holding her suddenly slid her in front of him. She sagged on her feet and he banded an arm around her waist to keep her upright. She was grateful until she felt the tip of a knife at her throat. She froze. *Seriously?*

"Lyla?"

Her heart skipped. "Blade?" she screamed through the gag.

Hope blossomed. Oh, God. Oh, God. Please be Blade. She would obey his dictates for the rest of her life if it was him.

"Let her go, Stark," Blade said.

Stark? The name tickled her memory, but eluded her for the moment. God, Blade was here. She was so close to getting the fuck out of here... She flexed her hands and this time embraced the shaft of pain. She stayed very still as the knife pressed hard enough against her throat to make her stomach flip. Ever since Sadist carved her up, she couldn't handle knives. The moment she saw the gleaming blade, she remembered what it felt like being stabbed. Why couldn't these bastards just shoot her and end it quick?

"It's over, Stark," Blade continued. "Let her go."

"What are you doing, Eli?" an unfamiliar voice asked.

Unlike Blade, this guy didn't sound worried, just curious.

"Pyre has my mother," the man holding her growled.

Lyla's mind scrambled, trying to figure out who he was and then it hit. Eli Stark, the dirty cop who approached them at Lux. The gorgeous one with turquoise eyes. His mother had been viciously attacked before he could testify in court and was in a coma. Gavin had his mother? Why?

"Let her go and I'll make your death quick."

Her heart nearly beat out of her chest. Gavin was here. She was going to live.

"I keep telling you, I have nothing to do with any of this shit," Eli growled. "Someone framed me."

He was so close, his breath fanned her cheek.

"Kinda hard to feel sympathy for the man who's holding a knife to my cousin's wife's throat." Angel's voice was soft but full of menace.

Lyla felt as if her heart was going to burst. They were all here. Okay, so maybe having family wasn't such a bad thing after all.

"Pyre took my mother. I have nothing else to bargain with," Eli hissed.

"You think Gavin's going to make a deal with a man who bound, gagged and tortured his wife?" Angel barked.

"I didn't do this," Eli snapped.

"Really? Who did?"

"Fuck if I know. I found her like this."

"If you're not involved, how did you know she was here?"

"I still have my contacts." Lyla grunted when the knife dug into her skin. "Stay the fuck back, Pyre!" Eli ordered.

"Did you kill Stark's mom?" It was that cool, detached voice.

No one answered.

"That would be a damn shame if you did," the bland voice continued.

"Why's that?" Angel asked.

"Because he's telling the truth."

There was a beat of silence.

"What?"

That was Gavin's voice, flat and remote. Whoever had that dry voice was seconds away from death, he just didn't know it.

"Eli's not working for my friend. He's been much too busy indulging in some vigilante justice. He's the perfect man to pin this on since he has the contacts and has been out of the spotlight and oh yes, you two had a falling out." The man's sigh was full of admiration.

"If Lucifer's telling the truth, what did you plan to do with Lyla?" Gavin's voice was soft and menacing.

"I needed insurance since you wouldn't listen to me," Eli said.

"I want to hear it from Lyla," Gavin snapped and he sounded closer.

Eli tightened his grip on her and took a step back, dragging her with him. "Stay where you are, Pyre."

"If you're innocent, let her go. If not, I'll kill you. You have thirty seconds."

Gavin sounded homicidal. It was music to her ears. For a long minute, Eli didn't shift. She mentally urged him to hurry the fuck up.

"You know I had nothing to do with this, right?" Eli murmured under his breath.

She nodded and the knife left her throat and the

gag loosened.

"He didn't bring me here," she said immediately and began to cough.

Eli's arm dropped away and she swayed only to be caught up against a solid chest. She didn't need to take the blindfold off to know who he was. She wrapped quivering arms around Gavin and felt her tears soak the blindfold. His hand cradled the back of her head.

"My mother, Pyre," Eli barked.

"One floor up in the hospital under the name Grace Stein," Gavin said as he held her so tight she could barely breathe. "I don't kill old, defenseless women."

"This is touching and all, but you're running out of time," the irritating voice said.

Gavin didn't release her when she tried to raise her head and see who the fuck that guy was. Gavin squeezed her so tight, she could barely breathe.

"Gaaaaavin," the man whined. "You promised."

Gavin eased his hold on her and tugged down the blindfold. Lyla shut her eyes against the blinding light.

"Who took you? Do you know who he is?" Gavin asked.

Lyla opened her eyes and peered into Gavin's dangerous golden eyes. He was really here. She ran her hand down his face with a trembling hand.

"I don't know," she said and began to wheeze again. "Water."

She heard a door open behind Gavin. The sound of someone being whipped made her push away from Gavin, but he didn't release her.

"What—? We have to help," she said.

Gavin shook his head. "No, we don't. We're in a brothel."

Lyla stilled. "Brothel?"

There was a fine hum of vicious energy around him. She wanted to burrow against him and beg for him to take her home, but knew that couldn't happen. They had unfinished business. Business, which included killing Sadist once and for all. She tried to suppress her shit and focus.

"Here."

It took considerable effort to look away from Gavin to the man standing beside him. She clutched Gavin tighter as she surveyed the beast holding a bottle of water in his humongous hand. This guy looked like a wild mountain man with a full beard, a braid halfway down his back and black, glittering eyes. He had to be over six foot five and was built like a warrior from an age past. He wore baggy beige pants and a fitted tunic top, which showed every muscle beneath the fabric. Lyla dimly registered that he wore red Crocs and had red nail polish, but was distracted by his eyes. He was staring at her with a hunger she normally associated with Gavin, but it wasn't sexual, it was something else. An eagerness for... something.

"You need water," he said.

His voice didn't match his appearance. A man like him should have the deep rumbling voice of a bear, not the airy lightness of a schoolboy. There was something about him that put her on edge. She didn't trust his smile or his hippy attire.

Lyla reached out for the water bottle and noted

that Gavin was eyeing Lucifer as if he hated him. What the fuck was going on here? Lyla gripped the water bottle and tilted it to her lips. She spilled a little on herself and Gavin, but he didn't release her. She downed half of it before she took a breath.

"I'm Lucifer," the mountain man/hippy said.

"Lucifer?" Lyla said sharply. "Gavin, he's working with Sadist. He—"

"He's double-crossing him," Gavin said.

She stared at him. "Why?"

"Gavin made me a better deal."

Before Lyla could ask what kind of fucked up deal, Gavin asked, "Who is he?"

Lucifer clapped his hands together. "He's so good at this! No one suspects him. A wolf in sheep's clothing. He's been a longtime patron of Hell. He does well up there," Lucifer pointed up at the ceiling, "*and* down here. I don't know how he does it. I admire him, actually."

"Who. Is. It?" Gavin bit out.

Lucifer gave him a sly look. "That's for you to figure out, isn't it?"

Gavin cupped her chin, forcing her to look at him. "You need to leave."

"I don't think so," Lucifer said.

Gavin tensed. "She's leaving."

"No one's leaving until I get my show," Lucifer said.

"Show?" She was beginning to hate that word. They were in a brothel. What kind of show was he talking about?

"I don't want her here for this," Gavin growled.

"Why? You're afraid she'll see the real you?"

Lucifer shook his head. "Besides, she has to come. She's the only one who knows who he is."

"I don't," Lyla put in.

"You do," Lucifer said with such certainty that her stomach lurched.

"Are you hurt?" Gavin asked.

She stared into his eyes and pushed all her inner turmoil aside. She needed this to be over. She needed to see this through. "No."

Gavin looked at Lucifer. "Take us to him."

Lucifer eyed Eli. "You in?"

Eli Stark looked at Gavin. "We're clear?"

Gavin glared at him. "We have things to talk about. Later."

"You in?" Lucifer pushed.

"To go into the Pit? There's nothing in it for me," Eli said.

"You get a *lot* out of it." Lucifer held up his thumb. "First of all, you're gonna get a great show." His pointer finger popped up. "Second, fighting at Gavin's side will make *him* owe *you*." He held up his pinky. "Third, you'll please me, which may get you a favor in the future." He held up a scarred ring finger. "Fourth, tonight's going to go down in history." The middle finger joined the others. "And last but not least, you'll find out the identity of the man who called the hit on your mother."

Eli didn't move, but the corridor suddenly seemed a little smaller than it had been a second ago.

"What did you say?" Eli's voice held no inflection, but his turquoise eyes were suddenly blazing.

360

"You didn't think some street thug called the hit on your mom, did you?" Lucifer examined his fingernails. "I thought you knew that came from someone higher up."

Eli clenched his fists at his sides. "Who is he?"

Lucifer's smile was chilling. "That's the big mystery, isn't it?"

Eli took a step towards Lucifer and then stopped. Lucifer's eyes were fixed eagerly on him, daring Eli to touch him. Lyla didn't know who the fuck Lucifer was, but she knew enough about dangerous men not to trust a smile, a sedate wardrobe or a man with a sweet voice. She watched Eli rein in his emotions.

"Are you in?" Lucifer asked.

Eli gave Lucifer a look that said he would love to dice this guy into pieces. Lucifer was completely unaffected. On the contrary, Lucifer looked as if Christmas came early.

"This is fantastic," Lucifer said and clapped his hands before he started down a god awful red hallway.

Gavin took her hand. There was a fine trembling in his hands. She knew it wasn't nerves. He was revved up.

"I'm okay, Gavin," she said.

He didn't look at her. "You're not."

She swallowed hard. No, she wasn't. "I will be once he's dead."

Gavin raised her hand to his lips and kissed the back of her hand.

"Where are we?" she asked over the shouts of a woman who had the filthiest mouth on the planet.

"This is Hell."

She looked up and was ensnared by his blistering gaze.

Gavin jerked his head at Lucifer's back. "He runs it. He's off his rocker."

They boarded an elevator. Gavin boxed her into the corner.

"How many men does he have with him?" Gavin asked.

"He has a board of twenty," Lucifer said.

"Twenty?" Angel echoed.

"Twenty," Lucifer confirmed with relish, "against you four."

"Fuck," Blade said.

"You got this," Lucifer encouraged them as the elevator traveled down. "Gavin and Blade are veterans." He pointed at Angel and Eli. "As for you two, I hope you have beginner's luck and know how to use something to defend yourself other than a gun."

Blade and Gavin were *veterans* of Hell?

"What about guards?" Gavin asked.

Lucifer snorted. "Their guards would wet their pants before they reached the door. You can't pay any run of the mill security guard enough to come into Hell."

"Good," Gavin said.

The elevator doors opened. Unlike the noisy, hideous red corridor, this place was whisper quiet and opulent with gleaming white marble floors, walls and shimmering chandeliers.

Lucifer stepped forward with his arms spread wide. "Nice, huh? I charge the rich fuckers who don't want to be in the stands a bundle to watch at ground zero. They like the gore just as much as the common folk, they just won't admit it."

Lucifer started down the wide hallway, Crocs squeaking.

Gavin's hand flexed on her. "Maybe you should stay here."

"No," Lyla said immediately. "I need to see this."

"There's twenty of them," Gavin growled.

"And you won't let any of them touch me," she snapped. "This is what we've been waiting for and I know his voice. You need me, Gavin."

"I do need you. I need you breathing."

"And I will be."

Gavin's eyes flicked to Blade. "One scratch and I'll kill you."

Blade inclined his head. Gavin whirled around and followed Lucifer who ran his finger along a gleaming table and frowned.

"Fucking dusty. Unacceptable," he muttered.

"Lucifer," Gavin clipped.

"Right. This way."

Gavin murmured to Angel, "You want the underworld? This is where you take it."

Angel nodded as Lyla and Blade brought up the rear. Blade had a knife the length of her forearm in his hand. A man who looked like a pirate was pushing a silver cart with two bottles of champagne and glasses to closed double doors. Lucifer said something to him and knocked on the door.

"Come."

Lucifer gave them a shit-eating grin before he

opened the door and rolled in the cart. This was it. Sadist was in this room. Years of death, nightmares and fear would be settled right here, right now. Her heart leapt into her throat when Gavin blithely walked in after Lucifer. No hesitation. She expected to hear the sound of gunshots, but there was nothing and that was worse. She moved forward swiftly, pulling against Blade's grip on her arm. She wasn't sure what she expected, but the sight that met her eyes took a few seconds to digest.

The room looked like an executive lounge with elegant furniture, a boardroom table and a wet bar all in snowy white. That's where normal stopped. Twenty men sat at the table, all in black suits and metal masks. Each mask was horrifying enough to induce nightmares whether it was a snarling animal or a demon. One wall of the room was made of glass. Two men with medieval weapons battled on sand. She caught a glimpse of an arena before the screaming tension in the room forced her to focus on the men at the table who were half standing, staring at Lucifer, Gavin, Eli and Angel. Blade forced her to stop behind him in the doorway.

"What the fuck are you doing here, Pyre?" a man wearing a horrifying clown mask asked.

Gavin slammed his fist into the man's face. There was the ping of metal and then the crunch of bone as the mask caved in. She saw a gush of blood slither down the man's throat and heard a gasping breath as the man crashed to the ground and clawed at the mask with his legs kicking.

Another man leapt up from the table with a dagger in each hand. Blade widened his stance to conceal her. Lyla leaned to the side, heart in her throat as Gavin eyed the man with a nonchalance that made her want to scream. Gavin dodged the first swing and the second. On the third swing, Gavin grabbed his wrist and reversed the knife. With a suddenness that stunned everyone, Gavin hit the butt of the dagger, which lodged in the man's chest. The man fell, gasping and twitching.

Four men converged on Gavin. She saw Eli and Angel engage with them before Blade shoved her back. A second later, a man barreled into him. Lyla saw the whites of his eyes through a snarling rabbit mask before she saw a flash of silver and he slid to the ground in front of Blade. Lyla pressed against Blade's back to look into the room and saw that Eli's face and neck were now splattered with red and Gavin's hands dripped with blood as he walked around the table.

"You all know why I'm here," Gavin said over the muted sound of the battle taking place in the sandy pit and the masked men's last rattling breaths. "And I know why you're here."

In the arena, a man wielded a weapon she had only seen in medieval movies. It was a stick with a chain and metal ball with spikes attached. She grasped the back of Blade's jacket as it imbedded into a man's skull with a sickening thud.

The scene with Gavin was just as disturbing. The steady clip of his shoes as he circled his prey gave her goose bumps. Despite the fact that Gavin was clearly outnumbered, none of the men moved. They watched his progress silently.

"Who the fuck do you think you are?" a

365

belligerent man wearing a wolf mask asked.

Gavin knocked the mask off his face and grabbed fistfuls of his suit. "I'm your fucking crime lord, bitch." Gavin released him and even as he staggered back, Gavin's fist flashed out. The man's head kicked back. He landed on his ass and shook his head, dazed.

"Lucifer here was kind enough to let me know where you were meeting," Gavin said with a politeness that clashed with the flashes of temper he was exhibiting. "Lucifer tells me there's some debate on whether I've lost my touch since I claimed my wife. Let's put it to the test, shall we?"

Gavin placed both hands on the table. Blood spread across white marble.

"I hear you had plans for my wife tonight."

No one spoke, no one even breathed.

"You dare to desecrate *mine*." Gavin hissed the last word, the veins on his neck popping as he tried to contain his fury. "I've been waiting two years for this moment. Two long years since my father and cousin were killed. Now, tonight, it ends."

A loud pop made everyone jump. Lucifer made a "carry on" gesture as he poured glasses of champagne.

"He's sitting here, in this room."

Gavin accepted the flute of champagne Lucifer offered and took a sip. She had seen Gavin go gonzo, but right now he was control personified. This was the crime lord. Absolute control, absolutely terrifying. She could feel the chill from across the room. This was the man who beat that man in the basement with single-minded focus and detachment. There was no doubt in her mind that no man in this room was a match for him. Gavin wasn't a mere man. He was born for this—to make others cower and beg for mercy. Wrath seeped from his pores. His sheer will was on display and it was beautiful to behold.

"Whoever my enemy is," Gavin said as he stepped on a body in his path. Bones cracked. "He's patient. He's a great planner..." Gavin finished his glass and set it in front of the man with an eagle mask. "And he's going to get everything that's coming to him. So much so that anyone half associated with him will be annihilated."

Gavin yanked the cord holding the mask in place. It clattered on the table and revealed a familiar face that sent Lyla inwardly reeling.

"Governor," Gavin acknowledged as casually as if they were at a dinner party. "I stopped by your office a week ago."

The Governor was ghost white and sweating profusely.

"You told me you didn't know the identity of the crime lord and that you weren't working with him," Gavin said pleasantly.

"I-I came here for—" the Governor began and then stopped abruptly.

"For what? The show?" Gavin picked up the eagle mask and leaned in close. "Did you choose the eagle because you're a patriot?"

The Governor's mouth opened and closed. "Gavin, please, I knew your father—"

"And he's dead."

Gavin smashed the beak of the metal mask into

the Governor's eye. The man's scream made every hair on her body stand up. Gavin slammed the Governor's face into the table until the mask was flat. The Governor slumped over the table and didn't move.

"I think there's been some confusion about my title," Gavin said calmly as he resumed his walk around the masked men who edged away. "Your presence here means you don't see me as the crime lord and have hedged your bets on the other guy, which means your lives are forfeit."

Gavin braced his legs apart as he surveyed the rest of the group.

"Give him up."

There was a beat of silence and then a man at the opposite end of the table stirred. He tipped back his troll mask, revealing a face that wasn't hard on the eyes.

"What are you going to do, Gavin? Kill us all?" the man asked with an insolence that made Lyla grip the back of Blade's jacket tighter.

"Detective Malone," Gavin acknowledged.

Malone looked at Eli. "What are you doing here, Stark? I thought you died in a hole somewhere months ago."

"I'm looking for the guy who ordered the hit on my mom," Eli said.

Malone's eyes moved to Angel and narrowed. "You can't bring another crime family into this. What happens in our city is our business."

"Angel's taking over so this is now his city as well," Gavin said.

There was a touch of unease in Malone's voice

as he said, "Roque hasn't served his entire sentence."

"I'm flattered that you know so much about my family," Angel said with a grin. "Raul can handle himself."

"Everyone knows the Romans," Malone muttered and switched his attention back to Gavin. "You can't kill us all."

"Can't I?"

A smug smile curved Malone's mouth. "You already killed the Governor. What are you gonna do? Kill a police detective, a senator, judge, gaming commissioner?"

"Why not?"

"You'll cripple the city! Every cop and FBI agent in the country will be gunning for you!" Malone shouted.

"I think we need new people at the top," Gavin mused, almost to himself and then glanced at Lucifer who was walking towards Lyla and Blade with champagne. "Hey, Lucifer, what do you do with the bodies in Hell?"

"I have my own crematory, of course. I'm not gonna waste time digging graves in the desert," Lucifer said.

"You hear that, Malone? No evidence to convict. Lucifer will turn you into ash and flush you down the toilet. No fucking FBI will find even a tooth. What happens in Hell, stays in Hell," Gavin said quietly. "That's why you should've never walked through those doors."

The masked men glanced at one another. The tension in the room rose to a screaming pitch.

Someone was going to make a move.

Gavin tugged on the string of a man with a wicked demon mask, revealing Steven Vega who was visibly trembling. He raised his hands to cover his head as if he expected a blow.

"Steven, what are you doing here?" Gavin asked.

When Steven didn't answer, Gavin gripped him by the hair and yanked viciously. Steven yelped.

"I asked you a question," Gavin hissed.

"Y-you k-killed my father!" Steven whimpered.

"So you joined the other side? I warned you what I'd do."

"What's the meaning of this, Lucifer?" one of the men at the table asked.

"What do you mean?" Lucifer asked as he tossed half of his glass down.

"You brought Pyre here?"

"He arrived early, promised me a good show *and* I get to play godfather to his kid."

Lyla jerked. "What?"

No one heard her. The men were all looking at one another, trying to communicate silently.

"Masks off," Gavin ordered.

Long seconds passed. No one moved. Lyla's throat closed up and she edged back. In the arena, two men fought with swords. Adrenaline, anticipation and fear stole her breath.

"Give him to me," Gavin said.

"And you'll let us go?" a man with a lizard mask asked.

"No."

"You can't take us all on," Malone said.

"You think not?" Gavin asked and then all hell broke loose.

Men pulled out knives, machetes and axes from beneath the table. Gavin narrowly dodged a ninja star that cut his cheek. Gavin brought his hands up, brass knuckles gleaming as men rushed him.

"Gavin!" She couldn't hold back the scream, but it was drowned out by the battle cries of the men.

Eli and Angel were lost in the scuffle and Blade backed her out of the room. She could feel him vibrating. The need to engage must be riding him hard. There were still too many men against Gavin, Angel and Eli and for some reason, no one had a gun. She heard something shatter and peeked through Blade's arm. A man was using his chair to break into the arena. Apparently, he thought his odds were better out there.

"Look at them run," Lucifer said gleefully.

Lyla caught a glimpse of a man on top of Gavin with a machete inches from his face. She shoved at Blade.

"Go to Gavin!"

"I can't."

Blade sounded pained.

"If he dies, I'll kill you," she screamed and shoved him again.

The knife in Blade's hand trembled. The glass shattered and the fight in the room poured into the arena. Another masked man raised his axe above Gavin's head.

"Blade!" she screamed.

Blade tossed his knife, which sank into the

man's belly. He screamed and dropped his weapon too close to Gavin's head for comfort. The man with the machete was distracted long enough for Gavin to gain the upper hand. The man left Gavin holding the machete and ran into the arena. The masked men tried to leave the sandy pit, but the spectators blocked off the stairs. The masked men scrambled towards a wall of weapons in the arena, which included whips, chains, swords, spears and other primitive weapons.

Gavin, Angel and Eli hopped into the arena. There was a moment of silence and then the spectators began to cheer. It was like they were at a football game. The masked men made a circle around Gavin, Angel and Eli who were unarmed aside from Gavin's brass knuckles and Eli's knife.

"Blade," she whispered. "Go."

"I can't!"

"I'll stay right here. There's no one in the room!" she shouted, shoving at him as one of the masked men began to whip a chain above his head.

"Fuck!" Blade whirled on Lucifer and gripped his shirt. "Watch her!"

"Sure, sure," Lucifer said. "You better get out there."

"You won't let anyone touch her?" Blade demanded.

"You said she could take care of herself."

"You—"

"Blade!" Lyla screamed as Eli staggered from a whiplash.

Blade snatched knives from bodies and the machete before he ran into the arena and broke the circle surrounding Gavin and the guys by cleaving a man's head in two. It was brutal, chaotic and gory. This was ten times worse than a gun battle.

Lyla skirted the bodies and ran to the shattered window. Eli's dagger landed in the throat of the man wielding the whip while Gavin played with a man who was trying to cut him in half with a sword. Gavin waited for his moment, pivoting while the man swung wildly, his actions becoming more desperate. When he miscalculated and staggered forward, Gavin's hand flashed out, brass knuckles flashing in the stadium lights. His victim's head snapped to the side. Blood and teeth splashed across the sand. Gavin followed this with a punch to the temple that made Lyla close her eyes and look away. Fuck.

She tapped the edge of the window anxiously, but wasn't able to look away for long. There was a piercing scream followed by the roaring crowd. She looked back in time to see Angel wielding a trident with the same ease he drove the car earlier today. The crowd leaned over the rails, yelling their heads off as Angel sliced a man's stomach open.

"Isn't it beautiful?"

Lucifer came up beside her with a champagne glass and a round metal shield. Lyla gave him a disbelieving look before Eli sliced a man's calf open and then followed it with an efficient throat slit. Blade stood back from the others, gauging and taking out the masked men with an efficiency that made her realize this was far from his first time in the Pit. Gavin claimed a sword. The sight of him in a bloody suit with a sword would be imprinted in her mind for all time. She was about to take a breath when a man wearing a wolf mask snapped the whip at Gavin's back. She let out a battle cry and would have launched herself forward, but Lucifer yanked her back.

"No women in the arena," he said.

"You—"

She whirled around to search the room for a weapon to toss and saw Steven Vega hiding beneath the table. Despite his position, there was something about his face that riveted her. He didn't look terrified. No, he was... seething. Something vicious flashed in the dark depths of his eyes and her world imploded.

CHAPTER TWENTY-THREE

Lyla

Even as Lyla was trying to come to terms with what her eyes were telling her, Steven crawled out from under the table. He straightened and smoothed a hand over his suit.

She would recognize the malevolence in those eyes anywhere. She had been *nice* to this fucker. She talked to him in the bar and helped him up when he fell in his father's hospital room. This man defiled her, used her parents as pawns and massacred Manny, the only father figure she'd ever known. He robbed Nora of the privilege of having Manny as a grandfather and Vinny as an uncle. The memory of this man tortured her every night for over two years and he had been hiding in plain sight. He was a true wolf in sheep's clothing. She built Sadist up in her mind to be an invincible monster when he was just a sicko in a mask. No one would dream that the timid lawyer was actually a sadistic killer capable of running the underworld, not when he left a trail of mutilated bodies in his wake.

"I told you, you're always at the wrong place at the wrong time," Steven said.

No stutter. That soft, gentle voice assaulted her

ears, making her stomach roil and head pound with nightmares.

"It's you," she whispered.

His eyes glittered with rage in his pale, angular face. "So you finally see me, do you? When we met at the bar, I thought you were different until I found out you were with Pyre. You're just like the rest of the whores." He picked up his cane and pointed it at her. "Time to finish what I started."

The way he was pointing the cane made it clear that it wasn't a normal walking stick. Lyla half turned to protect herself, even though she knew it was a futile gesture and squeezed her eyes shut. She heard a gunshot and then the sharp ping of metal.

"You know that's against the rules," Lucifer barked.

Lyla opened her eyes and saw that Lucifer had deflected the bullet with his shield. She looked at Steven who now had his cane pointed at Lucifer.

"You stay out of this," Steven said, his voice icy with control.

Lucifer handed the shield to Lyla who nearly dropped it. The shield felt as if it weighed fifty pounds, but it could deflect bullets so... She held it in front of her with both hands as Lucifer headed towards the madman.

"You know it's not allowed," Lucifer snapped.

Steven's expression twisted. "How could you betray me like this? You ruined everything!"

"I didn't ruin anything. I made a deal to get a better show, which is what you're interrupting. Give me the gun."

Steven jabbed the cane at him as he retreated.

"Pyre made fools of both of us. You hate him."

"I don't hate him," Lucifer said. "He's the closest thing I have to a brother."

Steven's mouth went slack with shock. "That's not what you made me believe!"

"I find your hatred for others amusing."

"Amusing?" Steven echoed.

Lucifer was walking towards a serial killer with a gun. He had no weapon that she could see and he was baiting him on top of it. Lucifer was obviously insane. Lyla looked for an escape route, but with Steven by the door, the only other place to go was the arena and that wasn't happening. Lyla caught a glimpse of Angel going for the death strike, the triton about his head before bringing it down and being sprayed in red mist.

"You find me *amusing*?" Steven shouted.

Lyla raised the shield just below her eyes and prepared to duck if Steven started firing wildly.

"You've been a source of entertainment for me," Lucifer continued on in a voice that was bored personified. "I gave you the skills you hungered for to work out your rage and I was amused by your ability to manipulate and fool Gavin and the others this long, but you can't hide behind the mask forever. It's time to step into the light."

"That wasn't your call to make!" Spit flew as Steven raged. "You kept my secrets. You made me believe I could do anything. I have the underworld in my hands and you turn against me now. Why?"

"You wanted me to *give* you your throne. I don't believe in giving anyone a handout. You want your throne, you take it." Lucifer gestured to the

Pit. "You want Gavin? He's right there. Take your throne, don't use me or anyone else to do it."

"You made me who I am!" Steven screamed. "I thought you were my friend."

"I don't have friends," Lucifer said, brutally blunt. "And I let you play in the brothel, but you never got in the Pit. You never step into the light because you don't have the confidence to take an enemy head on. No crime lord can lurk in the shadows forever. There has to be more to you than the mask because one day they'll find out the truth. This was your opportunity to show everyone what you're made of." Lucifer's voice became scathing. "Yet you hide under the table and insult me by bringing a gun into my house. If you can't survive without a gun or the mask, you're nothing. You're not worthy to claim the title. You're a coward."

There was the sharp crack of a gunshot. Lucifer jerked and a stain of red spread over his right shoulder. Lucifer looked at his shoulder and then back at Steven who took a wary step back despite the fact that Lucifer was unarmed.

"You always were a lousy shot," Lucifer said.

Yes, Lucifer was unhinged.

"I'll give you one more shot," Lucifer said and spread his arms wide.

What? Lyla looked over her shoulder at the arena for help but all four of the guys were engaged in bloody battle. Gavin now had two swords and was hacking body parts to the crowd's delight.

The second gunshot made Lyla duck. She peeked around the side of the shield, expecting to see Lucifer on the ground. Instead, she saw him launch himself at Steven. He ripped the cane out of his hands and broke it over his knee before he backhanded Steven with enough force to make the smaller man spin and fall on his hands and knees.

Lucifer met her gaze from across the room. "You want your revenge? Take it."

Lyla was so shocked that she didn't notice Steven crawl beneath the table and launch himself at her until it was too late. She saw the flash of metal and brought up the shield instinctively. The blade landed on the shield and scraped over it's surface.

Lyla backed up and shifted the shield in time to see Steven coming at her again. The impact made her stagger backwards. She grasped the shield desperately. The shield was too fucking heavy for her to lift it with one arm as it was intended to be used.

"Go on the offense," Lucifer called like a basketball coach.

Lyla jumped back as Steven aimed below the shield and tried to slice her legs or belly. He swung savagely. She wouldn't be able to hold the shield forever.

"I'm going to carve your heart out and shove it in Pyre's face," Steven ranted as his blows rained down on the shield. "He'll kill me, but he'll have *nothing*."

His vicious, mocking tone made her stop in her tracks. Something dark unfurled inside of her. No running. This would end here. Steven came at her again and she braced for impact. As he slashed down, she rammed the shield up and into his hand.

Steven screamed as the knife went flying. He cradled his hand and froze when Lyla blocked him from retrieving his weapon.

They stared at one another. In the arena, the crowd booed. She and Steven both turned to look. Eli was sprawled on the sand. Angel stood over him, trying to keep the last of the masked men at bay. Gavin ran towards Blade who was caged against the wall by three men who were tossing daggers at him as if he were a dartboard.

Steven glanced at her, his expression malevolent and sly. He hopped into the arena and grabbed a scythe. He was going to do what he did best—hit when no one was looking. Lyla whirled, searched for his knife and then turned back to the arena. Lyla took aim and tossed the knife as hard as she could. It sank into Steven's lower back. He staggered and howled in pain.

Lyla wasn't aware of anything but her prey. This was it. Lyla hefted Lucifer's shield, hopped through the window and rushed across the sand. She used both hands and all the momentum she could get and bashed Steven in the back of the head, sending him face first into the sand. Rage obliterated all thought. She gripped the shield, raised it over her head and brought it down with every ounce of strength she possessed. For Manny, for her mother, for Vinny, for Carmen—

The shield was ripped from her hands. She whirled, teeth bared and stared at a blood streaked Blade, Gavin, Angel and Eli. Beyond them, the arena was strewn with body parts and hundreds of silent spectators in the stands.

"You took the show, sweetheart," Angel said.

"You want to tell me why you're trying to dismember the Vega wimp?" Gavin asked.

"It's him," she panted.

"Who?"

"Sadist." No comprehension on his face. "The crime lord."

Gavin froze. "What?"

"It's him. He's the wolf in sheep's clothing. He doesn't have a stutter. He's the right body type, dark eyes, he's been here the whole time!"

Gavin kicked Steven onto his back. Lyla felt nothing when she saw the odd angles of his limbs. Blood trickled from Steven's mouth, but there was still activity in his eyes.

"I testified against your clients and caused you to lose some high profile cases," Eli said quietly.

"And you were at the hospital before Santana's men attacked," Gavin said quietly. "You're the one I talked to on the phone the night I killed your father."

Something evil stirred to life in Steven's eyes.

"You think you're big shots," Steven hissed, blood oozing from his mouth. "You're just like Rafael. You push your weight around. You think no one will challenge you." A deranged smile curved his mouth. "I showed you. I took everything from you."

"I should have killed you the night I killed your father," Gavin said.

"I did what my dad and Rafael could *never* do! If you hadn't shattered my knee and I didn't get my jaw wired shut, I would have killed you sooner."

"That explains the four months of silence," Gavin said.

"I *had* you," Steven snarled, his face twisting into something less human. "If Lucifer hadn't interfered, I would exterminate the Pyres and *rule—*"

Gavin ran Steven through the chest with his sword. The sound of the blade sliding through muscle and grazing bone made her feel sick, but she didn't look away. Steven screamed, the sound so high pitched and tortured that Lyla's hands fisted at her sides. It took every ounce of courage she possessed not to look away.

Gavin walked away and returned with another sword. The demon retreated as Steven realized he was going to be impaled again.

"Please—" Steven got out before another sword joined the first.

By the time Gavin was done, no less than six swords stuck out of Steven's body. He shuddered as his blood drained out of him. No one moved, no one spoke.

Lucifer grabbed his bloody shield as he approached. There was an angry murmur when the spectators saw his bullet wound. Lucifer eyed Lyla for a long moment before he held out a fist.

"That was awesome," he said solemnly.

Did he want a fist bump? She hesitated, but he didn't lower his fist. The setting was surreal enough that she hit his massive fist with her smaller one.

"He brought a gun into Hell." Lucifer shook his head. "Doesn't he know me at all?"

With a swift savageness that took her aback, he

brought his shield down. Steven's head rolled away and the spectators grunted in approval.

"I might have to revise my rules about no women in the arena. That was great," Lucifer said and smiled at Gavin, Blade, Angel and Eli who looked as if they walked through red rain. "How you feeling, boys?"

No one spoke. They were jacked and Lucifer knew it. Lyla couldn't stop shaking.

"Need to visit the whorehouse? First round's on me," Lucifer said graciously and then eyed Lyla. "I also have men—"

Gavin's hand moved. Lucifer raised his shield and a knife sparked as it collided and then toppled to the sand. Lucifer grinned unrepentantly at Gavin.

"Just a suggestion," Lucifer said.

Gavin turned to her and cupped her face with gritty hands. "Are you hurt?"

"No."

She glanced at Lucifer who was watching them with his head tilted to the side, eyes narrowed. "Lucifer saved my life."

Gavin dropped his forehead on hers. "Fuck."

"He stopped the bullet with his shield." She smoothed her hands over his tattered shirt. "You? You hurt?"

"Nothing that'll kill me." He wrapped his arms around her. "It's over."

She squeezed her eyes shut and grabbed handfuls of his shirt.

"You kept up your end of the agreement. That was a *bloody* good show," Lucifer said. "I knew Lyla would figure out it was Steven."

"All this time you knew," Gavin said.

"Yes," Lucifer said.

"Why didn't you tell me?"

"Why should I? I don't have an investment in the underworld and I admired Steven for having the balls to dethrone you Pyres. You've had it too easy for too long."

"It'll take a decade to right the wrong Steven's done in two years," Gavin hissed.

"Good thing Angel's hungry for it, huh? You're not planning on getting a hobby, are you, Roman?"

"Nope," Angel said dryly.

"You hear that? No harm, no foul."

Lyla whirled in the circle of Gavin's arm. "No harm?"

Lucifer eyed her coolly. "You're alive, aren't you?"

She tried to take a step forward, but Gavin held her back. "He left mutilated bodies all over the city!"

Lucifer glanced around. "You mean like this?"

She bared her teeth. "He *destroyed* Manny."

"Manny's an awful man."

"You didn't know him!" she shouted.

Lucifer took a step forward, eyes locked on her face. The bottom of his shield dripped with Steven's blood and other... stuff. Lyla was dimly aware of Blade, Angel and Eli drawing near.

"I know Manny," Lucifer said quietly. "He wasn't a good man."

She tossed her head back. "He changed."

Lucifer's eyes narrowed before they focused on Gavin who held her tight against him.

"Maybe," Lucifer conceded. "But the man I knew would sacrifice his son to the underworld."

"I survived," Gavin clipped

Lucifer nodded. "So you did." His eyes dipped to Lyla before he said, "You lucky fuck."

Lyla focused on the bullet wound, which was still oozing. She couldn't resist. "You should see to that."

Lucifer snorted. "My dad used to shoot me once a week so when the real thing came, I wouldn't go into shock. This is nothing."

She turned to Gavin. "Nora, Carmen?" she asked urgently.

"They're at the house."

"I want to call. She must be terrified. I need to hear her voice, tell her it's over."

Gavin lost his jacket at some point and his shirt was shredded and blood soaked. He ran a hand over his pockets and then looked around.

"Here." Blade offered his phone.

Lyla took it and swiped her finger over the screen, leaving a streak of red in her wake. Lyla paced away as the men talked in low tones and stopped in her tracks when she saw the body parts strewn over the arena. It had been a bloodbath. Even as her stomach rolled, she heard Carmen's breathy voice on the other end.

"Blade?"

"Carmen, it's me," Lyla said.

"Lyla?" Carmen sounded faint and then she screamed, *"Lyla?"*

"It's me," she whispered and tears threatened. Everything was catching up to her—being hunted in the desert, her mother's attack, being chained and witnessing a gory battle worthy of Roman times.

"Are you okay?" Carmen asked.

She nodded even as her mouth said, "No."

"Are you hurt?"

She shook her head before she realized Carmen couldn't see it. "N-no. A-are you guys okay?"

"Yes. Did Gavin get him?"

"Yes. It was Steven Vega."

"Vega? Rafael's brother?" Carmen sounded incredulous. "Are you sure?"

Lyla looked down at Steven Vega's head. His eyes were open and staring at her. This fucker tortured Manny, stabbed her, hunted her like some fucking dog while she was pregnant and would have killed Carmen and Nora—. With a scream, she drew back her foot and kicked Steven's head, which sailed across the two-story arena into the crowd of spectators. There was a yell as some men tried to dodge her missile and then a ringing silence filled the arena. For the first time, Lyla realized there were no women in the crowd and these men looked like gangbangers... or worse. She took a step back and prepared to run when Lucifer began to laugh.

He tossed an arm over her shoulders. "Your hand to hand combat needs work, but you have great potential."

"Who's that?" Carmen asked in her ear.

She didn't know what to think of Lucifer. He allowed Steven to jack off on her and would have watched her be tortured and then he fucking saved her from a bullet. He really was insane. She had the simultaneous urges to try to kill him, hug him and order him to see a doctor. She didn't care that he could handle the pain. She didn't want him to die... or did she? It was just her luck that she was indebted to an irritating, heartless psycho. "Fucking Lucifer."

"Lucifer?" Carmen sounded horrified. "Oh my God, Lyla. Get away from him."

"I'm trying." She shoved him, which made him laugh even harder. "Asshole."

"Lyla, he's a sociopath. He runs Hell. You have to—"

"It's fine." Lyla got away from him and tried to ignore the hooting and catcalling from the stands. She gave the crowd the middle finger, which made them even louder. She gave up and headed towards the ruined executive lounge. "Are you okay? How's Nora?"

"You took ten years off my life, but I'm okay. Nora's asleep. Are you coming home?"

"Yes."

Carmen sighed. "Lyla, is it really over?"

Lyla took a deep breath and glanced into the arena at the bodies of Sadist and his henchmen. "Yes."

"I love you."

Lyla closed her eyes and clung to her love and warmth. "I love you too. I'll see you soon."

She hung up as the guys came through the shattered window. She handed the phone back to Blade and did a double take. She grabbed his chin and went on tiptoe to examine the deep gash on his cheek.

"What happened?" she snapped and spotted two

deep lashes on Angel's chest. Eli was dragging his left leg and trailing blood from a wound she couldn't see. She whirled on Lucifer. "You have a doctor here?"

Lucifer stared at her. "No."

"They need stitches!"

Lucifer leaned towards her. "This is Hell, honey. They're not supposed to leave unscathed. Just be happy that they're breathing and so are you." Lucifer looked towards Gavin. "You might want to wash up before you leave Hell looking like you left a butcher shop."

Lucifer walked towards the exit and they followed. Gavin grabbed her hand and gripped tightly as he stomped over the fallen bodies and tracked bloody footprints over the white marble floor. Lucifer led them down a hallway and pointed to several doors before he disappeared.

Gavin pushed into a room fit for royalty. Like everything else on this floor, everything was blinding white. This bothered her on so many levels, especially because it didn't match with the sandy pit, the fact that this place was called Hell or that there was a brothel on another floor.

"I don't—" she began, trying to pull back.

Gavin grabbed her wrist and dragged her into a luxurious bathroom. There was a circular shower stall in the middle of the room along with a sunken bathtub. Lyla wasn't prepared for Gavin to drag her to the ground, rip her top down the middle and savagely yank off her jeans.

"Gavin," she whispered as he unbuttoned his slacks and pulled out his cock. "There's probably cameras—"

Gavin dragged her into position beneath him, spread her thighs and brushed his cock over her slit. Lyla bit back a moan and heard his growl of approval when he found her hot and slick. She tried to scoot away, but he grabbed her thighs and yanked her into place beneath him.

"They'll see!" she hissed.

"Let them watch. They'll never have what I have, the fuckers."

Gavin wouldn't be denied. He positioned her and slid inside. His eyes closed and he shuddered as if he couldn't handle the sensation. He didn't stop until he was in to the hilt. His hot breath fanned her face and she was pinned beneath his vibrating body. She could feel him holding back, trying to spare her whatever was going on inside of him.

"Gavin."

Metallic, golden eyes pierced hers. The monster that ruled the underworld stared back at her. She wasn't afraid. On the contrary, she stroked a hand down his bloody face. This man, this scary, wonderful man would die for her. He wouldn't give up and he wouldn't back down.

"I love you," she said and blinked back tears.

Gavin's mouth slammed down on hers and he began to move. She could taste blood, but didn't fucking care. She wrapped her arms around his neck and kissed him for all she was worth. Gavin growled into her mouth and fucked her against the unforgiving floor. After the horrors of the past hour, she needed to lose herself and Gavin was giving her an outlet. She dragged her nails down his back and clawed at him, begging for him to push her over the edge.

Gavin lifted her leg high and ground against her before he pulled back and then slammed home with a teeth jarring smack. It took less than five minute of his antics for her to climax, tipping her head back and screaming as it tore through her. Gavin joined her, clasping her desperately close and fucking her with a force that bordered on pain. So many emotions flickered through his eyes—fear, relief, rage, and bloodlust.

He gasped her name as he came and lay on top of her, nearly suffocating her beneath his bulk. She didn't care. She clutched him to her. They survived. Sadist was gone and they could finally move on.

Gavin stirred and raised his head. "Okay?" he husked.

She leaned up and kissed him gently. "Yeah." She would be.

Gavin hauled her up and bustled her into the circular shower stall and braced her against the wall when she weaved on her feet. He tapped a button on the floor with his foot. A massive showerhead rained over them and began to wash away the blood and fear.

They stared at one another. So much passed through her head, but she didn't know what to utter out loud. His energy pulsed in the enclosed space. He cupped her chin and kissed her, hard and deep. When he pulled back, his eyes roved over her face as if memorizing every line.

"I'm so fucking proud of you."

She blinked. "What?"

"I killed the last man, turn and see you toss the knife in Vega's back and then attack him with a fucking shield." His lips didn't move, but his eyes warmed fractionally. "You were a savage, out of control, after blood. You were magnificent. Every man in that arena would have killed to claim you."

"What?"

He brushed sweet kisses over her forehead, down her nose and over her cheeks. His hands moved over her as if he couldn't help himself. Lyla reached down for one of the bottles at her feet, read the label and began to bathe away the night. Neither of them said a word as they tended to one another.

When she was bundled into a robe, he went into the bedroom to see if there was anything in the closet and came back with a tiny slip of fabric, which turned out to be a dress. Lyla had no choice but to slip into it and was horrified by her reflection. The dress was obviously from one of the whores. It barely covered her pussy or nipples. It was slinky, tight and left nothing to the imagination. Her chest scars were on full display. Lyla was debating whether she should wear the robe out of Hell when she caught sight of Gavin.

Gavin was clad in clothes identical to the ones Lucifer had been wearing—loose beige pants and a tight Henley that showed off his muscles. Gavin plucked at the tight shirt as if it was a rag. He looked up and saw her biting her lip to hold in her laughter. He hauled her against him with his hands on her ass.

"You think this is funny?" he murmured as he nipped her neck.

"Yes." How she could find anything funny after the night they had, she didn't know.

"Fucking Lucifer."

"What's this about godfather duty?"

Gavin's hands tightened on her before he straightened. "He's going to teach Nora how to fight."

"What?" she snapped and shoved at him, but he didn't release her.

"He won't teach her until we're ready."

"Gavin, I don't want Nora a part of this life. You're passing the title to Angel."

He stared at her. "We can never let our guards down and neither will she."

Lyla moaned and rested her face against the hollow of his throat. "I don't want to think about that right now. Sadist is dead. That's all I care about. The end."

A knock on the bedroom door echoed into the bathroom. Blade stood on the other side. Lyla couldn't hold back her laughter. Blade was in identical clothes to Gavin and he looked even more ludicrous.

"Let's get out of here," Blade said.

Gavin put his arm around Lyla's shoulders. "Let's go."

Blade led the way down the white hallway. Angel and Eli were standing by the elevator waiting for them. They were dressed the same as Gavin and Blade. Angel looked her over and didn't flinch when he took in her scarred chest.

"Nice dress," he said with a grin.

She scowled at him and glanced at Eli. "Are you

okay?"

"I'll live."

The elevator doors opened and they got in.

"What are you doing for work?" Gavin asked.

It took her a second to realize he was talking to Eli who didn't answer.

"Your hospital bills are backed up," Gavin said casually.

"What's your point, Pyre?"

"You looking for a job?"

There was a beat of silence before, "Depends on the job."

"I hear there's a Detective position open with the Nevada PD."

Angel snickered.

"Or if you're looking for something more... flexible, Angel's taking my title and needs someone who knows the ins and outs of the underworld."

The elevator doors opened, revealing a long dark hallway.

"I'll give you a call, Pyre," Eli said as he limped in another direction.

"We still have to talk," Gavin said in a hard voice.

Eli nodded. "I know."

Gavin pulled Lyla into his side as they walked. There were no screams of torture of pleasure, but she wouldn't relax until they were out of here. They rounded the corner and walked into what felt like a sports book betting station. There were men everywhere and the largest TV screens she had ever seen on the walls. It was a circular floor with a bar and tables and chairs surrounding the arena and the sandy pit at the bottom. There was a lot of activity going on as they piled bodies on stretchers.

The noise level dimmed as they started through the crowd. No one smiled or spoke to them. She felt their eyes on her. After the night she had, she wasn't feeling remotely modest. These men fucking saw her kill a man. What were scars and tits in comparison?

Gavin led the way to a large metal door and swung the heavy thing open.

"Gavin!"

Gavin cursed under his breath before he turned to face Lucifer.

"Leaving so soon?" Lucifer asked.

"Got shit to do," Gavin said.

Lucifer's stared at her scars. She resisted the urge to cover her chest or belt him across the face. Lucifer's eyes locked with hers. There was something happening in the dark depths she couldn't define.

"You should wear your scars with pride. You survived and had your revenge. Every man here knows it," Lucifer said.

Lyla didn't know what to say to that.

"I look forward to hearing your stories in the future." Lucifer grinned. "And meeting your daughter. Are you planning on having more kids?"

"Lucifer," Gavin bit out.

"What? I want to know."

"We haven't talked about—" Lyla began.

"Yes," Gavin growled.

Lucifer clapped his hands. "Great."

"It's been a long night," Blade said.

"Yes, yes," Lucifer said and clapped them on the back. "The city lost some prominent leaders tonight. Watch your back."

"That's a given," Gavin said.

Gavin led her past a group of men smoking cigars and playing cards. A dark gloomy hallway led to rickety stairs and then Gavin pushed on a wall, which swung open. Lyla walked into a... closet? She heard the distant pulse of stripper music and glanced at the minimal costumes. She grabbed a feather boa and draped it around her neck as Blade's phone rang.

"Lyla."

She turned from her perusal of the empty dressing room. "What?"

"That was the hospital."

Fear grabbed her by the throat. "What happened? Did someone—?"

"She's awake."

Lyla froze. "What?"

"Your mother. She's awake."

"We have to go now. How do we get out of here?" she demanded.

Gavin took her hand. "This way."

He led her through the dressing room into a strip club with strobe lights. Lyla didn't glance at the strippers or the patrons. She hauled ass towards the door and emerged in a deserted parking lot. Blade beeped the lock on an SUV and they climbed in.

Angel and Gavin nodded as they slammed their doors and they were off. Gavin sat on the backseat with her, gripping her thigh.

"They weren't sure she would wake up," Lyla whispered.

"I know. This is good," Gavin said quietly.

"You think she remembers?" Lyla closed her eyes. "I hope she doesn't."

"We'll see," Gavin said.

The SUV was silent as Blade drove to the hospital. Since this was Las Vegas, no one glanced twice at the stripper with three hippy companions as they walked through the halls.

"You should all get checked out," she said absently.

None of them responded or broke away from their group. The ICU nurse didn't miss a beat when they walked up to her counter.

"Has she spoken?" Lyla asked urgently.

The woman's expression softened. "No. Let me take you to her." She glanced at Gavin, Blade and Angel. "We don't want to overwhelm her."

Gavin nodded and squeezed Lyla's hand before he released her. Lyla walked swiftly towards her mother's room. Her mother looked worse if that was possible. At Lyla's approach, her mother's eyes opened. The color of her eyes didn't seem as vibrant as before, but Lyla didn't care. Her mother was alive.

Lyla took her mother's hand carefully in hers and kissed her scarred fingers. "Mom, it's me."

Her mother blinked slowly. Lyla didn't see recognition in her eyes.

"It's Lyla," she said.

Her mother stared at her for a long moment. Her eyes were dull and lifeless.

"I'm sorry, Mom," she whispered.

Her mother closed her eyes, took a deep breath and then opened them again. Her bruised lips formed a word. Lyla leaned in close.

"What? What are you trying to say?"

Her mother said one word in a shaky whisper filled with pain. "Pat."

Lyla's heart stalled in her chest. Her father. Her mother loved him more than life itself. Of course his name would be the first one on her lips. Lyla bowed her head and tried to think of what to say. Her mother urgently squeezed her hand and said his name again. Her insides rebelled. She couldn't look into her mother's eyes and admit what she'd done.

"Lyla."

Her mother's voice sounded a little stronger, but doused with so much pain. Lyla raised her head. Her mother was watching her with tear filled eyes.

"Pat," her mother said urgently.

Lyla shook her head. A tear slipped down her mother's cheek. She closed her eyes and withdrew her hand from Lyla's. Lyla ground her teeth against the hurt that caused. She hadn't even told her mother that she was the one that pulled the trigger.

"M-mom? Do you need water or—"

"Leave."

Lyla opened her mouth to argue, but one glance at her mother's broken body made her obey. She kissed her mother's brow and walked out of the room.

"How is she?" Gavin asked.

She collided with his chest and he hugged her tight. He cupped the back of her head and kissed her temple.

"She's alive, Lyla. That's all that matters," he said.

"She asked about dad," she said against his chest.

"What did you say?"

"I just shook my head. I couldn't—I couldn't—"

Gavin raised her face to his. "You did what you had to, Lyla."

"But he was my dad." She swallowed hard. "I can't tell her."

"She has a long recovery ahead of her. Spare her that knowledge at least."

Gavin wrapped her securely against him. They stayed that way for a long minute. She thought of her father's last moments, the fallen men in the sandy pit and her mother's uphill battle. The knowledge of what was to come weighed heavily on her shoulders.

"How are we going to do this?" she whispered.

"One day at a time."

She looked up at her husband and saw that despite all that occurred, he didn't look weary or uncertain. He was focused and ready to take on the world. He would never back down and would protect his own with his last breath.

"I love you," she whispered.

His eyes heated. He cupped her jaw and kissed her long and slow. She clutched at him and felt his lips curve against her mouth. He hauled her into his arms and walked out of the ICU.

"Gavin, what—?"

"We're exhausted and I need to hold my daughter." Gavin's gaze slashed down to her. "We're spending the next week in bed. I don't give a fuck what comes up."

Angel snorted as he and Blade fell into step behind him.

"We'll do what we can for your mom, but I won't let you feel guilty for Pat's death. I would have done him in myself and made him suffer," Gavin continued as he stalked through the empty hospital corridors. "We're alive and that's all that matters. Vega's gone, along with most of those who have been conspiring against me for years. Fuck 'um."

Gavin walked out into the chilly night and deposited her into the back of the SUV while Blade and Angel got into the front seats. Gavin pulled her onto his lap so she straddled him. He looked up at her, the only illumination that of passing street lights.

Gavin clasped her face between his hands and pressed his face to hers. "I love you." The words reverberated with fierce emotion, enough to make tears fall. "We've been through hell, baby girl. That's at an end. I'm going to give you the paradise I promised. Whatever you want, it's yours."

"And if I just want you?" she whispered.

He closed his eyes and kept her curled tight around him. "That goes without saying. God, you're a fucking miracle."

She brushed kisses over his face and rocked against him. She felt him harden beneath her. She didn't give a shit about Blade and Angel.

Life was fleeting and fragile. She didn't want to think about tomorrow. She wanted to live in the now and right now, her husband was staring at her as if she was his reason for being. She took that in and let it wash away the guilt, rage and lingering fear.

It was done.

Blade pulled up to the house and the rest of Gavin's security surrounded them. Angel and Blade stayed outside to talk while Gavin led her inside. They made their way upstairs and went straight to the nursery.

Carmen was nowhere in sight and Nora was sleeping peacefully in her crib, arms over her head as if she were rocking out at a concert. Gavin picked her up and cradled her in his arm. They went to their bedroom. She sprawled out as Gavin sat with his back against the headboard. She rested her head on his thigh and stared at Nora. Images of the night slid through her mind and she clutched Gavin tight.

"It's over," she whispered.

"Yes."

"We're safe," she murmured.

"Yes."

She looked up. "And you're out of the underworld?"

"For the most part, yes. Angel's the crime lord."

She nodded, but she didn't believe him. Once a crime lord, always a crime lord.

Like Lucifer said, they would never really be out of the underworld. It would always be on the periphery of their lives. Lyla watched Gavin stroke his finger down Nora's cheek and felt a shaft of warmth push away her dark thoughts.

Sadist was dead, her mother would live and everyone she loved was breathing. Gavin was holding Nora who had no idea what kind of world she had been born into. They would move on and live their happily ever after... right?

Author's Note:

Hi All,

I hope you enjoyed Once A Crime Lord. I swear, I don't think I've ever sweated so much over a book! Lyla and Gavin have really led me on a wild ride (mostly Gavin), but the best thing about writing this series is the fans I've met who make the world come alive for me.

I originally intended for this to be a two book series and now I don't see an end in sight! I've had numerous requests for certain characters to have their own books, which I will be happy to oblige, all in good time, of course. A lot of people have been asking if there will be a prequel for Gavin and Lyla and I'm playing around with the idea. I promise we will see them in the books to come!

Love,
Mia

About the Author:

Mia lives in her head and is shadowed by her dogs who don't judge when she cries and laughs with imaginary characters. Mia comes from a big, conservative family that doesn't know how to handle her eccentricities, but with encouragement from her fans, has found the courage to put the characters in her head on paper.

Stalk Me:

Author Website: miaknight.com
Facebook: www.facebook.com/miaknightbooks/
Twitter: @authormiaknight
Email me at: authormiaknight@gmail.com

Cover Art by Kellie Dennis at Book Cover by Design
www.bookcoverbydesign.co.uk

Books by Mia Knight:

Crime Lord Series:

Crime Lord's Captive
Recaptured by the Crime Lord
Once A Crime Lord

Made in the USA
San Bernardino, CA
30 August 2017